THE GIRL WHO SHOULD BE DEAD

ALESSA WINTERS

1

After everything that had happened that day, Ambra doesn't begrudge herself a little light kidnapping.

Her head still pounds after all the alarms, her eyelids drag with each blink, and both the lingering gut wound and the slash on her face throb. Her mouth still tastes of iron, as it always does when the leash gets tightened, and whatever snap of death magic the necromancer had smashed in her face in the fight still echoes in her lungs.

All that's recoverable, of course, given some time outside the stasis chambers, and they would have to lobotomize her —again—in order for her to go back there willingly.

Straightening the moment her feet hit the floor, she drops her grip on the kidnappee's collar, dusting off her hands.

The kidnappee, a young man with floppy hair and thick rimmed glasses who shot one of the Five in the head, staggers back, gasping. He's still holding the gun in his hand, but thankfully, he doesn't aim it towards her.

"Where are we?" He chokes out, like the teleportation was less than perfect, which is rude.

She obviously took them to a safe house, so she blinks at him.

Ambra, like most demons she's come into contact with, instinctively crafts safe places to land. A place where she could run to, a place to think, a place to collect whatever catches her fancy, on the rare occasion something does.

She hasn't been to this one since the merge—her mind shies away from thinking about it directly in a way that's distinctively annoying—so a thin layer of dust coats the bench and the bookcase.

"Okay, okay," the kidnappee says, after her silence, as she obsessively lets her mind check her wards, lets it wander to see if anyone else has been in there. "Uh, why am I here?"

That, at least, is a question her mind doesn't have to think about.

"Because of the leash," she answers, and his brows furrow, like the answer isn't intuitive to him.

The leash, the incorporeal, magical leash tied so crudely around her throat by the College. The key to them controlling her. The key to her freedom and her safety.

He just raises an eyebrow at her, so she turns away.

One of her wards is smudged. Not broken, but someone else had clearly been sniffing around the edges, testing them.

Another demon, if the tang of the power is any indication, had probably noticed the emptiness and wanted to observe if the person who crafted it was dead or not.

She stalks towards the offending rune, and the kidnappee's eyes widen as she passes him, but despite pulling at the rune, despite squinting at it, she can't tell who it could be.

Another result of the merge. She just...can't do everything anymore.

Careful, his motions so careful it immediately sends up red flags in her awareness, her kidnappee sits on the bench, gripping the aged wood like it could help him.

The gun is still clutched in his hands, as if he forgot it.

He doesn't look too injured, near as she can tell, beyond the scrapes and bruises that come from breaking out of a prison.

He stares at her, his eyes a normal shade of human brown, and in between one moment and the next, she can see his brain kick in and something truly analytical lights up his face.

This, at least, she can talk to.

"You're a dud, you said," Ambra starts, and he nods. "Duds aren't supposed to know about any of human magic, yet you do."

He nods again, his mouth twisting down.

"You've been scarred by some magic, in a huge way," she continues, and it's obvious all over him. Like someone had taken a surge and shocked it directly into his system. "You knew how to read the runes, you knew a lot of the pathways, and you could instruct the necromancer and alchemist."

"Good assessment," he says, cautious, and his knuckles are white against the bench.

He's afraid of her, which is a bit nice.

"The necromancer killed Korhonen, and you killed Rastian," Ambra recites. "There's still Nalissa, Johnsin, and Boltiex out there."

"Boltiex is one of them?" the kidnappee says, immediately identifying the dangerous one out of all of them. It's good he's probably a bit smart, if he's catching on. "Why would they let him get access to a demon, he's almost insane."

"Once they piece through the wreckage your Half Demon left there, they're going to try to get me back," Ambra states, as matter of fact as she can, but a shudder still shakes down her spine at the thought. "Hence, you."

"Still don't follow," the kidnappee murmurs, but his eyebrows are still furrowed. "Can you return me back?"

The unease tightens across her shoulders. "I'm not going back to that prison."

"No, not the base, obviously, but...to my friends. They're heading to...a safe spot with backup. The College can't get to them there, you might be safe."

She squints at him, like that can give her clarity.

"Alright," her kidnappee says, clearly unnerved. "Ambra, that's your name, right?"

It had been a long time since anyone had actually called her that, and a shiver flickers across her body.

He raises an eyebrow, like he caught that. "It was on the nameplate outside your cell."

"I know that," she says, and in some odd mannerism left over from the body, hugs herself. "Yes, that's my name."

The smudged ward throbs against her awareness, again, the demon testing it. They must've set something, to see if someone would come back, and she likes that not one bit.

She hasn't faced another demon since the merge, and if her less than perfect control is an indication, she's not sure she would win any fight.

"Okay, Ambra," he starts again, the body shivers around her. "I need you to explain to me, in easy, human terms, what's going on."

She doesn't stop staring at the rune, and she doesn't think her protections have weakened enough so that another demon could just teleport in, but the itch to go elsewhere already eats at her gut.

Her gut, with the wound from the first fight at the bar still slowly bleeding. And hurting, far more than such wounds should.

Thankfully, the kidnappee stays silent, as she prods at the physical lines she etched into the wood of the safe room wall.

The safe room is little more than a single structure, deep underground, the air connected through an odd series of tunnels leading up to the surface. A few ages ago, she had teleported in wood plank by wood plank, then wired it when electricity became popular, and had a perfectly good collection of preserved books on the shelves.

It is also blessedly quiet, most of the time, and the presence of a living breathing human in it clashes.

One of the worst things about the merge is the noise.

That's a lie.

But it's an easy lie, kinder than thinking about it more.

"As long as the three are out there, they can pull me back," Ambra says, spinning and facing him with enough speed that he startles. "Needless to say, I don't want that."

"I'm not a fan of them being able to control a demon, either," the kidnappee agrees, which at least shows some common sense. "I don't know how they succeeded, but it's not good."

"I don't want to be controlled," she shoots back at him. "But you..." she lets her eyes wash over him, a direct motion that she observed her human handlers do to make people uncomfortable, and he grimaces in response. "I doubt you could."

He raises his hands, as if showing he's unarmed, despite

the gun he set down on the bench. "I'm not going to try to control you,"

"Good," Ambra replies, then, some strange quiver in her chest, some leftover response from the body, continues, "So you'll hold the leash, hold it tight, and they can't pull me back."

He listens, actively, and she can see his mind turning over her sentence, picking it apart, like it's some puzzle to be cracked.

She lets him, returning her attention to the runes, which buzz, and she prods it with the fingertip of the body.

Of course, that does nothing, which is even more annoying. Dead bodies gave her such better control, more fidelity in her actions and perceptions, and this living one is like fitting into a box a bit too small.

The fingertips tremble, just a bit, and she shakes out her hand, as if that could stop it.

"I have questions," he starts, and there's a tone in his voice like he's trying to project authority and failing miserably.

"Obviously," Ambra murmurs, and a different one of the runes buzz, the same demon now actively prodding at her. "I picked you because you most likely couldn't put me back in stasis. Your group saved the little wight, so you're unlikely to try to use this body for anything weird because of human morals. I didn't choose the necromancer because the Half Demon would kill me, and that alchemist is too powerful for me to want to try."

He swallows, his throat moving, and it's something she never noticed humans doing until the merge. "With her help, we might be able to remove the leash," he starts, and she can recognize someone bullshitting. "And the Half Demon might have some ideas."

"And you're just trying to get back to them," she replies, then stalks over to the other side of the room, to her little bookcase, scanning the traps she put behind the books.

Still untouched, the whisper thin wire all but invisible to the body's eyes.

She blinks at it, as if she could will the gaze to focus better, but it doesn't work.

Because she's stuck in this body, with its breathing, its pain, its eyelids, its shivers, and all of its unconscious movement that she has to be aware of.

Another buzz, and she twitches, as this other demon presses harder. She's going to have to go to another safe spot, going to have to abandon these books and the comfort and the silence, if this keeps up.

"Boltiex wanted full control, solo control, but he was overruled," Ambra continues, and at least if she has to have noise in the room it could be created by her. "He has some ideas about ruling the College using me, I don't like it, so I know the existence of the other four—two now—were to counterbalance. So there is a way to counterbalance."

Her captive says nothing, his lips thin.

"Boltiex is the most skilled at it, he's the one who…" she gestures at the body, and the body responds with a lump in her throat that threatens to momentarily choke her.

He nods, serious, like he understands what she's trying to communicate, which is nice, so she doesn't have to actually say it.

"Nalissa is the craftiest, she does experiments with my power," Ambra continues, twisting her face. "She knows all my limits, all the body's weird reactions."

"I thought she was in France," her kidnappee says, "doing research on the catacombs."

Another shudder of the body, at the claustrophobic,

echoing tunnels lined with bones that immediately pop into mind, but Ambra pushes onwards. "Johnsin is the one who liked pain, and he's the one that figured out how to tie the body's nerves into my own. I'd like to avoid him."

"Understandable," he says, and he hasn't relaxed, not really, but there's less tension in his shoulders and his face has softened into something pondering.

It's a bit gratifying, to have someone say that, after most of the humans in the College always act as if she's spouting nonsense.

"I also don't want another demon to find this," Ambra says, holding up the leash, but he doesn't track the motion.

Right. Because he can't see it.

"If one even for a second thinks I'm weak, thinks they can destroy me, they will. I don't want to be destroyed, no matter what they say happened to the other Terese project."

"The demon died, but the human lived," he says, and she rocks back, to digest it, the jealousy sending a twist to her stomach. "A necromancer killed the demon."

"And the body survived?" Ambra asks, before she can stop herself. "She didn't...die off?"

Her kidnappee falls silent, a blond brow raising over the glasses, and she hates that she said something, so she shakes her head.

"My point remains, I don't want to go back, I don't want to be controlled, I don't want to die," she says, the leash still in her hand. "I need someone useless to hold the leash."

He scoffs, like that's what he's upset about in all of this.

Another pull at the runes, something stronger, and she spins to stare at it, dread starting to drip down her back.

She also needs a place to recover. To sit with the body until she has enough energy to fix the annoying wounds, until she can think straight. To huddle away, find some sort of sustenance, whatever the body needs, and figure out what being at full power in the body would be.

Someplace out of stasis.

"I don't think that will work," he says, finally, his face carefully still.

A prod at the runes, and the electricity cording through the room flickers.

She snakes out a hand, grabbing his wrist, and he flinches.

"I don't care if you think it'll work," she says, and the skin around his wrist is warm, blood thudding against his pulse, and it momentarily derails her thoughts, at the warmth in front of her.

Before the electricity flickers again, plunging them into darkness for a split second, and she loops the leash around his warm wrist, knotting it down.

He jerks his hand away, but the knot holds true, and she gets a small corresponding tug around her neck.

"What—" he starts, before the lights slam off again, the room filling with another demon's power, and Ambra grips the collar of his shirt and flees.

2

Ambra's feet hit the floor of the motor home, and her kidnappee's knees buckle upon impact, knocking her off kilter.

"You're bad at that," she informs him, releasing his collar and letting him stagger away, to the comfortable plush couch she crammed into one side of the small space.

He all but collapses onto the couch, almost comically. "Why are we somewhere new?" Careful, he places the gun on the side table, the metal clattering against the cheap wood. Ambra's a bit grateful that he didn't try to shoot her with it. It wouldn't have done anything serious, but it would've been exceedingly annoying.

Despite the disorientation and the obvious physical effects of the teleportation, his words are sharp. Like his brain doesn't turn off, even when going through something strange.

It's not a bad thing. If someone has to hold the leash, at least she picked an intelligent one.

"Another demon was sniffing around the spot," Ambra answers, because a smart question deserves an actual response. "I haven't faced another since..." she gestures at the body. "And I don't want to try."

He stares up at her.

"The Half Demon not-withstanding," she amends, in case she offended him on behalf of his friend. "And that wasn't exactly a fun time."

He nods, then, obviously, as if hoping she would notice, looks around the room.

It's a small motor home, the sort on concrete bricks instead of wheels, and it creaks in high wind. The glass of the window is streaked with grime, barely letting in the light of the setting sun.

Snow powders the grounds outside, more slush than anything else, and tall trees stretch towards the pink streaked sky. Moss grows on most things, probably some on the outside walls of the motor home, and the mud darkens with all the moisture in the air.

"Pacific Northwest?" her kidnappee guesses, and she nods.

"The body liked the cold air," Ambra says before she can stop herself, then the lump threatens to choke her again. "I took her here a few times, she grew up within a hundred miles."

His brows raise over the glasses, then he lifts his hand, flexing it.

The hand with the leash.

A cold, irrational fear stabs into her, at the casual motion, despite the fact that she's the one that put that in place.

"First things first," he murmurs, squinting at his hand, "what did you do to me?"

"Tied the leash," she answers. If he's a dud, if he has no way of seeing what she did, then she at least needs to give him the information he needs. "If someone pulls on it, pulls me away, you'll feel it and be able to pull me back."

He nods, a bit pale, before an utterly bored expression settles across his face.

It's completely fake. Completely fabricated, and it's almost fascinating to see, so she takes a few seconds to stare at him before she checks the wards.

They're completely untouched, pristine, and perfect.

"This place will be safer than the last, it's in the territory of a demon who won't bother me if I don't bother them," Ambra supplies, squinting at him to see if the utterly fake expression falters. "I spoke to him about this place three years ago, it's outside of the area he really cares about. No other one would cause strife in these woods."

"And the leash?" he asks, and there's a flicker of panic under the expression, before it solidifies again. "Could they get you here?"

"If they think about it, they can get me anywhere, it's all a matter of who tries first." She has to swallow down again, and this might be the longest she's been without being in the stasis chamber since the merge, and the body is still giving her all the unconscious signals. "And how long it takes for them to sift through all the wreckage of the prison. I'm not the deadliest thing you let out."

"Good to know," he replies, before he glances around the room. "So, what, you're here to sleep? Get some food, get some power back?" He gestures at the still-bleeding gut wound, and there's a small tug on the leash at the motion. "Fix that?"

Unsteady again, she nods. "There's a bed in the other room, the body liked the pillows if you need rest."

"The body," he states, and she flinches, completely out

of her control, before he raises his hands in some obvious surrender. "Good, got it, okay—"

A shrill beep echoes in the small room, like a little spike into her brain, and she recoils back, then another, then another.

"It's just my phone," he states, digging into his pocket and pulling out one of the small electronics that all of her handlers kept on themselves. It beeps again in his hands, and he slowly, deliberately shows her how he can unlock it.

He's treating her like a spooked animal, instead of the other way around.

"It's my friends," he says, again slowly and deliberately. "They're worried."

"Why?" Ambra blurts out.

He stares at her, blank. "Because a demon grabbed me and then disappeared and that's not normal?"

"I wasn't going to hurt you, that'd be counter intuitive," Ambra says, gesturing to the room in some strange impulse she doesn't fully understand. "I want you to make sure I don't have to go back, not hurt you to the point where you willingly hand me over."

"Which they didn't know," he points out, then starts tapping on the electronics, and her heart jumps again.

"Let me see," she interrupts, and he sighs, turning the phone around.

It takes the body a few tries to focus her eyes, before the words swim into focus.

CHLOE A (7:30 PM): Are you okay?

CHLOE A (7:34 PM): I can't track your phone, where are you, are you alive?

DELINA N (7:36 PM): All I can tell is you're not dead.

FREDERICK HD (7:37 PM): The Wights can't track you right now.

CHLOE A (7:49 PM): Gurlien, can you answer?

"What's a Gurlien?" Ambra wonders aloud, and in front of her, he shuts his eyes.

"That's my name," he says wearily. "Chloe is the alchemist, she's my best friend. Delina is the Necromancer and Frederick—Maison—is the Half Demon."

She blinks up at him. "Okay, Gurlien."

"Here," he says, then types in front of her, pressing send.

GURLIEN (7:52 PM): I'm alive, with the demon, will explain later.

"No, you won't," Ambra protests, fear prickling over her skin. "How do you know they're not with the College? They could be captive, someone else could have their electronics and be impersonating them, they do that."

He sighs again, typing.

GURLIEN (7:53 PM): Chloe, code.

Immediately—

CHLOE A (7:53 PM): Charter Oak.

GURLIEN (7:54 PM): Ida Grove.

"There, it's her, she wouldn't give that up under torture," he says, dark. "Believe me, they've tried."

Ambra believes him, based on the amount of exhaustion and yet still power she saw in the alchemist, so she steps back, giving him a bit of space, as he continues to type out.

The wind creaks through the motor home, and the body shivers in the chill, outside of her control, but she stalks closer to the window in the meager kitchen.

Spiderwebs stretch between the faucet and the sink, but when she gives the sink an experimental twist, the water gushes out, bright and clear.

When she first took the body here, she had laughed in delight that such a run-down place could have such good plumbing, and Ambra hadn't wanted to tell her that she had done it with magic. The body had filled a glass with the water, drank from it, and it had been such a contradictory burst of sensations for Ambra that she almost teleported them away instantaneously.

The glass still sits, upside down, in the rack next to the sink, a thin layer of dust along the bottom.

Her kidnappee, Gurlien, taps out on the phone, his face serious, and gets corresponding beeps with every action.

The beeps are less painful with just that bit of distance.

"Did the rest of your team escape?" Ambra asks, still staring down at the dusty glass.

"Yes," Gurlien answers, curt. "They're in a safe house, Maison's mother is recovering, and they're going to find a hospital for Maison to get his knee checked out."

Right, because he can't self-heal.

Ambra scoffs, then stares down at the oozing gut wound, the blood still staining some of her clothing, sticking unpleasantly to her skin.

She pokes at it, and the pain sends edges of black at the periphery of her vision.

The damage cuts through the skin, into one of the secondary organs, but those are easy to fix with enough energy. The body had taken damage before, and she had fixed it then.

Her legs are less steady this time, though, so she sits herself down on the plastic tile and leans her head against the cabinet there, hearing the whisper of the water draining through the pipes.

The tapping of Gurlien's fingers stops, but she can't see him from her position. "Ambra?"

"I'm here, just sitting down." She pokes at the wound again, hissing involuntarily through her teeth, then focuses on the secondary organ, knitting the tissue back into place.

It's harder to do after the merge, and she hates that, bitterly.

There's maybe a few minutes of blessed silence, of letting her power focus in on that one little part of her, let it sink into the still breathing physical form she's stuck in.

Before Gurlien stands, the floor creaking with the movement, and in just a few steps is in front of her.

"What are you doing?"

She didn't want to have to explain.

"Healing the wound," she says, after he stares blankly at her, lifting the shirt to show.

The skin is still split, black blood spooling out, but with the absence of the cut in the secondary organ it feels significantly better.

He blanches.

"Don't be squeamish, your Half Demon was the one who did it," Ambra says, then pokes at the broken skin again, willing it back into place.

"No, I'm going to be squeamish about that," he says, his words faint. He's still looming over her, and it's too similar to being on an experiment table and looking up at her handlers.

"The body left some changes of clothing in the bedroom," Ambra mumbles, after a long moment of stitching the skin back into place, indeterminately slow. "Closet by the bed, can you find me something without blood?"

He dashes away, relieving the pressure of the looming, and she exhales, controlled.

Well, not as controlled as it would be in an actually dead body, but as controlled as all of the unconscious spasms this one allowed her.

She hadn't ever been so aware of blood in other bodies,

either. Of it sticking and drying against her skin, pulling on all the tiny hairs all over the body, flaking and tightening against her.

With another impulse, she lifts her hand to the shaved side of her head, where the leads once hung. The body had cried when she saw them in the mirror, with her beautiful long hair chopped so severely, but it...made sense. At least.

The handlers had spoken so many times of monitoring her brain patterns, at seeing how a demon soul in a human body would react, and, especially at first, Ambra had been so excited.

And now she's sitting on the floor, slowly stitching her skin back, as Gurlien audibly goes through the closet.

"Any shirt will do, it doesn't matter," she calls out, and her throat turns the words into something tight, something choked out.

He immediately comes back out, holding a perfectly functional pull over sweater, the type that the body would always reach for with the first hint of a chill.

Still working on the skin, she chucks the bloody shirt off, using it to scrub some of the dried viscera off her stomach, and Gurlien blinks away, visibly startled.

"Do you need bandages?" he asks, his voice a bit strangled.

"No, I'm almost done," she responds, taking the moment to squint at him, at his clear discomfort, before she clings to the side of the sink, hauling herself up.

Her legs shake at the action.

Firmly ignoring that, she runs the ruined shirt under the water, then dabs off the rest of the dried blood, until the only reminder of the wound is a thin pinkish scar, slightly raised.

She frowns at it, but the skin resists any of her effort to smooth that away, too.

The body has several other scars, raised in the same way, thin strips of skin poorly healed. Ones on her fingers, almost blended in with callouses. Some on her knees, like she fell. One on the side of her hip that aches a bit in bad weather, one curved against her breastbone, neatly hidden by the undergarments the body still wore.

It's somehow wrong for Ambra to be adding to them.

Besides the surgery scars, of course. Besides the places where they hacked the body open in their mad rush to fit Ambra's soul inside as well, then sealed them back up in the trap.

The rest of the blood dabbed away, she shrugs into the sweater, and it's soft, like the blankets on the bed.

"Thank you," she says to Gurlien, because that at least seemed appropriate, if she wants to keep him from handing her over.

He still watches her, sharp.

"You can go sleep, the leash will wake you if they pull me," she says.

"Is there food here?" he asks instead. "If you were hurt so badly, you need to replenish."

"Why?" she asks, but gestures to the small pantry where the body had requested sweets be stored. "Go ahead."

His forehead furrows, fascinatingly so, and if her legs were shaking less, she would've reached out and pressed her thumb into the wrinkle between his brows.

But even with his visible confusion, he opens the pantry, to the brightly colored snacks within. The candy, the preserved pastries, the thin bags of something called popcorn that the body had promised they would try together, and then never did.

Thankfully, his hand passes over that, pulling out a box of foil wrapped bars and popping them open.

"How often did they take you out of stasis?" he asks, and his casual tone sends the small hairs on Ambra's arms to raising.

"Not often," she replies, cautious.

"How long were you out each time?" He pulls out two of the bars, then, to her horror, hands her one and leans against the other side of the counter, tearing open the one in his hands. At her blank look, he continues, "Hours? Days? Minutes?"

"Never days," she answers, and he nods, like he expected that answer.

"And did they give you food?"

"You saw me with the necromancer," Ambra points out, and he wrinkles his nose. "That was only about...two and a half hours ago out of stasis."

Again, his eyes slate over to her, like he's evaluating something she can't see, but thankfully remains quiet.

At least he's not panicking anymore. At least this house has nobody else sniffing around, no other safety concerns. There's running water and a bed—two things important to humans—and the ambient temperature isn't too far outside of comfort.

The phone beeps in his pocket, and she flinches again.

"Do you have a plan?" he asks, after a long moment of scrolling over whatever messages he has.

She generally doesn't, never was one to craft elaborate schemes. Some demons excel at them, some spend their entire lives in one stratagem after another, but that usually bores her.

But.

After all that time in stasis, after all that time doing

nothing but pace, without the body or any other company, sure gave her time to think. All the times she was brought out, the leash choking her throat, all gave her ideas. All the experiments, all the humans looming over her and making decisions, ensured that her mind had been locked on too few of things.

Another strange sensation crawls over her, this one not wholly unwelcome.

"There's three more handlers still alive," she says, lifting her chin, watching him as he nonchalantly eats food she had purchased for the body, inhabiting the space that nobody else had. "Two dead, three more to go."

3

Gurlien stares at her, wholly unimpressed, and it's more interesting of an expression than she thought it would be.

"You described three of the highest profile members of the College," Gurlien starts, and he's not wrong, "and you want to just waltz in and kill them?"

"Oh, no," Ambra says, a fission of disgust going through her. "I never want to step foot in any of their bases ever again."

"Oh, okay, that's good, that makes it easier," he replies sarcastically, and it's far more interesting than him faking being bored. "You want to find three highly paranoid, highly secure individuals and off them?"

"They all have houses, they all have other places they live. They all have apartments in multiple cities, labs in weird parts of the world. They shop, they consume food, they leave footprints."

He says nothing, his eyebrows raised, until he finishes the bar he's eating and carefully folds up the wrapper, creasing the foil in precise lines.

"You can't talk, you broke into their base to save an old lady," Ambra preempts, when he opens his mouth to speak. "That's infinitely more insane than ambushing some individuals in places they aren't expecting it."

"It's not just some individuals, all of them could kill either of us—"

She scoffs at that.

"—could kill me with barely any effort, and they knew me." He sets the carefully folded piece of foil aside. "And apparently, they could control you, easily."

"That's why you're here," she interrupts, gesturing with the leash again, and he stares down at his wrist, like he gets some feedback with it. "You stop them from doing that, I kill them, then I'm..."

Her mind blanks out at that, for a few seconds, like the concept is just as foreign to her as the stasis chambers once were.

"Then I can do whatever I want," she finishes. "Figure out how long I'll live like this, be away from humans, hide from other demons. Simple."

"Simple," he echoes, brows still raised.

It, of course, isn't simple at all.

"So besides murder," Gurlien starts, "did you have any concrete plans?"

"Not terribly," Ambra replies. "It wasn't like I knew a rescue was coming today."

Or that the people letting her go were people she's faced in battle. Or that there would be someone so perfect for the leash.

Or that another of her handlers would be dead.

"Korhonen was the one I was most concerned about," she says, and he blinks, like it's a change of subject. "He's the fastest out of all of them, so thank you for that."

Gurlien swallows, before staring out the window.

"How close do I have to be for the leash?" Then, at something in his expression, he holds up his hands again. "I know, they can get you anywhere. But what about me?"

"We will have to test the limits," Ambra replies, because again, it's a good question, one showing a scientific mind that's not prone to assumptions. "I hope...I hope we have a day before they try anything."

"That long?" Idly, Gurlien starts inspecting the kitchen, opening the drawers and the cabinets, and it's the actions of someone who doesn't like to be lacking information about his surroundings.

"They'll want to control the beasts on site first," she murmurs, hugging herself again. "I shouldn't be a priority."

"No, you're just the first successful result of the Terese project, a controllable demon with massive amounts of power that could be in their hands, couldn't see how that would be a priority, not at all." Still, Gurlien shakes his head, grabbing the single glass out of the drying rack and filling it with water, drinking deeply.

She flinches, but doesn't stop him.

"I'm exhausted," he states. "I'm exhausted and very, very confused. I didn't fully expect to live through today, and now I'm somewhere unfamiliar, with a clearly unstable experiment, being asked to control a magical process I have not studied and have no abilities in."

"Exactly," Ambra says again, because he seems to be missing the point that that's entirely what she wanted.

"And my friends are still in Eastern Canada and I'm on an entirely different coast because I got teleported." He levels her with a glare over the top of his glasses, which spoils any sort of threat from it. "So pardon me if I'm not feeling comfortable with your level of plans."

It's fair enough, but Ambra scrapes at her mind for something else to do, some other lever to pull at this very moment, besides sitting back down on the chilly tile and recuperating.

"And you're still obviously not in good condition," he points at her, almost accusatory, and she stares down at his hand as if it personally offends her. "You're shaking, you keep on jumping at things that aren't there, there's still blood on your face—"

Instinctively, she reaches a hand to her face, and sure enough, some dried blood flakes off.

"—and I don't know if it's because you're a demon or if it's because nobody ever expected to have this experiment go well ever again or because you're in a human body and I don't think you know how to care for it." He crosses his arms, like it's the end of an argument.

It's not anything she didn't know, but there's still a sting to it.

She stares at him back. "Okay."

"Okay?" he repeats, face blank. "Just...okay?"

She shrugs one shoulder, and it reminds her of the muscle tightness that the body always had there, tightness verging on pain that she has never quite figured out how to heal. "You're not wrong on any of that."

"Good," he says, forcefully to the point of it being comical. "Thanks. Super validating."

"You're welcome," she murmurs, then pushes herself away from leaning against the sink, even though her legs wobble precariously. "Eat what you want, sleep on the bed. Don't leave the house until we have more information on the range, I'm going to clean up."

With a flick of her hand, she twists the wards tighter

around the windows, and the very structure creaks around them.

He jumps, eyes wide, before he spins back to her.

But instead of angry and scared, instead of the fake boredom or the sarcastic mask, he's fascinated.

The expression lasts just a split second before he schools his face back down, but another shiver winds its way down Ambra's back.

"That was just protection to make myself feel better," she informs him, then turns on her heel and marches to the meager bathroom, slamming the door behind her in the way her handlers used to do when they wanted her unnerved.

The bathroom in the motorhome is tiny, with barely enough room for her to turn around, but the plumbing still works and dust covered towels still hang over the sink.

Ambra inspects her appearance in the dirty mirror. Gurlien was right, she still has a rather ghastly amount of human blood on her face, along with some of her own. The wound from the necromancer, where she had the audacity to slam a strip of raw death into Ambra's face at the bar, still takes up the majority of Ambra's cheek, with flaking, peeling skin.

She pokes at it. It's not as painful anymore, but the skin around it is tight, like it's stretched too far over her cheekbone.

And no matter how much she prods it, how much she concentrates, it doesn't heal.

"Alright," she mutters, rubbing at the edge, which doesn't help. "Necromancer wounds don't heal."

In the cosmic balance of things, where most necromancers end up dead from demons while they're still a child, it makes sense that they could be one of the few things that could hurt a demon.

Ambra sheds the sweater again, then peels off the functional yet incredibly boring rough clothed pants the College always put her in, and cranks on the shower.

It's not an action natural to her, but the body had insisted on it, and they both always felt better after scrubbing the skin under hot water, and Ambra just hopes it still works. That she could get a glimpse of the peace with this action that she did before, despite everything that had happened in between.

She hisses, the impact of the water stinging against the new scar on her stomach, but holds still, letting it run over her hair and stream down her face, before she suds up the soap and attempts to get every last bit of blood off of her skin.

Through the thin door, Gurlien's voice carries, and she stills, as if her motion is the thing causing all of the noise and not the rush of water and the creak of pipes.

Not every word reaches her. "...northwest somewhere, judging...trees. Phone doesn't...location."

She tilts her head, and the water streams down her neck instead of her face, which is immediately better. It washes underneath the leash around her neck, almost startling her with the soothing sensation, and she bends her neck more, so more water runs underneath it, against the irritated skin and her own claw marks.

"Demon," he says, clearly, and his footsteps pace by the door, into the bedroom, then back out, circling the small motorhome. "Clearly suffering, very confused."

She raises an eyebrow at the plastic shower curtain. He's not wrong.

"I don't know!" He bursts out, clear as day. "I don't know,

that's why I'm calling you, since you apparently have been hiding…"

His voice fades out a bit, and she loses the next few sentences, so she hastily scrubs up and dries off the best she could, though now the one side of her hair is thoroughly tangled.

Gurlien's not speaking, but he's still pacing, making quiet sounds as if he's listening on the other side of the phone.

Ambra steps back into the undergarments, then shoves the sweater back over her head, but kicks the boring pants to the side. The body kept so many changes of clothes here, she never has to wear the ones the College put her in ever again.

It's a small thrill at the thought. Where she can dress in the clothing that would feel good against her skin, instead of the constricting and structured clothing they had forced her into.

"You can't be serious," Gurlien says, pacing back by the door, and a smile tugs on Ambra's lips. Someone has clearly given him news he didn't like, and the obviousness of his reaction is charming.

She attempts to finger comb through her hair, before giving up in boredom.

"What's not serious?" she asks, stepping out.

Gurlien stops in his tracks, the phone still in his hand and pressed against his ear, and blinks at her.

There's a whisper of someone speaking from the phone, but Gurlien just stares.

So she stares back, gesturing for him to answer.

"Hey, Axel, I need to go," Gurlien cuts off whatever monologue the other person's giving him, before he stuffs the phone back into his pocket. "It's a turn of phrase."

"Okay," Ambra replies, then steps into the bedroom for the first time since the merge, and gets a few steps to the closet before...something...slams into her.

Not something physical, but almost like a wave of emotions, a wave of chemicals flooding through her body, staggering her.

The body had slept in the bed, had curled up against the pillow and pulled the coverlet over her head, and it had been the most comfortable Ambra had ever been through the entire process. They had placed all the clothing in the closet, one bit by one bit, and Ambra had marveled at the fabrics, at the clean motions of folding each piece together. She organized it all by color, and the open doors show her the rainbow, all still meticulously in place. The body had chucked off her shoes, and they both stood, feeling the carpet between their toes, and Ambra had giggled at the sensation.

"Why aren't you wearing pants?" Gurlien calls from the hallway, voice dim behind the rushing of her ears.

Her lips part to answer, but no words come out.

Like he's expecting some sort of attacking creature or trap, Gurlien steps into the doorway, but instead it's just her, her legs wobbling.

The carpet is still plush under her feet, despite the time and the dust.

Gurlien cranes his neck to glance at the closet, then back at her. "Is it something I can't see?"

Mute, she shakes her head, then lowers herself to sit on the bed.

There's so much emotion, so many contradictory sensations flickering over her body. She's hot, but she shivers, tugging in her knees to her chest, as she stares at the rainbow of clothing, now only marred by dust.

"Okay," he murmurs, then disappears down the hallway, quickly returning, and tosses her the protein bar she had left on the counter. "Eat this."

She breaks her gaze on the closet to stare at the bar, half numb despite the growing pit of chemicals filtering through the body's blood. "What?"

"You were shaking like a leaf and staring at some clothing," he says, voice perfectly serious. "I don't know why, I don't know what the College told you, but if you're in a human body, you have to actually eat food."

She pokes at the foil package, and it's a bit easier to look at than the clothing. "I was just having some emotions, I think."

His brows draw together and he tilts his head, like he's calculating something, and that is just enough action to break through all the nonsense adrenaline flooding through her.

"I don't know what you know of demons," she says, as loftily as she can. Which isn't much, when her voice still quakes. "But we experience things very differently than humans."

"So I've read," he replies dryly.

"And some parts of that haven't translated very well to having actual nerve endings." She swallows down the lump, risking another glance towards the closet.

It's still the beautiful kaleidoscope of colors. All lovingly put into place by the body.

"Okay, logical," Gurlien says, interrupting another surge of sensations. "Probably disorienting, definitely an explanation for some of your twitchiness. Eat the bar."

She squints at him.

"If they try to bring you back right now, are you in fighting shape?"

The answer to that is a resounding no.

"If they pull you back now, and I get pulled into it, they'll probably kill me." His words are clinical, like he's stating a conclusion he already came to. "They kicked me out, definitely, over a year ago, and I just helped a high value prisoner escape. They're not going to be merciful to me."

It's probably true, and she nods. It's a good thing for him to keep in mind.

"I don't particularly want to die," he says, which again, makes sense. "So my best ticket to surviving the next few days is, until I convince you to undo whatever this is—" he gestures with his wrist, "—is to keep you alive and able to resist. So eat the food."

"Did your Axel give you that conclusion?" she asks, and his face twitches, like he's a bit unhappy with her figuring it out that quickly. "Is he a demonology expert?"

Gurlien opens his mouth, then closes it, obviously thinking better of his answer.

She waits, letting her eyes stray back to the closet.

"He's about as close to an expert as you can get to the Terese project who wasn't...actively involved in breaking the people," he says, guarded, and that catches her attention again. "So yes, he gave me a list of things to do, and unless we have a bad reaction to it, I plan on following his tips."

"I don't like the experts I've met," she mutters darkly, but picks up the bar, inspecting it.

It's one of the ones that came in a variety pack, not one of the flavors she tried with the body. Buzz words like 'protein' and 'muscle' are all over it in bright font, and the body had eaten a few of them when she had described herself as 'peckish.'

"Don't worry, he doesn't either," Gurlien says, heavily. "He's also kept his knowledge very quiet. He laughed,"

Gurlien says, suddenly, full of frustration. "He laughed when I told him what happened. He laughed at me for this."

She raises an eyebrow at him.

"I was literally kidnapped, and he laughed out loud."

"That doesn't sound like a great friend," Ambra ventures, peeling open the foil around the bar. It doesn't smell appealing, but the body's sense of smell has puzzled her since the beginning.

"Wouldn't call him a friend." Gurlien leans against the door jamb, watching her actions like a hawk. "If you don't like that, there's a cabinet full of food to pick from, but even if you don't think you need to, you should eat."

"Anyone ever tell you you're pushy?" Despite the casual words, Ambra glances back at the closet.

It's still so empty without the body with her, even while full to the brim.

And she has to exist like this, now. With evidence of the body existing all over the place, when she's left alone.

She shivers, suddenly, and Gurlien sighs, before he crosses to the closet and abruptly pulls a pair of sweatpants off the hanger. "Here, put these on, you'll be warmer."

Warmth had nothing to do with it, and Ambra had teased the body for even hanging up sweatpants, but she shucks them on anyways, then smoothes her hands on her hips in the unconscious way the body always did.

The fabric is, of course, much better than the rough canvas pants.

"Glad you're getting invested," Ambra says, pushing herself to standing, clutching the unappealing bar in her hand. "Did your friend know how to remove the leash entirely?"

Gurlien's lip twitches, and somehow she knows, deep down, that she's not gonna like the answer.

"He can't," he says, and despite the guarded tone, Ambra can tell he's not lying. "He's a dud like me. Had magic then had it taken away."

It wasn't something Ambra knew of happening, but she never paid all that much attention to too many humans to form observations of it before the merge.

She knew the body had had magic of her own, a small smidgen of power that was quickly eclipsed by Ambra's.

"Do you want to wash all the scuffs off of you?" Ambra asks, gesturing to the shower. "I can't imagine you like all the blood and dust caked on you."

He pinches the bridge of his nose. "Any of those clothes in there men's clothes?"

The body had some old T-shirts, worn soft with time and care, and a pair of men's pajama pants left over from a 'boyfriend,' so Ambra pulls them off the hanger. They're a lot easier to look at than the other clothing.

"She slept in these a few times, said it reminded her of her ex," Ambra supplies, at his blank look. "I don't understand it either."

"That's not the part of this I don't understand," Gurlien grumbles, but takes them anyway. He holds out the rumpled pajama pants, clearly meant for a shorter person. "Do you have anything else?"

"You can wear some of the body's clothes, but I don't think they'll fit any better," Ambra offers, and he closes his eyes. She's once again missing the point, the human conversation strange.

"Answer my phone if it's Chloe, Maison, Delina, or someone named Axel or Alette. Nobody else." He dumps the phone in her other hand. "Go eat some food."

4

Nobody calls for the brief time Gurlien's in the shower, but Ambra curls her legs underneath herself and gamely attempts to eat the thoroughly unpleasant energy bar, staring at the blank piece of electronics.

The couch is just as plush as she remembers it, at least, and she slumps backwards in it, like it's something that can embrace her. Even with the weirdness, even with the physical body sending so many contradictory sensations, it's a lot better than the blank fuzz of stasis, with the single cot.

And she goes over her plan, whatever it could look like. Her now much abridged plan, with only three targets instead of five.

She had always planned on going after Korhonen first, taking him out as quickly as possible. He used her for the most destruction, and she wanted to limit that the most.

Nalissa would be the easiest to kill but the hardest to track down, the most protected. She ruled the underground burial tunnels underneath Paris, and had laid all the traps possible for people to be caught off guard.

Even though she had walked Ambra through them like a friend, even though she had chatted amicably with the body, she didn't bother to step in during the merge, to stop the body from dying and leaving Ambra behind. She didn't help, and then afterwards put Ambra through a reeling array of tests, all for control.

Johnsin mostly stayed in Florida, the humid state with more marsh than forest, and the body had hated him with a passion. His mansion was slickly beautiful, smooth tiles and white walls overlooking a twinkling blue ocean, and Ambra had just thought it was all so very tacky.

He hadn't waited for the body to die before putting them through all the tests, and the body had screamed her throat bloody before Ambra could heal it.

Boltiex...Boltiex just wanted power. He lived wherever suited him, rarely keeping one home, and would be, by far, the hardest to kill.

She puzzles over it, as the shower turns off, her limbs somewhat heavy on the couch. Like they were unused to being out of stasis for so long.

"Nobody called," she says loudly, as soon as the tiny bathroom door opens up.

The pajama pants are somewhat comically short around Gurlien's ankles and his glasses are fogged up, but he shakes his head anyways.

"I hate these pants," he mutters, tugging at the hem. They don't look bad on him, just ill fitting, like something that he's never meant to wear.

Other than the tough work pants from the base, she's not sure why her mind makes that connection. Back at the bar, she had been too tunneled into focusing on the half-demon and the necromancer, and barely remembered Gurlien being there, except for the flash of his phone light and the reflection of it in his glasses. Nothing about his clothes or general presentation.

"I expect Axel's probably laughing it up with his friends," Gurlien mutters, swiping the phone back and sitting on the other side of the couch. "Do you want another bar?"

Ambra squints at him, weighing whether or not that was a normal thing.

The body had eaten more food than Ambra had thought necessary, but she had done a lot that Ambra wasn't sure of the purpose of.

"Why?" She finally settles on.

"Because humans," he starts, pushing himself up to the cupboard, "expend a lot of energy whenever they use any sort of power, and they need to replenish it. So if you want to be powerful enough to kill any of those three when they call for you, you need it."

"Sure," she says, "but if there's anything that's less awful than those, I'd appreciate it."

"Okay," he mutters, then tosses her a brightly wrapped candy bar. "Demon doesn't like protein bars."

She raises an eyebrow, unwrapping the candy and sinking further into the couch. On the table, the phone beeps, and she flinches.

But on the screen, even without him unlocking it, she can read:

AXEL (8:55 PM): She suggests that warm food is always better than cold, and that something ridiculous will get her to eat more than something boring.

"Are you asking your friends how to feed me?" Ambra asks, torn between being amused and absolutely horrified. "And who would Axel refer to as 'her?'"

Gurlien swoops in to pick up the phone with a clatter. "I

asked how to get you to full power," he snips, and once again, the glimpse of personality is fascinating. "And all of his suggestions are food and sleep and comfortable things."

"Who's 'she?'" Ambra asks, after a long moment of staring at Gurlien's fingers as he taps out responses.

"Could they compel you to answer if they get the leash?" he asks languidly, but she doesn't buy the casualness at all.

"Of course."

"Then I'm not telling you," he responds, with barely a flicker of a glance from behind the glasses.

It's fair, but it still sucks, so Ambra just leans further into the couch, mindlessly eating the candy. It's not bad, the sweetness a bit overpowering and artificial tasting, but again, not very interesting when one has consumed necromancer recently.

It's silent again in the small cabin, and she watches as Gurlien flicks a tiny button on the phone, quieting all the piercing beeps, but he continues typing, his eyes speeding over the screen with a quickness that almost astounds Ambra.

Sure, she's seen humans read, but not that fast.

"You said the other Terese project got killed by a Necromancer," she starts, after a long lull, and she's almost surprised at how much her voice has slowed down in the meantime. "But the one at the base—"

"Delina," Gurlien interrupts.

"Had only been unlocked recently, they said." She watches him underneath her eyelashes. "So there's more than one?"

"Yes," he replies, fast. "For once in history, there are two actual necromancers, and they're in the same country and around the same age."

She rests her head against the back of the couch, her eyelids strangely heavy. "Demons must be going nuts."

He shoots her another glare. "One of them is protected, we don't know how, but she is. Delina has Maison, and he's prepared to fight anyone for her."

"Convenient," she murmurs, letting her eyes flutter shut, letting them rest for the first time in the day.

With the bright lights of the stasis chamber, closing her eyes didn't provide much relief, and all since then had been a strange blur of alarms, of strobing lights, so the warm glow of the motor home lamps is soothing. Easily ignorable.

"Okay," Gurlien mutters, then sighs, pulling out a notebook from a drawer and rattling around for a pen.

She sits up straighter, opening her eyes again.

"Yes, I found this, I'm taking it," Gurlien says, holding up the cheaply spiral bound book. "It was empty and I need something to take notes on."

"Sure," Ambra says, gesturing at the motorhome. "Anything you need to take from here, as long as you help me."

This stalls his brain for a few moments, before he shakes his head and scribbles something down.

"But what are you writing?" she asks, unable to stop herself.

"A list," he replies curtly, and she recognizes the tone from other handlers to stop talking. He alternates between writing in the book and glancing at his phone, referencing something, and she'll have to steal it to check what he's writing later.

For a few minutes, the only sound is the whisper soft susurration of the snow outside and the scratch of the pen over the cheap paper, an almost lulling concoction of noises.

Until.

Almost imperceptibly, the leash tightens around her neck, cutting off the exhale of one breath.

Gurlien drops the pen, his other hand going to his wrist, before his eyes snap up to her.

And Ambra freezes, her heart jumping.

Before the leash loosens, just enough so she can pull in another breath.

Across the cheap plastic counter tops, Gurlien's lips part. "Was that…"

Ambra nods, as small as she could make it.

Dread pools into her stomach, and the leash stretches taught again, as if testing.

Moving slowly, deliberately, Gurlien puts his phone into his pocket, stepping around the counter, keeping a hand over the leash on his wrist.

Another tug, not enough to compel her, not enough to pull her away, but it jerks her chin up from her place on the couch.

She can't swallow, she can't speak, and air barely squeaks down her throat. Her hands shake like they're in the wind outside, and pain, sudden and vicious, rockets down her spine.

"Okay," Gurlien mutters, and he picks up the gun from the side table then, in a moment of foolishness, sits next to her on the couch.

All of Ambra's a single nerve, and it's on fire, and the leash loosens enough that she gasps in some air, before tightening again.

So it's one of the handlers that knows the unpleasantness of that motion. Knows the pain of the leash, of denying her breath for a few moments.

Her hands shake up, to clutch at the leash, and Gurlien catches them, startling a flinch out of her.

"Are they testing it right now?" he asks, voice low.

She can't speak, no words can leave her, but she nods, a single jerk of her head, before it tightens back up again.

"Don't respond," he whispers, and her jaw works against the leash, cutting into the skin on her neck. "If you don't respond, they might stop."

They won't, and she opens her mouth to say that, but no words come out.

The body's eyes water, uncontrolled, tears rolling cold down her cheeks.

The reactions to this are always the worst. The automatic systems, the nerves spiking, the parts of her that she can't control. The parts that the handlers manipulate, to tie her into the body.

Another jerk, just enough to hurt, not to bring her over. A gasp squeaks out of her, unbidden, and a drop of blood trickles from her neck.

His eyes are wide behind his glasses, and he cradles her hand, a contracting sensation, before he swipes his thumb over her palm.

If they pull her back now, before she's had a chance to figure out the leash with Gurlien, there's a chance she may never be free. They might shove her back into the stasis chamber, shove her somewhere nobody will ever dig up.

She grips his hand back, tight, digging her nails in, and abruptly, the leash slackens.

Like whoever was testing abruptly let go.

Ambra doubles over, a keening noise ripped away from her throat, and she shakes. Her hands shake, her face shakes, her breath shakes.

Gurlien inhales, like it had been choking him too, before he jolts up to standing, jerkily walking to the kitchen.

Ambra just squeezes her eyes shut, trying to stop her

lungs from aching. Her throat hurts, like the leash had cut into it.

Dimly, she hears Gurlien run the faucet, before his footsteps approach again.

"Here," he says, abrupt, shoving a wet towel into her view.

"Why?" She croaks out, attempting to straighten, but she lists to the side, unable to control even the most basic of motions of the body. "I'm..."

"Ugh," Gurlien mutters, sitting back down, propping her up. She leans forward, her head thumping against his shoulder, and even that motion hurts. "Here," he says, holding the wet towel against the broken skin on her neck, and she only manages a twitch in surprise at the touch. "It drew blood."

"It does that," she mumbles out, and she can't even control the body enough to speak clearly, so she clears her throat.

Which is, of course, awful.

"Well, that's vicious," he mutters, gently dabbing at the skin. "What medical care do they give you?"

She exhales through her nose, still keeping her head down. "I can heal myself."

"Right," he replies unsteadily, still cleaning up the black blood, and her stomach turns.

Straightening again, even though her head swims and her vision almost whites out, she snatches the wet paper towel from him, scrubbing at the abraded skin.

"It draws blood, it fucking hurts, and I can't fucking control this body," she snaps, and her voice is still raw, like sandpaper had been rubbed against her vocal cords.

He pulls back, and there's a calculation behind his eyes, one she can't parse.

"Which one?" Gurlien asks, and his face is pale. "Could you tell which one it was?"

She shakes her head, which is blindingly painful for a few seconds.

"Useful," Gurlien snips, but he pushes himself up to standing again, joining her in the kitchen, where she dunks the towel under the water again. "Any hints, though?"

Ambra exhales, leaning against the counter, letting her mind race. "It wasn't Boltiex."

"Good to know," Gurlien nods, and he's hardly alone in that.

"He wouldn't play with the pain, he would just..." she mimes jerking on the leash. "Nalissa and Johnsin might."

Gurlien faces her, drawing her gaze up at him in some unknown instinct. "So, a person who knows your nerves or a person who likes pain?"

He learns quickly.

"Johnsin had the best control over my body," she says, and the words hurt. "He could make me do anything with just a thought."

"So this wasn't him?" Gurlien asks. "He wouldn't need to tease you like that."

She shakes her head again, it's not the correct assumption. "He just might, just for the pain. Nalissa..." she trails off, trying to force her mind to think. "Nalissa might test, so she's not surprised by the results, and the pain wouldn't matter to her."

Gurlien's silent, for a minute, just watching her, and the surveillance is almost overwhelming, wholly different from the focus of scientists she usually endured.

"Let me call in Maison," he murmurs finally, and she flinches. "He's had connections with other demons, he could figure out how to fix this."

She shakes her head, as fast as she could without blacking out. "If he's had connection with demons, he could deliver me to them."

"His girlfriend is a Necromancer, he doesn't want anything to do with demons like that," Gurlien interjects, and Ambra gapes at him. "What."

"He's...fucking his necromancer?" she manages out, and it's almost distracting enough to erase the pain from her mind. "Intentionally?"

Gurlien just stares at her, blankly. "What did you...what did you think they were?"

She doesn't have a proper answer for that. "He's bonded to her, I didn't think..." she squeezes her eyes shut, to try to get a grip on her reactions, still horribly out of reach after the leash. "He's even more insane than I thought."

There. A trace of a smile on his face, like he couldn't help it, before he squashes that down. "When we aren't in the middle of a crisis, I will tell you that story, and it is more insane than you think it is," he says, fully serious, and suddenly, desperately, she wants to know it. "But we should call him."

"No," Ambra says, though now the curiosity of the story wars with the practicality of needing to stay away from the Half Demon. "I don't trust..."

If he's Half Demon, it means he's half human, too, which gives him more than enough power to fully control her.

To distract herself, she rewets the towel before placing it cool against her neck, a welcome distraction from the still burning abrasion.

"Plus, I think if given a chance, he'd absolutely just rather live somewhere and do his art rather than any combat," Gurlien says, and it's some sort of bid for her attention, for some reason. "And now with his mom out, I don't think he'd ever do anything for the College ever again."

She squints at him, at the shape of his lips forming words, at the pull of his skin on his face, as if it could give her more meaning. As if the moment slows down, as if the shaky pulse in her neck quiets its speeding, and—

Her head snaps back, the leash yanking tight, faster than she can yell out.

And.

And each time it does, each time it chokes, she gets the split second of warning. Of where the rest of the world flashes to white, where she can struggle and dig in. Where all sound slams away, a fuzz of static filling her mind instead. Where she can claw at the leash, drag her fingertips and nails into the skin, maybe get some purchase from it, and—

"Shit!"

A hand on her wrist, as the world explodes around her.

5

No matter what Ambra does, she always loses consciousness at first, and she's never sure if it's for a split second or if it's for an eternity, but she stumbles, her feet sliding on slick tile, until the leash around her straightens her, pulling her upright.

And Gurlien falls onto the tile in front of her, a sudden body weight not against her, clattering to the floor.

She gapes at him, she wants to, before her head snaps back again, ripping her eyes away from him and up to the room at large.

Warm lights.

Oppressive humidity, burrowing into her skin and weighing down her lungs.

Her arms prickle and the leash turns her around, to stare right at Johnsin, leaving Gurlien on the floor, scrabbling to get up.

Johnsin, with his black hair with streaks of gray in it, prematurely light. Or dyed, she never found out. He's younger than he looks, but cultivates a facade of handsome wisdom. Of someone who should be wealthy.

Johnsin, who lives in Florida, and would have been in the same time zone as the base and the fastest one to move.

Johnsin, who's holding a knife, casually, his other hand fisted around the leash.

Ambra tries to speak, tries to open the body's mouth and force words out, but her jaw doesn't move.

Because Johnsin is always the one with the most iron hand of control on the small things of her. He couldn't control her magic too well, so he never tried, but her body... he definitely controlled that.

The dread floods through her again, lighting her gut on fire.

And he looks past her, to where she can hear Gurlien pull himself to standing, and Johnsin's dashing eyebrows furrow. "Gurlien Banks? Is that you?"

She tries to turn to glance, but Johnsin's grip on the leash doesn't even allow that small of movement.

"Okay, this isn't what it looks like," Gurlien says, voice wheezy, like the teleportation winded him. "Uh, put down the knife?"

Johnson's face wrinkles with something resembling derision. "Hit any more ley lines lately? Get another concussion? Not gonna do that."

Gurlien's face spasms, before he controls it.

Johnsin meets Ambra's eyes. "You thought you could run off with a dud?" He pulls the leash tight, so tight the edges crowd around Ambra's vision, but still, she can't move an inch. "Surely you could tell."

He loosens the leash enough for her to nod, then chokes it back again. She gags, the unconscious movement happening despite his control, and her fingers spasm.

He always enjoyed gagging her.

Horror winds its way into her blood, sudden and vicious, and in front of her, Johnsin's lips twitch upwards.

"Okay, Kyle," Gurlien starts, and that must be Johnsin's first name, even though Ambra's never heard it. He straightens, and it's just out of the corner of her eye that she can see the flop of his hair, can see the edge of his silhouette. "Uh, this is a misunderstanding, stop choking her."

"What, and let Boltiex take her with no additional controls?" Johnsin shoots back, jerking the leash again. "I don't know how you're in all of this, but this isn't a person, you don't have to get all lawyer about this one."

Gurlien takes another step forward, and he has his hands up, as if showing he's unarmed, but the leash is still around his wrist.

Johnsin's eyes follow it down, then he snaps Ambra away, jerking her enough so she's across the room, teleported in between one breath and the next.

"What have you heard?" Johnsin asks, suddenly guarded, and the back of Ambra's neck prickles.

Gurlien wets his lips, but there's something working behind his eyes, some intelligence, some calculations. "Not much," he replies, voice cautious. "She took me by surprise."

Johnsin's not buying it, at all, and he tightens the leash around Ambra's neck, and her breath squeaks out again.

She hadn't had time to coach him, she hadn't had time to do anything. She doesn't even know if he could pull it yet, if he could counteract it.

"No, she literally kidnapped me," Gurlien emphasizes, "because of my…"

"Because of your accident?" Johnsin's skeptical, and it's a teasing bit of information, something just interesting enough that it derails the pain, derails the panic screaming through her. That Johnsin knows something she doesn't.

Gurlien swallows, his throat bobbing. "I think so." He blinks towards Ambra, some sort of message, attempting to say something with his eyes, but she can't tell what. "She said she didn't want me to control her."

It's the correct thing to say, but Ambra goes cold. It's correct, it's exactly what happened, but…

But if Gurlien's divulging it so easily, he could hand it over, and be done with all this.

She takes a big gulping breath. "He—"

Johnsin jerks on the leash, effectively cutting off her words, and she gags again, her eyes blurring. Blood wells up in her throat, but she can't even clear it out.

"Can you untie that" Johnsin asks, gesturing towards the leash, which of course Gurlien can't see. "I don't want to muddle the chain of command; this is a delicate project."

Gurlien shakes his head immediately. "I can't even see it."

Again, it's true, it's correct, but he's revealing too much. He's revealing too much and she's going to be handed back and she can't…

Unable to stop herself, she scrabbles at her neck for the leash, cutting into the skin, until Johnsin snaps the leash tight enough and her hands fall away, her muscles abruptly relaxing.

Outside of her bidding, she stands up straight, perfectly still, the body's shoulders settling back.

"It's okay," her voice says, Johnsin compelling the words out of her, and he mouths along with her.

Gurlien recoils back, as Johnsin turns her eyes to him.

"Did she work real hard at convincing you she was a person?" Her voice speaks, and it hurts to have them forced through her throat, after all the screaming and the tightness. "She does that."

Gurlien's pale, his hair firmly out of place after the teleportation, and the too short pajamas and hoodie stick out in all the slick white tile. Even though he showered, there's still a bruise on the underside of his jaw from whatever trials he had gone through in the base before they let her go.

"How hooked into the communications are you?" Johnsin asks, casually flipping the knife in his hand, and Gurlien doesn't stop staring at Ambra, fully spooked.

"Not very," he replies automatically. "I hear rumors."

"And did this one tell you what happened just yesterday?"

Ambra attempts to stare over at Johnsin, but he doesn't let her move her eyes, keeping her focus on Gurlien.

"She definitely didn't tell me anything," Gurlien replies, and Ambra blinks.

That's also the truth, but this time it's misleading.

Idly, Johnsin tugs against the leash, and all at once, all her nerves ignite. Flame up, the pain whitening out her vision and sealing her lungs and weakening her spine and

—

She can't move. Can't do anything from her passive position, standing next to Johnsin and observing Gurlien.

Johnsin doesn't let her knees buckle. Doesn't let her sag over, doesn't let her lose control of her body and fall to the ground.

"The entire Toronto base is gone," Ambra's voice says, perfectly even, despite the agony. "Years of experiments, monsters held there for decades if not centuries, all released. Took us this long to realize this one was one of them."

Always with a flare for the dramatic, Johnsin makes Ambra examine her own hand, as if the motion doesn't feel like her bones shatter in place.

Gurlien wets his lips again, and she can see the calculations flying through his eyes. "What are you doing to her?"

"What?" Johnsin blurts out, stopping the casual knife flipping. "I'm just holding her in place."

Gurlien's brow furrows, as if he very much doesn't buy that. "You're doing something." He takes a step forward, keeping his hands up, very much not grasping at the leash.

"Oh, she got you really convinced she's a person, didn't she?" Johnsin says, twisting his fingers around Ambra's leash, a telltale sign he's about to do something. "Demons do that, right up there with Wights, pretending to be human."

Gurlien flinches, like it's a personal attack, and Johnsin's lips curve up into a smirk.

Again, he knows something Ambra doesn't.

"Anyways, I heard you were exiled somewhere up north or something, how'd you end up getting kidnapped by a demon we buried in Toronto?"

He loosens up something in the leash, some sort of split concentration, and Ambra exhales, pushing the trapped air out of her lungs, past the agony and the rawness of her throat. Everything still bites of pain, tearing teeth into the nerves of the body, but if she could breathe...

How did you find him?" Johnsin asks, turning back to Ambra and...

Tangling his fingers in the leash, compels her.

The words spring, unbidden, without her consent, and she struggles with them for a few moments, her teeth cutting into her own cheek, before, "He freed me from the stasis."

Johnsin nods at her, as if she gets some sort of pleasure from the acknowledgement. "Good girl."

She twitches her hands out, but he catches her, smoothing out her body back to the peaceful stance.

Gurlien makes a choked off sound, something between horror and anger.

"And how did he get to the stasis chambers?"

Again, the same pull, and she digs in, tries to pull herself out of it. "He had a necromancer, a Half Demon, and an alchemist."

Johnsin's face twitches in some sort of surprise.

"She's lying," Gurlien says, and now desperation coats his voice. "I would never—"

"Sure you wouldn't," Johnsin says, smooth, turning his back to Ambra. "Of course not."

"I don't—"

With only a moment of warning, one Ambra only barely sees, barely gets out a quick inhale, Johnsin drops the physical control of Ambra, twisting his hands into the very fabric of the magic in the room, snapping out an attack towards Gurlien.

Ambra reels to the side, her vision blacking out and leaving her aimless for a split second, before she gets her feet underneath herself and braces.

Gurlien yells, something choked out, and everything snaps back into the laser focus of panic.

There's blood, sprayed finely over the slick white furniture, and Gurlien clutches at his arm, and Johnsin's already winding the strip of magic around his hand for another attack.

It's the arm with the leash. Johnsin's trying to get it off him.

Ambra jerks forward, the pain edging around her view, and Johnsin snaps the leash taut with nary a thought.

And in between one moment in the next, his eyes wide

with something resembling terror, Gurlien grapples for the leash tied on his wrist and yanks.

Yanks just hard enough to stagger Johnsin, breaking his concentration on her, and Ambra whips that around, her power flooding back into her control.

She gets a bare glimpse of the white of Johnsin's eyes, a flash of terror, before she clutches her fist into the magic.

And snaps his neck.

Snapping necks is her favorite way to kill someone.

There's no gore, there's no confusion, just between one moment and the next the person is no more.

For a split second, there's nothing, no sound, before he slumps to the ground, dead before he hits the tile.

Gurlien recoils back at the wet sound of Johnsin's body against the slick white floor, and he's panting, his chest heaving up and down.

"How—" he manages out, before he clutches at his forearm again, at the bloody gash Johnsin left in his attempt. "What?"

Ambra rolls her shoulder back and almost blacks out from the pain again, blinking out against it.

"He keeps bandages in the second drawer of the coffee table," she manages, before coughing again, spitting some blood onto the slick tile. "The gauze should be sterile, he hated infections."

"What the fuck," Gurlien whispers, and she turns her eyes to him.

Besides the gash on his arm, he's unharmed, though his pulse jumps at his throat, almost derailing Ambra's attention.

"Why the hell did he keep sterile gauze in his living room?"

"Do you really want to know that answer?" Ambra asks,

curious, and he's already shaking his head. "This wasn't the first time he did that pain surge on me."

"Jesus Christ," Gurlien mutters, and mechanically, he sits on the white couch, yanking open the drawer.

Sure enough, antibiotics, saline, and perfectly sealed paper packets of gauze sit in perfectly organized clear plastic containers.

Gurlien paws through them, and there's blood all over the hoodie, enough that Ambra knows the body would've been upset to see, so she examines Johnsin's corpse instead.

Every spark that made him threatening, every bit of control and malice, all gone, leaving behind a completely normal human corpse.

Ambra nudges him with her foot, and the body is still warm. If she could switch bodies into that dead one, she would, just for the satisfaction of controlling him instead of the other way around.

But instead, she's still in this one, and her shoulders slump with exhaustion from the pain, her nerves still firing wrong all down her spine.

"He has a lot of clothes in the other room, if you want to grab some," Ambra remarks, and she doesn't have to look at Gurlien to know he blanches. "They're good quality, he's a snob."

"I'm not stealing a dead guy's clothes," Gurlien replies faintly, but he studiously wipes the gash with an antibacterial wipe. It's a clean cut, the edges neat, and unless he does something stupid, it should heal up with just a normal scar.

She eyes him. In all the available skin to view, she can't see any other significant scars, and it sticks wrong in her that he would have one because of her.

He had been squeamish at the idea of her killing to begin with.

"Do you want to go to the other room?" Ambra asks him, finally, and he pauses in his cleaning to glance at her. "I'm going to make an example of his body, it could be upsetting."

He stares, his fingertips still against the paper wrapping of the gauze.

"I want Nalissa and Boltiex to think twice before trying," Ambra continues as gently as she could, but a shiver of pain chokes out her voice before she could finish. "This'll be the easiest way to."

Abruptly, he stands, clutching the medical wrapping to his chest, and stomps into the other room.

Leaving her with the dead body once more.

"Okay," Ambra whispers, before she crouches down next to the corpse.

The legs hate that move, but she forces herself to stay like that, to get some control over the body she's trapped in.

She seriously doubts she could permanently scare Boltiex away, but Nalissa likes pretty things. Likes comfort and control and 'vibes,' as the body once put it.

So time to thoroughly mess up the 'vibes' of the bright white room.

Ambra exhales, then funnels herself into the power of the room, as if the very air is hers to flex. As if she could grab it, rip it apart, and leave the entire house a shell.

But there's a living human just in the other room, so that idea is gone.

"Fine," she mumbles, then takes the strip of power, small in its scope, and shreds it.

Immediately, the world blooms gold, the bubble breathing out with her, surrounding the dead body. Ambra's hair flutters in the air, the clothes still on Johnsin's frame shifting as if in a breeze.

Stepping back, she lets the magic tear into his skin, drawing vicious lines of red, pooling it back. It's garish, but Nalissa would hate it.

Then, with just barely a thought, she sends a jolt into the bubble, until his bleeding body slumps up, levitating off the ground.

Still limp.

Ambra exhales, taking a few more steps back from the bubble.

If there is ever any indication of a demon, ever any style that anyone would spot, it's the ripped magic and the bubble surrounding it.

And a dead body hovering in the middle is certainly a message.

"Fuck you," Ambra whispers, in some weird instinct left behind in the body, then turns on her heel to the other room.

Gurlien's standing still in the middle of the bedroom, his face pale, and he twitches when he sees her.

She didn't get any blood on her, so he shouldn't.

"You done?" he asks, his voice strangled.

"Three dead, two more to go," she answers.

6

She teleports back to the underground bunker, before Gurlien bitches enough to take him back to the motorhome so he could grab his phone.

And the moment she does, the moment the body's feet hit the cheap linoleum floor, she sways.

Gurlien grips her by her elbow, then unceremoniously dumps her to sit on the plush couch.

"Hey," she protests mildly, but the couch is a welcome surface, so massively different from all the slick white.

"You're still in pain," he accuses, despite the fact that he's still the one with a bleeding wound, even with the rather professional level bandage job he gave himself. "No more teleporting until that's done."

"We don't know who he talked to," Ambra says, but lets the body melt into the couch. "We might need to go somewhere else, somewhere less obvious."

"No," Gurlien flat out refuses, "you're going to sit there and actually recover."

Stiffly, he tosses a foil wrapped pastry at her, then grabs his phone, staring her straight in the face as he dials.

If she had been less tired, she might've put a stop to that, but instead he places the phone on the counter, pressing the speaker.

"Yes?" a guarded male voice on the other end says. It's not a familiar voice, so it's not the Half Demon.

"Yes, hi, I need you to tell me how to give her some pain relief," Gurlien snaps out, and his hands are shaking, so he crosses his arms. "We just had an encounter with a higher up and he did something."

There's an inhale of breath, and Ambra's interested, she just can't bring herself to sit up out of the clutches of the couch.

A female voice speaks in the background, somewhat musical, but Ambra can't make out the words.

"There's not an easy answer to that question," the male voice replies, and Ambra anticipated that. "Morphine and most opioids don't work, and the ones that do leave withdrawals that are—"

"Not worth it," the female voice interrupts, clearly, and there's a hint of recognition behind it, something that Ambra half remembers.

"Not worth it," the male voice continues. "Make sure she's fed—"

"Why?" Ambra interrupts, and the phone goes silent.

Gurlien carefully folds his glasses and sets them on the counter, then rubs between his eyebrows.

"Oh, you're dealing with this stage of things," the male voice says, mischief thick in his words, and all at once, Ambra decides that he'd be annoying to actually speak to, outside of the direness of the situation. "We went through this with Mel, I'll chat with him on some particularities."

The female voice scoffs.

"Food, rest, and moving the body will help," the woman

says, and again, her voice itches at Ambra's mind. She should know her. "Trust me."

"Who are you?" Ambra wonders aloud, and there's silence before the line clicks off. "Who was that, do I know her?"

Gurlien rests his head against the counter, and it can't be comfortable. "I'm not going to answer that."

Ambra squints at him, but can't muster up the ability to get up from the couch, a shiver winding up her spine, some left over nerve firing a bit too hard.

Johnsin always left sensations and they always lasted for days. Always some ache or stab or throb, always where she doesn't think it would be.

"I was hoping there was an easily available drug to give you, but apparently not," Gurlien says, muffled, and the thought is nice, more than she thought she would get.

"It's just pain," Ambra points out.

"And human bodies aren't supposed to be in constant pain," Gurlien shoots back, before he shuffles around the small kitchen, pouring a glass of water—the same cup the body drank from all those months ago—and sets it in front of Ambra. "She's an expert, follow her advice."

"She sounded familiar," Ambra says, voice smaller than she would have liked. "Like I've heard her before."

He hesitates. "There's a non-zero chance you have," he replies, before disappearing into the bedroom, emerging with an armful of blankets which he dumps on Ambra's lap, then pointing at the foil wrapped pastry. "Eat that, drink that, then sleep."

Ambra splays her fingertips over the blankets in the way the body used to, and the blankets are soft to the touch, almost fuzzy. "You shouldn't have been able to feel the pain through the leash," she starts. "Otherwise, the other four would've stopped Johnsin long ago."

"I didn't."

She doesn't look up at him, instead staring down at the blankets. They're a cheery sort of light pink, the color the body smiled at when they were shopping for this place.

Exhaustion does blur at her eyes, some strange mixture of pain and tiredness and a surreal sort of lack.

It's the same surreal emptiness when she saw Korhonen killed in front of her. The same sort of lack when Gurlien shot Rastian in the head in the heat of battle.

And now, Johnsin is among those few who will never control her again. Never hurt her. Never light her nerves on fire and hold her in place in agony.

"Thank you," she says, after a long pause of staring at the flimsy foil packaging, of listening to Gurlien tap on his phone.

He shifts, glancing up.

"I don't think I would have gotten free without you."

Not even waiting for his response, she tears the flimsy packaging, and there's a frosting covered pastry inside, dry and powdery, but she eats it anyways, mechanically.

It's not great, coating the inside of her mouth, but she forces it down all the same.

"You're welcome," Gurlien responds, voice fake and neutral, and if she had more energy she would absolutely poke at that, prod to see what causes him to fake his response.

But instead, she just eats the pastry, then the next when he places it in front of her, drinks the water from the cup left by the body, then lets herself clutch at the blankets until she loses consciousness once more.

THE NEXT MORNING, wind creaks through the motorhome, shaking the plastic siding and rattling the windows and waking up Ambra with the chill on her nose.

She blinks awake, and underneath the blanket she's very close to comfortable. Sure, it's cold, and her face is almost numb from being above the warmth, but her muscles aren't clenched and her nerves are soft.

In the other room, Gurlien putters around, almost inaudible underneath the sound of the wind.

She lets herself wonder at that for probably longer than needed, then sits up, letting the blanket fall.

And immediately, the back cramps up, her spine aching, and she hisses out a breath.

"Oh good, you're awake," Gurlien breezes in. His hair is already perfectly combed, he's wearing the pants he stormed the base in, and somewhere he found another men's shirt. New bandages are wrapped neatly around his arm, precise in a way that suggests a long history of medical knowledge.

Meanwhile, Ambra's hair is tangled, sticking off to the side, and the shaved side of her scalp prickles when she raises her hand to touch it.

"How good are you with teleporting to specific places?" Gurlien asks, and she blinks at him. "Not just your safe houses, other places."

"Perfectly good, thank you very much," Ambra says, then makes a face, her mouth mealy.

She's now been out of stasis for two nights, and the human body continues to be disgusting.

He watches her like a hawk, as she unsteadily steps towards the bedroom.

On the bed, two backpacks sit open, and Ambra glances inside.

A few changes of clothes for her, the notebook, some of the food, sealed water bottles, and the single change of clothes for Gurlien.

So he doesn't intend for them to stay there.

A part of her should be offended that he thinks he's making the decisions, but the predominant part of her is just curious.

"You're still in pain," he calls, cautious, from the main room.

"Obviously," Ambra snips back. "Johnsin doesn't make it disappear when he stops his grip."

She turns to the rainbow closet, and again, her heart jumps in her throat, but she pulls out another soft shirt, one that hugs the body's skin, and another red sweater over the top of it as her arms prickle with the cold.

Gurlien steps in, glowering at her. "And how long does it last?"

Something prickly at the line of questioning, something halfway between pride and shame, stops her words, causing her to scowl at the closet before she pulls out a pair of slacks.

He leans against the doorway, crossing his arms at her, the fake bored expression filtering over his face once more.

And she needs to keep him on her side.

Especially after he was able to break the grip with Johnsin.

"It varies," she responds, finally, sitting on the bed and attempting to finger comb her hair. "Sometimes days, sometimes far less."

He nods, neutral.

"It doesn't have anything to do with him, it's a passive

wearing off, not an active decision," she supplies, and his brow furrows. "So we don't have to wait for someone to decide to take it off, we don't need to find someone else to relieve it, it just...is."

"Okay," he says, simple, and the hair on the back of her neck raises.

"You're planning something," she says, and he nods. "Tell me what you're planning."

"No," he says casually.

She raises an eyebrow at him, and he blanches for a split second before the bored mask falls again.

"Not until I have more information," he says instead. "Talking about it preemptively could weigh the results in one direction."

That's fair, but she still scowls at him.

"Get up, we are meeting some people." Gurlien says, almost curt.

"No," Ambra blurts out.

"Yes," Gurlien responds. "They're not going to hurt you, they're not going to tell the College, and best of all, they're going to have information for you."

She frowns at him.

"They're going to have information on Nalissa," he says, crossing his arms. He doesn't think she can tell, but he's bluffing. "And they're not going to give that over the phone."

That part, at least, seems true.

"Where is the meeting spot?" she asks, skeptical, but she swings her legs out to stand and wobbles.

They're sore, like the body had completed some sort of athletic feat, and she scrunches up her face all the same.

"Can you teleport by coordinates or do you need to visit first?" Gurlien asks, which is an interesting question, one most don't think about.

"Coordinates are difficult, but I'm fairly decent at them," Ambra says, cautiously.

"I've heard that's impressive," Gurlien says, just as cautious. "46.6652N by 122.9698W."

"That's deep inside another demon's territory," Ambra warns him. "I will run the moment I think I need to."

"And where we're going, I want you to let me do the talking," he continues, which is at least interesting. "We're getting there first, and if they feel threatened, they will leave maybe without even speaking to you."

"Interesting," Ambra replies cautiously, giving up on the finger combing and brushing past him to grab the brush in the bathroom, before startling at her appearance.

The hair on the shaved side of her head is starting to grow back, just barely prickling out of her scalp, like someone smeared a reddish-brown dust over one side of her skin.

She leans in close, rubbing her hand over it, and the texture is wholly unpleasant.

"Gurlien," she starts, and he glances inside, "how fast does living human hair grow?"

Again, the non-amused look.

"I've never had hair grow once inside a body, how…how fast does this happen?" Her voice tilts up, outside of her control, and it's a stupid thing to have an emotional reaction to, but here she is all the same. "Should it be this fast? This feels fast, I don't—"

"It varies," he says, parroting her own words at him. "Did they shave it every day?"

She nods, a lump in her throat.

He takes a very obvious glance at the shaved side of her head. "Human hair generally grows between half an inch and an inch a month. Some stubble after a few nights is within the statistical mean."

Still feels fast, but she just breathes hard out of her nose, then grabs the brush and attacks the non-shaved side.

"If it causes distress, we can pick up some razors and you can continue it," he says, and her throat just closes up further. "But that would be your decision."

It shouldn't be. It should be the body's, but she's gone.

"We should practice with the leash," Ambra says, instead of anything swirling inside of her. "Test the distance, in case you don't come with me when Nalissa or Boltiex summon."

"We will," he replies, and the neutrality once again shivers over her. Like in some way, while she slept, the balance between the two of them shifted in his favor.

Which is patiently ridiculous. She's a demon and he's a dud.

But he does hold her leash.

She braces herself on the sink, staring down at the spotted faucet, her mind briefly blanking out in terror.

He can't do much, he could barely grasp it enough to break Johnsin's concentration.

Gurlien gives her a last brow furrowed look, before going back to the backpacks, opening up the small room to a little more space for her, just enough for her to wrestle herself under control.

"Has there been any chatter about Johnsin yet?" she asks instead, finally wrangling the hair into something resembling neatness. It's far from styled, but it doesn't look like she slept on it anymore. "The faster we get chatter, the faster Nalissa or Boltiex will act."

"That's one thing we're going to find out," he says, zipping up the backpacks as she finishes. "I was going to have you take me to Chloe, but T...Axel thinks they'll be able to track your location through it so I'm not going to risk her and the others."

He says the words like it gives him a bad taste, and she wants to pry, wants to peel his mind open to understand how he processes all of the human emotions without being as affected as her, but instead she just grabs his shoulder, teleporting to the coordinates.

7

He stumbles away with a strangled gasp, the backpack slipping from his fingers.

The coordinates are outside a small rural building, some sort of cafe, and the word that bubbles up into her brain is 'cutesy.' Snow dusted trees surround it, a few tables under umbrellas outside the door, portable heaters glowing at them.

The sign on the cafe is faded and peeling, describing breakfasts and lunches, and the dim roar of a just out of sight freeway filters through the trees.

Some sort of truck stop.

Through the grimy windows, a few people sit, hunched over coffee cups and plates full of food.

There's nobody with magic in at least a mile radius, and Ambra holds her breath for a touch of the resident demon, but it doesn't come.

Gurlien takes in a deep, steeling breath, as if once again the teleportation is rough on him, before he squares his shoulders at the tiny cafe.

"Sit and wait out here," Gurlien orders, pointing to one

of the little tables next to the heater. "Don't do anything strange."

"Why," Ambra asks, skeptical.

He sighs, rubbing between his brows again. "I'm going to go order food, the others will be here soon, and you'll appear more normal if you wait at a table."

It's logical, so she sits primly on one of the cushioned chairs, letting the heater point directly at the ache in her legs.

It's not quite the comfort of under the blankets, but it's a different sort of soothing. Like the muscles and nerves need it.

Her warmest safety spot is in that nebulous area between Eastern Europe and the middle east, and it's still too close to Nalissa to want to teleport them there, but she briefly thinks of the desert sands and wiry green trees. The body had complained about the heat, but it had been quite a few months and Ambra doubted the weather is quite as severe now.

Gurlien disappears into the cafe, until she can only see his silhouette through the window, just the suggestion of his glasses and the cut of his chin, though he gestures enough with his hand that there's the barest hint of a tug at the leash with his motions.

It's the clumsy sensation that the Five all had in the first few months after the merge, but as they got used to controlling her, they all learned how to stop telegraphing all movement through the leash.

She's going to have to see if he could be taught to neutralize that, if the lack of magic in him will grant her that, or if she's just going to have to deal.

Then, suddenly, the back of her neck prickles, and she

straightens, as if her spine decides she needs to sit upwards in response.

She's being watched. She's being watched and it's someone she doesn't know.

It's not a threat, it's not quite a scan, but power flows into the tiny clearing, washing over her, until the hair on her arm raises and her heart jumps.

There's nobody else in the clearing, just her.

It's not another demon, not exactly, but there's something fundamentally wrong with it. Something twisted, something not quite human, and it settles over her for a moment before it vanishes.

Ambra blinks out at the clearing, her pulse pounding underneath the skin, and resists the urge to teleport away immediately.

It wasn't a demon. It definitely wasn't the College.

They didn't reach for her leash, and Gurlien's inside and she still can't tell if he could help her if she goes so far away and...

A sleek black car pulls up to the small gravel lot.

She eyes it, letting a scan of her own snake out, and there's just one person inside...

Another dud. Another person who once had ability, but the space where it should be is scarred over, the edges like a demon sliced it out of him.

She perks up. He's absolutely not the one who just flooded her with awareness, but...

The door kicks open, and it's a young man, face open and friendly, with curly black hair.

"Ambra?" he calls out to her, and she flinches, at yet another person knowing her name.

"Gurlien's inside," she lets the words fall out of her

mouth, not even bothering to control them. "What was that?"

He smiles so sudden it's startling, and she sits back. As if space could give her some room to process the discomfort. "So you did feel that."

"It wasn't you?" Her words trail upward, and she swallows down. "I know it wasn't you, you're a dud, it's obvious."

"Thanks," he replies cheerily, then grabs one of the chairs and sits across from her, entirely too close. "That was a friend, she was checking to make sure you weren't going to put me in danger."

Ambra doesn't know how someone could determine that from that sort of flood, but she scoots her chair back just a bit in case.

"What is she?" Ambra asks. "That wasn't a demon and that wasn't human."

The man across from her stares, a bit hardened, before defaulting back to friendly, leaning back casually in his chair. "Absolutely not telling someone with ties to the College."

"I don't have ties, they're the ones that tied me to them, and I'm trying to get away," Ambra shoots back, but her hands twitch up towards the leash anyways.

He smiles, wide, like she's a dear friend and this is expected, and her hackles rise again.

There's a small earpiece attached to the back of his ear, and Ambra's killed enough people with them to know that he's wired. That someone else is listening in, giving him information specifically so she can't hear them.

But thankfully, the door clacks open, and Gurlien steps back out, juggling four ceramic mugs filled with steaming black liquid.

"Just you?" Gurlien asks, setting down the mugs on the table, then briskly rubbing his hands together.

"Well," the man drawls, "I got spooked and Zoel didn't want to come."

"Zoel the Wight?" Ambra interjects, already skeptical. "That wasn't Wight magic right there."

Gurlien sighs, sitting at least on Ambra's side of the table and cradling his mug. "Zoel could have been a helpful neutral party," he says.

"Zoel hates you, that's far from neutral," the man shoots back, and Ambra cranks her head over to look at Gurlien.

"Why would a local Wight dislike you?" she asks, curious, leaning forward and resting her elbows on the chilled table. "Wights are famously easy to get along with."

"Yeah, Gurlien, why does Zoel hate you?" the man asks, and Ambra scowls at his sarcastic tone. "It's a good story, you should tell her."

Gurlien frowns at the man. "It's not important," he replies, and Ambra's absolutely going to needle him about it later. "We could've used his expertise."

"No," the man says, then grins at Ambra like they're friends. "We consulted, it's far outside of his expertise."

Then, horror of horrors, he extends his hand over to Ambra.

"I'm Axel," he introduces, and Ambra just leans further back, not reaching for his hand. "Gurlien said you killed Kyle Johnsin yesterday."

Ambra swallows, and almost at the memory, pain shivers over her. Like just thinking about it could make the body react outside of her control.

"To be technical, he was torturing her, that counts in self-defense," Gurlien points out.

"I'm definitely not going to be mourning him," Axel says,

still keeping too much of his attention on Ambra. "You want to be free of all of them?"

Ambra glances at Gurlien, almost to give herself a bit of a rest from the intensity of the attention. His fingers are wrapped around the mug, almost idly, and small lines of tension bracket his eyes underneath his glasses.

"Yes," she replies, and again, the shiver of pain.

"Then what are you planning on doing?" It's far too casual, far too friendly, and Ambra doesn't buy it one bit, so she scowls, crossing her arms. "I have a list of questions, if you want our help—and I'm not exaggerating when I say we're probably the most qualified in the world—you need to answer them."

Another quick glance to Gurlien, and he nods, minutely.

"Finding someplace to be alone," she answers, though it feels wrong, to divulge this to another person. "Exist."

"Any plans on destroying the world?" Axel asks dryly, and Ambra blinks at him, then wrinkles her nose. "Good answer."

"I told you—" Gurlien bursts out, and Axel waves him off.

"And you lie," Axel shoots back. "So yes, we're going to ask all the questions."

He leans back, sipping from his drink, then pulls out a tiny notebook, and Ambra tries to crane her neck to see the writing, but unfortunately this body doesn't have the ability to read upside down.

Gurlien sighs, then gestures to the mug in front of Ambra. "Have you tried coffee yet?"

"I didn't like it," Ambra replies, but the steam coming from it is appealing, especially when her nose is back to being cold. "Too bitter."

"Put sugar and cream in it," Axel murmurs. "All demons I know like that."

"All demons?" Ambra asks, her skin prickling. "Did you tell them I was here?" Preemptively, she grabs Gurlien's wrist, the curiosity over the list the only thing stopping her from teleporting away immediately.

"Believe me when I say they have no interest in harming you," Axel says, raising an eyebrow at the motion. "But yes, sugar and cream."

Ambra carefully releases her hand from Gurlien, and he rubs the inside of his wrist. She doesn't trust this Axel, but...

"If you have a way to sever the leashes, all of them, that would be preferable to me tracking them down and killing them."

Gurlien gives her another minute nod, like that's a good thing to say.

"The more interactions with them, the bigger chance they take me in," Ambra continues, then shivers again, even though the heater is quite nice. "I don't ever want to go there again."

"Good, we're on the same page," Axel replies cheerily. "Question two, are you in pain?"

"Yes," Ambra replies immediately, without any thought, and Axel writes that down.

"Johnsin was horrific," Gurlien says, and there's frustration coating his voice, frustration she can't quite pick out. "I told you, there was torture."

"Rich coming from you," Axel shoots back, and Ambra's absolutely going to get all of this story out of Gurlien later, but the door clacks open again, with a waiter carrying a tray full of food.

"Y'all sure you don't want to come inside?" the waiter asks, placing a plate directly in front of Ambra first, then distributing the food to the rest of the table. "It's going to snow in a bit."

"We're fine," Gurlien answers, and the waiter nods, setting down silverware and napkins, then leaving.

It's an extraordinary amount of food, the plate piled high with some sort of bread product covered in butter, with eggs and crispy meat to the side, and way more than Ambra thinks anyone could ever eat.

She blinks over to Gurlien, who's giving her the most bland expression over his glasses.

"I think that face answers question five," Axel says, cheerful.

"I ate last night," Ambra says to Gurlien, who obviously ordered it for her. "Two of those pastry things. Two."

"And human bodies need more food than that," Gurlien shoots back, then picks up his own fork. "You'll be better equipped to resist Nalissa if you have enough energy."

"And this is an unreasonable amount," Ambra retorts, but pokes at the crispy meat anyways. It breaks off in her fingers, so she eats it and it's…surprisingly salty, according to the words that spring up unbidden to her mind.

In all of her memories, she's not entirely certain she tasted something like it. The body preferred vegetables, eating bowls of leafy lettuce with very little taste or mugs of soup with more potatoes than Ambra thought feasible.

"Humans need around 1200-2000 calories a day," Gurlien recites, as if out of a textbook, and she pauses her next bite to stare at him. "When exporting large amounts of energy—which magic is, thank you very much—they need to increase that amount drastically."

"That can't be sustainable," Ambra says, though the textbook bit is clearly entertaining. "And that's way too large of a target to be at all useful."

Across the table, Axel's watching them, a funny sort of smile on his face, before he shakes his head, scooting his plate over to the side just enough to have the notebook out.

"Question three, what happened to your human?"

Ambra freezes, and the friendly expression drops from Axel's face, revealing something without a trace of mirth.

All of her senses, all of her alerts fire off, but it's nothing. He's just a dud in front of her, and Gurlien's there, but it's as if she's being attacked.

"It's a simple question." Axel sits back, crossing his arms.

Ambra swallows, her throat raw from the lack of screaming the day before.

Gurlien turns in his chair to watch Ambra, and there's something in his eyes, something closer to warmth, but it does nothing to eliminate the threat in front of her.

"She died," Ambra says, finally, after the moment stretches on far longer than it should.

Even saying it like that hurts.

"You sure about that?" As if this conversation costs him nothing, Axel sips at his coffee. "Are you absolutely, one hundred percent sure of that?"

"Yes," Ambra replies, small.

"How long into this process did she die?"

Ambra's hands shake, and she twists them in her lap to stop the motion, and Gurlien's eyebrows raise.

"Does it matter?" Gurlien asks, instead, when she struggles to speak, and a rush of gratitude floods through her, at those three words, saving her from answering.

"It very much so does," Axel shoots back.

"Look, just because you—" Gurlien starts, but Axel cuts him off.

"Not in front of the College plant," he says, curt. "The

demon can answer the question, or she can get absolutely no help from us."

"That's not fair, she was literally tortured—"

"And how long was the human tortured before she died?" Axel asks, lifting his chin, and Ambra can't believe she ever thought he would be friendly. "I think that has far more weight."

"Seven months ago," Ambra replies, forcing the words past the lump in her throat, and even clenching her hands doesn't stop the trembling. "She died seven months ago."

Both the men fall silent, watching her, and Ambra picks Gurlien to stare at, the far kinder face. "We knew each other for three years, were...in this..." she gestures at the body, "for about ten months before she died."

The sudden lack, the terror, the wrenching pain, all just as new as the day it happens, and Ambra swallows, then swallows again, trying to chase away the phantom sensations.

She's not on an operating table in a sterile white room, she's outside a little cafe, with food in front of her and steam still curling from the mug of coffee. The air still smells of the promise of snow, and cars rumble past on the freeway out of sight. A thin strip of magic flutters along the driveway, completely bypassing them, and if she wanted, she could jerk it towards her, detonate the table, and run away.

Axel sits back, but Ambra just stares harder at Gurlien, like he could get the conversation to end.

"And how did she feel about this," Axel mimics Ambra's gesture, "for the ten months?"

Ambra opens her mouth, but no words come out, her breath just as cut off as the leash had done, and her eyes water, beyond her control.

"Jesus Christ, and everyone says I'm the insensitive one,"

Gurlien interjects, and Ambra forces her jaw to unclench. "This is clearly a trauma response, can you back off?"

There's a trace of noise, someone speaking into the earpiece, and Axel listens, before nodding.

"Great," Gurlien says sarcastically. "Thanks. So kind."

"You're not one to talk," Axel says, and piece by piece, the friendly mask falls back into place, as foreign as anything Ambra's ever encountered. "Question four, and this one comes from an expert, did they tie you in through the cardiac or nervous system?"

"Nervous," Ambra says, and her voice is so much smaller than she wants.

Next to her, under the table, Gurlien presses his knee against hers, startling her, but she doesn't shift away from the sudden contact.

"Spinal or cerebral?"

"Both," Ambra says, even quieter, no matter how much she tries to project. "They said just cerebral failed."

"Depending on your definition of failure," Axel replies, then smiles fully back into friendly, and Ambra wants to throw the plate at him. "Good information, our Necromancer needed to know that piece for some reason."

"You shouldn't tell me where she is," Ambra says, before she can stop herself, before scowling at the plate. "Are we done?"

"You should still eat some," Gurlien says, an almost gentle reminder. "It'll help the pain heal faster."

"That it will," Axel agrees, and Ambra turns the scowl onto Gurlien for saying something that Axel would back him up on. "Though recognizing hunger signals will be something you struggle with...how were you dealing with those in the seven months?"

"They kept her in stasis chambers," Gurlien answers,

relieving Ambra of the need to do so, so she takes another bite of the crispy and salty meat. "Near as I can tell, only let her out tightly controlled and for specific missions."

Axel writes that down.

"So, you know, another form of torture," Gurlien shoots over, more aggressively. "More torture that she had nothing to do with and you're just digging at it like she's the instigator of it."

"Were you?" Axel asks mildly. "The instigator?"

"No," Ambra says, and her stomach turns over, unhappy, at the food. "We were approached by the College because we knew each other."

And they had been so excited.

She sets down her fork, shivering once.

"And I think we can all agree that the College does things unethically," Gurlien says bracingly, and Axel snorts like he told a joke. "So can you help us?"

Axel snaps the notebook closed, an open and practiced smile on his face. "I have to run this by my experts."

Gurlien scoffs.

"You realize you're dealing with an experiment that has, to our knowledge, only two living examples, right?" Axel says, and it jolts Ambra to remember the other one, the one where the demon died and the human lived, and how much kinder of a world that would be. "It's not like we have a lot of data to go off of, so we have to take this and actually research."

He turns to Ambra, and Ambra scoots her chair back a bit.

"Short term advice? Eat enough food, actually sleep on a bed, don't get taken by the College," he says, like those aren't equally as perplexing ideas. "Maybe kidnap someone a little less assholish next time?"

"He's not an asshole," Ambra says automatically.

Axel stares at her, like that's the one bit of information she's given that stretches his belief, before he turns to Gurlien.

"How'd you manage that?" Axel asks, before he stands, tossing a twenty on the table for his food, and striding off.

No strange scans follow his leaving, and the sleek black car rumbles out of the parking lot and out of view before Ambra lets her spine unwind.

"What the fuck," she mutters, pushing the plate away and burying her head in her arms, as if the lack of sight would help her stop the shaking.

"That went well," Gurlien mutters, clutching the mug of coffee like it'll save him.

8

Ambra doesn't speak for the rest of the day, teleporting them back to the cabin and burrowing herself underneath the blankets on the couch, and trying real hard to ignore Gurlien talking in low tones on the phone in the bedroom.

She should be practicing the leash with him. She should be taking him far, far away so they can test the limits of his ability to sense the leash, test how useful he'll be. Test if she can just let him back into his normal life, so she would just be a temporary interruption when needed, instead of trapped here away from his friends.

But her teeth chatter with the leftover pain from Johnsin and her stomach aches from the onslaught of chemicals following all the emotions, so she curls up the tightest she can and ignores Gurlien. Pretends to be asleep when he gets more food, only getting up to use the restroom when he has the door firmly shut, and drinks a glass of water only when her mouth is so dry she feels her teeth will fall out.

And attempts to not think.

THE NEXT MORNING, however, Gurlien has approximately no patience with her, breezing in and clattering around loud enough that Ambra lifts her head to glare at him.

"I don't think you're going to hurt me when you do that," he says, blasé, and Ambra regrets whatever niceties she's given him. "But I do need you to actually get up and do things."

She forces herself to sit upright, and her muscles protest, aching in ways she didn't even know were possible.

"Have you heard anything?" she asks, and her voice rasps unpleasantly after a day of not speaking. "Any news of Johnsin getting back?"

"Not yet," Gurlien replies, and his hair is carefully combed, so neatly in place. "But I got pretty strict instructions not to let you wallow for another day."

"I wasn't wallowing," Ambra protests, stretching out her legs in front of her, and her eyes water at the motion.

"No, someone just brought up some specific trauma and you sat on the couch for twenty hours, not wallowing at all." He tosses her a Power bar and she lets it thump against the couch, not touching it. "But Axel did hack into Johnsin's schedule and he has an event he is supposed to attend in three days. It's going to be conspicuous if he doesn't show up, I want to be better prepared for that."

That gets her attention, and she stands, using a jolt of her power deep into the earth to stabilize herself so she only sways once, and the house creaks around them.

He jerks back, his eyes wide.

"That was me," she informs him, then pushes past him down the hall to grab another sweater, this one bright red, that the body had laughed at while hanging up.

Ambra didn't understand why she laughed then, still doesn't, but still, it's soft and the color is cheery.

The backpacks are once more on the bed, and there's snacks and a change of clothing obviously in them, and she pokes through the one closer to her, not so much curious as her mind spinning around for distractions.

"I don't want to leave without at least one of these," Gurlien says, almost strict, and she raises an eyebrow at him. "If I end up somewhere separated, I want to be able to at least survive until I get help."

Ambra scoffs, but it makes sense. Even just two nights before was evidence that she is still horridly controllable.

"Hopefully, Nalissa will get pictures," she says, the image of Johnsin's corpse floating in her bubble flashing through her mind. "Hopefully she'll hold off."

Gurlien blanches before he covers it up, and she's immediately reminded of all the half secrets that Johnsin spoke about, of all of the mysteries surrounding Gurlien.

And yet, he's just standing in the doorway, completely harmless, wearing a T-shirt and the rough pants. All his magic seared out of him, not even able to see the leash still firmly tied around his wrist.

And Johnsin knew him, knew enough of his history to make snide comments, and she still didn't. And Axel hinted.

"I need additional supplies," he says, smooth, and of course he produces a list from his pocket.

She grabs it, almost ripping the paper, even though her neck aches at the fast movement.

It's all clothing, some toiletries, and more food. Nothing actually interesting.

Turning it over in her hands, she raises an eyebrow at him.

"I'd go back to the cabin, but that must be crawling with

College spies," he says, folding his arms over his chest, then unfolding them, wincing at the bandage.

"And the demon circle," she points out. "I can't get you in there."

"And the demon circle." For a long moment, he stares at her from behind his glasses, as if weighing some information. "Chloe, Delina, and Maison got to a safe place."

"Good?" Ambra ventures, and he nods. "If you want to keep them safe, I shouldn't...I shouldn't know where that is."

"I agree," he replies curtly, but still, he's almost sad. "They got my cat with them."

Ambra knew of pets, of course. Some demons kept them, friendly animals in their surroundings for companionship, though Ambra had never felt that particular sort of bond, and both Nalissa and Boltiex had dogs.

Gurlien doesn't seem like the type.

"I can get you another cat?" she offers, only half certain it's the correct thing to say, and he just shakes his head. "Or reunite you with this one once Boltiex and Nalissa are dead."

"You're really fumbling in the dark with all of this, aren't you?" he mutters, then pushes his hair away from his forehead, where it flops again immediately. "Can you teleport now?

In terms of power, of course she can, she always can, but the shaky lack of sensation in her chest doesn't breed any sort of confidence that she could do much more.

And here she wanted to test the leash, test his control. See what this man, this dud completely seared of all of his magic, could actually handle, but the body still feels like it's about to sway in a heavy wind.

"Do you want to get all of this," she brandishes the list back at him, "now? Later?"

He narrows his eyes.

"I can't reunite you with your cat, I can't get you back to your home or your friends, and I don't want to let you far away in case Nalissa or Boltiex try." He's still examining her with suspicion. "I have to make sure you don't get so fed up with everything that you leave me to them."

The moment stills, in the creaky little motorhome, with the dusty windows and the snow outside, as he stares at her, the falsely bored expression slipping from his face.

Leaving something dismayed.

"So, list," Ambra finishes, lamely, as he looks like he's reevaluating his entire life that led him up to this place. "I can do that."

Finally, he recovers. "Do you have money?"

The answer to that is no, but it's not difficult to get if you can teleport through walls.

9

After the briefest of stints where Ambra teleports them into a bank vault and then back out before Gurlien can yell about surveillance cameras and police, they sit outside in a temperate area, deep in a woods that Ambra doesn't know the name of.

Gurlien shakily counts the money, and Ambra perches herself on a gnarled tree stump, pulling her knees into her chest.

It's not a safe spot, per se, but it is comfortably warm. The ground is dry, the dirt halfway between sand and clay, and wiry trees with spikes instead of leaves twist their way up to the brilliantly blue sky.

Once, Ambra had gotten obsessed with learning all the different types of plants in the world, but besides 'low water, drought resistant,' she couldn't remember exactly what these types were.

Gurlien finishes counting, then types into his phone, sitting back. "How many times have you stolen from a bank?"

"Not many," Ambra replies truthfully. "The body didn't like it."

Those words were unintentional, and she scowls at the dirt the moment they leave her mouth.

"Right," Gurlien drawls. "The body."

Ambra flinches, before she stands herself up as Gurlien carefully folds a few of the dollars into his pocket, then stores the rest in the backpack.

"At least this will help if we get separated," Gurlien mutters. "I'll just rent a car and go somewhere else."

"Do you have coordinates for the shops?"

He's already nodding, holding out his phone, where incredibly precise coordinates are pre-typed into a note.

"My phone tells me we're in the mountains above Hemet in Southern California," Gurlien says, glancing around them, as if for the first time. "You commonly come here?"

"No," Ambra replies, still staring at the coordinates, trying to settle them in her mind. It's less easy while within a body, much less one that aches and shivers with each wrong movement. "Three times before, as just an in between spot to think and read."

His lips twitch with interest, but he doesn't ask, and only a small part of her is disappointed.

"Late summer it's beautiful," she continues, as if she could tease out more of his interest. "There's a lake with a pier, I sat there for a day and a half and read, and the sun hits the water enough to light up the trees around it."

If possible, she'll go back. Again. After all of this, take a book from her library and sit and read on the pier for a day or two. Take a soft sweater and some snacks, and lay there.

He hmms, something thoughtful and impatient, before showing her the coordinates again. "These are close and will have most of what we need."

Before he hesitates, obvious, his eyes slating over to her. "Have you been shopping before? While in the...body?"

She flinches, then nods. "We did for all the food, before the merge."

He hmms again, then holds out his hand.

It's the arm with the bandages, still pristine, but she grabs his warm skin anyways and teleports to the coordinates.

And it dumps them in a parking lot behind a behemoth of a building.

The pavement is dry, blisteringly so, and wind pushes fine dust across it in small waves. It's not much warmer, but the breeze dries up any moisture in Ambra's skin, rendering her eyes crunchy.

The very air smells almost foul. Like smoke and burning plastic and something else Ambra can't place.

"Bleh," Gurlien mutters, as if the scent is just as distasteful to him, before he adjusts the backpack on his shoulder.

It's out of place on him, rendering him more youthful than he probably appreciated.

"How old are you?" she asks, and he squeezes his eyes shut.

"Just thirty-four," he mutters. "Don't go around asking people that, people get offended."

He starts walking towards the entrance, and Ambra has to scramble to keep up with him, the body's legs far shorter than his, before he abruptly turns back to her.

"There's going to be loud noises and bright lights," he warns, almost brusque, "and everyone else is going to be ignoring them."

Wordless, she nods, then idly rubs the prickling of hair

on her scalp. "People always stared when they took me out in public."

"That'll probably happen again," he warns, his lips pursing, as he gives her an obvious once-over. "The best response to that is to ignore it. It's not a threat, it's just normal people reacting to something outside of what usually happens."

"Usually, the handlers have my leash too tight for me to react," Ambra says, and he grimaces.

"Do you want to risk sitting outside?"

Before he can even finish, she's shaking her head no. Too far away, too unknown, and to be so alone so shortly after Johnsin died...no. It would be too empty.

He sighs again, then gestures for her to follow, and they stride into the building.

Tall automatic sliding doors open for them, sending a puff of artificially cooled air into Ambra's face, and she wrinkles her nose at the sensation.

Instead of one store, like the grocery that the body took her to that one time, it's a collection of small stores, their doors all wide open into a grand hallway.

"This is a mall, isn't it?" Ambra asks, remembering to dip her voice low.

"Yes," Gurlien replies with a curt nod. "I felt it better than a Walmart, those are hell."

A gaggle of teenagers pass by them, too close, and Ambra shies closer to Gurlien. One of them stares at her, his eyebrows furrowing at her appearance, but they don't stop.

It's chaos inside.

Everywhere she looks people are walking, sometimes alone but often in groups, chatting. Bright lights flicker from some of the stores and giant signs in the middle, and even underneath the dim roar of conversation, twinkling music plays.

There's no spot of quiet, no break in the continuous noise, and it takes Ambra a few minutes of breathing out hard through her nose to not react.

Gurlien tugs her by her sleeve to lean against one wall, away from any store openings, and it's a lot better than being moved by the leash.

"Did you get this way before the...merge?" he asks, and her back prickles at the question.

"No," she replies sharply. "A live human body is way more...sensitive."

"And did the...body..." she still flinches, even at his careful tone, "...ever react like this?"

"No, she didn't even notice," Ambra says, past the lump in her throat. "I could be trying to clap our hands over my ears and she'd be fine."

He nods, as if she's saying logical things.

"Do these sounds ever stop in here?" Her voice is way smaller than she wants it to be. She's a demon, she has untold power, and she's acting like a hurt child.

She could destroy this entire building, flatten it to the ground. She could smother everyone around her, end the lives of countless people.

And she's scared by a little noise.

Her legs still ache and her shoulders are still tight, but it's not a good enough excuse.

"Not often," Gurlien replies, and she appreciates the honesty. "I take it they never gave you ear-pro?"

At her blank look, he pulls out the list again, clicking a pen and scribbling on it again.

He let go of her sleeve to do so, and it's a startling shock.

Gurlien strides, like he knows where to go, into a smaller

shop full of neatly pressed men's clothing, all arranged in perfectly sharp lines and neutral-colored stacks.

The cloth muffles some of the outside noise, as if the open door provided a barrier, leaving only a small chiming music and a few gossipy store clerks.

It's far better.

Ambra immediately heads to the obvious bench, sitting down before her legs start to shake, and a clerk swoops over to Gurlien, thankfully speaking to him instead of her, giving her mind a chance to wander once more.

He sets the backpack down at her feet with a significant glance, and she tucks it closer to her legs. Humans value money, this is important to keep safe for him.

Even if she could easily replace it with just another thought.

There are mirrors everywhere, and the body's face is sunken, her eyes ringed with dark circles. The one side of her hair is frizzy, unkempt, and looking in the mirror she can tell that the oversized soft red sweater clashes badly with the olive-green pants she picked out this morning.

Quite frankly, in terms of human behavior and human appearances, she looks like shit.

Vanity is not necessarily a demon's vice, what with the constantly switching out of bodies, but still, Ambra's... uncomfortable with the appearance. It's one thing when the vast majority of beings couldn't perceive her, it's an entire other when everyone can.

Idly, she lets her hand drape on a close rack of clothing, and the fabric is stiff to her touch, surprisingly thick. There's a thin strand of magic flowing through the store, barely more than a thread, and she watches it for a few seconds, watching the ebbs and flows.

"Do you want to try something on?" Another clerk is

almost immediately next to her and she startles. "Oh, it's okay, anyone can." The clerk's hair is dark, but a garish streak of yellow frames the front of his face, stylish and purposeful. He's wearing one of the suits, crisp and clean, with small connecting details in the pocket and of the tie.

Long story short, he's put together.

"Uh," Ambra starts, and this might be the first person outside of any magical order or the College to actually speak to her, so she swallows. "I'm okay."

It's a wholly inadequate statement.

"Okay, no problem!" he answers cheerfully, and there's even a gold chain connecting his tie to the pristine white shirt. "Let me know if there's anything that catches your fancy, we have no problems with girls in suits."

The fabric is way too rough for her to want to put it next to her skin, but the thought is nice.

"Or if there's any colors we should put on your boyfriend," the man continues, nodding over to where Gurlien's strongly conversing with the other clerk. "He strikes me as an aggressively neutral color palette."

The back of her neck prickles at the word boyfriend, as she knows that's weighty for humans, but it's easier than correcting him. "Try light blue," Ambra says, when the clerk waits expectantly for an answer. "For his shirt, he looks good in light blue."

She has no idea if it's true, but the clerk bundles himself away, thankfully leaving her alone.

She practices letting her shoulders unwind, letting the leg muscles relax. The body did a thing called meditation, where the entire physical body felt loose and soft, but Ambra never got the hang of it.

Sure enough, the clerk takes a sky-blue shirt over to

Gurlien, and he furrows his eyebrows at her like she's the mystery, but takes it anyway.

Ambra waits as he tries on some of the clothes, then as he pays for them with the stolen cash, and his face loses some of the tightness. Like wearing the same clothes and the pajama pants had caused him some strange stress as well.

It's an odd thought.

"Are you ready?" Gurlien asks, after another group of people filter in the store and all her work at relaxing her muscles immediately goes to waste. He's carrying two bags, each full, but the clean lines of the paper don't buckle out.

Unbidden, the thought that this must be a nice store pops into her mind.

"Sure," she says, and her legs shake a bit to stand, so he offers her an arm to help with a suspicious glance to the clerk.

Her ears pop the moment they leave the store, all the noise flooding in again.

"Just how much pain are you in?" Gurlien murmurs to her, watching her blink through the startle.

"Yes," she mumbles back, and his face draws up. "I'll be ok, I've done worse."

"Great," he sighs, before striding off to another store. "I miscalculated."

It's far louder, but he grabs a pack of undergarments in a plastic bag and some other small things, and pays, all without either of them needing to say anything, then another store for a few more casual items and a bigger jacket, and Ambra's head spins.

Gurlien gives her a sidelong glance from behind his glasses, and it's his planning look, so Ambra squints at him right back.

"What?" she asks, too prickly to be polite, and with him she shouldn't have to be so careful all the time anyways.

"I'm evaluating," he replies, just as prickly.

She bares her teeth at him, and he seems not at all fazed by that, as they continue to stroll through the mall, each carrying bags, as if they're completely normal.

"Your hands are still shaking," he states, and she clenches her hands into fists to stop them. "And it's been about fourteen hours since you ate."

Ambra just narrows her eyes more at him.

"And I've been in hiding for the last year and been unable to go to a mall food court," he continues, and she relaxes a bit at that. "Do you want to make the choice for your food or do you want me to make it for you?"

And he watches her, like it's some sort of test.

They stroll past a store with a dizzying selection of scents, almost enough to pull her attention away, but she makes herself stare back at him, makes her footsteps even.

"How many choices are there?" she asks, finally.

It's not like food sources for demons are terribly common, and it's not like they are offered very much variety.

"A lot," he emphasized.

"Go ahead and make it for me," she mutters. "That sounds like too much work."

"It's too much work for some humans," he replies, which is a bit gratifying. "I take it you have no idea of food allergies?"

She shakes her head. "The body ate a lot of vegetables and soups."

He raises an eyebrow, turning around the corner and tilting them towards an even more brightly lit area full of tables and loud chatter. "Well, you had Spam and jerky in your cupboard, I assume that the body approved of everything you bought." He waited for her to nod. "So she wasn't a vegetarian, so I don't need to worry about that."

"Why would you worry?" Ambra asks. "She's gone."

It still hurts to say, and she ducks her head to avoid looking at him.

"Okay," he murmurs, then tugs her by the sleeve again into the line of one booth. "Vegetables, I can aim towards that."

Someone steps into the line behind them and Ambra stiffens.

"Too much of humanity stands too close to each other," she mutters to Gurlien, at least knowing enough to not say that loudly.

"That is an objective amusing sentence," he replies, also low. "But yes."

Another person behind them, and the first person steps a bit nearer, and Ambra steps closer to Gurlien.

It's not something she should be frightened of, they're regular people, but it's something stored in the body. Like the body wants to pull away from humans, not her.

It's a confusing mess, and she sits with it, breathing hard out of her nose, trying to parse instincts from wants.

Gurlien pretends not to notice, but he's obviously bad at it.

If it keeps him from turning her in, it's worth it.

Another group of humans stride by, their gaze flickering up to Ambra, and one of them hides a laugh at something they see in her.

She bares her teeth in a grin, and the person startles, in term scooting away, an almost frightened expression on their face.

Good.

"Yeah, don't do that," Gurlien mutters to her. "It's not a threat."

"You just go around with people laughing at you?" Ambra asks, and they're next in line, thankfully.

Walking is easier than standing still on her legs, and this static line makes her knees quake.

"I've had people laugh at me in public since I was a child," Gurlien replies. "It's far, far better if you ignore it."

"Why would they laugh at you?" Ambra raises an eyebrow at him, making sure to do the up and down glance that makes humans uncomfortable. "Aren't you the most statistically normal type of human?"

He glares down at her over his glasses, then back to the line. "People will be cruel."

With Johnsin now dead, Ambra knows it the best, so she stands there, almost idle, as Gurlien rattles off an order and gets awarded with a tray full of food.

He nods at her to follow, and thankfully, he leads her past the hordes of teenaged humans, into a table that's almost tucked away in a corner, out of the oppressive bubble of noise.

She gratefully lowers herself into the hard plastic chair, gritting her teeth.

"They just expected you to move on from all this pain, didn't they?" he asks, placing an overly large salad bowl in front of her. "Did the stasis chamber take it away?" Precise, he gives her a fork, as if this is some routine of his.

She takes it; it does her no harm to protest that sort of movement. "Nope," she says, and he scowls at her like it's her fault. "You heard Johnsin, I'm not a person."

It comes out surprisingly bitter, so she stares down at the salad instead.

The human body always puts inflection on things she's not meaning to, and it's awful.

The salad itself is so covered with other things that the lettuce the body loved so much is barely visible. There are grains, fruit, some sort of meat, a bright vivid raspberry red dressing, and even something she only vaguely recognizes as cheese.

"You're going to make me eat all of this?" Ambra asks, pointing with her fork.

"Do I need to show you more texts from Axel?" he answers instead, and the interest must've shown in her eyes so he shakes his head. "Forget I said that, no."

She grins at him and he leans back, startled.

"Yeah, still unnerving," he mutters. "Here, put these on," he says, pulling out something from one of the bags and sliding it across the table.

It's a pair of glasses, the round lenses tinted green. Not as fully opaque as the sunglasses she's seen before, but still colored.

Wrinkling her brow, she slides them on her face, and immediately, the headache building behind her eyes lessen.

She blinks up at him, and with just that small amount of dimming, the lights in the crowded food court are way more tolerable.

He's studying her, intent.

"Good, they mask the eyes," he says clinically. "Green cancels out the red."

She takes them off, and the headache immediately returns, so she crams them back on her face. "These would've been great in the stasis chambers."

This seems to startle him again.

"The lights always hurt," she supplies. "They never varied and they were always just the same bright white."

This seems to stump him again, his jaw tight, before he rubs between his brows and grabs one of the shopping bags instead of sitting. "I'll be in there, actually putting on something that fits me."

That's why he sat them where he did, right next to the bathroom.

It's only a few feet away, less than the distance of the other room he was in the night before, but he's already striding away when she's nodding.

Leaving her immediately with the odd emptiness, the lack that still hadn't left her from Johnsin's death.

Which is patently bullshit, it's good that Johnsin is dead.

But if the lack gets worse each time one of them dies, then...

It's an odd, shifting fear inside of her, before she squashes it down and pokes at the salad.

Her freedom is far worth whatever loneliness she might feel from the end of the control. Any bonds could be recreated. Theoretically.

Maybe.

Who knows if she even can, if one of the central parts to being a demon had been taken away from her.

They say that's the only true way to happiness as a demon. That you can find contentment, find peace, but only happiness through a true bond.

The idea that they might've warped that in her, might've taken that away too, burns in her stomach.

With probably more viciousness than needed, she stabs the fork into the salad and shoves some into her mouth.

It's...fine. Not anything that inspires her, not anything that disgusts her, but after the line and everything, it's a letdown.

And the body had liked these to the point of seeking them out whenever possible.

A few people stride by, drifting to a nearby table, and Ambra watches them from behind the glasses, but they pay her no attention.

"Is the food at least good?" Gurlien says, interrupting her thoughts, and she swings her attention back up to him.

He's changed into the outfit he got at the suit store, with a crisp sky-blue button up and perfectly creased black slacks, and he's obviously re-combed his hair. He sits down across from her with something close to relief in his eyes. He looks good, at ease, like this is finally him fitting back into himself.

"You consider that more comfortable?" Ambra asks, remembering the stiffness of the fabric, but still, some part of her unwinds at having him in her view once more.

"I don't like being sloppy," he informs her, almost clinically. "I don't care about other people's clothing, but I can't stand it."

She doesn't know why he divulges that, but she shrugs all the same as he opens his takeout container.

"So I've been in clothes that don't fit and clothes that I bled and battled in the last three days, and I hated it."

Ambra nods, because that seems appropriate. "I can get more money if you want more," she offers.

"That's...that's not the point," he sighs, before starting to dig into the food in front of him, which appears way more fried than her salad, and she can see the cogs in his mind work, drawing conclusions, working towards something. "Like how the bright lights bother you, looking sloppy bothers me."

"Makes sense," she murmurs.

As he eats, he pulls the notebook out of the backpack, flipping it open, and that derails all of her attention.

"So," he starts, as if they aren't in the middle of a mall. As if they are somewhere secure. "Nalissa and Boltiex."

Once more, the panic rises in her, but she breathes out hard through her nose.

"Unless one tries to grab me," she starts, and her voice wavers, and he examines her as she has to get it under control. "Nalissa will be far easier to…"

"Yes," Gurlien agrees, and the light blue of the shirt and the cleanness of the lines elevates the expression, making him almost unattainably scholarly. "I want to put out feelers, see how the College is approaching Johnsin's…demise. See if there's any theories, anything we can mislead them with."

The fact that they're talking about this over food, in a public place, makes her skin crawl.

But data is data and information is power, so she nods. "Can you do that safely? Without leading back to me?"

"I've been officially on the run with a known fugitive for roughly a year and they didn't catch me," Gurlien replies, which is a far more intriguing conversation than the one about Ambra's list. "And I've been keeping up on the gossip and the general moving for the entire time."

So she picked well when she impulse kidnapped him.

Ignoring the salad, she props her chin in her hands, staring hard at him from behind the tinted glasses.

He sits back at the direct attention, brows raised from behind his own glasses.

"So you're good at gathering information," she starts, then grins at him in the way that unnerves most humans. "Whyever would they kick you out?"

Wrong thing to say, as his mouth thins and he falls silent, picking back over his own food.

"I don't consider it a bad thing," she ventures, eating another bite of salad, as if that would appease him. "The entire structure could collapse and I'd be happy for it."

"We're agreed with that," he mutters, and the crispness of his clothing directly counteracts with the casualness of his meal, fried foods in styrofoam containers, which he picks at with about as much appetite as she has. "Axel says..." he trails off, frowning at the food, before eating one of the fries.

She waits, raising an eyebrow at him when he doesn't continue. "He's going to help?"

There's still bitterness in her voice.

"Axel says we're going to have some culture differences," he says, almost bracing himself, as if it's anything but an indisputably correct sentence. "Until this is done, you're going to have to trust me."

"Obviously," Ambra says, getting a bite of a veggie, and has to pause in the sharpness of the taste, at the almost burn in the tip of her tongue, before her brain has a chance to interpret the sensation as something akin to pleasure. "Oh," she mumbles, picking through the salad to find a similar item. "I like this one."

Gurlien cranes his neck to glance at it. "You mean the raw jalapeños?" His voice is skeptical, before he shrugs, pulling out his phone, and it's her turn to look over to him.

GURLIEN (1:41 PM): Does your connection like spicy food?

Three dots appear, then disappear, then appear again.

AXEL D (1:42 PM): T does sometimes, M likes the flavor but dislikes the burn.

"So I can get more of this type of food?" Ambra asks, and

she gets the barest hint of Gurlien's lips curving into a smile. "Ask him where."

"I know how to buy spicy food, don't worry," he says, and his eyes crease nicely behind his glasses when he smiles like that. "Chloe'll want to introduce you to Thai food."

GURLIEN (1:44 PM): Well, she just ate a raw jalapeño and liked it enough to search for more.

AXEL D (1:45 PM): lol.

"That means he's laughing," Gurlien translates, almost unconsciously, before placing the phone on the table, face side up. "But yes. You need to trust me."

It's so close to a rehash of an old conversation that she briefly wonders what's different, but she takes another bite of the salad again, now actually enjoying it.

"That's what this all is, right?" she asks, after a few moments of silence. "This shopping, this food, it's for me to trust you." He hesitates in his reaction, so she sighs. "You had a chance to turn me over to Johnsin and probably go free. You had the opportunity to turn me over to Axel and his group of 'experts.' It's officially in your best interest at this moment to go along with my plan. I trust that."

"Alright," Gurlien replies, almost unsteadily. "So I need the trust for the small things, too."

She still doesn't know where he's going with it. "What do you need?" She gestures towards the food court in its expanse, at the mall at large. "I can get more money, get whatever you need. Whatever you want. If it keeps you on my side, you got it." They stare at each other, before she distracts herself with another bite. "If it's trust, then sure. I can try."

"Demons don't interact with each other a lot, do they?" he asks, voice almost a bit wobbly.

"I try not to," Ambra replies. "I know some tie themselves into society, get involved with humans and magicians, in wars and governments," It's strange enough to talk this much. "I've just always kept a few friends, found libraries, and let others do what they want."

There's a flash of interest in his eyes. "When you're less in fight or flight, I want to have a long discussion about culture."

"Sure," she replies, as again, it's the easiest thing he could ask for. If he wants to talk, she could do that.

"Okay," he says, bracing himself. "We're going to buy a few more things, then I'm going to get information for you."

She takes another bite, unable to find another jalapeño, but the rest of the salad is enriched by the fact they existed at all.

"After we do distance practicing," she warns, his words catching up with her. "You're not going away until after that."

His face pinched, he nods.

THE REST of the meal is a somber affair, and Ambra's about to jump out of her skin by the time he drags her into a small electronics store.

This time, however, he brings her up to the counter with him.

It's darker in there, somehow more grimy, and the human leaning against the counter is only wearing a beat up polo shirt and jeans, and looks like he hasn't shaved in a few days.

His eyes glance off Gurlien, focusing on Ambra instead. "And how can I help you?"

He doesn't sound like he wants to help her, and Ambra bristles.

"We want to buy a pay as you go phone with three months unlimited data, two SIM cards, and we're paying cash," Gurlien says, quick, and the man's brows flash up at the request. "And a case, something drop proof."

The man swings his gaze over to Gurlien, still wearing the perfectly crisp button up and pressed pants and a backpack, then back to Ambra, who's still not sure if her hair is brushed and is wearing the tinted glasses indoors.

So she grins at him, baring her teeth.

"Cash price is extra," the man says, and Gurlien scoffs. "Keeping the number unlisted is even more."

"Yes, unlisted," Gurlien says, disgruntled. "And noise canceling headphones."

The man mouths 'what the fuck' before disappearing into the back, and Ambra leans against the counter to hide her legs shaking.

"I could just go back there and get it," she offers, knowing well enough to keep her voice hushed.

"And then it wouldn't work, so don't," Gurlien whispers back, straightening the cuffs on the light blue shirt. "Trust me on the little things."

The glance he gives her is significant, though her eyes are drawn to the idle motions of his hands on the sleeves, and she lets her eyes rest there until the grimy man comes back from the back, carrying a variety of small boxes.

The man says nothing as he opens the boxes, plugging a sleek phone into his computer, and Gurlien scowls at him as he does so, until he slides it across the counter to Gurlien. "Two thousand dollars."

"Excuse me?" Gurlien asks, and Ambra bares her teeth at the man, who has the grace to step back at her expression.

"That's the cost for an unlisted number and the phone."

"This is a few years old," Gurlien protests, as if that matters. "For that cost..." He falls silent, crossing his arms and drawing Ambra's attention to that motion. "Do you have musician's ear-pro? Throw some of that in."

The man disappears into the back again, then comes back with a small plastic container and drops it on the pile of boxes.

"Anything else?" the man asks.

Gurlien counts out the cash from the backpack, and gets an almost disgruntled scoff from the man.

"You could afford it," the man says.

"It's the principle of the matter," Gurlien replies primly, and his clothing is the nicest thing in the entire store, but he adds the boxes to the bag and nods, almost formal, at Ambra. "You want to go home?"

Home is complicated, but she nods, following him back out through the mall, past the loud people and the jangling music that sets her teeth on edge. It's not fair, how easily he moves through the crowd, how everyone's eyes slip away from him and onto Ambra. How the attention slides onto her, until her skin crawls, and almost nobody pays attention to the man she's trailing behind.

"You've got to tell me how you do that," Ambra bursts out, the moment they're outside into the dry warmth that reeks of pavement.

"Do what?" he asks, nodding her to follow back behind the building, towards the uncrowded spot she teleported them into.

She rolls her eyes instead of answering him, and as soon as they're out of any sight lines she grabs his wrist, teleporting back to the motorhome.

Or, rather, where it should be.

10

Ambra breathes in, one moment so still, before power flashes around them.

Immediately, she slams up a shield around them, yanking Gurlien in close, and a crack splits the air.

Gurlien has a chance to inhale, to open his mouth to say something before the very motorhome around them...

Detonates.

Ambra clutches at him, plaster and wood crashing into the shield around them. Splinters fly through the air, blindingly fast, the very concrete pad beneath them shuddering.

Her ears pop, and in between one moment and the next, fire slams against the shield.

Gurlien staggers against her, the heat brutal even despite her shield, and she squeezes her eyes shut, tightening her fist in his shirt, doubling the shield, tripling it, coating more and more power into it, the effort catching in her throat.

Her feet slide on the broken linoleum, and fire flings around them, roaring into her ears, until...

All at once, it stops. The fire disappears, leaving a broken wreckage around them, a smoldering smoking wasteland.

Her breath hitches.

A trap.

Gurlien stumbles, almost clattering them to the ground, but she widens her stance, gripping the magic around her tight, holding him in place.

And there's...nothing.

Just the wind blowing snow through what should be a warm pocket of air.

Cautiously, Ambra lowers the shield, keeping her grip on Gurlien's collar, but nothing but wet slush hits them.

"What the fuck?" Gurlien sputters, still gripping the bags.

Her wards are in shreds, littered all over the forest floor, snow piling on the broken remains of the couch, scorched beyond recognition.

Ambra doesn't even let herself swallow, stilling herself, tasting the air.

No other demon had touched the place, and the stereotypical tang of wight or spirit magic is nowhere to be found.

Which means humans.

Shards of cupboard and splinters of the closet are spread all over the tiny clearing. Burnt scraps of fabric char against the snow, and a sleeve of a brightly colored sweater still smolders on the driveway.

It shouldn't be in the driveway. That had been safely in the closet just moments before.

Ambra's head lightens, and she forces herself to breathe, to get air into her system.

"Fuck," Gurlien mutters, and he's not struggling against her grip, just standing close, his shoulders broad. "What—"

"Shh," Ambra breathes, and there had been no attempt on the leash, none at all, since she had left Johnsin floating dead and bleeding.

Carefully, she loosens her hand on his collar, instead gripping his wrist where she had tied the leash, and the skin on the back of her neck crawls.

Someone had been here. Someone with enough knowledge to discard demon wards and then lay a trap that could systematically rip apart a protected space, all without alerting her. Someone with enough familiarity with her to suss out a hiding place so quickly.

Or knew of it from before, when Ambra had visited it with the body. Had taken the time to carefully hang up her clothes, had stocked the food for her, had shown her the beauty of this area.

Only a few people have that ability, and only a few people would dare.

Snow settles on the shaved side of her head, sticking uncomfortably to her scalp, but she can't move. Not when the very foundation of the ground, the concrete and the cinder blocks that were below the motorhome are cracked so deeply that nothing will ever sit easily on this place ever again.

"Ambra," Gurlien murmurs, and the sound of his voice makes the hair on the back of her neck rise. "Ambra, what was that?"

She doesn't tear her eyes away from the single smoldering sleeve of the sweater. It had been one that the body cherished, one she wore to all of the early meetings with the College, before they both knew what they had gotten themselves into. Back when the whole adventure had been new and fun and they had been together.

Only two people left alive would know to put that sweater there.

The nerves of her shoulder lock up, but she keeps her head high.

"Is there anything you can think of to salvage?" Ambra asks, and even her voice is remote, like it's yet another part of her that is alien and uncontrollable.

Gurlien exhales, strong, pushing his hair away from his face, grim, as he surveys the wreckage.

And she wishes, for one brief, wild moment, that she could see it through his eyes. Without the shreds of her runes, without the emotions of the clothing. Just as a place of destruction and fast accumulating snow and a sky that's quickly darkening towards night.

He's quiet for a few moments too long, so she grips him harder on the wrist and teleports again.

THE SMALL CONDO is perfectly intact, with the streetlights merrily shining through the window and a neighbor walking a dog outside.

And no disturbances to her wards, no disruptions to the floor, nothing.

Her knees pick that moment to buckle underneath her, and she clatters onto the hardwood floor, barely catching herself on the boring wooden table before she smashes her head against the ground.

Gurlien, breathing hard, sets down the bags he's still carrying, and his hands are shaking.

"This place is okay," Ambra says, and her legs don't want her to stand, so she lets her head rest against the floor.

He clutches at his wrist, right at where the leash is, and a tired, weary thrust of fear stabs through her heart.

She struggles to at least sit up, but all at once it's like the body has had enough. Enough of the pain, enough of the emotions, enough of the walking and activity. "You'll be safe here, at least for a little while."

Instead of walking away, he crouches next to her, and there's some ash on the hem of his new pants, incongruous.

Ash from the smolders of the motorhome.

Gentle, he places a hand behind her shoulder, guiding her to sit up and lean against the leg of the table, and her chest tightens, almost trembling from the effort.

She's weak. She thought she had been regaining strength, she thought she had been getting better.

"What sort of shield was that?" he murmurs, as he presses the back of his hand to her forehead, and his hand is chilled, cooler than her skin. "Never seen that before."

"Just a...normal shield?" she answers, voice lilting up. It's not the question he should be asking.

"Hell of a normal," he says, then moves the hand to the shaved side of her scalp, where it prickles at his touch.

"I don't know when they got there," she continues on, as if purging the words from her system will help. "I don't know how they shredded my wards, I don't know—"

He holds up his other hand and she falls silent.

"Are you injured?" he asks instead, it's a logical question, what with her literally sitting on the floor and shaking. "I didn't see any fire get through, but that doesn't mean anything." Careful, he checks the back of her head, moving her neck forward in some gentle sort of inspection.

She has to swallow down the lump. "No." She fists her hands by her sides, and they, at least, follow her command. "Not anything that's new. Just the pain from Johnsin."

He nods, as if that confirms his suspicions. "And can you tell who blew up your safe spot?" His hands still soft, he reaches down and holds her wrist, counting the beats of the heart against the thin skin next to the bones.

"Humans," she answers, voice rough. "Not another demon. They knew...," she bursts out, then squeezes her eyes shut.

Gentle, so gentle she barely feels it, he reaches up and slides the tinted glasses off her nose, and it startles her out of the anger.

"I see no sign of concussion," he says, examining her eyes in a way that's almost disorienting, and she blinks at the sudden brighter light. "I'm going to get you up off the floor, okay?"

After waiting for her nod, he grips her by her upper arm, hauling her up, and her knees wobble, before he guides her over to the beige couch.

It's far less comfortable than the now broken and burnt couch in the other home, but she sinks into it just the same.

"There's food in the cupboard I think," she says, and every time her eyes shut there's just the smoldering sleeve of the sweater.

"Where are we?" he asks instead. "This is a bit more populated."

"East coast of the continent," she supplies, and he raises an eyebrow. "The body liked the river."

"The river," he mutters, before he disappears into the other room, clearly checking it out.

"I should set up another human friendly safe spot," she calls to him, "in case they tracked me here with the body before the merge."

"Think that's how they found the last place?"

"It's that or they tracked me," she says, to the muffled sound of him opening the closet in the other room, then closing it.

The body liked this place for its nearness to the views, not the coziness of the space, and it lacks a lot of the cheerful warmth of the motorhome. Sure, there was an extraordinarily large bed and much larger kitchen, but it just wasn't the same.

And now the body's favorite place is gone. The place where she slept, the place where she smiled when setting everything up. The place where she felt so accomplished the emotion bled over into Ambra.

Ambra curls up on herself on the couch, checking the wards, listening to Gurlien putter around.

They're not going to give up on getting her back. They're not going to let her disappear easily away from them, not while they still have something resembling a way to control her.

And one of them found a way to tell her.

She refuses to shut her eyes.

The showy nature, the dramatics of leaving her wards like that, reads towards a sign. They weren't just destroying someplace for her to hide, they were showing she can't hide.

Though why wouldn't they just pull the leash and be done with it...

Gurlien steps back into the room carrying something, eyes her critically, then stomps over and flops dramatically on the couch next to her.

She startles upright. "What?"

"You look like you're having an internal meltdown. You shouldn't." He pulls out the small package he's carrying, and it's the first aid kit the body told her she needed to buy for each location under no arguments. Then his voice gentles. "They're awful. I had to learn how to keep my head above the water every time they did something."

"I'm not melting down," she protests as he unzips the package, setting aside some gauze, alcohol wipes, and medical tape. "I'm trying to plan."

He raises an eyebrow without even glancing at her. "Sure."

She struggles to sit up straighter, settling for half propped up against the back of the couch. "I have to plan, if they know all the spots I went to with the body, then we should be prepared—"

He unbuttons the cuffs of the sky-blue shirt, rolling it up to his elbows, revealing the bandages he placed while shaking in Johnsin's living room. Some blood had seeped through the top layer of the bandage, barely showing up against the white.

"Should that still be bleeding?" Ambra asks, almost whispering.

"Probably," Gurlien responds, but he doesn't sound perturbed by it. "Cuts like that, with how deep he got, usually take a while."

With an awful ripping sound, he peels up the medical tape, and Ambra winces.

"How can I help?" she asks, and to her dismay, despair leaks into her voice. "I need to help."

Barely a flicker in his brown eyes at that. "Just time is needed. Time and changing the bandages every few days." Even though the skin around is abraded by the bandage, the cut itself is mostly a thin line of scab, bloody and stiff, and Gurlien meticulously wipes at all remaining blood with the alcohol wipe.

It's still so strange to see the blood be so red, so close.

For the brief period before the body died but Ambra was still part of her, they had bled both black and red, and it was a shock to both of them.

Now, just black.

"On a scale from one to ten, how much pain are you in?" he murmurs, still focusing on his arm.

"That's too imprecise of a scale," she counters.

Of course she's heard that scale before. Back when they were tying in her nerves, back when the handlers were trying things, they asked it constantly.

It annoyed her back then, too.

"Then give me an accurate scale," he says, which is a far more difficult question, but he's letting her lean in and watch as he patches himself from an injury.

"It's not the worst pain I've been in," she starts, because they all seemed to want to know that. "It's more…weakness."

Another brief flicker of his eyes to hers.

"If I stand, it feels like the nerves would stop the muscles from working and make me fall down again," she supplies, and he nods. "Shooting pain when I do that, aches when I'm not."

He finishes with the alcohol wipe, folding it back and putting it in its open foil packet for safe keeping, then placing the gauze over the cut. "Hold this in place."

She does, of course, and the edges of his skin are warm, hot to the touch, but he doesn't react to the contact as he quickly wraps the area in medical tape.

"The pain during the spike was way worse, but this has less functionality," she continues.

"So we should evaluate in terms of severity and function?" he asks, business-like, before examining the bandage and wincing. "Did he have to cut up my good wrist?"

"What's wrong with the other?" she asks, and he rolls his eyes. "What?"

"Carpal tunnel," he replies sarcastically, and it's not a term she's familiar with. "It's a normal human injury, just lasts for a while." Then, after rotating his other wrist, says, "It's not bad on the severity scale, just have to take it easy on it or it'll bother me more."

Makes sense.

He neatens up the rest of the med kit, placing his trash precisely to the side and fitting everything back into its place, like the actions soothe him somehow. Like the day caused him distress as well, and this is how he needs to process it.

Humans are horrifically complicated.

"What do demons usually do when they need to recover?" he asks, raising another critical eyebrow at her, making his opinion of her physical state very obvious.

Which is fair, the body did collapse.

"Hide," she replies truthfully. "Usually, with something that can entertain the mind, a puzzle to solve, a book to read, a library to research, for however long it takes."

"Is hiding the answer for every demon ill?" he says, and she knows he's mocking her, but he's also not wrong.

"Hiding or fighting," she says. "Some...some go hard into sensation seeking, some collect influence over humans, some build power, but all that goes back to hiding or fighting."

He watches her face and she's acutely aware of it, and she almost prickles underneath his gaze, before something thoughtful crosses behind his eyes. "So you were the hiding sort of demon."

He's not saying it derogatorily, thankfully. "I saw no reason to risk myself in open conflict."

"Then the College made you into a puppet assassin."

She shrugs one shoulder. She's still wearing the reddish sweater, and it smells of ash, but the collection of clothes they left at this condo is way smaller and she doesn't want to stand to go look.

"And you have a library of hidden books and research. They could have made you an Archivist."

Unbidden, she smiles at the thought, and his eyebrows flash up.

"They didn't like it when I told them their research was wrong," she says. "Well, Boltiex usually indulged me in talking about it, but the rest always got irritated."

She lets her finger trace on the rough canvas of the couch, some design that she can't see.

"Turns out most humans don't like being told they're wrong and they should be ashamed of it," she drawls, and this time his eyes crinkle upwards. "And it doesn't matter how many primary or secondary sources you quote, they'll still be irritated."

"That's not limited to them," he says, before zipping up the med bag. "The moment you bring up primary sources, most people's eyes will just glaze."

"There was a scientist in the early days, back when..." back when the body was alive and chatting and Ambra wasn't alone. "Who obsessively asked questions, took notes, and tried to source all the books I talked about. I liked her."

Gurlien's face solemns, and Ambra eyes him.

"She was related to the Necromancer, wasn't she? Delina?" Ambra gestures at her head. "They had the same face."

"That was her mother, yes," Gurlien answers, cautious. "That scientist died at the hands of another demon."

Ambra shouldn't be surprised at that. "She asked some really risky questions, that tracks."

Outside the condo, a child calls out to another, and there's the merry sound of life, filtered through the walls of the safety spot.

"I want to ask so many questions," Gurlien murmurs. "There's so much scholarship around demons, and I feel like I have learned more in the last two days than I did in a lifetime of reading."

"Then ask," Ambra replies, and it's almost a sort of bravado that keeps her talking. "I'm never going to be accepted back among them, it won't matter if I divulge secrets. I'll get any answer I don't know for you once this is all done."

Once this is all done.

He's still for a few moments, obviously considering. "I'll include them in my notes," he says, finally, and it's a strange de-escalation to the conversation. "Is there anything we can do right now to protect this place better than the last?"

She swallows that down and assesses her own power levels. Body pain aside, she's not weak with her powers.

She should ward for alarms, protect this place within an inch of its life. Map out the line of powers until she controls it all.

This small city is outside the normal range of any demons, so it won't be offending territories, just other wandering demons. Such a high level of alert would absolutely draw their attention.

But is her risk from other demons or humans?

"I have some, but they should be done outside the walls," she says finally, mulling it over. "Alarms without beacons, etcetera."

Still, she pushes herself up and only wobbles slightly, before pushing aside the curtains to the road below.

It's a merry street, with a cafe across the corner and an ice cream shop next to that, and kids play, bundled against the cold.

Ambra closes her human eyes, letting all the light and sensory hell fall away, and settles more into herself.

It's harder to do in a living body.

But still, her awareness of the pulse of the world, of the

heartbeat of this small town, with the merriness and winter outside her window, grows.

There's the same strip of magic she remembers from when she set this up, pulsing down the street, twisted among the trees and fluttering with the cars. There's the ever-present thrum of the river, just a few blocks away, a conduit towards a major ley line, healthy and strong.

The strip of magic from the street flutters towards her, as if tasting the familiarity of her presence. She had been careful when setting up the safe spot, she's always careful with things like that, and most of the local magic appreciated it.

Maybe that's why the College put the wight next to her in the stasis.

She taps her hand against the strip of magic, compelling it into an easy twist around her windowsill, and it complies readily, flashing into the brick and teasing its way into the glass of the window.

Behind her, Gurlien hisses in a breath.

"Yes?" she asks, not opening her eyes.

"I can tell you're doing something, but I can't see it," he says, and even without looking she can tell his hand is on the leash, like he's testing it.

Which, if she's this close to him, it makes sense he would get that feedback.

"Do you want to?" she asks, keeping a hand on the magic, velvety soft against the human palm. "Come here."

Stillness behind her, carefully so. "I'm a dud."

"And I'm a demon," she responds, and the magic flutters against her touch. "Your ability has nothing to do with it."

She doesn't want to look at him, out of some strange knowledge that it would spook him. That this is something he would resent being watched for, resent the witness. That having someone watch whatever internal struggle he's so obviously having would render it useless and hurt.

It's a long moment, before the couch creaks with him standing.

He approaches, whisper quiet, and without the human sight, all he is, is a gaping raw scar where his magic had been torn from him, but he settles next to her, his weight against the brick of the windowsill.

"Here," she says, settling her other hand on his wrist, next to the leash, and sends a small pulse of energy into his warm skin.

He twitches, and she lets her eyes blink open.

His lips part, just barely, and she can see the whites of his eyes, vivid, and the gold magic of the world around them reflected in them.

His eyelids flutter, too fast, and for a split second she's afraid he's going to pass out, but she saw the Half Demon grant this sight to his necromancer so she knows it can't be too dangerous.

"I'm just reinforcing the window," she murmurs, tapping the strip of magic in her hands, and his gaze jerks down to it. "It's been a while since I've been here, I'm reminding it of my connection."

His pulse pounds in his neck as he swallows.

"You can just barely see the river over there," she says, pointing with her chin towards it. "It feeds into the ley line that feeds into the Atlantic crossing."

Barely, just barely, he flinches.

"It's friendly here," she continues, holding the strip of magic up, and it flickers around her hand, likely a playful animal. "If you treat it gently, it's always more willing to work with you."

His throat bobs, staring down at her hand, like his mind is desperately trying to catch up.

But he claimed to be a spell weaver before, he would have been able to see all of this without any issue. This wouldn't be new to him.

"I thought demons didn't need it to be friendly?" he says, his voice a rasp, and the back of her neck prickles, like she's in danger.

She shouldn't be.

"We don't," she responds, settling the magic back down on the window sill. "Still easier when the area is friendly."

He watches as the strip of magic flashes back into the brick, then jerks his hand away from her, breaking the contact.

"Did that hurt you?" she asks, curious. "It shouldn't."

"No."

He stares down at her from behind his glasses, and for the first time she realizes that even his lashes are blond. His lips part, like he's about to say something, like his thoughts are chasing around his mind, before he abruptly turns on his heel and strides into the bedroom, shutting the door with a firm click.

Interesting response.

Certainly, a reaction she didn't anticipate.

"Huh," Ambra murmurs to the magic now pulsing in her windowsill.

11

~

The next morning, after another night of sleeping under a mound of blankets on the couch, the far-off sound of someone speaking pulls her towards consciousness.

For a few minutes she flounders, the human brain she's trapped in unwilling to fully wake from the soft smudged comfort of sleep, before the voice continues.

Sitting up, the blankets slither from her, and sunlight trickles in past the curtains.

Dust motes dance in the beams, catching her attention, until, very clearly, Gurlien says something back past the closed door of the bedroom, then gets an answer through a speaker of a phone.

Ah.

Testing her balance, she stands, and though her legs ache, there's no shooting pain to accompany them.

So she's recovering.

Good to know.

Light on her feet, she steps towards the door, but his voice is still indistinct enough that she can't pick out words, the condo too well insulated.

And he had so clearly wanted to be alone the night before.

But he speaks, and she puzzles out her own name, so she turns the doorknob and pokes her head in.

He's dressed in a different button up, this one a light sage green with the sleeves rolled up to his elbows, and one phone is propped up in front of him and his head is bent over the other, the case off it's back, poking with a screwdriver into its innards.

There's a new set of bandages on his arm, pristine.

"Yes?" he asks, not glancing up at her.

Taking it as permission, she approaches, and on the other phone is the Half Demon on video, his brows raised at her appearance.

"How's your knee?" she asks, and the Half Demon rolls his eyes.

"I'll be in a brace for about a month," he replies. "Are you going to bring Gurlien back?"

This gets Gurlien to sit upright, raising an eyebrow.

"When it's safe," Ambra replies, nervy at the direct question.

"Good," the Half Demon responds, and briefly, behind him, the Necromancer walks through the view, a mere crossing of the frame, but he scowls at Ambra's gaze tracking the movement. "Back off."

"I didn't do a thing," Ambra protests, and Gurlien shakes his head at them. "What, I didn't."

"I don't know what you're talking about," Gurlien replies blandly, which is bullshit. "Maison's helping me with a remote device so we can get some data easier without being tracked."

The Half Demon—Maison, she should work on remembering his name—sits back, crossing his arms. He frowns at the phone, like he's deeply disappointed in them both. "Gurlien, mind if I talk to her alone?"

Instead of letting him stand up, Ambra drapes her arms over Gurlien's shoulders, leaning against him to be closer to the camera. "Why?" Still, her heart pounds, even though the Half Demon is hundreds of miles away and no danger to her or Gurlien.

Gurlien startles a bit. "Are you okay?" he asks, tilting his head up to her, as if the sudden contact is worrisome, and he's warmer than she thought he'd be, despite the relative coolness of the room.

"Depends," Ambra scowls at the phone, and Maison appears to be fighting a smile, "on whether or not the Half Demon is going to threaten me."

"I'm not," Maison replies, like her actions are amusing instead of a direct response to his posturing. "Just talking, Half Demon to trapped demon."

Ambra straightens, letting her arms fall away from Gurlien's shoulders, and he shoots her a bemused glance before stepping away, closing the door behind him.

The blankets on the bed lay rumpled, like he didn't bother to put them back when he got up, but she sits down at the simple desk chair, scowling at the phone.

And they sit in silence for about a minute, before Ambra sighs, leaning forward. "What?"

"You kidnapped him," Maison replies, almost incredulous. "You know he probably can't do anything for your problem and you kidnapped him."

"He was able to disorient one handler enough," Ambra

replies. It's strange, speaking to someone on a screen, despite the hundreds of times she saw someone do it before. "I call that something."

"He's been trying to be free of the College for over a year now," Maison says instead, and she sits up in interest, at the actual idea of getting more information. "And you're just drawing him back in."

"And getting him out," she says. "I teleported him away from the danger as well." She shifts, unsettled for some reason at the thought. "I'm not going to place him in needless danger, he's now my only way out of this mess."

"I take it you won't accept more help?" Maison asks, and for a split second, his voice distorts over the phone. "You don't have to be alone for this, we're not going to turn you over."

"But if I fail," she starts, and her throat closes up, beyond her control, but he just watches as she swallows through it. "If I fail, knowing where you are, knowing where the Necromancer is, is dangerous for you. He'd...he doesn't want to put you in danger, either."

He inclines his head in agreement.

"After this is done, I'll rob another bank, give him and you as much money as you ever need," Ambra says, bracing, "I just need to kill Nalissa and Boltiex, and then I can leave everyone alone forever."

His brows flash up, and he makes eye contact with someone off screen.

"Who else is there," she demands, baring her teeth at him.

"Chloe," he answers, "the alchemist who will absolutely kill you if her best friend is hurt."

"He already got hurt, Johnsin slashed at his arm," Ambra replies automatically. "I'll steer clear of her."

Maison rolls his eyes. "Sure," he replies sarcastically.

"What claim do you have on him?" Ambra asks, and his eyebrows flash up.

"Not like that," Maison says, his voice guarded, and even through the lines of the phone she can spot his eyes gleam red for a split second. "I've known him since we were children, but not like that."

"Good," Ambra says, crossing her arms.

"You've known him for all of five days," Maison continues, and there's a warning in his voice. "Is that wise?"

"Absolutely not," she answers, and he smiles at her, looking very suddenly human. "Nothing about this is wise."

He grins. "Work with him," Maison says. "He's a dick—"

"—no, he's not," Ambra protests.

"—but he knows his shit." Maison rolls his eyes. "Use his knowledge, is what I'm saying."

"Obviously."

He shakes his head, before his face falls into seriousness again. "The leash, that's the bond?"

Again, the lump in her throat.

"They split it, right?" he continues, and there's a fear, sudden, striking inside of her. "That's how they're doing it, right? A bastardization of a bond?"

She can't answer, so she just looks away, at the sleep rumpled room and the pillows with an indent of where Gurlien lay.

"So it would have to exist before, for them to do it?" At her silence, he sighs. "I'm trying to help Gurlien put it together."

"What would he know of the bond?" she murmurs, a pang lancing through her stomach. "Humans can't feel it."

The body hadn't, at least.

"No, but he's spent enough time with me to know what

they mean," Maison says, and there's no trace of laughing on his face, not now. "Did they break it for you?"

There's only one way to break a bond, and if he's a Half Demon, he knows that, so she jabs at the giant red button on the phone, ending the call.

"Your friend is an asshole," Ambra calls out, standing and almost knocking the chair over.

"Yes," Gurlien calls back through the door, and she rifles through the closet, quickly shucking off the reddish sweater for a dark blue shirt the body had loved. "He's been that way his entire life."

"Such great friends you have," Ambra says, breezing back into the main room, and her legs ache a bit at the quick movement. "Does this shirt look odd?"

He stares at her blankly.

"Yesterday at the store, my clothing looked out of place and odd. Does this look odd?"

"Well," he starts, "not really. You were just clashing yesterday."

"Okay," she grits out, then attempts to finger comb her hair, before giving up and flopping back on the couch. "Distance training or setting up another location to be human appropriate, one they didn't know about?"

"Safe spot," he says immediately. "Good way to track if they know your location or if they're just using historical data."

And this is why she appreciates him. An actual scientific approach to things, instead of poking at the sore emotional spots of her.

"And it'll give us a place to return to," he continues, which is a part she didn't anticipate. "Someplace with food, a bed, and relative safety."

"Good point," she says, and the frazzled edge inside of

her relaxes somewhat, away from the conversation with the Half Demon. "That's important."

"And I want breakfast before we go," he says, and she stills, like she had slithered right into a trap he laid before her. "Something that's actually filling."

She rubs the side of her head, and it still prickles uncomfortably.

"There's a cafe down the street, there's that strip of magic that runs through it, let's go there." He strides back into the bedroom, pocketing the phone and grabbing a sturdy jacket he bought the day before.

And he had remembered the lay of the magic with just a brief glimpse. A glimpse where he had been, at best, somewhat emotionally compromised.

"It'll be easy for you to grab and use if we're in there," he says, and he had obviously planned this in the however long he had been awake before her. "You can have your back to the wall, the magic in front of you, and I can get food."

He extends the green tinted glasses to her.

"You thought this through," she says, gingerly taking them from him.

12

The cafe is thankfully empty, the only conversations half-muted from behind the kitchen wall, and a bored looking waitress sits them in a tall back booth.

Highway signs and various car accessories adorn the walls, along with American flags and various star shaped paraphernalia. It's bright, so Ambra doesn't take off the tinted glasses.

The strip of magic pulses over to her, checking her out, before humming along its way, clearly not disturbed by the actual demon in its midst.

And the cafe is outside of Ambra's protections, so the back of her neck prickles the moment the waitress leaves.

"You're fine," Gurlien murmurs, glancing over the plastic covered menu, an eyebrow raised over his glasses. "What did Maison tell you?"

"Well, he called you a dick," Ambra replies, poking at the edge of the menu, instead of anything else. "He's also invasive and rude and asks insensitive questions."

"He's going to be using his access to some systems to

track Boltiex down, since he's going to be the harder of the two to find."

It's more kindness than Ambra had anticipated from the Half Demon, so she sits with that as the waitress drops off waters and looks expectantly at Gurlien.

With a sigh, Gurlien rattles off an order, before giving Ambra a critical glance. "You okay?"

Ambra shrugs, one shouldered.

"Maison says you're grieving." He drops that statement in the middle of the table, like it's the same weight as the frothy conversation about food, and watches her, sharp. "How do demons grieve?"

"He can fuck right off," Ambra says automatically.

"Fair enough." The waitress swings by with a steaming mug for Gurlien, who clutches it immediately. "What other locations are you thinking for setting up a safe spot?"

That, at least, is something that doesn't hurt to think about, so she leans forward as well, propping her elbows on the table.

"How okay are you with caves?"

"I'd prefer running water and a stove," he says dryly.

"That would narrow it down considerably," she says, before idly flicking the straw that came with the water. "Currently has running water or can get running water? I can get running water pretty easily in places with pipes."

There's a flash of interest before his eyes narrow. "How?"

"I can show you," she replies, a little bit of a taunt, and there's the same hunger of knowledge she saw on that very first night. "Pipes just make it easier. If it has a sink, I could make it happen." She sips from the water, and it's incredibly cold, almost startling her. "Do you want remote or city?"

"Does that matter in terms of getting supplies?"

"Only if you want to walk to a store instead of teleporting," Ambra says. "Or the ability to leave without me."

The moment the words leave her mouth she scowls, not meaning to say them.

"City," he confirms, and she takes another sip of water to distract herself from the lump in her throat. "I like to walk to coffee if I need to."

She could do that, get that for him at least, and lets her mind wander over where might be the best place, the most comfortable, and one she never took the body to before the merge.

There's a house in the mountains of Mexico, cracked in the foundation, but just a mile walk from a town. There's a cabin in the lavender fields in France—no, too close to Nalissa—that is the most beautiful out of all the locations. A high-rise studio apartment in a large city—Minneapolis?—with a beautiful view of a mighty river and unending grasslands probably covered with snow. A shack in the Rocky Mountains, only weatherproofed because the noise of rain was so annoying even without being in a live human body.

She could also probably swing running water in the old railway tunnel deep in Eastern Asia, but she doubts that he'd be terribly comfortable in it.

She raises an eyebrow at him, and the entire time she's been thinking, he's been watching her, like even her thought patterns were something he could observe.

The waitress drops off food without a word, and Gurlien silently switches the plates, giving her the large mound of eggs covered in bright red salsa.

"Mexico, Rocky Mountains, Minneapolis, or Tongliao?" she asks, picking up the fork. "All of those have or can get running water."

His brows flash up. "I can't speak Mandarin."

"They also speak Mongolian," she offers, but he's shaking his head.

"We'd both stick out there," he says, which is a good point. "There and Mexico, unless it's a big city. You're avoiding Europe?"

"Nalissa," she reminds him, before she pokes at the omelet. "It's a very small town in Mexico, I don't even know its name."

"Yeah, no," he replies, and he's eating his food like it takes no effort.

"I have other places, but not with the restrictions you gave me," she says, out of some odd want to make sure he doesn't think poorly of her. "The Rocky Mountains is a small town, too, along a highway."

"Minneapolis," he replies confidently, then points at the omelet with his fork. "Try it. You need the calories."

She wrinkles her nose at him, before taking a small nibble of the bright red salsa.

And immediately, heat blooms against her tongue, brilliant and amazing, watering her eyes. She coughs, once, before taking a larger bite, including the omelet this time.

It's sharp, the eggs not dulling the edge at all, and it is by far better than the salad the day before.

"Okay yes, spicy food," Gurlien says, and there's a hint of a smile on his lips, softening his entire face. "That doesn't hurt?"

"It burns, but it's good," Ambra replies, taking a long drink from the icy water. "Why would you eat food that doesn't do that?"

"It's not everyone's taste." He eats his food, the smile still around his eyes. "As long as it doesn't hurt your stomach, eat as much as you can."

It's a directive that's easy to achieve, at least, and she falls silent, mulling over the idea of the high-rise apartment.

It's hidden from the other apartments, a quick spell twisted around it to stop anyone from remembering it's there, no matter what documentation it exists on. There's a bed—no blankets—but a functioning fridge, stove, and pipes.

She hasn't been there for a few years before the merge, as it's too populous for her to spend too much time, though the demon who considers it his territory is somewhat friendly.

Or at least not antagonistic. At least not terribly interested in fights and struggles for power.

"I bargained with the demon in the area for a safe space, gave them art in exchange," Ambra says, after a long moment of almost companionable silence, her eating and him poking at his phone. "Unless something disrupted the power balance there in the last…four years? We should be okay."

"Demons collect art?" he asks.

"Some do," she answers. "I guess the same percentage that humans do. Picked the city because they liked the museums."

"Huh," he responds eloquently. "Well, that makes sense, with Maison and all."

She squints at him.

"If you ever spend any time with Maison, he paints excessively," he continues. "Says that if he hadn't been born as he was, that he would have gone to art school."

It's at odds with the competent fighter and frankly terrifying bond he had with his Necromancer.

His phone beeps again, and it takes Ambra a few

seconds to realize that it's a softer sound, like he softened it for her, and he prods at the phone.

"When I finish setting up this closed loop, you're going to take the extra phone," he says, then rolls his eyes at her wrinkled nose. "That way if we get split up, we can contact you."

"If we get split up it's because I've been captured," Ambra shoots back.

"And," he forges on, "so Maison and Axel can text you directly so I don't have to play translator."

"Do I have to?" Ambra asks, and Gurlien briefly grins. "I want to talk to neither of those people."

"And Axel's experts," he says, and Ambra sits up. "For very obvious reasons they don't want you to talk face to face, but text it could be good."

"Alright," she agrees cautiously, falling back to her food, into the silence, as they finish up the meal and Gurlien pays, only stepping outside the diner before she teleports.

The apartment is immediately much warmer, even though storm clouds brew outside the tall windows, and Gurlien still stumbles the moment she releases the grip on his wrist.

"Is Axel any better in text?" she asks, shaking out her hands at the memory of his grilling. "Or is he just as pushy?"

Instead of answering, Gurlien just gulps in breaths, before he half staggers to the bare bed.

The single room apartment is unchanged, of course. No speck of dust, no fold of fabrics, just the empty furniture and light streaming in from the windows.

Her books still cram together on the shelf, the one sign that this isn't just a model floor.

Her footsteps echo as she crosses the wooden floor to the window, craning her head to see down. They're far from the top floor, but still, people are mostly small dots on the streets below, between shining white piles of plowed snow lining the sidewalks.

"Are there lights in here?" Gurlien asks, and there's a hint of nerves behind his question, so she flexes her power to the switches, flicking them on all at once.

One bulb crackles, but the other bloom on, flooding the space with warm light.

"Right," Gurlien says, still unsteady. "When you said studio apartment, I thought much smaller."

He stands, and even in the nice clothing the space dwarfs him.

"Is this...is this the entire floor of this building?"

She shakes her head. "Just a corner."

"This place must be...Christ, a few million dollars?"

"Probably," she answers. "If I paid for it."

This stumps him, and he gapes at her for a long moment, before digging his phone out and snapping a picture of her in front of the window.

She jerks back, one hand up to snatch the phone away from him, before she stops herself.

"Why?" she demands, baring her teeth.

"Because Chloe won't believe this," he informs her, already tapping on the phone. "Because we've been living in a tiny cabin for a year and you casually have places like this."

She swallows down whatever reaction she's having, letting him have the moment, before he stuffs the phone into his pocket and surveys more of the room.

The kitchen is nestled into one corner, with an expansive wooden table left unused. A fridge runs, completely empty, but still thrums with electricity.

A makeshift office, only marked off from the room with

the packed double-sided bookshelves, and a grand mahogany desk and a plush chair in the center. They still gleam with newness.

The bed is nestled against one wall, giant curtains around it, as if it could shield from the light pouring in from the windows. A wardrobe rod stands alone, wire hangers carefully placed on it, and empty.

"And this place is safe?" he asks.

"Safe enough," she replies. The wards shine through, barely any degradation over time, easy to fix.

The ley line of the city pours through, far enough away that she's out of the main thoroughfare, close enough that she could reach out and taste it if she wants.

Huffing out another breath, Gurlien wanders over to the bookshelves, and she smiles at his back. Of course he went there first.

"You can hang up any clothing you want," she says, and he startles away from the books, like he's doing something he's not supposed to. "You'll need food, but otherwise it's fine."

She crosses to the other corner of the apartment, gauging the distance with her steps. It's not the cave, but there's more room than the motorhome and the bunker combined.

"Pull the leash, first," she instructs, and he blinks at her, owlish behind his glasses. "Compel me over there."

It takes a moment, before he straightens, any smile and friendliness evaporating from his face.

"You still think I can do this?"

"You disrupted Johnsin," she challenges, though her heart is pounding, "I want to see what else you can do."

"There's a big difference between breaking a concentration and compelling someone," he cautions and just then, there's a flicker of something in his eyes, something in between insecurity and...eagerness.

"Yeah," Ambra replies. "Practice."

Of course there's more, he'd know it, too.

His chin lifts, jaw tight and shoulders back, and his hands loosen in a stance she's seen from hundreds of magicians.

A thrill goes down her back.

Dud or not, traumatic accident or not, this is Gurlien the magician, and each line of his body belies years upon years of training.

She grins at him, at the change.

"Do you know the theory?" She taunts, and his lips twitch. Not quite a smile, not quite a smirk.

"I just talked Maison and Delina through a few weeks of theory," he shoots right back, "All without seeing any of it."

Considering the fidelity the Necromancer had, at the utter destruction she unleashed when she compelled the Half Demon, he did a good job of it.

"From what, reading a few books in a warded cabin?" she says, shaking out her hands and lifting her chin. "I made it easy for you, it's tied on your wrist. See what you can do."

Again, the flash of insecurity, visible from across the room, before he wraps the leash around his free hand, tangling his fingers in it.

It twitches around her throat, the hint of movement. Not tightening, not hurting, just reminding her of its existence.

She swallows, as he tests the sensation of it against his palm, obviously calculating.

"You can feel that?" he murmurs, but his words carry across the hardwood floor.

"Of course," she replies, then paces, and his hand briefly

tightens on the leash. "Just like if you're paying attention, you can feel that."

"Intent, control, and willpower," he mutters, and she wants to laugh at the three words. It's a massive simplification of the theory, boiled down to a child's understanding, but still accurate.

Ambra herself had told the body that, before the merge. Before they shared a space.

She exhales past the ghosts of the moment. The body never visited this apartment, there are no memories in this space tainted by the grief.

Instead, there's Gurlien, testing the feel of the leash, a scholar's intellect behind his brown eyes and a traitorous eagerness in his stance, mulling over the best way to achieve what he wants, even at the disadvantage he's at.

"Is it dangerous to do this in a city?" he asks, the leash twisting against his fingertips, sending a resulting shiver down Ambra's back. "It was dangerous for Delina and Maison."

"I'm gonna assume that was because he had zero experience with that side of him," Ambra says, and Gurlien nods, thoughtful. "And the Necromancer had so little subtlety in any of her actions."

Another twitch of a smirk before his hand closes fully on the leash and he pulls.

It's not much, it's not nearly enough to make her do anything, but she jerks forward, teleporting a few steps towards him, halfway between instinct and compelled to do so.

And her breath squeaks out of her throat and he drops the leash like it burns him.

"Sorry," he blurts out, holding up his hands, as if to show he's unarmed. "I didn't—"

Ambra coughs once, then straightens, and he blanches.

"No, you were fine," she says, running her fingertips under the leash. He didn't break any skin, it wouldn't leave a bruise. "Not bad for a first effort."

But he's pale, the white of his eyes visible from across the room.

"Do it again, it's good practice," Ambra says, resetting her stance, widening her legs. "Don't you think it'd be nice to have a demon at your beck and call? Good weapon?"

"No," he blurts out, drawing her up short.

She tilts her head up at him, and even across the grand wooden floor, he's pale.

He shakes out his hand, turning away, so she stalks across the apartment.

"We're going to be practicing that more," she warns him, her brow furrowing. "This is the best opportunity for me to avoid them."

"I understand that," he says curtly, then shuts his mouth with a click, crossing his arms.

She raises an eyebrow, stepping close to him, and his jaw tightens.

He's taller than the body—most humans are, it's not a shock to anyone—but even still, he raises his chin.

It's such a sharp departure from the confidence of just a few short moments ago, and she aches to poke at it, aches to peel apart what could be causing this reaction.

"You didn't hurt me," she starts, guarded. "Believe me that I would tell you if you did."

He swallows. "Good."

That's not it, or, rather, that's not the whole picture.

"We practice this, we practice distance, there's a bigger chance you can go back to your friends and I can be out of your life," she says, and he nods. Of course he understands that. "I'm offering you security. Anytime you need backup, anytime there's anything out of your league, I'll be in your hands."

There. A twitch on his jaw, a tightening around his eyes.

She leans back, so she can regard him a bit better, giving him space to answer, where he obviously struggles with his words.

The moment stretches on, and his phone beeps quietly in his pocket, but he doesn't shift to pull it out.

"I'm not someone who should have a weapon," he says, finally, his voice low.

That's definitely not what she thought he'd say.

"You literally have a gun," she protests, and despite the tenseness, his lips twitch up a brief moment. "And a knife, you took one from the trap."

"There's a little bit of a scale difference," he starts, heated, "between a normal human gun and an actual demon."

She shrugs, loose, and that gets a ghost of a smile.

"I'm not the College, I'm not a part of the College, I shouldn't be...wielding anything—anyone—that could cause mass death." There's an inflection in his tone, something reflected onto himself.

Despite his words, this has nothing to do with her.

"Hmm," she says, instead of anything else. "This have anything to do with how practically everyone calls you an asshole?"

That diffuses the tension, and he huffs out a sigh, rubbing his face. "Pretty much," he says, then shakes out his hands. "Distance and disrupting their grip is one thing, causing more destruction...I shouldn't be able to do that."

"Okay," she responds.

"Okay?"

"Sure, no problem, I won't teach you that." She shrugs again, even though her skin buzzes to find out more. No human she's ever met turns down free power, not without substantial reasons.

But she steps back, disengages, and puzzles over what his mystery could be.

13

After a perfunctory trip to a local grocer and another quick teleport back to the small condo for actual blankets for the too large bed, Ambra gets Gurlien to help her drag the bed into the center of the room.

"Why?" he asks, after they already did all the effort. She could've done it with magic, but she'd have to reset more of the wards then the effort would have saved her.

"I'm gonna build that as the most secure spot," she says, pointing. "Redo some of the wards, put alarms in the mix, concurrent circles, that sort of thing."

He nods absentmindedly, and there's a trace of dust on his pristine shirt, but otherwise unbothered by the physical activity.

"Feel free to read, this'll be boring for you," she instructs, and he raises an eyebrow.

He's still on edge, the jittery sort of energy when someone's jaw is too tight or their hands are a bit too active, like he hasn't fully unwound from the conversation earlier.

She doesn't know how to stop the tension.

"And lose a chance to see a demon put up security?" He challenges back, then bounces on his toes, too much energy. "A topic of scholarship and discussion and debate that's been going on for centuries?"

She squints at him. "It's not that interesting."

"Yes, it is," he replies immediately.

"All you'll be able to see is me walking around in circles," she informs him, and gets a twitch of a smile in return. "I have to concentrate to do them so I can't narrate them, and this," she gestures to the body, "is full of distractions on every turn."

"Hmm," he says, and she scowls at the vague answer. "So what I'm understanding is demons don't have as many nerve endings to deal with on a daily basis."

"Yes," she says cautiously.

Sitting on the bed, he rummages through the bags from the shopping trip, until he pulls out one of the smaller packages from the phone store.

"Put this in your ear, they'll block up to 22 decimals of sound," he instructs, and she turns the package over in her hand. "It won't be everything, but it'll help."

She peels the pack open, then sits on the bed next to him, fiddling with them.

"Like how the glasses mute some of the light, these mute some of the sound," he continues, taking them out of her hand. "You put them on like this." He demonstrates on his own ear, then at her blank expression holds back the hair on the side of Ambra's head, pressing it against her ear.

Ambra freezes, like the touch itself is a compelling order, even though none has been given.

But his hands are gentle, businesslike and efficient, before he offers her the other one.

Still rather feeling like a deer caught in the lights, she gingerly takes it from his palm, fixing it to her other ear.

All the small sounds of the apartment fall away. The crackle of electricity through the lights, the hum of the pipes, the creak of the wind on the building, all small annoyances she hadn't even recognized were weighing on her, all gone.

"This way you can still function, some people get these attached to earrings, so they can use them when needed," Gurlien says, and his voice is still audible, if muted. More like he's speaking to her through a layer of foam, instead of sitting so close to her on the bed.

"Huh," Ambra says, and her own words are tinny, echoing strangely through her mind. "Never seen a human use one of these."

"They're not...common common," he says, leaning back. "Musicians use them to make sure they don't damage their hearing but still able to stay on tune, kids who have trouble focusing use them to help, that sort of thing."

She touches the small loop on the outside of her ear and it shifts, but doesn't break the seal.

It's a kindness from Gurlien, one akin to the tinted glasses, even after she had made him upset earlier. Not something necessary for their mission, it's not going to enable her to kill Nalissa and Boltiex easier, it won't get him back to his friends faster, but just...

Something to make her existence a little less cruel. A little less grating against her very self.

It's not an exchange for something, it's not a bargain or a deal where she's expected to produce something in return. It's not a manipulation, it's not a plea for help.

It's just nice.

"Thank you," she says, after too long of a silence, where

he had gone back to poking on his phone.

"Not a problem," Gurlien replies casually, eyes still reading something flash fast on the tiny screen. "You're the one who stole the money to buy them."

So instead, she climbs to her feet, somewhat unsteady, and toes off her shoes so she can pace across the hardwood barefoot. So she can tie the power directly through the skin she inhabits, without another barrier between them.

"Does it matter if I stay in one place?" he asks, now typing something in return. "Or can I cross at will."

"Cross at will," she replies, testing the floor. It's chilled but not horrifically so. There's another apartment beneath her, and another one after that, so she has just a barrier of a few feet to tie it into without disrupting more of the property.

His phone lights up, which means it beeped as well, but so soft the earplugs block it out.

"I would've done better at the mall with these," she says, and gets an amused nod from Gurlien. "And the alarms at the base, and the stasis chambers, and at the bar—"

"If the College ever gave a thought about basic accommodations, they would be in a much more successful place in general," he says dryly. "It's not like Magicians are a well-adjusted normal group of people in any stretch of the imagination."

She shrugs, one shoulder, then twists the magic into her hand, filling up the body until crackles down into her bare feet.

And with the glasses and the earplugs, it's almost like she's back as her own self. Like she's a full demon, unbound by all the restrictions and annoyances, full of power and the ability to wreck as much havoc as she wants.

But instead, she begins to pace, feeding the power into

her steps, laying them down into the very matter of the wood. Sparks swirl with every motion, a beautiful little light show, nestling among her skin and the grains of the floor.

Even without glancing up, she knows Gurlien is watching her. He can't see the beauty of her actions, can't tell how precise she's being with each step, but still.

If he had thought to grab the notebook she has full faith he would be taking notes.

So she keeps that smile to herself, and focuses on stepping protections into place.

THE SUN SETS before Ambra's done, and by the time she emerges from the trance-like tying of the magic, her hands shake and Gurlien is putting something into the oven.

She blinks over at him, as he putters around the kitchen area like he knows it like the back of his hand.

A few of her books are on the bed now, where he obviously did some research, and his notebook is splayed open, a few new pages full.

So he did go grab it.

Ambra opens her mouth to say something, but all that comes out is a halfhearted croak.

"Yeah, humans have to take breaks," Gurlien says, already in motion and filling up a glass with water from the tap.

She makes a face at the dryness of her mouth, then pads over to the kitchen island, leaning against the counter. Her ears are sweaty, a somewhat novel and unpleasant experience, so she gingerly pops out the earplugs.

"I thought about making you stop after hour six, but nobody has any research on if it has to be completed in one go. I checked." He points to the books on the bed. "Maison didn't know either and Axel's contact didn't know if it would be different in a human vs demon body."

Her fingertips tremble as she downs the water in one long motion, and it's almost as good as the spicy food was that morning. Gurlien takes the glass from her again and refills it, before setting another bottle from the fridge in front of her.

It's a brand that Nalissa always drank, so Ambra eyes it.

"Protein drink," he says, when she makes no move to touch it. "I'm making an actual meal, but this will help."

It doesn't smell good when she cracks it open, but she sips it, before scrunching up her nose at the taste.

"Understandable," he mutters, but she drinks it anyway. "Anyways, if I'm keeping count, I just disproved about eight theories of demons just by watching you."

"Just eight?" she responds, chasing the protein drink with another glug of water.

She gets another crinkly eyed smile in return.

"It may not be that much more secure, but I'll have more warning now," she continues, then leans across the counter towards him to hide her legs trembling. "Distance practice?"

"Uh, no," he says, eyebrows drawing together. "You need food and rest." Still, his lips quirk together. "Demons aren't good at resting, are you?"

She rolls her eyes. "I could practice, it's not terribly difficult," she says, and to completely undermine her point, her hands shake against the glass.

"Well, I won't. Not till tomorrow." He idly starts to clean up the kitchen area, the motions natural, existing in the space as if he belongs. "I don't want to get somewhere and then have you faint and leave me stranded in the Alaskan wilderness or something."

It's mildly annoying.

"Besides," he continues casually, and the hair on the back of her neck raises. "Here. The contacts 'T' and 'Mel' are your experts."

He pulls the extra phone from his pocket, tossing it at her.

She tugs one of the stools over to her with nary a thought, poking at it apprehensively.

"Chloe's in there as well, so is Maison, they have opinions."

He watches her, so she scowls at him.

"I don't want to talk to your Half Demon," she says, but unlocks the phone anyways. "Why would they want to talk to me?"

"Do you want an honest answer?" Gurlien asks, like he's actually curious, not like he's mocking her. At her nod, he shrugs. "They feel sorry for you."

"He's the one who can't self-heal," she points out.

Her pride smarts, just a bit, but she'd pity any other demon forced into her position. Wouldn't volunteer to help them, wouldn't put herself in harm's way, but pity...yes.

She's seen enough humans operate phones, knows where the apps are, where to send text messages to, but it's still clumsy in her hands. The body texted obsessively, to the point where Ambra had teased her and made her laugh, but the motions feel foreign with just Ambra operating her fingers.

Still, she pokes her way over to the messages, and sips from the water, musing what to send first.

"I'm assuming one of the experts would have told you already if they suddenly found a way to untie the leash, right?"

"Absolutely," he confirms, leaning against the other side

of the counter, and the stark white bandage of his arm catches her eyes.

He obviously re-wrapped it while she warded.

AMBRA (7:41 PM): Sorry, he got injured.

CHLOE A (7:42 PM): That's your first text?

"Already did something wrong," Ambra says, flipping the phone around so Gurlien can see it.

"That's not wrong, she's just being sarcastic," Gurlien murmurs.

AMBRA (7:43 PM): Seems applicable.

Then, before she can stop herself, she flips over to the other contacts, filling a text with both the experts.

Gurlien's eyebrows raise, but she ignores that.

AMBRA (7:45 PM): Why does Gurlien think you can help me?

Three dots appear, then disappear, a few times.

"I am," Gurlien starts, "so glad I don't have to play translator for you right now. Though..." he trails off, the scholarly expression filtering over his eyes once more. "Who knows, maybe this will be good. Similar conversation styles and all."

She squints at him, before her phone buzzes.

MEL (7:47 PM): Shared life experiences.

"They're being intentionally vague, aren't they?" Ambra puzzles aloud, and Gurlien nods. "There's only been one other of the Terese experiment and she's dead, so it's not that." She stares down at the words. "It'd be a lot easier if I didn't have to worry about the College yanking the information out of me."

"Which is why we're not confirming anything for you," Gurlien says, clinical, and she raises an eyebrow at him. "You can have your own conclusions, but they'd be unsubstantiated."

"And there's nothing they hate more than untested theories," Ambra finishes, and gets a half smile in return. "So I don't have to know anything solidly, and they'll discount it."

"Exactly." The oven beeps, and Gurlien checks it, but ultimately leaves it alone.

"So shared life experiences, some sort of demon or demon-like, now existing in a solid, relatively alive body, whether they're trapped or not."

His brows flash up.

"You're not the only scholar," she points over to the bookshelves crammed with books. "If the experts have shared life experiences, if you take their words as gold, there's not terribly many other conclusions to come to."

T (7:51 PM): And a shared desire to never fall into the College's hands.

AMBRA (7:52 PM): Good enough for me. Research the perversion of soul bonds split towards control.

MEL (7:55 PM): Are you serious. They did that?

It's a little validating.

MEL (7:55 PM): How are you sane?

AMBRA (7:56 PM): That's up in the air.

"Of course Maison likes him," Gurlien mutters, obviously reading over her shoulder, before the oven beeps again. "Why does that not surprise me in the least."

T (7:57 PM): This isn't going to be an easy thing to untangle. Other than death of one party, those last forever.

Like she didn't know.

AMBRA (7:58 PM): Hence why I want to kill Nalissa and Boltiex. They killed my human, I get to kill them.

MEL (8:00 PM): Good.

Gurlien's phone beeps, but he's pulling the food out of the oven and it, quite frankly, smells far too good to be human food.

MEL (8:01 PM): I have been informed to tell you to not kill Gurlien at the end of this, but I'm neutral on that.

"Seriously, does nobody like you?" Ambra asks, and he sighs. "What did you do to these people?"

He doesn't answer, pulling the baking dish out and setting it on the stovetop.

"What is that?" she asks, when he doesn't speak. She hadn't paid too much attention to what he bought while shopping for the groceries, instead tracking the ley line through the store wall and twitching at every other sound.

"It's a basic casserole," he replies. "Chloe's from the Midwest, so when we connected again, she taught me how to cook everything she knows. Which is only very complicated Thai food and weird casseroles." His brown eyes flicker to hers, before away. He's avoiding the other conversation. "Chloe actually lived outside of the College until she was twelve, she has other life skills that I never got a chance to learn."

Still holding onto the dish with the oven mitt, he scoops out some onto the plates that came with the apartment, before sliding it across the counter to where she sits.

"Chicken, tater tots, a weird amount of cream cheese, and buffalo sauce," he lists off. "It's not fancy, but..." he shrugs.

As if he's self-conscious.

"I don't think I have any skill at cooking at all," Ambra offers him. "I tuned out when the body did it, and she usually just put a salad into a bowl with some sauce on top."

There's a glimmer of something, maybe relief, that she's following him away from the other subject, and she burns with curiosity, but instead pokes at the luridly colored food in front of her.

And puzzles at him more.

14

There's something soft about spending an evening with someone in silence.

Her wards are pristine, perfect and whole, and after dinner she props herself up on one side of the too-large bed, alternating between poking at the phone and reading an old book she hasn't touched in a few decades. Gurlien alternates between leafing through old pages of research and writing down an impromptu catalog of the topics she kept in the bookshelves.

He's going to love the library in the castle.

When it's all over, when she's free to do what she wants and he has no more obligations to her, she's going to let him spend as much time in the castle as he wants. Going to let him sift through the books, find which ones to read and which ones to merely record their existence.

The bed is kind, the blankets plush against her skin, and even though exhaustion pulls at her eyelids and at her very bones, she's not...she's not uncomfortable.

"You look like you're about to nap on a pile of books," Gurlien mutters, after a few hours of the peace, and the interruption isn't even an imposition. "Are you going to be weird if we sleep on the same bed?"

She blinks at him, slow. "That's a human thing, right?"

"Yes," Gurlien says, glancing at her over his glasses. "But despite the bookcases and the desks, you're the one who didn't put a couch or anything in this apartment."

She shrugs, still not getting up.

"This bed could probably fit four people on it without anyone making physical contact," Gurlien continues, and she's not sure if he's attempting to convince her or convince himself.

"And it's the safest place in here, now," Ambra says, pointing at the runes before she belatedly remembers he can't see them, that it wouldn't be an instinctive decision.

He nods, his mouth thin, before he exhales, shaking out his hands, and abruptly striding to the bathroom.

Definitely convincing himself.

Humans have hang-ups on strange things, but she rests her head back on one of the pillows, staring up at the ceiling, trying to piece it out on her own, despite the sleepiness.

Humans associate it with intimacy, with safety. And with Gurlien being fundamentally unsafe just by the nature of her mission, and with her still not knowing too terribly many things about him and his past, they don't qualify for either of the criteria.

But that's not enough motivation for her to leave the first truly comfortable position she's been in for ages.

Since that one night with the body in the motor home.

Without getting off the bed, she shifts the books to the floor next to it, pulling one of the two blankets up over her, nestling further into the embrace of the bed, and lets her eyes close, listening to the small sounds of the apartment at night, until Gurlien steps back into the main room.

She doesn't open her eyes at that, lets him deal with his own hang ups in the only privacy she can really afford him. His footsteps pace across the room, to all the many different light switches, flicking them off one by one.

"You are incredibly obvious when you're faking being asleep," he mutters at her, before he slides into the other side of the bed.

"You're the one who was being weird," she points out, still turned the other direction. "This is the most comfortable I've been in at least a year."

He's silent for a long moment, his breathing evening out into something predictable.

"You should seek out this comfort," he speaks; after so long, she thinks he must be asleep already. "If you're stuck in that body, you should treat it well. For yourself."

His words should hurt, should poke at the tender part of herself, but spoken across the softness of the bed and the gentleness of the blankets, they don't.

IN THE MIDDLE of the night, when even the city outside seems to hold its breath, something whispers against Ambra's wards.

Her eyes pop open, but there's nobody else in the apartment, and despite the vast distance across the bed, Gurlien's foot is hooked around her ankle. Like in sleep his body unconsciously reached out to her, even in that small way.

Ambra exhales into the expanse of the room, and the same whisper against her wards.

Not antagonistic, but curious. Hoping to draw her attention.

A flicker of her mind out towards the edge of her runes,

and another demon paces, outside the door to the apartment.

When originally setting up the wards, way back when she had all the time and ability in the world, she had placed them a few feet into the hallway, so even a malicious force couldn't break through to the door, do damage against the wall.

The whisper again, an acknowledgement that the other demon knows she's awake, but clearly not an attack. The most polite of queries, the sort that demons dance around when not wishing to embroil themselves in a fight.

Ambra pulls her foot away from Gurlien, and he makes a soft sleepy noise, before burrowing his head deeper into the blanket. She hesitates, but his breathing returns to its rhythm.

Her feet bare against the cool hardwood, she pads her way to the door. The city lights cast shadows through her long windows, just enough to tint the whole room a deep blue.

She sends back the same sort of polite whisper, a communication of something like peace, before she gently creaks open the door, stepping out into the hall, staying behind her wards.

In front of her, wearing the most nondescript dead body imaginable, some sort of businessman who could be anywhere between thirty and sixty years old, is the demon of Minneapolis. The one she traded for artwork all those ages ago.

If he wanted, he could have easily torn down her wards and rend her into many, many fragments of a soul.

She shuts the door as quietly as she could, to not wake Gurlien.

"What happened to you?" the demon of Minneapolis

asks, the brow of the body furrowing. "I thought it was you, but..."

Ambra hugs her arms, acutely aware of the stark difference between a living and a dead body when presented with it in front of her.

There are only so many things she can say, none of them good, but she weighs them all the same. "Human experimentation."

His head tilts, halfway between a predator sizing up the prey and a scientist looking beneath a microscope.

"I still mean you no harm, still using this place for safety and not for power," Ambra says, keeping her voice hushed in case it spreads to the room behind her. Gurlien wouldn't be able to hear the demon in front of her, but her words would be perfectly audible.

"Of course," he replies neutrally, then, "can you escape?"

He means the body, the body that breathes and aches and still tastes like sleep.

"No," she responds.

"Who did it?" he asks, still expressionless. "Who would do this, so I can avoid?"

Because he, like her, is more likely to run than fight. Despite his base of power, despite the ley line coursing through his city like an onslaught, he'd still pick fleeing over whatever happened to her.

It prickles at the edge of her eyes. "The human research College," she says, and his face twists. "They tried many times to tie demons into human bodies, don't fall into their traps."

He nods, frowning, before his eyes flicker to her door. "You have one in there."

"Oh, he's harmless," Ambra forces out, though her heart

jumps at his implications. "He's helping me, he's under my protection, don't touch him."

"Understood."

They stand there, in the middle of the night, before he glances away. "Looking at you is like a nightmare, don't draw attention to my city."

And he disappears, leaving her alone.

Ambra stares out at the hallway, as if she could will her human eyes to see where he teleported to, but there's nothing.

Just empty air, recirculated from the building.

And she's the nightmare.

She withdraws back into the apartment, letting the runes and wards wash over her with comfort.

Someone of her own kind can't bear to look at her.

Whatever was done, whatever part she has yet to uncover, is so monstrous and so unnatural that even someone she considered at least partially an ally is so disgusted by her very existence.

It hurts.

It hurts viscerally, in the way that such slights never would have before. It hurts behind the breastbone, where the heart beats blood up through to the brain and fills the lungs. It hurts in the scar on her gut, in the aches in the back of her legs, in the prickles of her hair growing out.

She backs away from the door, still staring at it, into the inner circle of her wards.

The hurt burrows into her stomach, into her throat, closing it off far more effectively than Johnsin ever could, and her very fingertips tremble with it.

She's known her own nightmare, she's known every horrid thing done to her, every small pain and every small bit of control. But to think, to know, that even looking at her would scare someone like that.

A lump in her throat, she turns on her heel, all but stomping back to the bed, before she climbs back into her side, pulling the blanket up over her head like it could keep out all the thoughts.

It doesn't.

She curls up on her side, staring out at the door, as if her watch could keep another bludgeon of emotion from hitting her unaware.

Tears prickle at the corners of her eyes, but she keeps them wide open out of some sort of sullen stubbornness. Keeps them open to prove that she has this control over her body, that she is the one in charge. That despite all that had been done to her, despite all the experiments and the surgeries and the fine lines cut into the brain, she could still do this one thing.

With another sleepy sound, Gurlien rolls over, flopping his arm over her midsection.

She freezes.

But he just makes a contented noise deep in the back of his throat before his breathing settles out again, regular, tugging her in close.

His chest against her back is warm, almost obsessively so, and she can feel each crest of his breath, and if she imagines hard, hear each beat of his heart. His arm is heavy, not restrictive, not holding her down, but rather some sort of protectant.

Like just this touch is to keep her safe.

Ambra stays still, barely letting herself breathe, for as long as she can.

15

Ambra shivers herself awake, and the bed is empty. No other breathing person, no weight against her waist, nothing to keep her down against the bed.

Just chills and the expanse of the room in front of her, pointing her towards the door.

Light spills across the hardwood floor from the windows, giant and shining, and the dim roar of the morning traffic reaches even this far up.

Her heart hammers, jumping into her throat, before the whisper soft turn of a piece of paper kicks the rest of her brain into action.

She jolts upright, twisting, and Gurlien sits hunched over a scroll, propping himself up on the desk, fingers tracing along the aged page.

He's wearing another one of the nice shirts, this one a beautiful deep maroon, darker than the color of blood. It draws the morning sun to his face, filling color in his skin, until he's almost pristine with perfection.

Ambra swallows, reaching up and touching the shaved

side of her head. It's still prickly, but softer somehow against her palm.

"Good morning," Gurlien mutters. "You sleep hard."

Her mouth is dry, so she pulls herself up to the kitchen, filling the glass with water again, her heart hammering.

"Nalissa has an event in a week," Gurlien continues, and she almost drops the cup. "Some sort of show she's putting on, some sort of concert in the catacombs. Loose protections, tons of public, very few magical staff."

She stares at him across the room. "How long have you been awake?"

He stretches, drawing more of her attention. "Hour and a half? Either we need to get a coffee maker for this place or we should go to a coffee shop."

She stares at the glass of water, before taking a large gulp. Her skin feels gross, like the emotions somehow washed all over her from the night before and left their residue in the physical.

"A week?" she asks again, and her voice is small, unfortunately so.

"One week," he confirms. "She'll be out of her enclave, out from her protections, and surrounded by people."

It's officially too much of a good opportunity and too much for her to comprehend at the moment, so she grabs a change of clothes and marches over to the shower.

Once clean, her hair actually combed, and once dressed in a stretchy soft shirt that hugs the body, she deigns to follow Gurlien down the elevator and into the lobby of the building. He carries a heavy wool coat she saw him buy, and bullies her into carrying at least another sweater.

A few people stare at her tinted glasses and bright orange ear plugs, but Gurlien ignores them, instead striding straight out into the city.

Even with the ear protection, a wall of noise buffers against Ambra, but she blinks through it, letting her attention focus more on the cutting wind and the frigid air slicing against her skin.

Thankfully, Gurlien doesn't speak, just lets her have the moment, before nodding and forging on. It's a short walk to the small shop, and it's full of people and bustling workers dressed in black.

"The noise will die down in approximately ten minutes," Gurlien mutters to her, and despite everything, despite the volume and the earplugs, if she's standing next to him, she can hear him perfectly. "This is just a rush around the start of business hours."

"That's good," she mutters back, casting a glance behind her at the person who stepped way too close, but they don't notice, and after the night before her heart jumps.

"Anything in particular you want?" Gurlien asks, and the menu doesn't have anything particularly enlightening on it. "Want some coffee? You don't look like you slept enough."

She doesn't exactly know what that means for her, but she rolls her eyes. "It tastes bitter."

"I guarantee I can get something here that doesn't taste bitter," he challenges, as if he's being aggressive to distract from her twitchiness. "You might feel better with some food."

"Sure," she replies, and another person steps in, forcing the line to compact a bit more.

"I'll grab hot sauce," he continues, obviously seeing her reaction.

"There's an open table on the edge, I'm going to take it." Barely waiting for him to nod in receipt, she ducks out of the line, sliding into the table before anyone else can take it.

It provides her with a decent view of the little cafe, with

all the people bustling around, and Gurlien a solid figure in the middle, as if the rest of the world flows around him, leaving him untouched. Her back is to a wall, and the other side of the table is against the large floor to ceiling windows.

She touches her fingertips to the glass, and the chill from outside barely touches her back.

The city outside streams along, people blurring together from their fast motion, as if everyone needs to get to their location faster than the next. It's almost hypnotic, something akin to sitting on the edge of a smaller ley line and watching the magic shift across the world.

Maybe that's why the other demon chose to stay here. Unending views, never the same but startlingly uniform, so similar to the natural world that they were born for.

"You look hilariously punk with those glasses," Gurlien says, startling her out of her thoughts, sitting down with a huff. He pushes a large, frothy drink across the table to her, plastic cup glowing with the cold, topped with whipped cream, then hands her a small sandwich.

"Is that an insult?" she asks, poking the cup.

"Not really," he replies, setting down a plain cup of his own. "Axel swears that his 'experts' like that drink."

Ambra raises an eyebrow at him over the tinted glasses, and Gurlien snaps a picture in the moment before she resets her expression.

"Why?" she asks, suspicious.

"Because it's a bit funny," he informs her. "When Chloe and I have cell signal, which we both do right now, we try to send ridiculous things to each other."

A smidgen of discomfort worms its way inside of her, that she's so easily perceived, so she unpeels the sandwich instead.

"So. You and Chloe," she starts, then frowns at the food,

despite the fact that Gurlien's already casually eating his pastry. "How'd a dud like you end up working so closely with someone so powerful to break through the locking pits?"

He blinks at her, owlishly, like her words caught him off guard, before he sets down his coffee cup. "She heard I was kicked out and remembered me from school."

Ambra pokes at the entirely unappealing sandwich, before Gurlien places a bottle of self-described 'hot sauce' in front of her.

"Use that," he instructs. "Chloe's like the little sister who annoys the shit out of you but also saved your life."

Ambra nods, not quite sure what the emotions she's experiencing are, but decides they're something close to relief.

"Do Demons have siblings?" Gurlien asks, leaning forward and ducking his voice down just enough that the ear protection almost blurs out his words. "Is that a concept I should explain?"

"We have genetic siblings," Ambra answers, idly taking a bite of the sandwich, and it's a lot more appealing with the hot sauce. "Not the family structures of humans, but I'm familiar with how they work. Wights have huge, sprawling families, and we interact with them enough to know."

A hint of a flinch, one barely caught, but Ambra seizes on it with both hands.

"You dislike wights," she states, not a question but so he could deny it if he wants, "and yet you saved the crying one in the cell. Stella."

"Wights dislike me is more accurate," he mutters, and the lines around his eyes tighten.

"And Johnsin referenced them," she forces the words past the same pang of loss, "and Axel said Zoel hated you, which seems like an awfully strong word for someone as utterly mild as him." To act casually, she takes a sip from the frothy concoction, then jerks in surprise at the insane rush of sugar. "What the fuck?"

"Doesn't taste bitter, does it?" Gurlien mutters, scowling at the remains of his pastry.

She takes another drink, and the chill of it numbs the roof of her mouth, derailing her thoughts completely. "And people consume this? On a regular basis?"

"Far more regular than you think," Gurlien says, and for a split second, there's a hint of panic behind the false mask of boredom. "Zoel and I had a...conflict...and I was on the wrong side of it."

It's wholly incomplete, but she just puzzles another sip of the drink.

"I'm still having trouble imagining him in 'conflict,'" she says, and Gurlien looks away, out at the shop instead of her, and she doesn't like that. "Do I need to be on the watch out for any Wights?"

"What?"

"Do I need to protect you from them? I can," she says. "Even limited, there's no way I wouldn't win in that battle, and I can guarantee I'll fight dirtier than any Wight ever would."

"I believe that," Gurlien replies dryly. "No, I don't think I'm in any danger from them. They just don't like me, and it's for a reason I don't like me either."

She tilts her head at him, and her stomach drops.

"They're far more likely to ignore me than hurt me," he continues. "Which I can't see them, so it's fine."

"You should like you," she murmurs.

"That ship sailed a while back," he says, sarcastic, before he rubs his eyes. "I don't want you to fight for me."

It's similar enough to his freak out about using her as a

weapon, so she doesn't quibble about the differences in what she meant.

So she just takes another drink of the overly sweet concoction, and even though she makes a face at it reflexively, she doesn't stop consuming it.

"I'm going to, though," Ambra says, after a long moment of quiet between the two of them, in the bustle of humans moving around the shop, ever changing in volume and stasis. "Especially during this..." she points to herself. "If someone attacks you, I'm gonna attack back. You're a necessary part in all of this, and I'm not going to lose that just because you're weird with Wights."

His lips twitch up at that.

"Though you're statistically going to be in much more danger from other humans," she continues, eating more of the sandwich after dumping another generous few shakes of the hot sauce on it. "Both as a reality of being human and because we're gonna go after them."

This shakes him from his slump, and he sits up straight, pulling out his phone.

"So Nalissa," he starts, and she doesn't flinch at the name, somehow, as he taps away, pulling up a few documents and spinning the phone around to her. "Axel pulled up these plans and Mel translated them."

It's a map of the catacombs, with the wide sprawling caverns marked with stages and crowd areas, and the skin on her arms prickles. There are gaps, large ones they'll need to fill, but it's a start.

"She loves music," Ambra murmurs. "Always played it during the experiments."

"Ghastly," Gurlien remarks dryly. "Look."

He points on the phone, at the ghost drawing of runes on the floors. Nalissa's protections.

Wholly incomplete, but still, something to work with.

Stopping weaponry, controlling the sound to just the area, amplifying people on the stage but protecting their ears. Alarms for anyone teleporting in—there goes that idea—and alarms for anyone who is trying to attack the musicians.

"She thinks the musicians are in the most danger, not her," Ambra says, and he nods, like he came to the same conclusion.

Which if he could read sketches of runes so easily, that's good. It's more fluency than most humans she's encountered.

"She has to have heard about Johnsin, though," Ambra says, and Gurlien equivocates. "Anyone would look at that attack and know it's me."

"His so called 'public event' is tomorrow," Gurlien says, leaning back in his chair, and Ambra's eyes are immediately drawn to him, at the straightness of his shoulders and the draw of the light to his skin from the color of the shirt.

Nobody else is watching him, which sits wrong. He's striking in a room full of mundane, solid when everyone around seems transient.

"So if she finds out, it'll be then."

Ambra breathes out of her nose, shaking off the sudden lack of attention she had. "So we have to expect her defenses will strengthen."

"Around her home, yes," he says. "Did she know you hated loud noises?"

Ambra nods, of course.

"And lots of crowds?"

"Wasn't around terribly many of those," Ambra replies honestly. "But probably."

"Then she'll view it as a defense as well." His phone beeps and he pauses, reading lightning fast. "Chloe says she likes your style."

"What does that even mean?" Ambra asks, almost exasperated. Of course she's heard that slang, of course humans would say things like that to each other with her around, but she's never had the freedom to fully ask about it.

"It means she thinks your appearance is distinctive and unique and not in a bad way," he defines, typing back. "It's a casual way of communicating approval."

Which isn't something Ambra ever thought she'd get from the alchemist.

Still, in the picture, the stubble on the side of her head sticks out, so she rubs at it, making a face at the texture, even as it's softening.

"My hair never grew in dead bodies," she mutters.

"And, see, she sent back a picture of my cat," Gurlien continues, ignoring that last bit, showing the phone to her.

Indeed, there's an image of a sleek looking tabby with narrowed green eyes, curled up on a couch pillow, appearing both content and peeved.

"It's...cute?" Ambra ventures.

"Proper response," he answers. "Unconvincing, but correct words."

She rolls her eyes at him, but finds herself smiling all the same, before she shakes herself out of it. "So. Plan."

He nods.

"We should be in the apartment for the time frame around them finding Johnsin," she says. "It'll be more secure and defensible if they choose the stupid option and try to attack me directly."

"And not just pull you immediately," he says, which she nods along.

"I'm hoping the scene persuades them that it would be a bad idea," she says, then dumps a bit more hot sauce on the sandwich. "Enough that they think I'd be more...able to defend myself with less of them."

"Do you think they'd buy it?" he asks, completely serious. Not patronizing, not talking down, but curious. "Axel and Maison are looking into the control, there's no real theory behind that idea."

She knows this, but she swallows. "I hope they'll see the destruction and have enough doubt. Enough doubt to not...hurt me."

He watches her for a long second, then nods. "So we plan."

The lump still sticks in her throat, so she swallows again, and someone passes a bit too close to them in the shop, giving Ambra a stare that makes her cringe away.

"Oh, hey, you're okay," he says, at something in her expression, reaching out and grabbing her hand over the half-eaten sandwich. "We'll prep. We'll gather information. We'll get through this."

"Thanks," she replies, aiming for sarcastic and missing it completely. "It's...weird. Spending your existence not being able to be perceived, able to fight or flee or be wherever you wanted, with no sensations to bother you."

He nods, serious, and there's some gratification that someone is taking her seriously. That someone is hearing her words, hearing how ridiculous they are, and still treating them as worthy.

"And then with this...the entire world is sharper," she continues, a little bit softer, "light that didn't faze you now hurts. Someone could strike me, and it'd cause pain. Things you did effortlessly take up a finite amount of energy that doesn't just...spring back. Your fingers hurt if you move them wrong. You can feel all the magic around and touch all of it all but like a child, fumbling in the dark."

"And your hair grows," he murmurs, and he's getting it. Relief courses through her, as sudden and as striking as a blow to the side of her head. "And the world isn't kind and there's a gaping cavern between your internal picture of yourself and where you are now."

"Yeah," Ambra says, muted, but holding herself still, holding the very air still around them. "Things are different and everyone can hurt you now."

For a long moment, he doesn't move, his face carved from perfect marble, before he nods, curt. "Exactly."

As if brushing himself off from the conversation, he stands, the only remnant of stress in his jaw. "Do you want to sit here in this coffee shop and plan, or do you want to practice up in Alaska?"

16

Gurlien bullies Ambra into dressing in more layers than she thinks is probably necessary, but she lets him, an odd sort of contentment in the growing familiarity of his actions. He makes her take his large wool coat, which dwarfs her comically, and he layers on a few extra sweaters.

"I can't practice with the leash if it's tucked under my coat," he protests, which after the discussion she laughs in his face.

"It definitely goes through solid objects and that includes clothing," she informs him when he has the temerity to press his hand against his chest, offended. "Or else I could just go to the other side of the world and be safe."

"Still," he replies, packing one of the backpacks with a change of clothes and his gun. "I'm not putting nearly as much faith in my ability as you are."

She narrows her eyes at him, some hint of the past conversation threading through her mind.

He had been changed, just as her.

"One day," she starts, tugging the lapels of the wool coat closer to her skin, "I want to know the secret of how you lost your power." His face falls, dropping into a mask. "Maybe you can tell me when we get to the library."

He scowls at her, before pulling on another wool sweater, and the collar of his maroon shirt peeks over the top, still drawing her eyes to his complexion. "It's not a secret."

"You can tell me now," Ambra nudges him with her elbow, as if the brief physical contact could soften the world as quickly as his hand on her shoulder did. "I'm not gonna turn down free information."

"Of course you're not," he mutters, then straightens. "You promised me an abandoned mining cavern in Alaska."

There's some small tenderness in his words, some nuance she hadn't heard before, and it's just as warm as the woolen coat.

And a mining cavern in Alaska. She could do that.

She clasps her hand over his wrist, right over the knot of the leash, and pulls them there.

∼

EVEN BEFORE SHE has a chance to pull in a breath, even before she can think to blink, the cold stings her eyelashes.

"Woah," Gurlien mumbles, up into the open air around them. "What—"

It's pitch black in the cavern, and his hand grasps hers right back, the only warmth in the entire place.

Her wards still seal the entrance, untouched by the ravages of time, and her circle of protection still glows against her mind, perfectly whole.

"Like I said, Alaska," Ambra says, her words echoing

back at her from the opposite wall, as if she has more power than she does.

She moves to brush off her hands, but he grips hers tight, almost desperate.

"Ambra," he starts, and the faux bored tone is back, desperate. "Ambra, I can't see in here."

She can't either, besides the oft familiar shine of her magic, not enough to light the physical, and he shifts closer to her, the edge of his sweater sleeve brushing up against the woolen coat.

So Ambra lets her eyes flutter shut, lets her magic expand, creak out towards the cavern walls, to where rushing water and metal tools carved into the very stone. Let's her magic find the lantern sconces, where candles and torches once hung. A few rotting pieces of wood, almost dust in age, still sit in the sconces.

And, with a flick of her mind, she ignites them.

Light spills across the ground, rock smoothed by the hundreds of footsteps, illuminating the far reaches of the cavern. Flame licks along the wood, and with barely a thought she freezes it there, so it gives light but doesn't consume the wood in its entirety.

The firelight flickers over Gurlien's face, reflecting in his glasses, and his hand gentles in hers. Not letting go, just his fingers going slack against her palm, his thumb still curved along her knuckles.

"Is there an alternate source of oxygen?" he asks, almost dumbly, like it's been struck from him.

"What?"

"There's fire, it'll...it'll use up all the oxygen, we'll suffocate, or..."

"Magic fire," she reminds him. "But yeah, that pathway leads to a crack in the surface." She points across the cavern, over to where the hall tapers off, tilts upwards. Where they stopped digging. "It drips in the summer."

His breath puffs around his face, a wispy trace of the air showing where he is. Absolute truth that he's there with her, that the very environment is changed by him standing there, in too many sweaters and his hair flopped on his forehead.

Ambra exhales, and the air clouds around her, too.

It never used to do that.

"Okay," Gurlien says, and his voice echoes. "Yes, alright, this is impressive." He drops her hand to rub his together, warming them. "It must be, I don't know, eight degrees?"

"It's warmer in here than on the surface," she says, then bounces on her toes, the movement helping something, some unrest inside her, and grins at him.

Startled, his brows flash up.

"This existed before mankind, and it'll exist after them," Ambra says. "They hollowed it out, they smoothed out the walls and widened it until it creaks with the snow, and still couldn't find anything of worth. It's perfect."

His eyes crinkle around the edges.

"Sure, there's no gold or silver or whatever the fuck they were mining, but this—" She spreads her arms wide, as if she could take up the entire cavern, "—is worth more than any gold they could have mined."

"And you have this entire place protected?" he asks, mouth sloping upwards.

"Both this floor," she scuffs her shoe against the smoothed rock, "and the forest moss above."

Slow, the smile spreads across his face, like even he doesn't believe that he's making that expression. That after the morning they've had, after the discussion and the sudden realization that he understands her, understands what frightens her and how everything is different than it once was, that this, this is what amazes him.

"Okay, alright," he says, "and you just can casually come here. No problem."

"No problem," she echoes, then, impulsively, teleports across the giant room, between one blink and the next.

Over here, the roof slopes closer to the floor, and frost from the damp glitters in the light of her fire.

Even across the cavern, she can see him startle.

"Try to pull me," she calls out to him, her own voice dwarfed by the room. The firelight casts steep shadows across the floor, against the hewn walls, catching in the natural quartz ingrained in the stone. Rusted metal tools, grating and pipes and rebar, lay bundled against one side, a rat's nest of old industry.

And in the middle stands Gurlien, the air puffed around him.

Again, the straightening of his shoulders and the exaggeration of the motion in the shadows, and her heart jumps a beat.

At the anticipation of the compelling, at how painful that can be.

And at the competency of the man in front of her, at the care he takes in the soft touch to the leash around his wrist.

Even at this distance, the pads of his fingertips send a shiver of sensation around her neck.

This time, however, he doesn't just yank. He lets his fingertips run across the leash, as if trying to memorize by touch what he cannot see.

Even at a distance, even though she can't see his eyes, she can almost feel the calculations in his mind.

He mutters something, too quiet for anything but the

softest of sounds to reach her, before he twists it between his fingers.

Immediately, all the hair on her arms raise, her scalp prickling, and her chin jerks up.

"Does that hurt you?" he calls out.

The answer is no, but it's also incredibly strange.

"No," she answers, and he hasn't restricted her airflow, hasn't done anything that could stop her from breathing.

So even with a firm grip on the leash, even with someone else undeniably there, she's not in pain.

"Tell me if I do," he commands, and a thrill slams into her, softer than a normal compulsion but still...

She would obey that. It would be pulled from her if she tried to stop it, even if she didn't want to tell him.

And with equal certainty, she knows he has no clue that he could hold that power over her.

Dud or not, he must've been so fluent before.

"Were you a spell weaver?" she calls out, and he nods, the shadow dancing across the floor. "I can tell!"

Even being so far away, his smile lights up his face.

He clenches his hand around the leash again, drawing it tight, until all of her is at attention to him. All she can do is watch him, try to piece out the details dimmed by the firelight, her heart hammering in her chest.

"Still okay?"

"Yeah," she manages out. He's not restricting her airflow, he's not making it impossible to breathe at all, but each rise and fall of the lungs is shallow.

Finally, his eyes glance up from whatever he could see in the leash, and even across the distance they glitter at her in the darkness.

And she doesn't even see the motion, doesn't even catch a glimpse of his hand working on the leash, until between one moment and the next she's beside him, her feet catching on the uneven ground.

He catches her by the shoulders, bracing her upwards, his grip on the leash dropped, and just like that all compulsion to answer, all commands and all strange knots of confusion is gone.

"You good?" he asks, and she could swear his hands are burning hot, even through the wool coat and even though the skin on his knuckles is already chapping from the chill of the air.

"I'm good," she manages out, blinking. She's dazed, as she normally is when someone summons her, but she didn't black out. She didn't suddenly lose consciousness in the transition.

Whatever Gurlien can or cannot do, it's kinder. And she's not sure if that's something innate to him, something to do with his abilities, or if it's something he chose to do.

She straightens herself and his hands fall away from her shoulders. "Good," she says simply. "That was good. Well done."

He squints at her, like waiting for her to trick him.

"You do that with me, you can disrupt them easily," she continues, and a bubble of hope wells up in her. Hope that this is possible. That she could be successful, that she could escape, actually escape, and be okay.

That one day, the hold the College wields against her, could be gone.

"And I didn't hurt you?" he restates.

"Not at all," she says, then grins at him, and his eyebrows flash up. "Do it again, take a few steps back, let's dial down on your limits."

17

Gurlien's limits end up being roughly forty-five meters away with his back turned, before all he can do is manage a whisper of sensation around her neck and no compulsion. The work, whatever it may seem to him, draws sweat from his brow despite the cold and bright pink to the tops of his cheeks.

So Ambra takes him back to the apartment with the too large bed, and he immediately chugs one of the protein drinks and then a glass of water, all before resting his forehead against the cool granite counter.

Ambra sits on one of the stools after shedding the giant wool coat, resting her chin in her hands.

"I haven't done anything like that in a year," he grumbles at her waiting expression. "That's not easy to do."

"Lie, you did it two days ago, in this very room," Ambra remarks.

"Not like that I didn't," he mutters, then pushes himself up straight, grabbing a stick of...cheese?...from the fridge.

She tilts her head at him, observing his motions.

"Do you need more food?" he asks, staring down at the fridge.

"No," Ambra replies honestly, bouncing her leg against the stool. "That took nothing out of me, I could rush into battle and be fine."

He eyes her.

"Really," she reassures him, giving him a quick smile. "That was fun."

Her skin still thrills with the excitement of the summoning, and if the College had ever even thought to work with her like that, she doubts she would be on this quest to end them.

All that it would take to change the course of her existence would have been to treat her a little more like Gurlien does.

It's a somewhat sobering thought, that an organization so obsessed with power and structure could have just... thought of kindness instead of brutality and been so much more successful.

"Why are you making that expression?" Gurlien asks, swallowing down his food. "You're making an expression. Why?"

She squints at him, appraising the risks and details of giving him that information.

But he had just done what she asked, practiced when he thought he couldn't, she at least owes him that to keep him on her side.

"I find it ironic that all the College would have had to do with me is treat me a bit more like you do and I would be there willingly," she says, and he blanches. "No, no, you're fine, just that was the first time anyone's done anything like that with the leash and...not hurt me."

"Jesus Christ," Gurlien mutters. "I have got to get you

exposed to more people." He clears his throat and straightens, like he's a professor and about to give a lecture, and she smiles at the thought. "One. That's not the first time I've heard of a similar sentiment and it's depressing that it's not."

"From who?" Ambra interjects.

"And two," Gurlien pushes forward, "I am not some... paradigm of kindness and it's not good for you to think of me that way."

She stares at him, tilting down the tinted glasses so she can get a better look at him.

He shifts, before refilling the water.

Whatever it is in his background, whatever the thing that's haunting him, he must think it's bad. Horrible. Laughably vile.

"You know they made me kill people, right?" Ambra checks, somewhat suspicious that he seems to forget that. "You make sure I eat food and try not to hurt me. That's a massive improvement."

"Jesus Christ," he repeats, then scrubs his face. "I'm gonna go shower."

Abruptly, leaving half the cheese stick on a plate by the sink, he turns on his heel, shutting the bathroom door behind him with a click.

Alright.

Ambra slips off the stool, getting a glass of water for her own, then drifts around the apartment, checking on the books, checking to see if there's anything she should be immediately researching, before she sits at her desk and pulls out the phone.

AMBRA (1:02 PM): What did Gurlien do that made him think he's a bad person?

Immediately—

CHLOE (1:02 PM): That's his story to tell, not mine.

AMBRA (1:03 PM): Obviously. But he seems to think he's a piece of shit and it's not matching with any of his actions.

AMBRA (1:03 PM): Also, nobody besides you likes him and it's weird.

CHLOE (1:04 PM): Maison and Delina are his friends too, but yes.

Ambra puzzles over this, listening to the sound of the shower run through the pipes. She leans back in the chair, and it's some comfort against the lower back, in an area she hadn't even noticed was aching until it wasn't.

AMBRA (1:07 PM): He has a lot of good knowledge. Even with whatever happened, he's able to grasp theory and use it effectively and learn it fast.

CHLOE (1:07 PM): Lol.

CHLOE (1:07 PM): Yes, but that doesn't make him any friends.

AMBRA (1:08 PM): It should.

It should, because who else, when faced with a gaping maw of ability, would stare down a demon and control them cleanly. And with kindness.

CHLOE (1:11 PM): Look, Gurlien can be prickly and some people find that off putting, and he has some history of doing some very questionable things before he was kicked out of the College. The kindness you see now is the result of hard work on his part, and more people should be seeing it, but it takes time.

Ambra blinks at the wall of text, practically filling up her phone screen.

It makes sense, with how everyone knows him, that he had been part of the College, but even more impressive that he somehow did something to get himself kicked out. After all the unethical things that she saw while in stasis, all the unethical ways they cut into Ambra's mind after the death of the body, to have someone do something so interesting that even they couldn't stand it...

Her estimation of him kicks up a notch.

And if the kindness doesn't come naturally, if the care he put into making sure she was okay and unhurt and always fed isn't an instinct for him, that's astoundingly impressive.

AMBRA (1:18 PM): Kindness by effort is more impressive than kindness by nature. And I'll fight anyone who says otherwise.

AMBRA (1:19 PM): Though he did say to not fight anyone on his behalf. Which is foolish.

Across the room, on the marble countertop next to the cheese wrapper, Gurlien's phone buzzes.

Ambra lifts her head to stare at it, but the shower turns off and he could emerge at any time and she doesn't want to be caught snooping on his phone if he does.

AMBRA (1:20 PM): So how do I get him to tell me what happened to get him kicked out because that sounds like a fun story.

CHLOE (1:21 PM): Lol. Wait until he's not spooked by accessing magic for the first time in a year. Bribe him with books.

AMBRA (1:22 PM): I've bribed him with an entire library if we deal with Nalissa.

CHLOE (1:23 PM): Omg.

AMBRA (1:23 PM): It's too close to her base to go now or else I would.

The door to the bathroom swings open, and Ambra bounces up to her feet.

"Your phone went off," she calls out across the large room.

Gurlien blinks at her, as his hair is sopping wet, hanging in his face, a few shades darker than its usual color, and a new button up is open, revealing a plain black undershirt. A towel drapes over his shoulders, one of the ones that came with the apartment, fluffy and light blue.

"Is this because I made you drink coffee?" he asks, suspicious. "Is that what this is?"

"Is this what what is?" Ambra responds.

He shakes his head at her, before scrubbing at his hair with the towel.

Smiling at the motion, Ambra sits back down, something settling in her chest.

Until Gurlien rolls up his sleeve, revealing the cut left by Johnsin.

The edges are red, visible even from this distance, as he picks up his phone. He hasn't rebandaged yet, and Ambra doesn't fully know enough about human biology to know if it's normal, if he needs care, if he needs help...

Beyond her consciousness, her shoulders stiffen, the muscles freezing into place. Her stomach drops at just the glimpse.

"What did you tell Chloe?" Gurlien asks puzzled, gesturing with his phone.

"I texted," Ambra says, the words falling out of her mouth outside of her control.

His mouth tilts up into some sort of half smile as he taps out a response.

"Check with your experts to see what they experienced around coffee," he says, almost lazily, scrubbing his hair with the towel again.

And he's so vulnerable like this. His attention split, halfway between a mundane automatic behavior such as maintaining his body and whatever he's reading and writing on his phone. The ruddy ness of his cheeks, from the hot water. The bright red of the cut.

"Do you need more medical care?" She blurts out.

"Hmm?" he asks, glancing back up at her, and even his glasses are still a bit fogged from the steam. "Wait, this? No, I was just letting it dry before bandaging."

She creeps upwards again, drawing near him. "It looks bad?"

He twists his arm to get a better glance at it. "It'll definitely scar," he replies, matter of factly. "It's not terrible, I'll recover."

It still sits poorly, and that must've shown on her face.

"It's just a normal stage of human healing," he informs her. "It's not infected, it's clean, and the skin is connecting again, which means it wasn't too deep. Stop making that face."

"What face?" She shoots back immediately.

"Like you're grossed out by normal biology," he says. "It's just a healing cut. It takes a while."

"I'm not grossed," she starts, then shuts her eyes, forcing the lungs to inflate and her ribcage to flex, to see if that'll calm her down. It doesn't. "How do we make it heal faster?"

He gives her a blank look. "We don't."

"But there has to be something we can do."

"There isn't," he says, running the towel through his hair again, making it stand on end. "Or, rather, this. This is what we do. We let it air out while clean, until the skin is dry, then put on more antibiotic gel and rebandage it. That's what we can do."

She scowls at him.

"No, really," he says, returning to hang up the towel, even though his hair is still out of place. "It's doing fine, I'm not concerned with it."

Out of a fit of frustration, she sits on the bed, but her leg still jangles with the want for motion.

"Do you need any help healing that?" he asks, gesturing at her face, where the blackened wound from the Necromancer Delina—still annoys. "That looks way worse than this."

Impulsive, she reaches a hand up to touch it, and while it stings, it's not even registering on her awareness of her general pain.

"Why didn't you heal that one?" he asks, giving his hair one more go through before hanging the towel back up.

"Apparently, necromancer wounds don't heal nice," she answers, before lifting her chin at him. "Teach me how to help rebandage that."

He raises an eyebrow at her, bemused.

"If I have to be 'among humans' then I should know how to help them," she says, mirroring the quotation marks with her fingers the body occasionally did. "And I don't like that…" She trails off, actually hearing herself approach something emotional and actually able to stop herself from going too much further.

"I can do that," he replies cautiously, because of course he caught that hesitation. "Give me about an hour for this to dry."

18

~

Ambra regrets that, as bandaging humans turns out to be intensely boring, but the knot inside her chest loosens the moment the pristine white bandage is back in its place.

"See," Gurlien says, twisting his arm around once the final bit of tape is in place. "I'm fine."

"He still shouldn't have injured you," Ambra mutters, for what feels like the hundredth time in this process. "There were other things he could do."

There obviously were, but even in saying that she knows that Johnsin never would have picked them. He liked blood too much and the pain, to miss a chance to do it to someone unsuspecting.

And now he never would again.

Gurlien flicks his sleeves back down, buttoning the cuffs around his wrists, right as both of their phones buzz.

Ambra freezes and Gurlien's brown eyes widen, almost

imperceptibly, before he slowly reaches for his phone and Ambra pulls hers out of her pocket.

It's a group text, with her, Gurlien, Maison, and Chloe.

MAISON (3:02 PM): They know about Johnsin.

"How would he know?" Ambra asks, suspicious. "Isn't he just as out of the loop as you?"

GURLIEN (3:03 PM): Thank you for the intel.

CHLOE (3:04 PM): Jose has a report that they're circling some forensic mages in Miami, flying them in from Washington.

"That's not good," Gurlien murmurs, then gives Ambra a grim look, his lips flattening. "So they'll know about you."

Instinctive, she reaches a hand up to the leash, where there've been no traces of attempts, nothing, and her pulse flutters in her neck. Careful, she steps backwards, back into the concurrent circles of progressively more complex wards, the hair on the side of her scalp prickling, until she sits down on the overlarge bed in the center.

Another buzz of the phone, and even though it's quiet, she flinches.

MAISON (3:06 PM): Someone sent me a query to help consult, someone who isn't kept in the know.

"They want demon experts," Gurlien mutters grimly, then refills two glasses of water, carrying them over to the bedside table.

Ambra's heart pounds.

She knew this would happen, that they would discover Johnsin. That someone would put it together, would see the incredibly obvious trail of clues.

And she left them intentionally. Left them as a warning.

And despite that, she shivers in fear.

Gurlien drops off the water, then brings over one of the

boxes of protein bars and a bag of chips that Ambra had bought specifically because the word spicy was written all over them.

"Is this the safest place in the apartment?" he asks, even though she had said so many times. Even though he had watched her put the protections down.

She nods, jerky.

"Then we'll stay here," he replies grimly, before going back to the bookshelves, pulling out some tomes, and grabbing the extension cord and her phone charger. "See if they make some moves, decide safety after a few hours."

It's another bit of kindness.

"You can be 45 meters outside of it," Ambra says, almost automatically.

"I probably will be at some point," he says, before flopping down onto the bed, staring up at the ceiling. "I'm tired from the practice and all the everything, so I'm staying here."

She can't tell if he's indulging her or if he actually needs rest, but still, the closeness is…nice.

Carefully, she lays down on the other side of the bed, the heart hammering hard.

HOURS PASS, as Gurlien reads, naps, and reads again, but Ambra just lays still, the adrenaline never leaving her limbs, before…there.

The leash flexes, and Gurlien drops the pen he was jotting notes with, grabbing at his wrist.

Saying nothing, Ambra just nods, a lump in her throat.

"Okay," he whispers, then weaves the leash through his fingers, sending a shiver down Ambra's spine.

There's another flex, something barely against her neck, and Ambra flinches.

"Here," Gurlien says, before scooting closer to her on the giant bed, until he's right next to her, the fabric of his shirt grazing her shoulder. Quick, he wraps the leash around his hand, and she shivers once more. "How much of that do you feel?"

Ambra swallows, and the leash isn't cutting off her air or anything, but the tension might as well. "A fair amount," she manages out. "It doesn't hurt, but it's like..." her mind flashes blank, trying to find an equivalent sensation. "How sensitive were you? Before your injury?" She blurts out.

His lips part, and he's very close. "Fairly."

Another tightening, a jerk, and she grabs his shoulder, flailing, in some strange fear. "Did you ever dive into a ley stream?" The words are torn from her, even then they make little sense. "Did you ever tap into too much magic that you weren't supposed to grasp?"

A minute widening of his eyes.

"Did you ever plug into something and know, just know, that it's too strong for you?" It tightens, vicious, cutting off her words with a squeak.

She fights against it, clawing up at her neck, before Gurlien catches her hand, holding it tight.

"Yes," he replies strongly. "Yes, I know what that's like."

It's still too taut for her to speak, so she struggles, before it loosens just a bit.

"It's like that but around your neck." It closes again, a vicious jerk, and her mind blacks out, her back arching off the bed.

Before Gurlien's hand around the leash tightens, and he slams his hand against the bed, crashing her back down into the room with him.

She gasps, the air torn out of her lungs, and pain snaps down her back.

Gurlien grabs her shoulder, pinning her down, and that touch will do nothing if they try again, will do nothing against their pull. "I got you, you're here," he says, serious, and her whole body shakes against the bed.

Another attempt, slicing through the skin on her neck, and Gurlien grips the leash just as tight back. She sputters, choking on the leash, on blood welling up in her throat.

But his hand on her shoulder digs in, as she jerks with another attempt, fear coating her blood and pumping through her veins like acid, washing through her stomach and her lungs.

"You're okay," he murmurs, after a keening noise tears from her throat, and she's manifestly not, but she turns her head towards him on the bed, the shaved side of her head gross with sweat against the pillow.

She blinks at him, and her eyelashes stick together.

He's pale, a grim determination in his jaw, and she's close enough to see the small variations of colors in his eyes, the flickers of lighter brown and even green.

They stare at each other, in the silence after the attempt, the only sound Ambra's harsh breathing.

His lips part again. "Did I hurt you?"

It's so laughably wrong that she huffs out, her throat raw.

"You're bleeding," he says, serious, because of course she is. "Your neck, your eyes, and your mouth. And nose."

She lifts a shaking hand to her mouth, dabbing and coming away with a black smudge.

He's still gripping her shoulder, still pressing her into the bed, and a rush of gratefulness floods through her.

"You..." she rasps, before she coughs, the taste bitter.

"I'm okay," he informs her, holding up the hand with the leash. "This wasn't...this was okay. I didn't hurt you?"

He's shaken, too.

Not trusting her voice, she shakes her head.

"Are they about to try again?"

She has no way of knowing, no way of predicting, but the leash is slack against her stinging neck.

"I don't think so," she manages out, her voice wrecked, and he releases her shoulder, a sudden lack.

Sitting up, suddenly terribly far away, he swings his feet over the other side of the bed and pads to the bathroom, emerging with a wet washcloth.

"Sit up," he orders, and even though there's no compulsion, she shakily pushes herself up.

Blood, hot and sticky, trickles down her shoulders, and some is smudged on the pillowcase.

He sits next to her, his knees touching hers, and carefully wipes under the leash. "So this is just abraded, I think," he murmurs at her, as if the injury is just as mundane as a skinned knee in a child. "This should be easy to heal."

It will be, but her fingertips tremble as she reaches up to slide her hand under the leash.

The very skin is hot to the touch, slick with sweat, and it mixes with the blood.

"Oh," he murmurs, at something he sees in her face, at the trembling of her hands, at the shivering of her shoulders. "That took a lot out of you."

Her breath hitches, and he's not wrong.

She's weak. She's so weak the body fights her in staying upright, wanting to just slump over and for her eyes to close. Her stomach roils, simultaneously empty and full of bile, and she doesn't know if she could even hold the glass of water still enough to take a sip, to wash out the taste of her own blood in her mouth.

All because the College wanted her again. Wanted to claim her, to shove her in a stasis chamber and never let her out. Wanted to take her from this small, carved out pocket of comfort and place her in the unending brightness and volume of the jail cell.

All because they couldn't let her just live.

"Here," he murmurs, and gently, as if she would break from something so small as a touch, wipes the blood streaked down her cheeks.

Her eyes blur, and to her horror, she's crying.

She's actually crying, her lungs hiccuping with the effort, her throat closing up until a sob wrenches its way out. She's crying, sitting there on the blankets from the condo, on the too large bed, and no matter how much she wrestles to get the body under control, no matter how much she tries to stop these somehow automatic functions, the tears spill down her face, almost as hot as the blood.

Not saying a word, Gurlien shifts closer, then wraps his arms around her shoulders, pulling her into a tight embrace.

She slumps forward, pressing her face into the crook of his shoulder, as if that could stop the tears falling from her.

It doesn't, and her shoulders shake with the effort.

Almost idle, Gurlien rubs a hand against the middle of her shoulder blades, and it sets off another wave of horrid, gut tightening sobs.

The College couldn't just let her go. They saw the carnage and wanted her back. They saw the threat she wrote into the very magic of the room and decided that meant she was still theirs. That they had to keep her. That they had to pull at her to the point of pain, to the point of cutting into the body, instead of letting her have some peace.

Cutting into the body, the very body they had forced her into and then killed off her only companion. Harming the very place Ambra is forced into, the very vessel she can never leave and the constant reminder of everything she lost.

"It's okay," Gurlien says, almost clinically, placing his chin on top of her head, and she clings to him like he's the only thing keeping her afloat. "You're okay, you'll be okay."

She won't be, but she lets her hands fist into the back of his shirt, as if the touch could somehow make his words true.

"They didn't get you, we kept you here, you're okay," he repeats, and this close, she feels the rumble in his chest at his words.

He brushes some of her hair back, still in the hug, and she squeezes her eyes shut at the sudden shock of emotion that wells up at that motion.

"Why am I crying," she mumbles, keeping her face pressed against his shoulder. Her throat is somehow even more raw than with the leash, and her head starts to pound, her pulse loud against her skull. "This is stupid, why am I crying?"

It's not stupid, she knows that even as she says it, but the lack of control aches at her behind her breastbone.

"Well," Gurlien drawls, as if this is a normal conversation and she's not tucked against him. "I'd put my money on an intense situation, physical pain, fear, and still not knowing how to process those in this body. Yet."

It has the intonation of an insult, but he's not wrong, so she lets herself be lulled into silence, the exhaustion so heavy that if she releases her grip on Gurlien, she's certain the weight of it would press the body into the bed and never let her go.

"Have you cried before?" he asks, which isn't helpful. "I'm not talking about tears. I'm talking about actually sitting down and crying."

"I know the body did," Ambra replies truthfully, before pulling herself away. "More than I knew why."

Shakily, she reaches for the glass of water, and it's cool against the fingertips.

Gurlien watches her like a hawk, and there's a smear of her blood against the collar of his undershirt.

"Crying is one of the ways the human body processes stress chemicals," he says matter of factly. "Yes, it's emotions, but it's biological. You'll be dealing with it again and it won't be some sort of failing."

That helps, so she nods, washing the blood out of her mouth with a grimace, and weighs getting out of the safety to make her way to the shower. To get the blood off of her, to focus on healing the skin on her neck and the stinging in her eyes while under hot water. To peel off the sweaty clothing sticking unpleasantly to her skin.

"Tell me," Gurlien starts, and all her attention snaps to him, laser focused, "what exactly were they trying to do?"

He's rubbing his hand along his wrist, right where the leash is still tied.

"They tried to take me," she murmurs. "And you stopped them."

"More specific," he requests. "Were they trying to gain control? To force you to teleport to them? What was it?" At her blank look, he sighs. "I want to get familiar with the specificities. So I can block them better."

"Teleport," she replies curtly, putting her own hand on

the leash and tugging it slightly, to generate the sensation on him. "Like snapping a rope around a dog."

He blanches but recovers well, ducking his head. "They call you that?"

"When they called me anything at all," Ambra replies darkly.

He watches her, like he's debating telling her something, and she can't parse it together. Her curiosity worn out by the competing pulls against her neck, all her brain seems to be able to do is just...spin.

Ambra stands, testing her weight on her knees, and they wobble annoyingly.

"My head hurts," she announces, as authoritatively as she can. "My head hurts and I feel so completely gross." Completely undercutting herself, she scrubs at the tears on her cheeks, and her face is still too damp.

"I'm not shocked," Gurlien replies, then rubs his own forehead, grabbing one of the protein bars. "Eat something?"

That sounds like the worst possible idea, and she scowls at him, before something twists inside of her and she sighs, bracing herself on the bed so she doesn't slump forward.

"Thank you," she says, and there's something horrible about it, about once again finding weakness. "Thank you. You...you saved me. I think."

His lips part to respond, but she turns on her heel and all but stumbles towards the shower.

19

After the shower, she crawls right back into the bed, her head pounding, and flexes her power across the room to plunge the lights off in one large movement.

Gurlien doesn't say anything, just turning on the one desk lamp to illuminate his reading with a small motion. It's not passive aggressive, it's not denying her the want for darkness, instead just a tiny movement for himself.

The light spills out the large floor, just enough to send a shadow of his silhouette across the wall, and that too is something comforting. That even with the darkness she so desperately wants, there's still a hint of him in her vision.

With exhaustion pressing down against her body and dragging her eyelids to close, she curls up on the bed, shuffling so she's under the blankets the best she can, and tries to sleep.

∼

In the small hours of the night, she drifts back up towards awareness, the sleep clinging to her like a fog on a lake, but it's just Gurlien climbing into the other side of the bed, whisper soft in the darkness.

Not a threat at all, and she drifts back to sleep within moments.

She awakes in the morning with a start, and sun streams through the windows, piercing through her eyelids and stabbing her in the brain.

Gurlien's arm is tight around her middle, his body warm under the blankets, and he's still breathing deep, still asleep.

Ambra jerks slightly, before getting the body under her control, and blinks up at the big room.

Somehow, she slept through him cuddling against her; somehow, she rolled over until she's in the center of the bed with him, and her limbs are loose with warmth and comfort. His foot is once more hooked around her ankle, as if keeping her in place.

She breathes out, and dust mites dance in the morning sunlight. It's bright, clear and cold, and the far away howling of wind across the building just prods her to stay in place. To stay under the blankets and against the pillows.

Gurlien had changed the pillowcase to one she didn't bleed on.

She knows enough about humans to know that this level of contact isn't normal, that humans don't just do this with one another unprompted. That the body had dreamt of contact like this, in her most loneliness, and Ambra had marveled at the specificity of the images.

Yes, some demons chase after contact with humans, rare

and difficult with the realities of their biology, but Ambra never had. Never had the impulse to lose herself with touch, to intentionally overwhelm her senses, with this close of physical connection.

This doesn't feel overwhelming, not in the way she's become accustomed to. Other demons had described it as incandescent, as burning a hole through their sense of self until all they can think about is the physical need. But this, with his arm around her and her back against his chest, is much closer to just...comfort.

She breathes out again, and he sighs in his sleep, a small sound.

And he had saved her. Had, despite all his own misgivings of the leash, despite all his own doubts about his own ability, been able to grasp the leash right back and slam her into place.

And then cuddle her.

Now well and truly awake, she wiggles out from underneath his arm, and he makes another sleepy noise, deep in the back of his throat, before he flops over to the other side of the bed, his blond hair sticking up in the back.

Even his glasses are by the side of the bed, rendering him almost entirely without armor.

Ambra takes a few moments to slip on her tinted glasses and some socks and grab her phone, then carefully creeps over to the fridge. Gone is the acid wash of fear in her stomach, leaving her with an almost contented hunger.

It's wholly unreal. Wholly unlike her.

She shivers the moment she strides out of her strongest protections, but no jerk of the leash strikes her, no otherwise demon interference.

And she lets herself hope, until she squashes it down.

It's too much to hope that they'd give up. It's too much to hope that they'll view the night before as a final act.

Instead, Nalissa or Boltiex is out there, scheming a way around her defenses, as much as they don't understand them. Scheming and researching and poking around them until they figure something out.

And here Ambra is, wearing socks that were bought just because they're soft, and staring at the fridge like it could solve her problems.

Balefully she opens it, and finds no more elucidation. There are protein drinks and some leftover casserole that Gurlien made, which was nice but not appetizing at the moment. There's more cheese sticks, which appear far too rubbery for her taste, and a few things she would categorize as ingredients but not necessarily 'food.'

She's going to have to learn how to cook and clean and do all the small things humans do to fill up their time. And if the mere act of rebandaging a wound is boring...this isn't going to be great.

She grabs a bottle of juice, and the warm comfort of sleeping next to Gurlien is almost already gone, so she settles into the desk chair, poking on the phone.

Somewhere in the middle of the night, her phone must've lit up like crazy, but that too didn't wake her up.

It's the contact 'T,' not in the group chat, just to her.

T (2:03 AM): Are you alright?

T (2:23 AM): To clarify, Gurlien told us you fought off an attack.

Ambra scoffs, because she did no such fighting and to call it an attack is almost a misnomer.

T (2:24 AM): Everyone was focusing on how it's exciting that Gurlien was able to do something and the implications, but I wanted to check on you.

T (2:24 AM): And I know something about how terrifying it is to not be in control of yourself.

It's another small hint of the mystery, and Ambra lets her eyes flicker to Gurlien's still sleeping form. All she can see of him is his hair, the blankets pulled up to his ears.

AMBRA (9:12 AM): I feel like shit. Gurlien did all the fighting and I just got bloody. Then I slept for about twelve hours.

Even though not enough time for this person to get enough sleep has passed, immediately three dots fill the screen.

T (9:13 AM): And let me guess, now he's bothering you to eat and that sounds horrible.

AMBRA (9:14 AM): He's still asleep and there's nothing appetizing in the apartment.

Then—

AMBRA (9:14 AM): How much can I talk to you? How much do you know?

She sips from the juice—it's fine, if cloyingly sweet—and props the phone up on the desk, so she can see the response without holding it up.

The three dots appear, then disappear, a few times.

With a start, Gurlien jerks himself awake, flailing in the blankets, and Ambra blinks over to him.

"Are you okay?" she asks, and she hadn't spoken yet, her own voice almost foreign against her throat.

He stares wildly at her, then scrambles for his glasses.

"Just how bad is your eyesight?" she asks, sipping from the juice again, the idle motion somewhat entertaining while he's so flustered.

He shakes his head, more of getting himself together than a negative.

"Are you doing okay?" he asks, voice still bewildered.

The answer is not terribly, but not critical at that very moment. "We can discount the idea that they're going to give up on retrieving me."

He rubs his entire face, still disoriented. "Are you a morning person?"

"I didn't need a sleep schedule before the merge," she points out, "so who knows."

"Right," he says heavily, then swings his feet to the side of the bed, right as her phone buzzes again.

T (9:32 AM): I don't want to give too much information in case of a success from them.

Ambra expected that, with how secretive they seemed to be.

T (9:32 AM): And Axel halfway thinks that Gurlien is going to turn on you, if push comes to shove.

Ambra slates her eyes over to Gurlien, who's staring blankly at the middle distance, blinking behind his glasses.

AMBRA (9:35 AM): He's saved me twice now.

T (9:36 AM): Axel has his reasons and they're good.

It's still puzzlingly vague, and Ambra scowls at the phone.

T (9:37 AM): All of that to say, no specifics. But I can talk emotions, and I know that in times like these emotions get pushed to the back of the priorities and that can be just as hard.

And with that, right then, Ambra decides that there's no way this expert is a demon trapped in a human body. No demon would talk like that, no demon would offer that unprompted.

It's still nice, though, and the temptation to push on it, to needle it out, still digs underneath Ambra's skin.

AMBRA (9:39 AM): So human emotions are odd and don't make sense, right?

T (9;39 AM): Lol.

AMBRA (9:40 AM): They all manifest in physical ways and I can't stop the reactions even when I want to.

"Did you eat already?" Gurlien mumbles, stripping off his undershirt and reaching for a clean one, facing the other direction.

Ambra raises an eyebrow at his back. Again, not behavior she associated with normal human interactions with each other, right in line with the cuddling.

"No," she replies, not making herself glance away. If he, the one actual human in her life, isn't going to act normal, then neither is she.

Plus, his shoulders are nice to look at. All the humans Ambra has been around since the merge, have either been older scientist types who viewed her as an object of experimentation or excessively muscular combat types who seemed unpleasant to touch.

He glances back at her, catching her eyes as he throws on another button up shirt, this one the color of deep olive green. "What?" he asks suspiciously.

"Axel thinks you're going to betray me?" Ambra says, and Gurlien shuts his eyes with a sigh. "And T isn't a demon, that's for sure."

"Yes," he shoots back at her. "You're a morning person, that's what this is." He rakes a hand through his hair, and it's nowhere near as neat as it normally is. There are circles under his eyes, even visible from this distance.

Ambra sits up straight, but he ignores that.

It's alarming, and she squints at him across the bright early morning light.

"You need food," she declares, pushing authority behind her voice to force out the question. "You did more than you anticipated, and now you need food."

He sighs. "Probably."

Ambra bounces to her feet, and her head only aches a bit with that action. "No, you do. It's been what, a year, since you've done any sort of combat magic?"

He stares at her, baleful underneath his glasses. "That wasn't combat magic."

"Bullshit," she informs him, and his lips tug into a smile before he stops himself. "You were controlling a demon, actively against another force trying to control her, and you won. If there's a winner, then it's combat."

"That is so incredibly reductive," he mutters, but stands, reaching for his heavy wool coat.

Despite the rush of terror at being beyond her wards, despite the headache that bubbled up after only five minutes outside in the bright cold, she follows Gurlien along to a restaurant and coffee shop, and doesn't say a thing about leaving until the color returns to his cheeks and the analytical light flickers back on behind his eyes.

And she lets him bully her into walking, actually walking, back, in an almost familiar action now. Even though they have only done this once before.

But Gurlien turns up the collar of his woolen coat against the wind and Ambra tucks her hands into the sleeves of her sweater and, for a split second, they actually look normal. They look like two absolutely run of the mill humans walking around the busy downtown, huddled close for the wind.

And for the first time, it doesn't quite feel like a bad thing.

"So," Gurlien starts, as they're strolling back, and she

tilts her face towards him. She's not wearing the earplugs, but outside the noise isn't as severe. "Do you think that was Nalissa or Boltiex?"

A shiver of fear winds up her back, but it's far away, now that she's out in the bright sun with the clear blue sky overhead.

"I'm not sure," she murmurs, keeping her eyes on the snippets of sky visible from in between the sky scrapers. "Felt like Boltiex, but I think...he's generally stronger," she says, and it's so strange to be speaking so freely. "He's more instantaneous, we had...that bit of warning."

He nods, almost neutral. "And I would think that Nalissa would be busy preparing for her event," he says, and the wind has turned his cheeks pink. "I'm surprised she didn't cancel, with the Toronto base."

"She never thought much of the Toronto base," Ambra supplies. "She hated the weather, hated the culture. When she...worked on me..." she swallows. Even the clear air can't stop her throat from seizing. "She had me transported to Paris. Once Italy."

The body had found it glamorous, with the old-world beauty and fields of lavender, and Ambra had been struck by the extremes of sensations. Of the beauty of nature, at how sharp the scents surrounding them, at the difference in the magic flowing through them.

"She hated that they kept me on the other continent," Ambra forces on, kicking a pebble and watching it skitter into the gutter. "But three of the Five lived there full time, so she was outvoted."

And now just two of the Five remained.

It's still weird to think about.

"So she wouldn't stop something she liked just because her least favorite base fell," Ambra continues. "She likes her music, she likes her spectacle, she likes when they come together. Did you know," Ambra pivots to face him while walking, "that she brought in a specialty record player into her labs? Not just a speaker, everyone had those, but an actual record player that took up almost an entire desk."

"I only met her three times," Gurlien says, and it's a bit of a jolt to imagine him speaking with Nalissa. "I had to draw up a contract for her once, she was not...very responsive."

She raises an eyebrow at him, and he had the temerity to shrug, embarrassed.

"I wasn't the most interesting of person," he says. "I mostly did legal work, I did diagnostic spells, I did magically binding contracts. Not a combat mage, not someone terribly important."

It tickles her all the more that he still did something to get kicked out.

"I wasn't the sort of magician to be invited to fancy musical spectacles," he says, his face soft in some sort of self-deprecation. "When people saw me, they knew I was there to fix a mess that was mostly paperwork."

"I'm glad," Ambra declares, and he gives her such a startled glance that she almost feels bad. "If I had met you on the experimentation table, I would've absolutely killed you."

"Right," he says, unnerved. "You and murder." He takes a deep breath, like physically moving himself on. "Nalissa. Any friends to manipulate?"

"She didn't make a lot of friends, unless you were an artist," Ambra says. "I don't think any of the Five liked her terribly much."

"Did anyone in the Five like each other at all?" Gurlien asks dryly. "They're not a group of people I can imagine being friends."

"I think that was the point," Ambra says, before she falls silent, the hint of a plan unfolding in her mind. "She had her enemies."

Gurlien gives her a brief smile, like he could read her mind. "Any particulars you want to try?"

∼

THEY SPEND the day sketching out ideas, playing with potentials, before having a completely uneventful night's sleep, one where Ambra doesn't dream and wakes up with her chin tucked against Gurlien's shoulder.

But it's another day closer to the possibility of Nalissa with her guard down, and Ambra doesn't want to spend time in the warm comfort.

After some arguing and some agreeing and back to arguing, they settle on a target.

Bianchi Layton. A rival in research funding and someone who once yelled at Nalissa's research assistants when they had the body's brain peeled open and Ambra was aware during all of it.

She didn't stop the assistants, just disagreed with their tactics, and Ambra could hear her argue with Nalissa the entire time her skull bled over the sterile experimentation table.

They track her location down to her flat in rural Scotland, where Nalissa once took Ambra after the leash was tied to show off, and Gurlien managed to figure out a schedule of behavior, aided by Axel and one of Gurlien's contacts titled 'Alette, do not message.'

"She hates me," he supplies, again somewhat embarrassed. "Axel at least sympathizes with me, but Alette can't stand me."

"She's helping you," Ambra shoots back.

"No, she's helping you," he replies. "She feels bad that her aunt's research ruined another life and likes that you saved her cousin. After this is all done, you could probably meet her, she would kick me out of her house."

Ambra crosses her arms and squints at him. "She'd rather help a demon than you?"

"Absolutely," he says, crossing his arms right back.

"She also hates the College, though," Ambra needles out. "Why is she even not on your side?"

She half expects him to sigh, she half expects him to shut up and withdraw, but instead he scrunches his face at her in such an expression that it surprises a smile out of her.

"If I promise to tell you the story of that, can you promise to not kill Bianchi?" he asks, which is a strange sticking point for him once again.

"She's not a good person either," Ambra reminds him, the knife sharp memory of the skin peeled open still sitting underneath her gut.

"Nobody is," he says. "Let's keep the murder down to the Five. The story in exchange for keeping the murder to a minimum."

She's not entirely sure how feasible that would be, but the want of information about Gurlien wins over the bone deep need for revenge.

"Fine," she says, then grins at him, baring all her teeth. "Unless she tries to kill you, then she's fair game."

"Not this again," he mutters, but at least doesn't argue, so she watches him pack a bag with some quick energy food and throw the woolen coat back on, before she grabs him by the shoulder, teleporting him directly into the kitchen of Bianchi's flat.

And into chaos.

20

Immediately, Ambra releases Gurlien, flashing a shield up around him, as an automatic trap snaps around them, tearing into Ambra's exposed skin and drawing lines of fire across her face.

Bianchi, with her yellow hair curling wildly around her round face, staggers backwards, kicking up the kitchen table towards Ambra, who bats it away with a flick of her hand.

If the trap didn't kill her, a single piece of wooden furniture certainly isn't going to.

Between one moment and the next, Ambra snaps out her power, drawing it close to herself, tearing the strip right out of Bianchi's hands, leaving them bloody.

And just like that, Bianchi freezes, going stock still, pale.

"Remember me?" Ambra asks, and the skin on her cheek stings, so she sends a bit of the power to seal it up, heal the wound in real time.

Behind her, still in the protective shield, she feels more than hears Gurlien backup, getting out of the way of any battle.

Good. She likes him being smart about this.

"What do you want?" Bianchi whispers, her voice the same soft accent that Ambra remembers. "I didn't do anything, I never touched you, I never hurt you."

She raises her hands, dripping viciously red blood, an obvious surrender.

At least she knows she's overpowered in this situation.

"Is this about Toronto?" Bianchi continues, her eyes flickering past Ambra, towards the hallway to the other room. "I didn't do any protections in Toronto, I didn't keep you there."

It's an odd tactic, one that Ambra didn't quite anticipate. She had expected more of a fight, expected more chaos than this.

"We want information," Gurlien says from behind her, faster in the uptake than Ambra. "Nobody has to be hurt if you give it to us."

"Anything," Bianchi breathes, immediate. "Anything you want."

Ambra narrows her eyes at her, and she blanches. It's a far cry from the scientist willing to berate people cutting into the skull of an active demon.

"Nalissa's event," Ambra says finally, before she pokes a wound on her hand to close. "I know you have your contacts in Paris, you know about it."

Bianchi's eyes widen further, and Ambra bares her teeth at her, no hint of a smile.

"What do you need to know?" Bianchi asks, slow, and her shoulders are tight, like she thinks she can grab some magic from Ambra, tear it away from her if she only catches her off guard. "Nalissa hates me, she doesn't share her information with me."

It's a lie, a small tightening around her eyes, like she hopes Ambra doesn't notice.

"You still have all your maps," Ambra says, and Bianchi winces. "I saw you sketching them, saw you keeping track of everything. Or did you think I wasn't aware?"

Gurlien draws in a breath at that.

"I didn't think you were conscious," Bianchi replies, voice hushed, and her eyes flicker down the hallway again. "You were...aware?"

"Every bit," Ambra replies, and to her horror, the anger turns her voice into a growl.

"Was Misia?" Bianchi asks.

Misia.

Immediately, fear slams into her, fear so strong it floods her mouth with bitterness.

Terror, at the surge of protection Ambra couldn't give her. At the helplessness of the strings of her soul tearing into pieces, at the slow and steady ripping apart of what made her—her. Of the screaming that Ambra couldn't stop, of the pain that she couldn't soothe.

Of the helplessness that drowned Ambra, helplessness that she couldn't do a single thing.

Of the vicious hot tears she left on the face, even when she disappeared and it was just Ambra.

In front of her, Bianchi cowers away, her hands above her head.

"Misia," Ambra starts, and she hadn't let herself speak, think, or remember the name, "was already dead by then."

Ambra snaps a bit of her power out, grabbing onto the wood of the chair, a provincial carved bit of decoration, old with age, and shreds it, sending shards around the kitchen, peppering into Bianchi's arms.

It doesn't help, even when Bianchi screams.

Standing there, in the kitchen, all the power in her

hands and all the control possible, and Ambra still aches with the uselessness of that exam table.

"I didn't know," Bianchi rasps out, her heart beating so hard Ambra can see it pounding at her throat. "I didn't know, I thought...I thought it was theoretical, they said you felt nothing."

"And you believed them?" Ambra growls, taking a step forward, and the magic swirls around her feet, kicking up splinters of wood. "You would believe someone like that? You would—"

A rush behind her, a tangle of motion, and Gurlien grabs her hand.

Ambra jerks, but he grips her tight, and she catches a glimpse of the white of his eyes behind his glasses, of his face devoid of color, of fear drawing lines sharp next to his lips.

He's still untouched, the shards of wood no match for her shield, and he stares at her.

And he doesn't have to say a word, his hand in hers.

Ambra lets the power seep away from her, lets it relax back into its place, and Bianchi whimpers.

Gurlien inclines his head at her, and she's not sure why, but it's some sort of recognition, some sort of acknowledgment of her.

"Give us your maps," Gurlien says, and his voice is quiet in the aftermath. "Give us your maps and all your research on the defense."

"Desk drawer, false bottom, scroll protector," Bianchi blurts out, pointing. "Everything's there, take everything, please."

Gurlien nods, then squeezes Ambra's hand, before stepping into the other room.

Leaving Bianchi and Ambra alone, Ambra turns her attention back towards her.

"If you tell anyone I was here, I will know," Ambra says, as neutral as she can, her voice still tight and sore. "I will know and I will kill you then."

Bianchi's already nodding along, her face screwed up and turned away, her eyes squeezed shut. "I didn't know," she repeats.

Ambra forces herself to take a step back, and she had cracked the very tile she had stood on.

"Nalissa knew," Ambra says, into the silence only broken by Bianchi's harsh breathing. "Korhonen knew. Rastian knew. Johnsin knew."

"Oh my god," Bianchi whispers. "Oh my god."

Then, finally, she lifts her head, and streaks of blood have mixed with sawdust and tears.

Something similar to shame eats at Ambra, worming its way into her gut.

"Nalissa tried three other times after you," Bianchi says, and a chill shoots down Ambra's spine. "They're beneath her catacombs. She wanted full control. None of them were successful."

Ambra rocks back on her heels, as Bianchi watches her.

Gurlien emerges from the other room, carrying three poster protectors, the type found in art stores to protect drawings.

"You'll find more like you," Bianchi continues, "but wrong. Corpses that you could have been." Incongruent, she hiccups, and a few more tears run down the sludge on her face. "I didn't know, I thought it was humane."

And here Ambra stands, a living, breathing example about how none of it was humane.

Stepping forward, Gurlien brushes his shoulders against

Ambra's, tilting his body towards her, and Ambra tears her eyes away from the destruction she just wrought to meet his gaze.

"Let's go," he says, voice dipping low.

"Gurlien Banks?" Bianchi asks incredulously, as if that's the confusing part of all of this. "Wait, is that you? What are you doing involved?"

Gurlien opens his mouth to respond, but Ambra grabs him by his shoulder, teleporting away.

21

Gurlien carefully sets down the scroll protectors on the oversized bed, his face sharp.

If they didn't have to stay in a 45-meter radius of each other, Ambra would teleport herself to somewhere far away. Somewhere in nature, where she can sit alone for as long as she needs, and doesn't have to see the look on his face.

"That was an interesting shield," Gurlien says finally, and she squints at him. "That trap had a subroutine that tears through human shields. Thank you."

Ambra hadn't even noticed.

Gurlien pops off the top to one of the scroll protectors, pulling out the giant roll of whisper thin onion paper.

"Good call on the maps," he says, and her skin prickles, like he's building to something. He unrolls it, spreading it across the wooden floor, and it's far more detailed than the version on his phone. Water lines, electricity, magical conduits, all of it. "So all that was horrifying."

There it is.

She sits on the bed, watching him smooth the paper down, his actions neat, economical.

Like he's used to doing this. Like the time in the compound, when she barely knew him, was definitely not the first time he handled maps like this.

"I am horrifying," Ambra replies back, and her voice still hurts from even the memory of all the screaming. "There is no part of me that isn't an abomination. I shouldn't exist."

"Okay, edgy," Gurlien says, his normal sarcasm creeping in. "I meant how she expertly triggered you into a rage and then had the temerity to cry about how scary you were." He sits up, so he's staring at her. "I've known her for years. I've seen her cry hundreds of times. It's never been genuine."

It's not what she expected.

"You're not angry?" Ambra asks.

That seems to throw him. "I can recognize manipulation when I see it. Spend enough years among people like that, you have to."

"I meant at me," she says, and a bit of frustration filters back into her tone. "I'm the one who lost control."

"Ambra," he starts, sharp, and she straightens, her spine drawing up, "in the last month and a half I have seen a Necromancer bring back someone from the dead who had a bleeding hole stabbed through his chest. I've seen a Half Demon disappear before my eyes and almost kill his girlfriend on pure instinct. I saw the same Necromancer turn a combat mage into dust without knowing what she was doing."

"That was terrifying," Ambra murmurs in agreement.

"I have broken into a protected compound that I used to be loyal to, I saw an entire hallway of experiments that could never live outside of stasis. I saw a captive pre-teen held in what amounts to a torture chamber, and she had been there long before I got kicked out, so that happened while I was there." He thumps a book down on a corner of the map so it doesn't roll up, then scowls in frustration at it. "You not quite having a grasp on regulating traumatic emotions when deliberately provoked does not even register on the things that get me angry."

He stares at her, hard, like he could impact more meaning with it, and her mouth goes dry.

"Did I wish that you weren't provoked like that? Yeah, it was terrifying, you literally damaged the foundation of a fucking house. Do I hold that against you? No!" He scowls. "Do you need to do a bunch of work so you don't get manipulated like that? Absolutely. Do I think that's something you do in, what, a week and a half since you've been out of stasis? Not at all. It took me years—years!—to recognize when someone was manipulating me like that, and that was with me dealing with it every day, all day."

Ambra doesn't know much about human development, but she does know that the College generally takes children with a grip on magic at a very young age, molding them and raising them to be what it wants them to be.

And the idea of Gurlien like that, a scared kid, underneath the brunt of all of the expectations and emotions and trainings, is just...sad.

"Did they kick you out because you were too kind?" Ambra murmurs, pulling the plush blanket off the bed and wrapping it around herself, sitting on the floor next to the maps as well.

"God no," Gurlien mutters, then he rakes his hand through his hair, completely messing up the neat precision. "Can you heal yourself so you don't bleed on the maps?"

"All of these are superficial," she informs him, before

poking at one of the cuts on her arm, prodding the skin together, feeding a bit of energy into it.

It stings, still.

Gurlien spreads out another one of the maps, another detailed drawing of the catacombs, elongating down into the experimentation rooms.

It's more detailed than even Ambra knew, more rooms and more storage than she ever saw.

"Just when I think I can't get more disgusted by them, something else happens, and I'm right back where I was a year ago," Gurlien mutters, marking with a pencil the placement of a rune, matching it with the map on his phone. "I thought Bianchi would be logical, would jump at the chance to get back at Nalissa, but no, she immediately went for the most hurtful thing."

"I didn't even know she knew...Misia's...name," Ambra says, forcing the shape of the name past the lump in her throat.

Misia would've scoffed at Bianchi, at the cruelty that Gurlien just described. Would've smiled at the homeliness of the little cabin in Scotland, would've liked the carving on the chair.

Misia would've been vastly entertained by the floor full of maps, would've appreciated watching someone like Gurlien sketch on them.

Gurlien stills the pencil on the paper. "Does it hurt to say her name?"

Ambra nods, swallowing.

His eyes are unreadable behind his glasses for a long moment, before the pencil starts to move again. "That's grief," he says simply, and she watches his hands instead of him, through the silence that follows.

It's close to an hour before they speak again, as Gurlien sits back and cracks his neck from hunching over on the floor.

"A year ago, after the spectacular crash of the Terese project, the College sent me to deal with the will of the scientist behind it and check for magical anomalies," he starts, as if this is any other conversation. "I found a cagey and heartbroken spell weaver, an alchemist who lost his magic, and a series of ley lines so twisted on themselves that they were breaking."

"Alette and Axel?" Ambra murmurs, and he nods, not looking at her.

"Alette was the beneficiary of the will, but the magic of her aunt's compound was fragmenting around her and she had no way of repairing it. The demon—Terese—had ripped into the very matrix of power in the region and shredded it to her will, decaying it until entire regions were going dark. It was...perilously close to the main Line through Washington state."

Having been to that Line, having walked through the pebbly beaches of the bay and sat with the magic coursing through her, it's hard to imagine it in any other way but strong.

"The College told me I had to stop it before it took down the Line, and that I had to cleanse the Line itself if it got infected."

"That's insane," Ambra replies flatly, and he startles, almost like he didn't quite realize that she'd have her opinions about this as well. "That'd kill someone who did that. That was a death sentence."

"They told me two people could do it safely," he says, and she scoffs at that. "Well, I tried to enlist Alette, she resisted. She was working with Zoel—not that I knew it at the time—to untangle on her own, got injured a few times, but was far more successful than my monitoring and scans were. I was, to put it mildly, a dick about it."

This brings the hint of a smile to Ambra's face, and he shakes his head at her expression.

"I dangled the idea of being able to heal Axel—"

"—no human could, I felt that scar," Ambra interjected.

"Over Alette, to try to get her cooperation. Here she was, growing a relationship with the Wight community and saving them, and I was telling her she had to choose between killing all of them and getting her best friend his abilities back." His face twists. "Like I said. Manipulation. You stay in it long enough and you think it's normal."

"Ah," Ambra says.

"Yeah, you'd hate me, too."

Ambra shrugs, because she doesn't have a good answer for that.

"They told me the world could end if I let the Ley Line break, that it was all my responsibility, and that I had to do everything to fix it. Then...no backup. No help. No battle mages or healers or experts, just me staying in the compound of a dead scientist with her angry niece and an ever-growing awareness of magic decaying around me, piece by piece."

It's a ghastly thought.

"It got worse, until the Ley Line was about to break, and I went down to try to cleanse it alone. It broke, with me in the middle of it."

Ambra eyes him, because the Ley Line was perfectly healthy when she touched it briefly while in the motor home.

And because Gurlien's still alive. That would have absolutely ended any human near it.

Any demon, too. Any anything.

"Alette fixed it, literally stitched it back together with her needle like a fucking spell weaver would repair a thread, and I..." he gestures at all of himself with the pencil. "Couldn't touch magic anymore. Gone. Completely erased."

"You're lucky," Ambra murmurs, and he shuts his eyes, like he's heard that so many times before. "That should have killed you."

And his College should have hailed him as a hero, for putting himself into harm's way so thoroughly he couldn't have hoped to get out.

"It didn't, and the moment I recovered from the concussion and rib fractures and punctured lung, they exiled me and told me I was useless." Finally, he lifts his eyes to hers. "So that's the story of why everyone hates me, all neatly wrapped with why they kicked me out and why I'm a dud with nothing more but a spectacular education."

"That's bullshit," Ambra informs him.

"Well, that's what happened," he snips back, then rubs his face. "Chloe reached out, I tried to put my life back together—twice—and failed both times. Read some psychology books, those didn't help. She gave me a book on getting out of cults, that one did, and then ended up in a cabin in northern Washington with no cell signal until Delina waltzed in with her Necromancy locked up and now..." he gestures over to her.

He sits back, exhausted once more, like the discussion and the talking is just as difficult as the combat magic.

And Ambra's fragile herself, from the pain of losing control and the grief and from the pain in Gurlien's words, at his distaste for his own actions and the obvious self-loathing.

"They're even more foolish than I thought," Ambra says, and he cracks a smile at her, like the effort took out any control of his expressions, leaving him entirely unguarded. "Any place that rejects those that gave the most for them will die a slow and painful decline."

He shrugs, and he has a smudge of dust on his cheek, still from Ambra almost destroying Bianchi's cabin, that she's just now noticing.

"Do you need to take a break?" Ambra asks, gesturing down towards the well-marked up map, with the runes and protections lightly penciled over the ink. "Do something that has nothing to do with this? Forget about it for a little while?"

It's something that Misia used to say, whenever she noticed someone with the look in Gurlien's eye, and Ambra's not sure she fully understood why until that moment.

Would letting her—and his—guard down be a bad idea? Absolutely, the College could decide at any time to pull her back.

But deep in her skin, behind the scratches and the still healing wounds from the trap, she desperately wants to erase that expression from his face.

He eyes her, like it's a trick.

"Tomorrow, we'll continue this," Ambra says, pointing at the maps. "We'll continue this and go to Europe, find some more info there. But it's..." she flounders, trying to figure out the words to say. "I don't think there's anything else our brains could do productively tonight."

This seems to be the correct thing to say.

He sighs, almost explosive. "You know what? Yeah. I saw a chair explode today. Let's do something else."

22

∼

After a quick shower to get rid of the still pervasive blood remaining on top of the scratches, Ambra throws on a deep green shirt that sits close to her skin, the fabric moving and flexing with her motions. It shows off a bit more of her chest than she's used to, but in a way that her skin is a shocking contrast with the color.

She frowns down at her chest. The hint of the scars, from where they carved up the body in the merge, trail up from underneath the left breast, visible with the cut of the shirt.

The few times the body had seen them, she had cried. Had cried that nobody would want them, that they were ugly with the vicious marks.

Gurlien dresses in another one of his button ups, a bright cardinal blue, and Ambra's getting the sneaking suspicion that no color truly looks horrible on him. That everything he puts on will find a way to be complimentary.

He raises an eyebrow at her outfit, as she fits on the

green-tinted sunglasses on her face. "In a different world, you'd be very popular at a punk bar."

She glances down at herself, but nothing stands out terribly much.

"They're a bit loud," he says, which makes more sense. "Loud and generally crowded. But with the shaved head and those boots, you'd have a lot of attention."

She wrinkles her nose at him, touching the side of her head, where now a soft smudge of hair covers her scalp. It's past the prickling stage, thankfully, but it still sticks in the back of her mind as wrong.

"Misia," she starts, and it's almost a bit easier to say her name this time, "liked fancy cocktail bars. Or wine bars. The types with cheese and bread and olives and we could sit and read without anyone interrupting us."

"She took you to a few of those?" Gurlien asks, packing an extra shirt into the backpack.

"A few," Ambra hedges, then shrugs, not quite embarrassed but not quite settled. "Didn't have much time to do things like that."

Gurlien hesitates, as if thinking through his options, and she could watch him contemplate things for a while.

"Want to go back to one?"

SHE TAKES him to a small one in the southern side of the West Coast, where the air is far less chilled and controlled fire burns in a brazier on the patio. Twinkling lights are hung, criss crossed over the small outdoor area, and plush furniture is tucked into every corner.

It's one that they went to all of twice, and Ambra had enjoyed the looseness that Misia felt after three glasses of the light wine, had enjoyed the sensation of the muscle between her shoulder blades relaxing until it no longer felt tight.

Ambra tugged Gurlien along to a two-person lounge chair in the back, with a low sitting table of wood next to it. It has a wonderful view of the entire patio, while being relatively tucked away, and a standing heater next to it casts a warm glow over it.

"Okay, alright," Gurlien says begrudgingly, "this is far better than I thought it'd be."

"No one bothered us here, it was great," Ambra says, and it's dim enough she folds up the glasses and slides them into the front pocket of the backpack.

There are a few people on the patio with them: three men with many empty wine glasses in front of them—their collars loosened and their faces open, two young women with glossy lips leaving smudges on their glasses, and a couple sitting close on a bench, their legs touching and their heads bowing together as they whisper.

It's just warm enough that Gurlien sheds his jacket, rolling up his sleeves.

"This is why I try to stay in the northwest," he says, before a waiter drops off the menus printed on thick, textured paper.

The waiter, dressed in a crisp black shirt, gives Ambra a warm smile. "Good to see you back," he says, and the back of Ambra's neck prickles at something in his tone.

She sits back, deeper into the couch, and the smile doesn't fade as he turns his attention onto Gurlien, handing him the menu.

"We do wine by the glass and the bottle, depending on tastes," he narrates to Gurlien, who nods, and even though

Ambra's the one who's been here before, he's far more comfortable than she is.

But still, his expression is far away and grim, even while reading the wine list.

"The body liked these two," Ambra says, pointing at the menu. "I enjoyed these ones the most."

They're two different sections entirely, and the body—Misia—had been incredibly delighted that their tastes could be so far away from each other, even when they were using the same taste buds.

"Interesting ramifications," Gurlien mutters, "so a demon has different preferences than the body they're in. Does this extend to dead bodies?"

It's the wrong way of looking at things. "You don't really eat in dead bodies," Ambra says. "You can, but everything is the same taste, like everything feels somewhat the same to the touch and everywhere is the same temperature outside."

Gurlien pauses to consider something, before reading more of the menu. "That falls in line with what the other experts say."

It's enough of a tendril of a hint that Ambra sits up.

"I'm not telling you more," he grumbles, without even glancing at her, like he knows what she was reacting to. "How are the reds here?"

Neither Ambra nor Misia had appreciated them that much. "Too bitter," Ambra replies. "Felt like our mouth was drying out and stained the teeth."

"Fair enough, sounds like what I like," Gurlien says, flagging down the waiter again.

He ordered one of the cheese and bread plates—a spicy one, apparently, Ambra didn't even know those were a thing—and they both ordered a glass, the emotional exhaustion eating away at both of their motions.

The wine comes first, and it's one of the pale pink wines that Ambra had enjoyed before, so she settles back into the lounge chair, curling her legs underneath her.

Gurlien sips at his, then nods, as if impressed, relaxing in the chair next to her.

"I don't think you're a dick," Ambra starts, and Gurlien just raises an eyebrow down at his glass. "I think the College chews people up and makes them act in ways they never would have if they had any other options."

"Sure," Gurlien mutters. "I could have very well done everything without attempting to manipulate them."

She watches him from underneath her eyelashes. "True."

He doesn't quite flinch from her words, but takes a long drink from his glass, the wine so dark no light can shine through it.

"I tried to apologize a few months ago, before Delina showed up," Gurlien says, voice even quieter than before. "But they didn't believe it was sincere, and I don't blame them, and I got frustrated and made it worse."

Ambra can easily imagine that happening, with how prickly and pointed Axel was to Gurlien.

"And?" Ambra asks, and he squints at her. "I'm not great at human morality, we know that, but you tried to make it better, and now you're trying to live differently." She takes a sip of the wine—it's just as light as she remembers, and she's briefly grateful that it's the same. "Isn't that the core of trying to be better?"

"I guess," he mutters, before his face twists. "You're a lot more forgiving than people are."

"They don't, I don't know, need to forgive you for you to be better, right?" she asks, curious, and he slates his eyes towards her, like he's expecting her to be sarcastic. "Humans have done so many wrongs in the world, nothing would ever be accomplished if they all stood in one place feeling bad after they tried to make it better."

"Would you forgive Nalissa? Or Boltiex?" he asks, and she scowls at him. "If they would swear to never control you, swear to never contact you again, would you let them go?"

"Are you asking that to just the attention off of you?"

That surprises a smile out of him, brief.

Ambra sets the glass down so her hands don't shake. "If they released the leash, I might let them go," she says, but it still reeks of a lie, after the torture and the control. "I wouldn't believe them if they just swore. They swore to the body that she'd be safe."

"Fair enough," Gurlien says, before they lapse into equally moody silences.

The breeze through the patio ruffles in the shaved side of Ambra's scalp, ruffling the short hair there, almost to the point of distraction.

Before Gurlien sighs, like the quiet gets to him too, even though they've had entire days where they've barely spoken.

"The last drink I had was the night at the bar that you interrupted," he says. "This is a far better drink."

Ambra has vague memories of a neon green cocktail splashing against the wall when Maison flipped the table, but she hadn't paid it too much attention, all her focus on the orders flowing through the leash and the compulsion locking her limbs into movement.

"I would hope so, that place had sticky floors," Ambra responds. "I would know, your Half Demon tackled me to them."

"He would absolutely get insulted if you call him my Half Demon," Gurlien says, grasping onto the distraction, before she sees his analytical mind finally kick in, sees the hunger for knowledge light up behind his eyes.

She settles back on the couch. This Gurlien, this want for information, this she can handle. This she can speak to.

She'd say anything to him to keep him in this place.

"How much of your actions and words were controlled?" he asks, gripping the stem of his wine glass like a pencil he could take notes with. "I know there were orders, how much individual parts were controlled?"

Ambra opens her mouth to respond, but he pushes onwards.

"For example," he continues, and she grins at him, "before the bubble, you did a motion like this," he gestures with his hand, and it must've been her shattering a piece of furniture. "Did he control that or did you? Why the motion if it's just power?"

"It was compulsion, not strict control," Ambra replies, and he nods, encouraging her on. "With the compulsion, like following an order, it makes me do whatever the command is, but it doesn't always—strictly—determine how. My orders were to capture the Half Demon, maybe the necromancer, and to kill you and the alchemist." The horror of what almost happened that day, that she was so close to never be able to have this conversation with Gurlien, if they had been just a little less competent. "I was focusing on the nec…Delina…because…obviously," she says. "With a Necromancer in the room, it was hard to even glance anywhere else."

"So the strict control, you wouldn't have focused on her, instead been more methodical?"

"Depends on the handler," she says. "Korhonen was good at crafting the compulsion to leave as much room for combat as possible while not letting me do my own thing.

His philosophy," she pauses for a brief second, to comprehend how easy it is to talk about all of the sudden, "was that I would always be better at combat than he could think to control, so he would let me determine the order of actions."

"See, this would all be interesting in the theoretical," Gurlien says, and the waiter drops off a slate slab full of meats and cheeses and strange jellies. "All interesting ramifications, all absolutely horrific in the real world."

One of Boltiex's assistants had once said something to that account. But had still done the experiments nonetheless.

So instead of answering, Ambra just swishes the wine in her glass, in the idle motion that the body would always do. "Korhonen honestly thought the bar fight would be done within seconds," she says, as if speaking around her existence, speaking around her presence then, would make it easier. "He thought that faced with me, the Half Demon would immediately fold."

"Yeah, that was a stupid thought. He literally died for her. Literally. Necromancer's bringing anyone back is terrifying."

Ambra nods, staring out at the small patio, something small and disquieted inside of her. Like they should be talking about something else, doing something else, besides just talking about their violent pasts. Like some sort of small talk, some sort of normal conversation, something where they could both forget the relative nightmare they're in.

"What do normal humans talk about when they're not dealing with unstable magical experiments?" she murmurs. "Most of my interactions before this were with scholars, and...Misia...certainly taught me that that's not the norm."

"What was she like?" he asks, and his voice is way, way more gentle than she's used to.

"Fairly sure that goes into unstable magical experiments," she says.

He shrugs, his fingers idle around the stem of the wine glass. "People talk about their past. Current interests, events, what they did. Past friends, family members, past lovers."

That certainly explains that, and Ambra curls her feet underneath herself on the lounge seat, staring at the wine.

"All my ice breakers usually revolve around me trying to show how smart I am," Gurlien says, which surprises a smile out of her. "Right out of the gate, impress them with intelligence."

"That'd be easy for you," Ambra murmurs.

"Before I got kicked out, I tried to impress people with being competent. They weren't going to like me because of everything else about me, but they might if they saw how good I was at anything." He sets the wine glass down, idly picking at the plate in front of them. "It worked maybe thirty percent of the time."

"When I communicated with scholars, about half the time they ran in fear," Ambra says. "The other half were intensely curious and willing to barter knowledge for...a variety of things."

"Sounds about right."

The waiter swings by with another glass for Ambra, and they both eye it.

"Have you ever been drunk?" Gurlien asks. "I feel like this is something we should know before too long."

"Not alone," Ambra answers honestly. "And with Misia, we just got relaxed."

Gurlien considers for a second. "Can you teleport while impaired?"

She raises an eyebrow at him, and he lifts his hands in defense.

"I don't know, demons are a mystery, can demons even get drunk without human bodies? Nobody knows."

"Wights have an alcohol that can get us impaired, but it leaves a horrific headache so I avoided it," Ambra says, then pulls out her phone. "What do we want to bet that the experts would have ideas on if I can?"

"Oh, they'll find that amusing," Gurlien says, scooting close to her so he can see her type on the screen.

It's not lost on her that he didn't press her further about Misia. That he briefly touched on the topic, received her brush off, and then pivoted.

It's another little kindness.

AMBRA (7:42 PM): Any red flags around getting drunk?

Immediately, both people start typing, and Ambra and Gurlien share a smile.

"I've never met either of these people, not in person," Gurlien says, then equivocates. "Well, I've been near one, but I wasn't conscious for it."

"Ridiculous," Ambra informs him, before her phone buzzes.

T (7:43 PM): Drink lots of water and have a meal with it.

MEL (7:43 PM): Don't blow things up.

T (7:44 PM): I have NEVER blown anything up while drunk.

MEL (7:44 PM): Liar.

Ambra gives Gurlien a quick, impish smile, before typing.

AMBRA (7:45 PM): But all my abilities will be the same?

T (7:46 PM): If you're anything like me, yes. Just less precise.

MEL (7:47 PM): Don't teleport anywhere new.

MEL (4:47 PM): Or sleep with anyone new.

"Oh that has interesting connotations for them," Gurlien murmurs, and Ambra elbows him. "What?"

"You keep on dropping hints about something I'm not allowed to know!" she says, and Gurlien's phone buzzes.

She raises an eyebrow at him.

"It's just...it's Chloe, asking me what the hell I'm doing, and a picture of Chance," he says, glancing at it, and as he's reading it, Ambra snaps a picture of him with her phone. "Are you serious?"

"She sends you pictures of your cat, she'll probably appreciate a picture back," Ambra says, sending it over.

The motions of the phone are starting to feel natural to her.

It's a good picture, regardless. Gurlien's lit by the glow of the heater and the twinkling of patio lights, holding his phone in one hand and the glass of deep red wine in the other.

Three dots show up from Chloe as she types, before it disappears, and Gurlien's phone buzzes instead.

"You are doing a decent job at endearing yourself to her," he informs Ambra, the hint of a smile on his face.

She grins at him in return, then pokes at the platter of food.

When here before, she had let the body control their actions, let Misia decide what to eat and drink, with Ambra mostly existing in the background.

But still, the act of putting the meat and cheese on a thin wafer is almost automatic.

"So this 'T' says to eat a meal?" Ambra starts, holding up one of the wafers. "Does this count?"

"Traditionally," Gurlien replies dryly, still tapping on his phone. "According to Axel—" Ambra wrinkles her nose, "—

T got very drunk once and didn't eat and was hungover for almost three days."

"Can she heal?" Ambra asks, and Gurlien eyes her, like he doesn't want to answer that. "Fine."

AMBRA (7:53 PM): Important question: is it possible to heal away a hangover?

T (7:53 PM): No.

Mel (7:53 PM): Yes.

AMBRA (7:54 PM): Great.

Ambra sets her phone down on the table, then raises an eyebrow down at the food again.

There's a strange detachment inside of her, twisting and growing at the day.

She had almost lost control, had almost killed someone who wasn't one of the Five. Who didn't have any defenses that could hold her back, regardless of the traps she had set. Manipulations or not, pressing all of her emotional buttons or not, Ambra shouldn't have lost control like that.

It would've been better to leave no trace.

And if she's being completely honest with herself, it had been Gurlien's presence there that held her back.

Had been Gurlien's presence, had been him talking so candidly about his past, had been him answering her questions, that had calmed her down. That had stopped her from spiraling into despair, that had pulled her out of the quagmire of emotions she had no real way of escaping on her own.

And here she is, having a glass of wine with him, joking and texting people, as if she hadn't been trapped by the chemicals in her brain just a few scant hours before.

"I have a human question," she says, turning towards him and setting down her wine.

He raises an eyebrow, tucking his phone into his pocket.

"What, you ask demon questions all the time," she says.

"I didn't say a thing," he informs her, and there's a looseness about him right now as well, as he gestures for her to go on. "Go ahead, ask."

"How do humans form bonds?"

He listens to her question, absorbs it, then holds up a finger.

"One, not nearly on the same level as demons, we're just not like that," he says, and a rush of gratefulness hits her, that he's listening to her question seriously and treating it like any other scholastic approach. "Most humans don't have intrinsic mental connections to other beings, that's just not the truth of biology like demons do."

That's not new information, having observed and read about humans for ages, but it's still nice to hear.

"Two, emotionally..." he trails off, pinching his lips together. "Emotionally, it varies human to human. Some will form affections and loyalties to people incredibly fast, some it takes ages. Some form friendships with dozens of people and care about them all deeply and truthfully, while some only care about maybe two other people."

"Misia was like that," Ambra murmurs, taking another sip of the wine to drown out the immediate tightening of her throat.

It's so strange to say her name.

"Some are friendly with many but close to few, some are friendly to only a few people but care deeply about them, it varies so drastically it never stops being confusing." Gurlien watches her, like he's expecting to read something across her face. "Some people fall in love many times, deeply and quickly. Some it takes years to develop to just one person and they never get over the loss."

"That sounds more like demons," Ambra says. "If your

Necromancer ever left the Half Demon, he'd never get over it."

"So demons are hopeless romantics, got it," Gurlien says, and the sarcastic tone makes her smile. "Never would have thought, what with all the murder."

"The murder ones are the more emotional ones," she informs him, and gets a smile in return, a relaxing around his eyes. "Still can't believe Maison slept with a necromancer."

"To be completely fair, he didn't know she was one until about a month and a half ago." For a few seconds, he stares into his glass, as if he could read something from it. "Chloe gets crushes fast, decides she likes a person but takes forever to trust them fully. She's fast to be friendly, fast to be kind and nice, but I think she trusts maybe two people."

"You're one of them," Ambra points out.

"And the other is someone she won't even tell me about," Gurlien says, then fixates his gaze on her, under the twinkling lights of the patio. "I tend to like people long before they like me and most people never do."

Ambra resists the urge to roll her eyes at him, instead presses her knee to his, like he did to her when Axel was grilling her at the restaurant. "Then most people have a limited view," she declares.

And a revelation like that deserves one in return, a balancing of the books. He answered her question, he deserves to ask one back.

"Go ahead," Ambra says, when the silence tilts towards long. "Ask me something."

"Dangerous thing to say," he teases back, then narrows his eyes, as if his brain is stuck.

"What?"

"No, there's just ages of demonology studies and I have

no idea which question I should ask first," he says, taking another sip, and the waiter sets down another glass for him. "How old are you?"

She blinks at him. "I don't know."

"Off to a good start. Do you know any demons who've had more than one bond?" His eyes are sharp, despite the glass of wine he's already drunk.

"That can't be the most pressing question of demonologists for centuries," Ambra says, before settling back in the chair again.

There's the immediate wish to deflect, to get the attention off of the question and all it implies. He would know what it implies, spending the time with her and hearing who knows what from Maison and his 'experts.'

"Do I know any, no," Ambra hedges, and she can see it dawn on him, immediate. "I don't know…exactly what will happen to me."

Impulsive, she reaches up, sliding a finger underneath the leash, at the still sore skin, and Gurlien's hand settles on his wrist in return.

"I've never seen a bond last beyond the death of one of the members, and this one still exists," Ambra says softly, and the words settle between them. "I don't know if it's because of the experiments or if because they used it to control me."

He regards her, and there's something different than the scholastic lens he's been tracking her with.

"So, more experimentation nonsense," she says, forcing cheerfulness in her voice. "Every demon I've talked to has been horrified, so I have that going for me."

Surprising her, he clinks his glass against hers. "And I've been exiled away from the only social group I know how to interact with, cheers."

It's a nice bit of levity, and despite all the drama of the day, despite all the emotions, she lets the wine seep over her tongue, lets the small bit of camaraderie keep her above water.

He takes a somewhat large sip from his glass, the deep red liquid shining in the twinkling lights. "Do demons have gender preferences?"

It's a relatively ridiculous question. "Demons don't have a gender unless they're in a body, not really," she says, then shrugs. "It's not set in stone, I've known some who only find male bodies, some that only find female, some that make it a priority to switch around. I never paid attention to it, mostly."

His lips twitch. "Such a different experience than humanity."

"It is astoundingly weird to be in one form for so long," she says, and it still hurts. "I don't know how humans can for their entire lives."

"So you don't pay attention to gender," Gurlien says, almost to himself.

"I mean, I observe it," Ambra says. "Humans and some Wights get very angry if you don't at least recognize what they're doing with that."

Another twitch of his lips, this time into something resembling a smile.

The patio is slowly filling up, people trickling in, and besides a few curious glances their way, nobody pays them that much attention. Like they're two normal people having a drink together, as common as anything else in this world.

It's a soothing thought, somehow, that despite everything, she could be...normal. Have a life others wouldn't blink at. That maybe she won't need to exile herself away, avoid the world for forever. That despite the heartbreak, despite the loneliness and the loss inside of her, that she'd be okay.

"Try this one," Gurlien instructs, drawing her attention back to the present, pointing at one of the luridly reddish meats. "It's too spicy for me."

Before she can even shift, he's already piling some of the meat together with some cheese on one of the wafers, handing it to her.

"I think, after all of this, we should really find out all your limits in terms of spicy food," he says, just as seriously as before, as if just as worthy of scientific experimentation as her power. "See if there's something you actually can't handle out there."

After all this.

"Sure," Ambra says, and her heart beats a little bit faster at the idea.

23

Hours pass, and the small table is full of empty wine glasses, the platter of food empty besides a few crumbs, and Ambra's entire sense of self is...loose.

Her shoulder blades don't hurt, the tips of her fingers don't hurt, and there's a red flush on the top of Gurlien's cheekbones.

He's animated, more animated than she thought possible, leaning back on the lounge chair with her, an arm slung over the back. They've moved from talking about their past, to books, to scholarly theories, to the weirdest of adventures that Gurlien's had since being kicked out.

And it's all...fine. Not emotionally charged. Like the wine has taken all the sharpness of conversation and dulled it to an enjoyable touch, and spending it with someone else has taken away the loneliness that usually accompanies those moments.

For the barest hint of a second, she even thinks it might be 'fun.'

Gurlien's hand touches her shoulder, startling her out of

her thoughts, and he's been doing that. The small idle touches, like pulling her out of herself with just the hint of contact.

"Your face got maudlin again," he says, and it's amusing how he pulls out the larger, somewhat more obscure words the more wine he has.

And that he could pinpoint it in her so quickly.

"I don't even know what my face was doing," Ambra informs him, and he smiles at her. "Half the time this face makes expressions I have no way of controlling."

"Again, very human trait," he says, and there's a teasing note to his voice. "Very normal."

"I refuse to believe that," Ambra says, and his hand dangles from the back of the couch cushion, barely touching her shoulder again. "Humans have got to be better, they were born in these bodies, there's no way they all just lose control of their faces."

She's not going to move away from the touch if he's not.

"I mean, some can, sure," Gurlien says, expansive. "Some have such meticulous control that nobody has any idea what they're thinking ever. But," he taps her shoulder, "most just go through their day with only a loose idea of what expressions they're showing and what they're communicating with them. Most just don't care."

She's learned more about humans than she has ever, just sitting here and chatting, more than centuries of research with scholars and observations.

She watches him from under her lashes, sipping her wine. There's something beautiful about his face like this, so open, like he's carefully showing her all his inner thoughts, revealing bits of himself until she doesn't cringe away.

He hasn't cringed away from her, in all of this.

It's a heady thought, colored by all the wine. That

despite her horrifying existence and the rather traumatic and emotional day they've had, that he's not scared of her at that moment. That sure, she may have cracked the very foundation of a house, but he's not frightened of her. Doesn't believe she's a threat to him.

And right at that moment, she'd rather turn herself in than do anything to harm him.

She sets her glass of wine down at that realization, almost unsteady.

Gurlien arches an eyebrow at her. "Do you need water?"

"Probably," she responds, her mouth dry, though her heart is pounding.

Gurlien gestures for the waiter, gets water for both of them, and she envies that smooth confidence, before he drapes his arm back on the couch.

"I don't know how old Misia was," he starts, voice gentle, his words rounded along the edges. "But how you deal with a hangover will hinge on that number."

"She was twenty-eight," Ambra replies, and she doesn't even need to think about it. "We celebrated her birthday in January."

They were in captivity then, everything had been uncertain and fearful, but the College was still pretending to care about them.

One assistant had baked cake.

"So almost a year ago," Gurlien murmurs, then makes a face. "Well, do you have a different birthday? Is that something a demon tracks?" She's already shaking her head. "I guess you can celebrate then if you want."

Ambra's still reeling from the strength of conviction in herself, that she'd let her own self come to harm if it'd protect Gurlien, and the temptation to run away, run far away, almost overwhelms her.

"I'll text Fr-Maison, see if he's ever been privy to any demon parties," Gurlien continues, and it's a vaguely amusing thought, even through her utter shock at herself.

"Demons don't do parties like that," Ambra murmurs, staring out at the patio, at the twinkling lights, at the warmth flickering from the heaters and the fireplaces.

It's such a profoundly human place, in such a profoundly human activity, sitting next to someone and drinking wine and talking. They had been there for hours, had been sitting there together, and she hadn't thought about time passing or about panicking throughout the evening.

He taps her shoulder again, just the barest of grazing of fingertips.

"Sense something?" he asks, sharp, but there's no danger, other than what's represented by his closeness, by her fondness of him. By the risks she would be willing to take, by the sudden strength of all of the emotions.

"Nothing," she answers, swallowing, then taking a sip of the provided water, and it's only out of sheer force of will that her hands don't shake. "Emotions are just weird and I don't understand them."

He clinks the water glass with hers, and they're so exposed, in this world with no protective runes, with nothing to keep them safe. There's nothing to stop a random crime, a demon deciding to obliterate them, nothing.

Instead, humans just go about their days like this, never protected, never knowing what is happening around them.

Without her saying anything, Gurlien digs through the backpack, pulling out the money and counting it out.

"I'm living a big tip," he says, almost primly, as if it's something she'd reject. "If we can get more money, then I am not going to be skimpy on that."

Ambra still doesn't quite have a grasp on all of those intricacies, but she stands when he does, all of her limbs loose from the wine.

He throws his arm around her shoulders, still much warmer than she is, and she leans against him like she fits there.

"I'm a bit unsteady," he declares, even though he's walking fine, even though his steps are just as even as before. "And tomorrow I'll absolutely need coffee before I can function, you won't be able to get out of that."

She wouldn't dream of it.

Still nestled up against her, he guides her to the spot in the alleyway they teleported in from, so close to the bar that she can still hear the clink of glassware and the far-off murmur of polite conversation.

"This was great," Gurlien says, almost too loud this close to her. "I haven't had that good of wine in about a year."

"We can come back," Ambra promises, the words falling from her mouth, and Gurlien's eyes go down to her lips before flickering back up. "We should come back. After everything, bring all your friends, bring everyone who helped."

He smiles, actually smiles, and everything about him is softer. Like the wine took away all his prickliness and all his protective shields and rendered him easier to get close to. Easier to touch.

And his arm is already around her shoulders, warm.

She turns towards him, so her fingertips graze the edge of his shirt. "Where do you want to go?" she asks, something halfway between boldness and shyness welling up in her. "We can go anywhere in the world—not Europe—but anywhere else."

"How about back to the apartment with the bed," he

says, almost teasing. "With all the protections and the runes so you stop being so twitchy."

It's smart, so she curls her hand on the collar of his shirt, where the buttons connect the fine fabric, and she's not sure she's ever chosen to be so close to a human before of her own free will. Sure, there's grabbing them in combat, there's the times when the Five would get close to test something, test reactions, test the nerve endings in the body to make sure everything was connected, or just to inflict pain to see her reactions, but not like this.

It's even different than waking up curled next to Gurlien, when they got into that position when unconscious. It's different than when he hugged her and she cried on him.

It's her stepping in close. Her controlling the body, her controlling the hands, her controlling the face, tilting towards him.

His eyes widen, ever so slightly, and this close she can see the small striations of color in his brown eyes, see the small lighter streaks and the hint of honey.

"How drunk are you?" he murmurs, his other hand settling on her waist, warm and secure. Nobody's ever really held her there, not even Johnsin in his most cruel and most creative.

"Yes," she replies honestly, and his eyes crinkle up. "My shoulders don't hurt, everything is warm, and I...had fun tonight."

It's an odd statement to say, and the analytical light in his eyes briefly flares.

"When was the last time you had fun?" There's an undercurrent in his words, something wholly welcome but she can't quite parse out.

"Well, breaking out of the base was somewhat fun," she

answers, and again gets a smile. "But like this...not in ten months."

"Good," Gurlien declares, and she wrinkles her nose at him. "You're out of their grasp, you should be having fun. All this...all this violence and all this planning, it should be so you can live, not just get free."

Still, his hand on her lower back presses strong.

"Maybe," she says fancifully, teasing the thought from herself, letting herself lean against him, and there's another sort of drunkenness in that as well. A tightening of her gut, a warmth lower.

His eyes flicker down to her lips again, and she would swear she could feel the sensation of his gaze, the heaviness of that small motion.

"We should really go back to the apartment," he says, his voice low, and her breath catches, but not from pain or fear. "I think you're drunker than you realize."

"You're probably correct," she whispers back, curling her hand around his collar once more, and feels the heat of his skin beneath the fabric, the concrete under her feet, the far-off clink of glasses, the street lights reflecting in Gurlien's glasses.

Before she inhales, between one moment and the next teleporting back into her circle of runes, next to the grand bed and the nightstand they dragged over and the thin paper maps held down on the floor from books.

And he doesn't let her go, his fingers splaying wide on the small of her back.

Instead, he raises his eyebrow at her again, like he's waiting to see what her action will be. Like he's skeptical of what she will do next, like he needs some guidance, some permission, before making whatever move he will make next.

"Does wine always make you this warm?" Ambra asks, letting her fingertips graze his cheeks, which are still deep red, even under the brighter lights of the apartment.

"Often," he murmurs back, blinking rapidly, like he's at war with himself. "Not in...not in ages. Not when I'm by myself."

It's a fascinating little idea, that the looseness and the comfort would be different alone than with another person. That the most integral part of this, the desire and the warmth for the one in front of her, may be absent from this entire affair.

Desire.

It's a strange word for the moment, and she mulls it over, with him stock still next to her, her hand on his cheek. It should scare her, it should terrify, that this is what the body is feeding her in such a time, but instead it just unspools inside of her.

His lips part, and she presses herself up to him, pulling his chin towards her and kissing him.

He freezes, his entire body going stiff, and for a split second she panics that this isn't what he wants, before his hand comes up, his fingers weaving through her hair and gripping tight.

He kisses her back, like he's starving. Like he's had nobody to touch for far too long, bereft in the world. Like he's drowning and the salvation is in her lips, like he could steal the very breath from her lungs to keep himself alive.

Like the very control he holds himself with snaps, and she is in the way.

A thrill shoots down Ambra's back, wholly new, and she gasps, opening her mouth against his, and his hand twists harder in her hair. Seizing the weakness, seizing the gap in her shield, his tongue grazes her lips, like he could taste her and find wholeness in that touch.

She grabs his collar with both hands, holding on, as if that could save her, and pushes back. Winds her own way into his defenses, lets her focus flex until all that is within it is him, his lips, his tongue, and the brutal heat of his body pressed against hers. Until all she can sense is his blood thudding through his veins, his hand tight in her hair, the scarred edge where his magic used to be, and the very want of her coursing through her like nothing she's ever, ever experienced.

A small sound escapes her, something outside her control, and he still once more, before breaking the kiss.

His pulse hammers in his throat, and his lips are wet as he stares down at her, his brown eyes wide.

Ambra's heart freezes, something halfway between fear and a need, as he loosens his grip on her hair, gently smoothing it back down.

"I'm..." he trails off, and he's still pressed against her, she still grasps his collar.

He blinks, fast, and despite his magnificent brain, despite all his intellect, he's flustered. He's confused.

Ambra drops his collar, takes a step back, and her lips sting as she does so, every fiber in her body wanting the opposite. Her mouth dry, she swallows, but no words flash into her mind to say.

Even the tips of his collarbones, barely visible beneath his shirt, are flushed red.

"That's...different in a human body," she says numbly, and her fingertips tremble with the hunger to reach out again to him.

He huffs out a breath, something between a gut punch

and a laugh, and his hand flexes, as if his sensations echoes hers.

"Not something we should do while drunk," he says, as if he too has been struck by lightning. "Trust me, not drunk."

She nods, slow, her mouth dry.

He leans back, breaking eye contact and running a hand through his blond hair, thoroughly messing it up.

"Okay," he says, visibly steadying himself, visibly getting himself back under control, back into his own sense of self. "Okay. Not what I expected."

"Me neither," she murmurs, then between one breath and the next, lets her grip on her powers relax, lets her awareness fill something besides just him, besides just the sensations currently warring within her.

The wards are perfectly fine, still and steady, no touches or grazes among them. Nobody stepped into her apartment, nobody attempted anything while they were away. No further tugs on the leash, no further pokes and prods at her consciousness.

She's still safe. They're still safe, despite the adrenaline shooting through her.

Gurlien steps away, another bit of distance between them, walking softly over to the kitchen and filling another glass of water, and with each foot further, Ambra's heart hurts, just a little.

24

Despite everything else, despite the two other glasses of water Gurlien bullies her into drinking, Ambra wakes with his arm loose around her waist and his breathing steady behind her, and her head aches.

"Oh," she mumbles, and his arm briefly tightens, but the rise and fall of his chest remains steady.

Her head pounds, her mouth tastes like something dead crawled inside, and her stomach turns, despite the stillness of her limbs. Light winds its way underneath her eyelids, too piercing and too

This is what the experts meant by hangover.

Forcing herself to exhale through her nose, she sends a tendril of power to the thudding in her head, to the blood vessels throbbing, and it eases, just enough that she squints her eyes open.

Immediate mistake, and the light slams into her so hard she flinches back, the pain blooming brilliant once more.

Gurlien hmms behind her, a soft sleepy sound, not quite awake.

And if he's going to feel a fraction of what she is right now, she doesn't want to wake him further.

Gone is the looseness of her shoulders, leaving her with a stiff neck.

On the side table, her phone buzzes, and that must've been what woke her, and she mentally curses it for a few seconds, before it buzzes again.

"Okay," she mumbles again, and snakes a hand out to it, wholly unwilling to move from underneath Gurlien's arm.

Outside the floor to ceiling windows, snow batters the glass, swirling against it, and all she can see is the cloud and the snow. Even the other building across the city street is obscured.

And still the light is too bright for her.

Awkward, she slides the tinted glasses over her face, and it helps. Not as much as it usually does, but a bit.

T (9:22 AM): Food and caffeine and time will help the hangover.

T (9:23 AM): But everyone is different. Axel likes walks to get rid of his. If you learn what Gurlien does, it'll be helpful.

Ambra blinks at her phone, and even her eyelashes stick to each other.

She sends another tendril of power to help with her headache, and it briefly offers relief, but the moment she focuses even a fraction of her mind on something else, the pounding returns.

AMBRA (9:24 AM): Gurlien's still asleep, I'm not waking him.

She worries at her lip, the faint ghost of his kiss lingering like a bruise.

AMBRA (9:25 AM): My head hurts and food sounds awful. I ate last night, I don't need to today.

T (9:25 AM): take it from me, you absolutely do. Even if

you don't have hunger impulses, you need it. It will calm the stomach and it will help with energy regeneration and steadiness and ability to grasp any magic.

Ambra raises an eyebrow at her phone. So this T person isn't emotionally a demon, but that's a very demon way of interpreting power.

AMBRA (9:27 AM): Why is kissing humans different in a live body?

T (9:27 AM): Oh good lord, I am not talking about that.

AMBRA (9:28 AM): Thanks.

Ambra lets her head thump back against the pillows, but they're not even comfortable at this moment.

T (9:31 AM): I take that back. How drunk were you to kiss Gurlien?? Unless you're talking about an entirely different human, which has different problems.

Ambra weighs being offended on Gurlien's behalf, especially since this T person wasn't even involved in Gurlien's story of the ley lines.

And Gurlien says he's never even met her.

But other people can dislike him, and from the glimpse of his story, she can understand why that entire group would have their defenses up, why they would judge him. If they hadn't taken the time to learn him after getting out of the College's grasp, then they would be stuck in their perspective of him.

Which is their loss. They don't get to know the sharp intelligence, that hunger for knowledge, or the intentional, careful kindness, the sort of kindness that comes with a second thought instead of a first.

It means she doesn't have to share with them, either, and that warms her.

AMBRA (9:32 AM): I think I had six glasses of wine.

She doesn't know if he'll kiss her while sober, and even with her head hurting, she hopes he does.

T (9:33 AM): Oh wow, yeah, you're probably hungover as fuck.

That's accurate.

T (9:34 AM): Don't count on doing anything productive today. Today is a loss.

AMBRA (9:34 AM): I was planning on scoping out some of the outside protections in Paris.

T (9:35 AM): Don't. Also, find time to get a passport if you can.

On the other side of the bed, Gurlien's phone chimes, and he flails awake, sitting bolt upright with a gasp.

Ambra immediately misses the contact.

She turns over to face him. "It's just your phone." Her words croak out instead of anything smooth, and she scrunches her face at the sound.

He stares wildly down at her, before cramming his glasses on his face. "Oh my god, you're already awake."

She holds up her phone. "Your experts were texting about hangovers."

He cradles his head, squinting against the brightness of the swirling snow outside.

"I'm so sorry," he says, and there's panic in his voice. "I didn't mean to cuddle you, I..."

She blinks at him slowly. That's what he's upset about? "Gurlien, you've been doing that all week."

He gapes at her.

She sits up carefully, and her head swims all the same. "Did you think I didn't notice?"

"You didn't say anything..." he trails off, then squeezes his eyes shut. "I can't handle this right now."

"You want coffee?" Ambra offers, thinking back to his words the night before and to T's advice. "My head hurts."

"No shit," he snips, before he rubs his face.

He's still in the undershirt from the night before, and the shirt she grabbed by the collar lays crumpled next to the bed.

"What time did we get back?" he mumbles from behind his hand.

Ambra didn't look at a clock when they did, so she shrugs, and her neck is way too stiff after the looseness of the wine.

Hand still on his face, he glances at her, like he's searching for a clue in her appearance.

"What do you need?" Ambra asks, after the moment stretches on too long. "You're trying to figure something out, what is it? I can't help if I don't know what it is."

There's another flicker of panic, before something akin to fondness crosses his face, and it's so out of place among the physical misery he's putting off. "Right, you're a demon. Different cultural mores." He sighs, rubbing his eyes once more, before he swings his legs over his side of the bed, steadying himself. "My memory is very fuzzy from last night," he informs her, not looking at her, instead leafing through his bag of clothing.

She eyes his shoulders. "Define fuzzy."

"I'm not sure what happened," he says, and there's a trace of embarrassment in his tone. "I was trying to figure out if I needed to apologize more."

"No," Ambra replies, and despite her stomach and despite her head, there's a little bit of amusement worming inside of her. "No, you don't need to apologize."

It's not something she'd considered, that he might not have even been aware of what happened. That he might not have a strong emotion about it, because he doesn't even know it happened.

She hopes he doesn't dislike the thought.

Instead of grabbing another button up, he shrugs a plain black shirt on over his head.

"Yes, coffee," he says, attempting to comb through his hair with his hands and sending it sticking upright in every which way. "Coffee is needed. Yeah."

TWO ANNOYINGLY SWEET espresso milkshakes and a muffin later, Ambra doesn't quite feel better so much as she's a little less miserable, though Gurlien still struggles to make it through his pastry, on his third cup of black coffee.

He's surly, barely speaking, leaving Ambra to observe the world from their little corner of the coffee shop. Now the third day in a row, and the patterns of the noise have grown a touch more familiar, a touch less jarring, a touch less frightening. The same people work it, recognizing them with a smile, and the music playing over the speakers repeats.

And despite the unpleasantness of the physical body, Ambra definitely wants to sidle up to Gurlien, to lean against him, to have his hand touching her shoulder like it did at the bar.

"What parts of the night are fuzzy?" she asks, after he's torn more of the pastry apart than eaten it.

He sighs, put upon.

"It's not fuzzy for me, I can put it together for you," she continues.

"I really don't want to talk about it," he mutters, then,

"did I...do anything untoward? By whatever standards you want to use?"

And Ambra's first instinct is to immediately tell him no, to immediately make sure he knows he did no wrong, but she tilts her head, takes the moment to observe him.

Does he even want to know?

"I kissed you," Ambra says evenly, after a long pause, and he groans, burying his head in his arms on the table. "And you broke it off and told me to not do so while drunk, but I wouldn't...categorize that as untoward."

Not for the first time, Ambra desperately wishes she could understand humans a bit better, but even when she shared a mind with one, they were still a mystery.

"I sort of remember that," he says, muffled. "Sorry."

She squints at him, and her head hurts just enough that she's not sure she wants to be nice at the moment. "It wasn't bad."

"Thanks," comes the rather sarcastic response.

But a twist of motion catches her eye, one that's not in the human range of action, so she jerks up to look.

Outside of the window, giving her the most puzzled of stare, is a Wight.

It's not one she knows—not that she knows or takes care to remember very many of them—but the Wight has wiry grey hair and lines on her face that echoes someone Ambra should know.

Careful, Ambra lets a bit of her power out to flex, making sure not to stomp over any protections or lines that the main demon would have left, just enough to entwine around the Wight.

She grimaces, and Ambra releases immediately.

Gurlien's hand goes to his wrist, to the leash around it. "Did you do something?" he asks, voice still muffled, and Ambra remembers his story of the Wights, why they dislike him.

"Just investigating," Ambra replies, and her stomach turns over, like accessing that part of her upsets the delicate balance of her body at the moment.

It's odd to see Wights so far into a city, so far into a place of industrialization and pollution, but the Wight stays put, eyes locked onto Ambra.

So this one wants to talk to her.

Or Gurlien.

Which she wouldn't let.

Finally, Gurlien lifts his head, and whatever he sees on her face sits him up bolt straight. "What is it?"

Ambra doesn't let her attention wander, even though her head still throbs.

The Wight's gaze flickers to Gurlien for a split second, the often familiar evaluation, before right back to Ambra.

So her.

"A Wight's outside and she wants to speak to me," Ambra says, and to her ears her words sound remote. "Nothing I can think to say can convey how much I really don't want to deal with the Wight population right now."

He grimaces. "In a city?"

"Right?" Ambra responds, and, finally, a trace of a smile flickers over Gurlien's face. "I don't...my head hurts and I don't want to talk about anything they'll talk about."

Gurlien glances over his shoulder, towards her focus, then shakes his head. "Yeah, they're not showing themselves to me."

"Naturally, that'd be convenient," Ambra says, then rubs her face, her eyes still too crunchy. "Stay here, I'll be...I'll be within 45 meters."

But the moment Ambra pushes herself up to standing, the Wight teleports away, because of course she did.

"Ugh," Ambra says again, letting herself flop back into the chair. "She disappeared. Why...ugh."

"Why would they talk to you?" Gurlien supplies, and she nods. "Either because you're here with me and they know my face, or because you're completely out of the norm and puzzling."

"I'm not so puzzling that I couldn't destroy her with a thought," Ambra replies darkly, staring at the straw of her now empty espresso drink.

"I am too hungover for murder talk," Gurlien mumbles, which is fair, then he sighs again, put upon. "I'm going to really regret this—"

This catches Ambra's attention, and she sits up straighter.

"—but we should focus on what's going to happen in Paris in a few days." He pokes at the shreds of his pastry, a sour expression over his face. "Even if we get in there, even if we get through all the security and past the literal...metal music festival, we're still going to have to see her."

Ambra sits back, her stomach turning all over again. "Well, I'm not going to do it when I'm like this," she mutters, gesturing at her head, then chews on her lip. "If she's among the crowd I'll just break her neck from a distance," she says, and a passing human gives her an alarmed expression.

"That would be ideal, wouldn't it?" Gurlien responds, then scowls at his pastry. "Let's go get greasy food, this isn't cutting it."

25

Greasy food is absolutely worse, but Gurlien gets a much better pep into his step, and Ambra's not going to stop that.

Instead, afterwards, she lets him convince her to teleport back to the Pacific Northwest, on the advice about the passport.

"I can teleport in and out, I don't see why I need to care about this," Ambra says, surly, the moment her feet hit the forest floor.

It's cold, but a different sort of cold than the ones on the street of Minneapolis. Here, clouds hang low in the sky, ominously grey, and the snow crunches sparsely along the gravel sidewalk.

It's a small town, with nary more than a few boarded up shops and a meager coffee stand next to a lumber mill. There's a church with an ancient graveyard, a dubious looking animal hospital, and a long road leading up to some motorhomes, more run down than not.

Ambra squints at them, at the memory of the sleeve of the sweater and the house that was no more.

It sits poorly with her still sour stomach.

"I don't like this," Ambra mutters. "This isn't needed and we could be preparing."

Gurlien just turns the collar up on his wool coat, nonplussed. "Same reason I have this bag," he says, shifting the weight of the backpack. "In case we get separated."

The thought sends a shiver down her spine, even worse than it used to.

Because if they get separated, she doesn't think she'd ever see him again.

As they walk, there's the same wight, staring at her.

And her arm is protectively around...

Stella. The little wight who cried.

Her hair is brushed now, less of a mess, though there's a sunken depth to her eyes, a hollowness to her shoulders.

Ambra stills, her footsteps stopping in the low mist.

Stella gazes out at Ambra, half numb, and she's still so thin, so fragile, like Ambra could reach out a single finger and break her.

Ambra thought that many times during stasis. That there was no way a little wight could be so important to be locked away next to her, that she was too small, too young, too breakable.

Ambra doesn't quite have the life cycle of the Wights memorized, but this one is far from adulthood.

The woman's arms tighten around Stella, and with a jolt, Ambra realizes their faces match. That there's some familial relation, some genetic kinship.

Ambra opens her mouth to say something, and Stella's face crumples, before the older Wight whisks her away, both of them vanishing.

Gurlien glances back at her, where she pauses on the

sidewalk, and she just shakes her head and continues after him.

She shifts, her skin prickling, before Gurlien steps towards the single gas station. Still, Ambra glances around, at the tall trees and the mist vanishing up into the clouds.

"I miss this," she murmurs, and Gurlien glances back at her. "The motorhome. I liked being there. Seeing this outside."

Another small smile. "This area is pretty unparalleled in beauty."

While it's a true sentence, it still rings incomplete.

"Feels more like home."

Home is still an odd sensation, sitting deep in her chest, and it must come from the human body. Demons want their comfortable places, want their hidey-holes, but beyond that...the location matters much less than most would think.

But the air is crisp, smells correct, and the cold humidity dances along Ambra's scalp like it's welcoming her.

Gurlien's eyes dip to her lips, sending a shock down her back, before back up to her, as if it never happened.

"I'll run it by Delina, but I know her mother held many properties in the area," he starts, and the cool air puffs around his face. "If one doesn't have a demon trap, she'll probably let you set it up as a hiding spot." He shrugs, almost embarrassed. "Delina now has more property than she could ever hope to manage and more money than entirely normal, it wouldn't hurt to ask."

Ambra's absolutely not gonna ask the necromancer for anything.

"I've lived in this area for the last year," he says, almost wistful, as he tilts his head towards the cloud-laden sky. "Before, I had only lived in big cities. Toronto, Atlanta. It's different in a small town."

She could believe that, especially with humanities crushing need to be around others.

"Nobody cared who I was, nobody cared that I had failed so spectacularly, nobody cared that I had lost all ability. I was just another person living out in the woods."

The bar Ambra tracked them down to is about thirty miles away, deeper into the mountains than along the coast, and it must've been near there.

"Sorry about wrecking the bar," she murmurs. "I was just very happy to be out of stasis. And to see a necromancer."

He squints at her, but it's good natured.

"I'm not going to go after her," Ambra reassures. "Your Half Demon would kill me, and he'd be able to."

"Good to know," he replies sarcastically.

Ambra follows him, until...

Turning the corner to the gas station, in front of a cheery convenience store, is the remnants of a demon bubble.

A demon bubble gone horribly, horribly wrong.

She stops dead in her tracks, and Gurlien turns towards her at the scrape of her shoes.

"What?" he asks, suspicious, and he seems perfectly fine, now, after the greasy food. Like the malaise of physical awfulness has completely left him. "It's just a Buggees."

"Why..." she lifts her chin, staring hard at the remnants of magic, before she bares her teeth at him. "Why are you taking me here?"

"Chloe said she'll meet us here," he replies, and whatever had happened between the two of them completely erased any fear he had at her expressions, and she's not exactly sure when that occurred. "It's close enough to where she is that she can, you know, get here in a reasonable time, but far enough away that it's anonymous."

"It's not anonymous," Ambra blurts out, and there are threads of necromancy, twisted in the decay of magic. "Did a battle happen here? In the last few years?"

He opens his mouth to answer, before shutting it, a peculiar expression on his face, but he strides back to where she's stuck in place. "It may be," he says, picking his words carefully enough that her curiosity briefly raises its head. "I know that Alette was hospitalized after something that happened here, but when I checked it out later, I could see nothing." Gently, his fingertips graze the elbow of her sweater, and she's not sure he knows he's doing so. "What do you see?"

"A demon tried to explode something," she says, staring out at the twisted magic. "A necromancer was here? I think? Whatever it is, it's wrong."

"Hmm," he says, his eyes narrowed, like he's slotting together a puzzle that's bothered him for quite some time. "So something that would possibly affect someone who's been raised from the dead, but not a normal spell weaver or random human."

"Maybe?" Ambra says, and the hair on the side of her scalp prickles, before something he said a few moments ago trickles in. "Do I need to worry about the alchemist trying to kill me?"

"No," he replies, and his lips tilt upwards, drawing her attention. "Let's pretend to be normal people—" she scoffs at that, but he pushes onwards, "—and buy some Gatorade or something, then wait for Chloe."

"Did Chloe pick this specifically because of this?" She gestures towards the sparking decay, where glints of light still dance across the pavement, sick. "Is this a test or something?"

He shrugs, which isn't a good enough answer, before

dropping his hand from her elbow, severing the bit of contact, striding confidently through the rat's nest of sickly magic and through the automatic doors, obviously expecting her to follow.

She scowls at his back, before stepping carefully around it.

A few sparks swirl against her boots, digging into her skin, stinging ever so slightly.

Still, she watches, and they're sluggish, not what they should be. Flinging themselves across the concrete, as if something, anything, could help them.

Whoever did this, whatever demon caused this destruction, was sick. Ill. Wracked with pain.

She can understand that a little.

With a glance to make sure that Gurlien is within 45 meters, she squats down, letting her fingertips graze the concrete, next to the tattered magic.

It sparks up to her, arcing up from the gray pavement, nestling into her palm.

As gentle as she can, Ambra rolls the magic in her hand, stretching it, teasing it out, and it flickers, weak. It can't hurt her, not beyond a few nerves firing where it hits her skin, but beyond that...it's not a threat.

It's just sad.

A completely normal car pulls into the parking lot, and Ambra straightens to standing, dropping the magic in her hand, her neck prickling, before the Alchemist—Chloe—steps out, a cheerful smile across her face. Her shiny black hair's pulled into a tight ponytail and she's wearing steel toed boots, but other than that she's pretty much exactly the same as she was in the base.

Chloe waves at her. There's nobody else in the car, there's no strange scan like last time, everything's safe.

"You found it!" Chloe says, way more energetic than Ambra's feeling, bounding across the decayed magic like she can't see it. "We weren't sure if the coordinates were good enough."

The coordinates had dumped them down the street and in the woods of someone's yard, but Ambra's not going to quibble.

Chloe's eyes flicker past her, into the store, obviously finding Gurlien, before she smiles even larger at Ambra.

"You're not going to hurt him?" she asks sweetly, and all the hair on the back of Ambra's neck raises at the tone.

"He already got hurt," Ambra replies, and if Gurlien hadn't still been in the store, she would've teleported away immediately. "It's healing, though."

Gurlien hadn't even bandaged it that morning, saying that it was 'fine.'

"That's not what I meant," Chloe says, and she's still smiling, but Ambra remembers the sheer amount of power that Chloe had flexed, even after making her way through the locking pits.

"I'm not going to intentionally do anything to harm him?" Ambra ventures, her voice lilting up beyond her control.

"That's closer," Chloe says, before scuffing her boot on a bit of crusted ice, completely ignoring the tainted magic, before her face sharpens.

There. There's the alchemist warrior Ambra had seen.

"He's a hell of a lot more sensitive than he thinks he is and I don't care that you're some superpowered demon person, he's like my brother and I will cut you," Chloe continues. "I want him safe and I want him happy. Kay?"

"Okay," Ambra repeats, unnerved, but Chloe plasters the cheerful smile back on her face, and it's somehow not fake.

"I've spent too much time teaching him to rebuild himself, I don't want that to be thrown away just because a pretty girl kidnapped him and turned out to be an interesting mystery," Chloe says, but there's no ire in the sentence.

Ambra reaches a hand up to the shaved side of her head, before she slides the tinted glasses off her face, staring hard at Chloe, twisting herself into the sick magic of the cracked pavement of the gas station.

The alchemist recoils back.

"I don't want to upset him," Ambra says, voice deathly quiet, the sort of tone that makes far stronger magicians blanch in fear, and Chloe's eyes are wider than Ambra thought possible. "But don't threaten me."

To her credit, Chloe stands her ground, face pale, and Ambra fits the glasses back on her face.

"I'm apparently hungover for the first time in my life and existence is miserable," Ambra continues, and Chloe blinks, like that's not what she thought she would say. "And Gurlien is the only person who's been consistently kind to me. I'll kill anyone who does him harm."

"Good," Chloe replies, a bit unsteady, before she smiles, almost bloodthirsty. "Give them hell."

This, Ambra can respect.

"The only reason they got a shot in was because Johnsin was controlling me," Ambra says. "And Johnsin's dead."

Chloe nods, and she's probably heard that information before, but Gurlien bustles out of the convenience store before she can say anything else.

Immediately, Chloe all but tackles him into a hug, staggering him, before shaking him by both his shoulders.

"Hi, Chloe," he says, disgruntled. "I'm fine."

"You got kidnapped," Chloe shoots back, and Ambra

takes a step back. She doesn't need to intrude on this. "You're not allowed to do that, I was so fucking worried it's not okay."

Gurlien's brown eyes flicker over to Ambra before he gently extricates himself from Chloe's grip, digging into the plastic bag he bought and handing a bottle of toxic blue liquid to Ambra.

"Drink this," he orders, but there's no compulsion behind it. "I guarantee you'll feel better."

It looks like it'd poison her, so she stares at him instead.

"You do look hungover," Chloe says, almost thoughtfully, which isn't better. "Have you given her coffee?"

CHLOE INSISTS on dragging them to the small library in town, and Ambra trails behind them within the 45 feet, but giving them that little bit of privacy as they walk across the otherwise abandoned sidewalks.

Gurlien and Chloe whisper as they walk, their heads bent close, and Ambra kicks a pebble at the disquiet sensation that builds inside her chest.

It's obvious they've known each other for years, in the fast conversation and shorthand of words, but they visibly squabble, a scowl tugging on Gurlien's lips.

But it's not true distress, obvious from the slope of his shoulders and the ease around his eyes. It's just evidence of knowledge of another person, of his history and past before he met her.

Humans and their bonds and how massively different they are than demons. This isn't a threat to her—not at all, not even in the short term—but it still chafes against her.

And if she's going to fit into this world, if she's going to at all exist around Gurlien after this is all done, she has to accept it and she has to be the one to deal.

Her eyes trail onto the leash, shifting slightly as he gestures emphatically with that arm. It's not uncomfortable, not exactly, but after the kiss from before she could swear that she's more aware of it.

Like it's ever something she could ignore.

The library is a puff of warm air and a familiar scent of old books, stronger in a living body but nonetheless welcome. There's a rich carpet under her feet, well-trod along the paths of the bookcases, and it's empty but for one librarian and one homeless man nodding off in the corner.

Chloe tugs Gurlien into one of the small study rooms, then waves Ambra inside when she hesitates.

"This is about as private as we can get," Chloe says, digging into her backpack and tugging out a small smooth stone. Casually, she taps it against the table, and it transforms into some sort of speaker with a small twist of magic, and Ambra's ears pop.

And all sound from outside the room fades away, small susurrations of pages turning and air conditioner creaking and the cars on the street outside.

It's immediate relief, and Ambra's shoulders fall away from her ears.

"Neat trick," Ambra says despite herself.

"It's nothing," Chloe replies, far more casually than is entirely natural, before she sits forward, propping her elbows up on the table. "I need some information from you for the passports."

"I don't need one," Ambra replies, but sits on the cold metal chair next to Gurlien, and her knee grazes his, grabbing all her attention.

"It'll make things easier," Chloe says, "and if you have

identification after all of this, it'll make life go more smoothly than not."

It's another thing Ambra never considered, and it must show on her face.

"Even if your plan is to disappear from society, it'll be useful," Gurlien continues for her, and that's...not nearly as appealing of a plan as before. "And if we go to Europe and get stopped, it'll get us out of some trouble without needing to teleport out and potentially trip alarms."

"That's the most compelling thing you've said," Ambra points out, and he gives her a self-satisfied smile that sits well on his face. "If you had said that first, I would've complained less."

He puts the same blue drink in front of her, as if a punctuation.

Chloe watches Gurlien with a raised eyebrow like he did something startling. "Do you have any preferences on names, ages, or country of origin?" At Ambra's headshake, Chloe pulls out a blue passport, recognizable from the paperwork Nalissa would flash around at customs, before they learned to control Ambra's teleportation. She slides one to Gurlien, who flips it open before shoving it in the front pocket of the backpack. "The goal is to avoid officials, these are good but not perfect," Chloe recites, like it's something she's had to say many times. "They hold up to a glance and a cheap scanner, not a fancy one. So don't try to fly with it if you can avoid it."

"I can teleport," Ambra says dryly. "I've flown on a plane before, it was hellish."

"Too loud?" Gurlien murmurs, and Ambra nods instead of glancing at him.

Chloe's eyebrows do the funny thing again, before she prods the extra passport, twisting the ink to resettle on the page. The picture isn't of Ambra, not exactly, but it's of someone with similar hair and a similar enough nose to Misia that she could probably get away with it.

"Are you going to take the gun?" Chloe asks, her head still bent over the passport, and the fact that she can talk at the same time as she works is impressive.

"As far as I can," Gurlien says grimly, and Chloe makes grabby hands for it without even looking up. "Don't break it."

"I'm not gonna break it, I'm gonna make it hidden from metal detectors," she replies.

Ambra sits back, and there's something charming about the back and forth. A different side of Gurlien from the one he shows her, not a false one, but different.

"I spoke to Axel—he's brilliant, by the way—and he told me how to make it more effective against shields."

"More effective against shields?" Gurlien answers, skeptical.

"Against all sorts of magical things," Chloe says, and despite her almost insane amount of power she just put out, she's almost bouncing in her seat. "Against shields, wights, it won't kill a demon but it will hurt them, through some wards, it's fantastic."

"Won't kill me?" Ambra says, bemused.

"Te...Axel said it is significantly annoying and delays the healing process," Chloe says, almost fumbling the name, and Ambra smirks at her. "They knocked out a full demon for a good twenty minutes."

It'll be useful if any other demon decides Ambra's easy pickings.

"I like that," Ambra says, and they both glance at her in surprise. "I would've liked that in Minneapolis."

"That one just threatened you, he didn't actually hurt

you," Gurlien points out, then sighs, put upon. "Of course Axel would have a magic gun." Throwing a look out the small window on the door, he adjusts himself so he blocks it, pulling out the gun.

Chloe grabs it, fluently checking the chamber and ejecting the magazine, before tracing on it with her fingertips.

"It would've been nice to have a weapon," Ambra says, before Gurlien can even give her a look. "I was useless."

"Need I remind you that you cracked the foundation of a house yesterday?" Gurlien grumbles, but Chloe doesn't even react to that. "Useless is an exaggeration."

"Maison thinks it'll go through most of Nalissa's wards," Chloe says, her head bent over the gun as she prods it. "So if you can get a clean shot off, that'll work." Her eyes flicker up to Ambra. "Unless you need to make the kill, I don't know how these things work."

"I don't," Ambra replies, somewhat charmed. "He killed Rastian and the Necroman…Delina killed Korhonen."

He catches her eye, and his face is serious, but there's a lack of stress in him at this interaction. That he could be so used to someone that it doesn't cause any issues. "It'll be more effective at killing then throwing a punch, probably," he says, miming a punching motion.

"That's not how you throw a punch," Ambra says, moderately amused. "Did they really never teach you how to throw a basic punch in a human body?"

Ambra didn't know how to at first, but the body did and laughed endlessly at her.

"I wasn't exactly a combat mage in my heyday," Gurlien snips back, but he shakes out his hand. "Not a lot of punches in magical contracts."

"Here," Ambra says, grabbing his hand and he leans back, startled. "More like this."

She curls the fingers into a fist, straightening the wrist, tucking her thumb around the knuckles instead of inside. "Don't twist your hand like that, you'll break something and you take forever to heal, apparently."

Gurlien rolls his eyes. "I know how to throw a punch," he assures her, despite all evidence to the contrary and Chloe snorts, still bent over the gun. "It's just not usually my normal course of action in situations like that."

Ambra grins at him, his strange bravado tickling her. "And you know how to actually fight?"

He rolls his eyes once more, as if for emphasis, but there's the beginning of a smile tugging at his lips, and she wants more.

"I'm more of a talk my way out of things kind of person," he says, which is hilarious given how much everyone seems dead bent on hating him. "Wound them with words, not punches."

"And a gun," Ambra points out. "You wound them with the gun."

He rolls his eyes, then prods her knee with his. "How's the hangover?"

"Everything is awful," she informs him, but without any real heat to it. "How do humans exist when things like this happen?"

This close, she can read his amusement, even though his expression doesn't really change. "It's temporary and we forget it happens just enough to be willing to drink that much again."

"Impractical," Ambra says, and he reaches over and opens the bottle for her, like the simple seal was enough to keep her from consuming it.

"I've been talking with Mel," Chloe starts, now prodding the gun with one hand and the paperwork with the other, "and he says it took him eight months of just existing in a human body before he got used to it."

Ambra sits up straight and Gurlien groans. "He was trapped like me?"

"Thanks, Chloe, we're not giving her specifics because it can literally be compelled out of her," Gurlien snips, then grimaces at Ambra in a sort of apology. "No, not like you, it's an entirely different scenario."

"But demon in human body," Ambra clarifies, then grins at him when he rolls his eyes. "You have to remember that I'm still smart."

"He never remembers anyone is smart," Chloe murmurs. "Mel has no access to any of his demon powers."

"Thanks, Chloe," Gurlien repeats, throwing up his hands. "I'm sure Boltiex will just love that little bit of information when he gets it."

"That would be beyond Boltiex's interest," Ambra says, though her mind is racing, bit by bit, and she sips the blue drink before sputtering.

"It's fine," Gurlien says, before she can complain.

"This is...just sugar and salt," Ambra shoots back, before setting the lid back on it. "But he is only interested in the power, so someone with none will be...literally useless to him."

Gurlien takes the cap off the drink again. "And hungover human bodies need sugar and salt. Trust me."

There's something heavy in the words, and she hesitates, before he raises an eyebrow at her.

Of course she trusts him, of course she...

She takes another sip, and it still tastes vile.

"Thank you," Gurlien snips, but it's without any sort of

heat behind it. "I'd rather you be able to fight if you have to instead of complaining about a headache."

"I can absolutely still fight right now," Ambra replies, and his lips twitch up before he controls his face. "How does Mel deal with humans, then?" She leans on the table, but twists the body towards Gurlien. "He has to have specific tips, your psychology is the worst."

"He's dating one," Chloe murmurs, as if only half paying attention to her. "Dotes on her and threatens to fight anyone who looks at her wrong. Doesn't like Maison at all."

"I can't imagine Maison appreciating a demon around Delina, powers or not," Gurlien says. "No offense."

"None taken," Ambra replies. "I wouldn't want a demon around a necromancer I cared about either."

Or a demon around anyone she cares about, to be honest.

But she'll have to text him with that in mind, dig through his brain about how to actually communicate with humanity.

The words on the passport twist again, bright against Ambra's awareness, before Chloe sits back, pushing the passport over to Ambra. "Here," she says, and there's a tiny bead of sweat on her brow. "It should work, ish."

It's still hot to Ambra's touch, but she peers at it.

"Anyone ever tell you you're very good at that?" Ambra asks, turning it over in her hands. "That took you what, ten minutes?"

"I did the prep work at…the base," Chloe says, after a warning glance from Gurlien.

"I have research I can give you," Ambra murmurs, letting her mind wander over to the library, over to the catalogs of books she's kept and lost over the years. "It'll be antiquated, but some of it should have ancient lock making."

Chloe blinks at her.

"Thank you," Ambra says instead, since her message seems to have been completely missed. "I don't think this'll be important, but I appreciate the effort and the artistry."

Another half-smile from Gurlien, like she did something correct.

"So that's what you meant when you said she communicates like you," Chloe says, almost an aside to Gurlien. "I get it."

"That's absolutely not what I meant," Gurlien says.

It takes Chloe an additional hour to make whatever changes she needs to make with the gun, and Ambra sips more at the Gatorade and mulls over feeling better despite it. Gurlien adds to his notes on the catacombs (and Ambra tries really hard not to look at the section with the medical wing) and the small contact of his knee against hers keeps her...grounded.

Somehow.

But there's the itch for action, the itch to do something, and every small shift of Gurlien's wrist pulls slightly on the leash.

Chloe notices, too.

"Is that...is that painful for you?" Chloe asks, after Ambra fails to keep her expression neutral as they stand to pack up, return the small room to its normal state.

"What?" Gurlien asks, twisting to turn to look at her.

Ambra scowls at Chloe, who blanches at the expression.

Gurlien lifts his chin, raising an eyebrow. "Is what painful?"

"She's asking about the leash," Ambra informs him, the words bitter in her mouth.

"Right, because you can see it," Gurlien grumbles. "Because I'm the only person who can't."

"It is a bit odd," Chloe starts, which is an understatement, "from the—very limited—history of demons that I've been able to glean from Mel and Maison."

"It's not painful right now," Ambra interrupts, staring hard at Chloe. "The remaining two haven't done anything in two days."

Chloe's eyes flicker between them, and Ambra would do anything to fall through the floor at the moment, before Chloe just plasters on a bright smile that raises Ambra's hackles. "If it's not hurting, that's good," she says cheerfully.

"Do you want to come as well?" Ambra offers, and both the humans stare at her as if caught. "I saw your alchemy in the base, you're more than capable."

"I'm banned in Europe," Chloe blurts out.

"We'll avoid the College officials, I can get you in and out easily," Ambra continues, before Gurlien taps her on the arm, drawing her attention.

"She's banned from about eight countries, not just in the magical community," he informs her, which is delightful, and despite the hangover a smile tugs at her lips. "She can't do any of that."

"Why?" Ambra asks, leaning forward, and Chloe responds by rolling her eyes at Gurlien.

"I ruffled feathers with my research," Chloe says simply. "The College got my passport pulled and put me in some do not fly lists."

Ambra squints, even more curious. "Research?"

Chloe just waves her hand, as if that could dismiss it. "It's no big deal."

"I like research," Ambra offers.

Chloe smiles, a dimple appearing, then packs the stone back into her bag as an obvious change of subject, and all the sounds of the library comes roaring back, popping Ambra's ears. "And, here. Courtesy of Maison."

She hands Gurlien a ticket, then to Ambra. It's laminated, plasticky, and Nalissa's familiar script covers the entire thing.

"Turns out he's useful at copying tacky art tickets from the internet," Chloe says glibly. "Took him very little time to paint this."

Ambra turns it over in her hands, her skin crawling at the handwriting.

The amount of help that's been given to them all of the sudden piles up, overwhelming, and Ambra sits back down, heavy on the metal chair.

"He doesn't even like me," Ambra says, beyond her control. "I almost killed his necromancer."

"Turns out he's very willing to throw the College under the bus," Chloe says, zipping up the backpack. "Combine that with a weird art project and he was all in."

"And he was the first one to defend you," Gurlien murmurs, and his hand grazes her shoulder, something between a touch and a reassurance, and she glances up at him.

He nods, as if he understands the emotions.

Before she can convince herself otherwise, she reaches up, curling her fingers around his, and he gives her hand a brief squeeze.

"This also gives you an entry into the catacombs," Chloe says, though her brows are also raised. "So you don't have to sneak in or teleport."

Gurlien examines the ticket. "Is she really doing punk

metal?" he asks, derisive. "She's doing punk metal in the fucking catacombs?"

"Three bands, too," Chloe replies. "That was the difficult part for Maison, fitting all the band names so tiny."

Ambra nods, the lump in her throat. "I'll text him thank you," she says, and her voice barely trembles at that. "That was help he didn't need to give."

She stands up again, trying to ignore all the chemicals flooding through her body, and with another nod to Chloe, teleports herself and Gurlien away.

THEY'RE silent as they pack up the corner apartment, a heavy silence, the only sounds their soft footsteps and the paper crinkling as Gurlien rolls up the maps.

"Will our base be the library?" Gurlien asks, after the long quiet.

"It's not set up for human habitation," Ambra replies, and her voice is scratchy with the combined emotions and hangovers. "No running water. I have...I know of a small house near Paris, it'll be far easier."

If they get separated, Gurlien could go there by himself, make it back to somewhere safe.

He's watching her, but she doesn't look over as she folds up another sweater into the duffle bag.

The tickets make it all the more real. That in just a short amount of time, she'll see Nalissa again. Have the potential to end her, to sever one remaining part of the leash.

To see the smile Nalissa always had when music was playing—regardless of the type of music—and to see her fingers twitch whenever she controls something. To see her face, always so animated.

And see her reaction when she spots Ambra.

"If you need to, we can stop by the library first," Ambra rambles, a cold shiver down her back. "We can get you whatever material you need, anything."

He shoots her a look, one she has not a prayer of interpreting.

"Paris is nice, there are wine bars and any restaurant you could ever need," she continues, her stomach turning over again. "I can steal more money—they use euros, right?—and you could buy whatever you need, anything."

"I've been to Paris before," Gurlien replies neutrally. "The College has their entire European base of learning there."

Which doesn't make the fear any better. There are hundreds of people in the city who might recognize her, might recognize Gurlien. Experts they could bring in, runes that could be drawn, anything.

"They'll mock my accent because I learned French in Quebec, but I'll be able to play translator," he continues.

"French is easy," Ambra shoots back, then rubs her face, her stomach turning over. "I don't need a translator."

"Right," Gurlien drawls, before switching seamlessly to French. "If I speak in French, will you stop freaking out?"

"I'm not freaking out," Ambra snips back, and he just raises his eyebrows at her, and she sighs. "You'd be afraid, too."

"Of Nalissa?"

It's too much of a magnifying glass on her, so Ambra paces across the apartment, the heart pounding in the body.

Before Gurlien's hand touches the leash on his wrist, and she stills, turning towards him.

He's watching her, a funny look on his face.

"Were you trying to get my attention with that?" Ambra

asks, stalking back towards him, but he doesn't blanch away, not like Chloe did.

"Yes," he replies, precise.

Ambra narrows her eyes at him, but he doesn't back down.

"You're panicking about something, I can feel it through this, and I want to understand a bit better so I can help," he continues. "I don't know why I could tell, but I could."

This changes things, and she straightens.

"You shouldn't." Nobody ever has. Or, rather, none of the Five have ever reported getting any emotions from her, and she felt so many that she can't imagine that they'd just ignore them.

If they did get emotions, if they did get the cast off of her feelings, they're even more heartless for ignoring them all this time.

Gurlien's face twitches, like he's about to say something but thinks better of it, as he weighs his words, his fingertips still against the leash. "It doesn't hurt you." It's more of a question than a declaration.

"You haven't hurt me," Ambra repeats, a curiosity starting to well up inside of her, at his actions. At the calculations flying behind his eyes. "But really, you shouldn't get anything from that."

"Interesting," he says, cautious. "You have any demon research at that library?"

She bares her teeth at him, and, surprisingly, he smiles back. "More than you can ever read."

26

She teleports him to the house in France, still pristine perfect from her protections, not a speck of dust anywhere, and watches as Gurlien gets his feet underneath himself, his eyes sharp.

Her skin crawls, this close to Nalissa's territory.

"Okay, this place is older than I anticipated," Gurlien says, at the green counters and the rounded edges on the refrigerator. It's dark outside, the lights twinkling from the street below.

She had found it after it had been left for a year, the family disappearing after a sickness, and hidden it away from the world. People would pass right by it and not think anything was strange, the utility companies would ignore it on their balance sheet, and other demons would see her claim on it and shift right on by.

"A few decades," Ambra says, after it becomes clear he wanted an answer.

"Try close to seventy?" he says, tapping a foot against the bright tile. "How land-rich are you?"

It's not something demons track.

"Because you could sell this place and not have to steal from banks for quite a few decades," he says, pulling out his phone and glancing at it. "And everything still works?"

She lets him putter around, pulling her power into herself, checking her wards, and—

Her eyes pop open.

Someone had been here.

Specifically, Nalissa had been here.

"Don't touch anything," she breathes, as he runs his hand over the countertop, and he freezes.

Nalissa had been there, her tang of magic distinct and clear, within the last two years.

Exhaling as quietly as she can, Ambra tracks the motions Nalissa made, tracks the point of contact.

She hadn't left any traps, but had instead trailed her hand over the bookcase, scanned the fridge, and touched her wards, reading them like they were a book.

And had done so before they had contacted Ambra and Misia.

"What is it?" Gurlien asks, voice sharp, as Ambra shakes herself back to the present. "Is it a trap, do we need to leave, what—"

"Nalissa came in here," Ambra says, and her own voice is remote. "Before the merge. Before I knew her."

A thread of anger worms its way inside her stomach.

Nalissa had found one of her spots, had entered it, had investigated it, back when her experiments were only ideas.

Gurlien lifts his hand from the counter.

"No, it's safe, she left nothing behind," Ambra says, shaking her head, blinking. "She investigated, she must've come across a demon spot and..."

It might've been what gave her the idea to contact

Ambra. To put her aim onto her, onto Misia. To find a perfect candidate for the experiments.

It could've been Ambra's own house, Ambra's own safe place, that had doomed them, and—

Gurlien's hand closes around her elbow, and Ambra jumps, almost teleporting away from panic.

"Do we need to go somewhere else?" he asks, voice dipping down. "Is she tracking it?"

Ambra shakes her head, and once again, there have been too many emotions in the day, too many conflicting sensations, even as the hangover has receded and the body feels less hostile.

"Just another part of me that she took uninvited," Ambra says, and her voice is almost a growl, before she squeezes her eyes shut, trying to get a hold of the chemicals flooding through her limbs.

Before she's even fully aware, Gurlien guides her to the plastic covered couch, sitting her down onto it, still focused on her. "Breathe," he mutters, his voice low. "She's awful, feel angry, but breathe."

Ambra does, a big gulping breath, and tears prickle at the edges of her eyes, a leftover automatic function.

"I'm going to kill her," Ambra declares, and her words wobble out of her. "She found this before she found me, it could've taken her to me, she planned me—"

Gurlien glances up at the house, at the perfectly preserved furniture, at the decor that's seven decades out of date, before he lifts his hand to her back, rubbing in small circles.

"Do we need to leave?" he asks again, careful. "Go somewhere she hasn't taken away?"

It'd be impossible for her, when she's breathing through Misia's body.

But there's a frisson of anger there, too, at the idea of running, and Ambra straightens. "No," she answers, before swallowing. "No, she doesn't get to ruin this."

His lips curve upwards at that. "Good."

So she watches as he explores the small house, puttering around the antique hardware of the kitchen, the sourness back in her stomach.

It would be so much better if he had a magical trace. If he could leave hints of himself behind, overshadow the ones left by Nalissa.

She would need to re-ward the place, write in more protections. Mask her presence in Paris, render her invisible.

Most of the demons around this part of France are like her. Transient, not setting up a base of power beyond the minimum needed for hiding spots, so she doesn't have to worry about appeasing anyone. Too many people—demons, spirits, everyone—flock here to search for knowledge, to find answers, that nobody would be able to defend it for long enough.

Gurlien disappears into the other room, poking around, so she pushes herself up to standing to follow.

"We'll have to buy you groceries," Ambra says, following him into the little office area, with its dizzying collection of thin-papered science fiction books and its outdated maps on the wall. "There's a little store down the street ran by a magician; he couldn't see me, but he could sense when I or some wights were around."

"Who is it?" Gurlien asks with a curved brow.

"Not in the College," Ambra says, letting her fingertips trace over the spines of the books. The sensation is different now, with a live body and actual nerve endings against her skin. "Not strong enough in anything practical, so they ignored him. They're very...snobbish around here about that."

He nods, it's not new information. "Have you read all of those?" he asks, gesturing to the bookcase, to the brightly colored books. "Half of those books don't exist anymore, they're out of print and most copies are non-existent."

"Of course," Ambra replies, tapping her finger against the books. "What use would books be if you don't read them?"

He smiles at her, something soft and unguarded, and for a few seconds, Ambra's heart kicks up a beat.

"Here," she says, quickly pulling out one of them, a dashing tale of a fighter pilot in a world taken over by fantastical aliens. "This one is ridiculous, I adored it."

He cradles the book, giving it so much care that it pulls at her heart again. "This is a legitimate antique, you know that, right?" he asks, running his fingertip over the spine and creaking the cover open to glance at the publication date. "You would revolutionize the collectors' market with all of these."

Ambra, having come across a few collectors in her time, just shrugs. "They don't read their books."

Another smile, paired with the gleam of knowledge in his eyes, and it helps against the traces of Nalissa.

GURLIEN READS, curled up on the one bed (a much smaller one than the apartment, Ambra's not sure if he'll still sleep next to her with it), the entire time that Ambra sets up the wards, so when the sun starts to peek into the windows, his hair is tousled and his eyes look scratchy when he blinks at her.

"This book is awful," he informs her, and he's a good two-thirds of the way through. "I love it."

"Right," Ambra says, then makes a face at her voice, at the dry rasp across her vocal cords as she swallows. "I forgot to drink water for this."

"Same here," Gurlien mutters, and he did stay put the entire time she laid down wards, not shifting from his place on the bed, and his back pops when he shifts and stretches. "Food?"

Instead of answering, she sits next to him on the smaller bed, and he blinks up at her, owlish.

"Can I kiss you again?" she asks, now that her head isn't pounding and her words don't feel like they're slipping out of her mouth.

Deliberate and precise, he fits a piece of paper in as a bookmark before closing the book, smoothing its cover, and it's just as obvious of a stalling tactic as anything else.

"Do you want to?" he asks, sitting up so they're on an even level.

She wrinkles her nose at him. "I wouldn't ask if I didn't."

"Fair enough," he murmurs, then places his hand over hers, a gentle tangle of fingers.

"And I want to when you remember it," she continues, though the graze of skin contact on their hands distracts, derailing her thoughts. "Seems unfair."

A twitch of a smile on his lips, before he leans in, pressing them against hers, and she stills.

It's wholly different. More of an affection, of comfort and contentment, instead of a mad rush of consumption.

∽

THE CLERK at the small store blinks rapidly at her, but doesn't say anything, besides being obviously puzzled by the leash. He's gone completely grey haired, frizzy and wrinkled, but he still peers at Ambra before dismissing her with a shrug.

"When we're done," Gurlien starts, on the stroll back, as Ambra glances over her shoulder at every small noise, "when this place is clear, we should come back and visit a few proper French wine bars."

His face is carefully neutral, a blond brow raised as he scans the small neighborhood. The trees are mostly sticks with a few browned leaves, and it must've rained at some point in the night, for the sunset bathes the cobblestones in a reflective gleam.

And he's beautiful in it, his wool coat shrugged on, the circles under his eyes, carrying a paper bag with bread and cheeses and soda. Beautiful in the way Ambra rarely describes anything, handsome and, for a human, unreal.

"After the hangover I didn't think you'd want to do that," Ambra says as carefully as she can.

With the hangover and his mortification at sleeping next to her, she can't imagine him wanting to. He had bought a pocket knife, too, with a multitool attachment, one that would open wines if they needed.

He shrugs. "I wouldn't want to today, but give me enough time to recover and I will." She gets a sidelong smile. "I don't think I'll do seven glasses at once again. I don't like forgetting things."

Ambra doesn't have anything to say about that, ducking her head from the flutters in her stomach.

~

THEY BOTH FALL asleep after a quick meal, and she wakes up as the sun sets, his arm around her middle and his face buried in the crook of her shoulder.

And it's a day closer to facing Nalissa.

Her phone is full of texts of research sent to her from the Half Demon, Mel, and Chloe. Some psychology links from Mel, which she files away. Something called Instagram posts sent by Maison from past concerts thrown by Nalissa in the catacombs, showing person after person dressed in fanciful black and stylized leather.

From Chloe, a picture of Gurlien, obviously months old, of him sitting on a couch with a scrawny cat curled up on his lap.

The same cat that Gurlien had shown her, with a glossy coat and well filled out.

Gurlien in the picture looks slightly annoyed, and there are dark circles under his eyes and his cheeks sunk in. His hair is shorter, and even how he's sitting he's favoring one side of his chest.

AMBRA (7:02 PM): Was he healthy for this?

CHLOE (7:03 PM): He was getting there.

It's good to know.

AMBRA (7:04 PM): He smiles when you send him pictures of the cat.

On the other bedside table, Gurlien's phone buzzes.

CHLOE (7:08 PM): Keep him safe tomorrow, I don't like the thought of him going into the catacombs.

AMBRA (7:09 PM): If I safely could leave him out, I would. The control on the leash is only 45 meters right now.

CHLOE (7:10 PM): That is a brutally short distance.

CHLOE (7:11 PM): I'm surprised he hasn't dragged you to do more scientific testing of it. It's got to be bugging him to not have more information on how it works.

There hasn't been time, not really, and she knows the hungry look in his eyes each time she does something unexplainable, the poking and prodding for knowledge.

Gurlien's phone buzzes again, and he flops over with something of a sleepy grumble.

And she's going to put him in danger.

Careful, Ambra slides out from underneath the blankets, and is immediately colder for it.

All her instincts, all the warped thoughts inside her, tell her to crawl back in. The demon part of her screams to curl up against him, never let anyone else hurt him, do anything and everything to protect him, possess him. The human part, that wants the warm comfort, wants the press of his skin against hers. Wants the casual touch, the heaviness of sleeping limbs, the sensation of being wrapped up in safety.

It's a mess. It's a knotted, mortifying mess, and the physical side of it just adds to the confusion.

So she flees, teleporting just to the kitchen, well within their distance restriction but outside of the line of sight.

27

They spend the night walking the cobblestones of Paris, tracing the motions of the next night. Finding the entrances, finding the spots where the magic bleeds to the surface, evidence of the experiments done below.

They don't talk much, the nerves skittering underneath Ambra's skin, but she trails as Gurlien buys himself a new outfit to not stand out as much in the concert, and doesn't protest when he adds a few things for her onto that.

They fall into bed again once the sun rises, and Ambra doesn't wait for him to fall asleep before turning towards him, burying her face into his shoulder, and he inhales.

"Are you okay?" he murmurs, and there's sun starting to peek in through the curtains.

"I'm fine," Ambra declares, slightly muffled and he huffs out a laugh. "Human bodies process things differently than demons."

It's a wholly incomplete sentence.

"So you've said," he replies, almost lazily, but his hand

curls around the small of her back all the same. "Describe it to me?"

It's another small, warm comfort. "Every emotion—and I mean every single one—has a physical component," she grumbles. "And right now, I…"

He doesn't say anything, but the hand traces a motion across the thin fabric of her sleep shirt.

"I'm having a lot of them," she finishes, frustrated with the impreciseness of the language. "I can hardly sort through them and pull-out specifics."

"I'm worried," he says, and she pulls away enough to look at his face, read his expression. "What, I am!"

"Why?" she asks, instead pillowing her head on her arms, her leg still touching his.

He scowls, before his face softens, his brown eyes staring up at the patterned ceiling. "I keep on trying to predict what their behaviors are going to be, what actions they're going to take, and they've taken none of them."

She blinks at him, and the morning sun is gentle on the colors of the room, sending pastel pinks and yellows through the window.

"If I were them, I would firstly follow any written containment procedures," he says, rubbing his nose. "Barring that, I would stop at nothing to get you back in custody. They've…they've given up too easily. Or there are bigger things they have to deal with, and that frightens me. And Nalissa is still pushing on with her plans…I don't know what to make of it."

He frowns up at the ceiling for punctuation.

"I can't figure out why they wouldn't wait for you to be asleep and pull you then. Just try every hour or so until they get lucky. But here we are, relatively unharmed, in Paris, and they've tried little."

"I don't want them to hurt you," Ambra says, softly into the dawning room, and his eyes flicker over to hers. "Whenever I try to plan, I see them hurting you and all my thoughts crumble away."

"Not to be glib," he says dryly, and she arches an eyebrow at him. "If they kill me, you can always teleport my body to Delina and I'm sure she'll be fine with taking care of that problem."

"There's other things they can do to you besides kill you," Ambra says, and she shivers, even in the warmth next to him. "I would know."

And even a Necromancer in her prime wouldn't be able to bring back Misia.

He remains quiet, breathing next to her on the bed, filling the space with his presence as indelibly as if he struck a chord.

"I don't know if that's the human brain chemistry or the demon...way of thinking," Ambra says delicately, not quite able to force her mind to think of it head on. "Or if it's some leftover trauma from all of this." She gestures to herself, to the body she's stuck in all alone, and swallows past the lump in her throat.

"Trauma sounds like a good way of talking about it," he murmurs, still not looking away. She's exposed, completely vulnerable. This man in front of her could do anything to her and she wouldn't stop him, wouldn't even think of it.

"I think they took away a very part of me." Ambra says, and he reaches over, touching the exposed skin on her arm, sending goosebumps down to her hand. "I don't know how to put it in words, and when I think about them harming you, I feel the same way as that fear."

It washes over his face, brilliant in real time, and he gentles his touch on her arm, a soothing back and forth.

There aren't tears in Ambra's eyes, but the pressure's there, building.

"When this is all done," he starts, hushed in the morning air, "we can spend all the time in the world figuring out how to put things into words."

When it's all done.

She stills, blinking at him in the soft lights.

"It's hard to think about," she says, after a long moment. "What after would be."

"I could believe that," he says, just as quietly. "When your entire existence is bent towards one thing, comprehending anything else is foreign."

And that's exactly it.

And he would know.

His hand is still on her back, warm against the sleep shirt, and he's still wearing the pajamas from the motor home, even though they're too short on his ankles.

His face is tired, he had complained after about hour three of walking along the Paris streets, but his eyes are sharp and aware, like he knows how weighty it is for her as well.

"I'm glad I'm here with you," she whispers, and it's far more vulnerable than she wanted it to be. "I can't imagine what it would be like to do this alone."

His lips part, his eyes flickering down.

"I'll admit, the kidnapping was a rough way to start," he says, and she huffs out a laugh at that. "But..." He trails off, deliberately so, like he's trying to suggest something she can't quite understand.

She raises an eyebrow at him. "You're using subtext and I'm not getting it."

This breaks his face into a smile, before he pulls her

tightly in, so her head leans against the crook of his shoulder and her chest is pressed against his.

She squeaks in surprise and feels rather than hears his chuckle.

"I'm glad I get to take them down with you."

She briefly considers squirming out of the hold, before she settles her forehead and listens to the rise and fall of his breathing.

"I never thought I'd be this far along in taking them down," he continues, his voice a low rumble against her ear. "But before three weeks ago I didn't think I'd ever break into their base and release a bunch of stasis chambers, so everything's new."

She tilts her head at him. He had done so much for the College and they had cast him aside, and now they're getting what they deserve.

"And I didn't think I would be...so close with a vastly unpredictable demon through the whole process," he says, and his other hand settles in her hair, threading through the one side of her scalp in an almost hypnotizing mirror of the tight grip he had when they kissed. "But I'm not complaining. About that."

Another laugh, and she smiles at him, impulsive. "You complain about a lot of things."

"It's one of my talents," he replies dryly, then his eyes flicker down to her lips again, and the seriousness of it strikes her.

He's not drunk this time. She's not impaired.

His hand is already in her hair, the other on the small of her back, and they're already touching so much there's hardly a part of her body that's not in contact with his.

And she wants more. Again.

He inhales, like the want is across her face, and it very well may be.

"Ambra," he starts, voice low, but he's not pulling away. "Stop me if I do something you don't want me to do."

"Of course," she replies. "I can blow up buildings, I'll stop you if I need to."

His brain visibly skips a beat. "Stop me before we get to that point." And his eyes, his intelligent eyes, focus down on her lips again.

"Of course," she murmurs, struck by something halfway between embarrassment and need, and the tip of her nose burns warm.

His lips quirk up into the barest hint of a smile, before he gently, ever so gently, tilts her head towards his and kisses her.

It's different from the drunken night.

Before, he had been so full of fury, like every bit of control had left his body and all that was remaining was the want for her, but now his lips are tender against hers, softer, like he's taking his time to explore her.

She curves her hand on the collar of his sleep shirt, holding him in place, kissing back.

This time, kissing Gurlien is like a thorough examination, like he's discovering her and sharing in the act of knowledge. Like each motion and small adjustment is an instruction, a revelation of more of herself that he gets to guide, and the fingers in her hair tangles lazily.

Instead of a fire roaring until it consumes everything about her, it's a slow growth of warmth, like a steady lighting of a candle, until even her fingertips tingle with the potential.

His lips part, and she mirrors him, and the skin on the palm of her hand warms at each moment of touch. It's a safer burn, she's not on the precipice of losing control, and she can experience it all.

He makes a small noise in the back of his throat, something gentle, and she pulls away, breaking the kiss.

"Is that okay?" he whispers, brushing the hair that had fallen in her face.

Without words, she nods. It's a different sort of sensation, not the lump in her throat choking her out, but the knowledge that no words she can think of would come close to expressing what is in her.

Except warmth, and with that warmth, a sort of profound safety.

He smiles at her, heartbreakingly so, before settling back in the pillow, and she settles with him, an easy relaxation through her body.

Yes, there's the want there, but without the stressful ever pushing need behind it.

Instead, comfort.

His hand traces a circle on the thin stripe of skin where her sleep shirt rides up, and it's almost overwhelming all over again.

And she never wants him to stop.

She splays her fingers out on his chest, on the collar of the thin T-shirt he wore to bed, and there's the same want she had at the bar, lurking beneath the knot in her throat.

She's not a stranger to sex, not really, but never before has she had this strong of physical desire to go along with it. It's almost a wave, threatening to drown her, and all they're doing is some idle touching while lying next to each other.

He's not even wearing his glasses, they're neatly folded up on the side table, leaving him entirely without armor.

"Your eyes did a thing," he murmurs, and she's close enough she guesses he could tell. "Most of the time they just glow, but they flickered off right then."

"That happens," Ambra says, debating being embarrassed, but that would entail her pulling away. "Part of the... side effects of the processes."

He hmms in the back of his throat, and she could press a kiss to his neck so easily. Anyone could, if they were this close, and the level of vulnerability he's at is astounding.

That anyone without powers would let anyone get this close.

And that despite all that, he's letting her.

So she leans in, pressing her lips to the tender point right on the side of his neck, and for a brief moment she can feel his pulse.

His breath hitches and the hand on her back briefly spasms.

"Ambra," he murmurs warningly, and another thrill goes down her spine.

"Yes?" she asks, propping herself up on her elbows to watch his face. "You're going to tell me if I overstep, right? If I get to stop you, you get to stop me."

A thousand emotions flicker over his face, starting with the widening of his eyes and a looseness to his jaw.

"Right?" She pokes him on his rib cage, and he squirms at that, the corners of his eyes creasing into a smile. "That goes both ways?"

"You're a menace," he informs her, and she smiles at him. His arm still around her back, smiling and getting those small expressions in return. "Are you going to turn every comment about how to be a person back on me?"

"Of course," she replies sweetly, before leaning forward and kissing his mouth, catching him off guard.

She would kiss that mouth a hundred times if the world let her.

"I just want to make sure you know what you're doing,"

he mumbles into her lips, definitely not stopping her. "I don't want to do something to you that you don't know what it is."

"May I remind you that I am literally centuries old?" She breathes, letting her own hand drift to the elastic band of his pajama pants, her thumb grazing the skin below his belly button, and he twitches beautifully.

But still, his words deserve to be taken seriously, so she pauses, keeping her palm against his skin there. If he's helping her with context and subtext and understanding things, she should extend that.

"I'm proposing sex," she says blatantly, and he nods. Behind the seriousness and the attentiveness, there's an almost manic hunger behind his brown eyes. "Or at least things on the way there."

His throat bobs as he swallows, and her mind is briefly derailed at the thought of kissing there again.

"Have you, before?" he asks, haltingly, his eyes flickering down to her chest, to the skin revealed at her waist, to the slope of her shoulder.

"Of course," she answers, and he briefly shuts his eyes in relief. "It's going to be...different. In this body." Which is an understatement. "But there's a different sort of...desire in it. That I want to try."

For a long moment, the only sound that reaches her ears is the rasp of his breath and the ever so slight buzz of the lighting fixtures.

"If you do," Ambra amends, a strange, almost mortifying shyness creeping over her, flushing her cheeks.

Gurlien's eyebrow twitches up, but he keeps his eyes on her, and even his lashes are blond this close, and there's a smattering of almost invisible freckles that she's never seen before across his nose.

He holds up a finger, like he's going to list something out, and somehow, it's the most charming thing he's done that night.

"One," he starts, almost imperious, and Ambra giggles at his tone. "Hey, I'm being serious. One, is it safe? I have heard so many stories about demons forming odd attachments after sex."

"Hey," Ambra says, then shrugs, and she's still next to him, his other hand still on the small of her back, fingertips touching her skin. "They broke my bond. I don't think I could ever form one again."

His touch briefly tightens, chasing away the lump in her throat.

"And also, that's such a reduction, demons have all sorts of sex without forming bonds."

"Right," he replies. "Then two, are you going to be weird about it?"

"Are you?" Ambra asks, and his eyes flicker down to her lips again, then to her chin, like he's studying her. "I don't know what weird would be in your mind. Probably?"

His lips twitch up. "This is why I like you, Ambra, you're fine with me asking questions that anyone else would be annoyed by and you answer honestly."

"Light kidnapping aside?" Ambra teases, and gets another smile in return. "I like it. Gives me a base idea of expectations."

"I like knowing where I stand," Gurlien murmurs, then gently, ever so gently, cradles her chin.

She stills, his hand blister hot against her skin, and her lips part. Her blood seemingly swirls, like just that touch could boil up something inside of her, leaving only the small sensation of the contact in her awareness.

He swipes the pad of his thumb over her lips, and everything inside Ambra pulls her attention to that one little motion. All of her focus, all of her intensity, all of her mind.

"Tell me to stop if you need me to," he murmurs again, then tugs her into a kiss, a slow kiss, achingly slow, like this one he's taking his time in learning her lips. Like each moment is a scholastic study, an observation, and he can't help but implement the research immediately.

She pushes back, unable to stop herself, and his mouth opens to hers, eager, and it's wonderful. Absolutely wonderful, sending a thrill down her back, straightening her spine and catching in her lungs.

His hand on the hem of her shirt shifts, pulling it up, and she breaks the kiss so she can pull it over her head, so his hands can touch more of her, can have more of her skin against him.

Immediately, he presses a kiss to her neck, down her shoulder, drawing a line with his lips on her body, before his hands traces on the scar underneath her breastbone, twisting around her ribs.

"What happened here?" he murmurs, running the pads of his fingertips along the scar, where it rests between the body's breasts.

She shudders at the graze to her chest, all of her skin wanting more of his hands there.

"Unstable magical experimentation," she replies, her own voice high and airy from the desire, and he crooks a smile at her reaction. "You can ignore it."

"Hmm, no," he says, then shifts, pressing a kiss where it starts along her rib cage, and she shivers. "It's a part of you, I don't need to ignore it."

Unable to do anything else, she twists her hands in his pale hair, and he smiles against her skin.

It's a breathtaking image, of his lips against her scar, of

the soft, almost reverent worship of her skin, of the soft places on her body. Of the attention he pays to every small part of her, of the meticulous focus on her reactions, every small twitch recorded away.

"You are beautiful," he murmurs, and she shivers again, the compliment somehow unwarranted. "All of these," his other hand moves to the scar left on her stomach, from the injury at the bar, caressing it, "are a part of that."

She opens her mouth, but no words come out, like he's stolen them away.

His hand reaches up, cradling her breast, and she jerks from the sudden shock of the intensity. "Okay?" He checks, gentling the touch, rubbing his thumb along the underside, sending another shudder down her back. "Too much?"

"No," she squeaks out, and he grins at her again. The only physical contact she's had there has been clinical or violent, and this, this is far from that.

But before she can verbalize it, before she can think otherwise or change her actions or anything, he kisses the skin right above her nipple, and she jerks again.

She wants more of that. More of the touches, more contact, more anything, and she scrabbles at the hem of his shirt until he pulls it up over his head, thoroughly messing his hair.

There's a smattering of freckles across his chest, belying curiously strong muscles underneath the skin, and Ambra lets herself see it in a blink before she grabs him, jerking him towards her into a kiss. Until her entire body is against him, all lean long lines and his arms twist around her back.

This time, he kisses like he did while drunk. Like all semblance of self-control is gone, like she has snapped a central part of him, and she's in his crosshairs. His tongue swipes against hers, hitching her breath, like he could taste all of her in just that greedy motion.

And she wants more of that.

He makes a small sound in the back of his throat, and she wants to hear him do that again. Wants to hear more of those noises, more of the unconscious, uncontrolled sounds, anything she's able to wrench from him.

Anything.

His hand falls to the waistband of her pajama pants, tugging them down, and she kicks them off, her breath hitching one more. Pulling back, he glances down at her, at the body before him, at the scars and the marred skin and the small tuft of reddish hair between her legs.

Gentle, he strokes along her hip, and a shiver sends goosebumps up her arms and tightens her nipples, completely new.

"Oh, you like that," he murmurs, trailing his hand up and thumbing over her nipple, sending sparks behind her eyes.

"Yes," she squeaks out, and again he smiles, something almost mischievous in his face, and he does it again, watching her reaction as she twists underneath his hand.

"You're so very sensitive, aren't you?" he asks, like it's something good about her and not a liability. "So when I do this—"

He pinches her nipple, just hard enough, and she just about levitates off the bed, a gasp wrenched from her throat.

"—it gets a reaction," he finishes smugly. "So beautifully."

"Fuck," she mumbles, and he soothes it over with a swipe of his thumb, the brief moment of intensity trailing into an all too pleasant tingle. "How..."

"Some people are like that," he says, pressing a kiss

against her breast, and her breath hitches once more. "Some people need more, some people need less."

"And you?" She breathes out, and surprise briefly flickers over his face, before he kisses her lips so sweetly, teasing out another little gasp from her. "What do you need?"

"This is good," he murmurs, before turning his attention lower to her body, resting a hand between her thighs, before he pauses, as if waiting for some sort of permission.

Heat coils inside her, at the touch and everything it suggests.

She stares down at him, swallowing, and he grins at her expression, winding his hand between her thighs.

"See the good thing about this, though," he says, running a finger along the seam between her legs, parting her and wringing another little gasp from her. "Is that when people are sensitive like this, it's so much more fun."

All of her attention is there, on the sensation of his finger, and each breath is its own little exquisite torture.

This was nothing like sex without a human body. Nothing.

He runs his finger over her clit, and everything in her clenches, her breath, her heart, everything, before he dips inside of her. She's wet, of course she is, and he smiles at her, slow.

Again, she jerks, as he works his finger into her core, every small twitch and motion more sensitive than the one before, before he crooks his finger inside of her.

The world explodes behind her eyes, stealing the air from her lungs, forcing a small sound from her throat, and he leans her against him, tracing a small circle on her inside wall.

"You're good," he mumbles, as she struggles to catch her

breath, and even that small bit of reassurance crumbles away with the slow, languid touch inside of her. "I've got you, you're good."

Wordless, she nods against him, then reaches over and flattens her hand against his crotch. He hisses against her, and a thrill of triumph runs down her back, that she could make him make that sound.

If all of that was just his hand, then she's amazed.

"I want you to enjoy this, too," Ambra starts, and her voice is raspy, like the body forgot what it needed to do to keep that part of her functioning.

"Believe me, I am," he responds, voice dipping low with another circle of motion inside of her, causing her to clench unconsciously.

Still, he pulls his hand out, and she makes a small noise of protest in response. He tugs the too-short pajama pants off, and he's hard, magnificently so, and heat just tightens more behind Ambra's stomach.

There's a moment, a pause, a breath, as they stare at each other. At her heaving chest and his steady still. At the splotches of red at the tops of his cheekbones, so close to the color of when he gets upset. At the small blond curls around his cock, somehow neater than the hair on his head.

At the waiting, as every bit of her trembles with curiosity at what he'll do next. At what sensations he will wrought from her, at how the body will react.

At how she will react.

The small lines around his eyes crease into a smile, and that's the warning she gets, before he's on top of her, an arm on each side of her, bracing himself over her.

He kisses her neck, small gentle kisses, and she needs more. Needs way more, so much more than the gentleness.

So much more than the small kisses, so much more than the hints of action.

"Please," she breathes, voice high, and she never thought she'd be one to beg for something like this.

"Hmmm," he says simply, and before she can think, he lines up against her and presses in.

She twitches in his arms with another little gasp, and she's so wet every little bit of skin is magnified. Every touch, every slide, everything.

Her back arching up to him, he cradles her, catching her right when she thinks she's going to fall, right when everything threatens to overwhelm her, threatens to crest over her and drown her, taking away all it means to be her.

It's magnificent, all the sensations and the contact and the pleasure, magnificent and so, so much, and tears crowd her eyes, despite herself.

He freezes, and she breathes out, something halfway between a pant and a moan.

"Are you okay?" he asks, alarmed.

"Yeah," she manages out, her voice wrecked, and clenches around him, eliciting another low hiss. She scrubs a hand over her face, despite it all, and he twitches inside of her, sending another little cascade of sensation down her back. "Do that again."

He grins, something vulnerable once again behind the smile, and he languidly thrusts in her again. "I like it when you boss me around like that," he says, and he's far too composed, far too coherent, when she's on the edge of being a mess.

And so Ambra's on the edge of something, and it sticks in her throat.

She can't compel him, of course. Can't make him, not in the way that people think Demons can.

But here he is, fully naked with her, and he's telling her to be in control. She could tell him anything, make him give her as many orgasms as possible, make him lose control. Even out this complicated wretch of a playing field, until they can both be the same.

Or make him push her fully over the edge.

So she clenches again, and gets another small sound from him. "I want you to fuck me as hard as you can."

It dawns on his face slow, before the intelligence flashes behind his eyes. Faster than she can think, his hands close over her wrists, pinning her to the bed.

She could teleport out, if she needs. Get out before anything happens to her, recover like nothing happened.

She doesn't want that.

Instead, she grins at him, baring her teeth at him, daring him.

"You're going to kill me if you look like that all night," he murmurs, leaning over her, his hair across his forehead.

He's gonna kill her if he doesn't do something soon, if he doesn't work towards that need clawing inside of her.

"I'm going to kill you if you don't do something," she challenges right back, and he thrusts into her, hard, drawing another gasp.

Then another, then another.

~

SHE AWAKES to a nervous pound in her heart as the sun sets, and it's the night of the concert. The night she has to kill Nalissa, the night she has to face Nalissa, the night she has to do whatever she can to make sure Gurlien isn't harmed.

She pulls herself out from his cuddles, and his hair sticks up on the pillow.

They have a few hours, and Ambra can just tell by the pit of her stomach that she's going to hate all of them.

Quickly, she changes into the outfit Gurlien bought for her, then grimaces in the bathroom mirror at herself, leaving the door open enough that she can hear everything in the house.

The pants make her legs look like unsteady sticks, and the top, made out of a stretchy and almost transparent black material, gives the impression of the torso being covered in a black mesh net.

It also shows off the scar curving underneath her chest, like it's something to be proud of. Like she's trying to show off where they carved her to pieces, show the world where the body cried.

Ambra adjusts the shirt, but any angle she lets it lay reveals the scars. Tempted to chuck the shirt and grab one of her normal ones, she scrolls through the reference photos on her phone, and frowns when she comes across picture after picture of other people, men and women, wearing similar shirts.

So Gurlien knew what he was doing when he bought it.

There's now a fine layer of reddish hair on the side of the scalp, almost half a centimeter long, and when Ambra swipes her hand over it, it's softer instead of prickly. Like it might actually grow back and be normal hair.

She can't feel the skin beneath the hair anymore with such a touch.

"You're definitely going to look the part," Gurlien grumbles from right outside the bathroom, and she jumps, startled.

His hair is still a mess, falling over his face, and he's wearing a plain black t shirt and black jeans and looks incredibly discomforted by it.

"The scar isn't going to stick out too much?" Ambra asks, tracing it over the shirt, and his eyes trail down.

There's a moment of silence, where he considers her blankly, before shaking himself out of it.

"Generally speaking, these shows are friendlier to bodily oddities than normal concerts," he recites, like it's from a textbook, which is an interesting response. "They won't be looking at the scar."

Ambra glances back in the mirror, and it's the first thing she spots.

"It'll be dark in there, and they'll look at everything else before they notice the scar," he continues, and she raises an eyebrow at him in the mirror. "Jesus Christ, you're going to have guys hanging off of you."

"Strangers?" Ambra asks skeptically.

His lips twitch into a smile before he smothers it. "A non-zero amount of people go to these shows just to pick up strangers for sex."

She makes a face at him through the mirror, and he cackles a bit, before reaching around her and into one of the grocery bags by the sink, pulling out an eyeliner stick.

And they're so close in the little bathroom, with the rounded mirror and pastel colors.

Without saying anything, he begins to apply the eyeliner on himself with practiced hands, and that's absolutely not a skill she would've thought he had, and she watches with fascination.

"Stop looking at me like that," he grumbles.

"No," Ambra replies easily. "This is far too interesting."

"I used to be edgy when I was a teen, it lasted for maybe six months," he says, but he's watching her in the mirror, like he's waiting for some sort of reaction.

"I'm going to keep you safe," she insists again, and his

mouth quirks up.

"I believe you," he answers, leaning back from the mirror and blinking at himself. "God, I look like I'm trying to be an edge lord or something, this is awful."

"It's not a bad look," she offers.

It's not, though distinctly out of place for him, like a costume he's put on instead of an addition to his face.

She ducks a kiss to his collarbone, and his eyes crinkle up into a smile in the mirror.

"Wouldn't it be easier to do that without your glasses?" Ambra asks, as he shifts them up his nose to access his eyes with the liner?

"Not at all," he replies, but the hint of a smile still lingers on his lips. "I look considerably more uptight than you, I need to do something to blend in."

Ambra brushes the side of her scalp, where the reddish hair sticks a bit haphazardly. It's less than neat, but they wouldn't be able to easily stick the EKG's to it anymore.

"Yup, exactly that," Gurlien says. "I'm not going to spike my hair," he informs her, and she shrugs at that. "And don't you dare send any pictures to Chloe."

She wasn't going to, but now she's tempted.

"No," he says, at the look on her face, and despite all the nerves and the terror and the fact she's going to be facing one of the Five in less than a few hours, she finds herself smiling. "Stop that. Let's get you some food before we go down there."

28

Nerves fill her stomach more than the food does, but before she has time to get a grip on herself, before she can firm up her personality to actually be ready for the night in front of her, they find themselves in a crowded staircase in line to get into the catacombs, the silly little multi-tool pressed into her pocket

The stairs are rough-hewn from the same white stone as the stone beneath the bones, and the air is muggy from the crush of humanity all around them.

Ambra stands embarrassingly close to Gurlien, as if she isn't the most powerful person among them and could flatten everyone within a wide mile.

He holds himself straight, sticking out in the crowd, and throws his arm casually around her shoulders like that could protect her.

Several other people in the line stand similarly close to those next to them, so it's not the worst camouflage. Before these last three weeks, Ambra couldn't imagine letting anyone touch the body like that willingly, so it's probably not what the College is looking for.

If they're looking for her at all there. If they're expecting her to show up.

Music thumps up, even up the stairs, and Gurlien flashes the two false tickets at the guard, who barely glances at the artwork before waving them through, his eyes too focused on the scar on Ambra's chest to check carefully.

"And that is why I bought you that shirt," Gurlien mutters to her, as they descend down another set of sweaty stairs and the thumping music grows louder.

"So they can stare at my scars?" Ambra shoots back, and it's so dim she might remove the sunglasses.

"He was absolutely not staring at your scar," Gurlien informs her, before his face twists, like he's trying to judge if something is amusing or not. "You have no idea what humans find attractive, do you?"

It's an odd question, so she shrugs.

Again, he makes the distinct expression of trying to squash a smile, before his hand tangles in hers, pulling her forward, into the main antechamber.

Skulls line the crease between the wall and the ceiling, and rib cages adorn the sconces of the lights, grim and dirty, and Misia had stared at them the first time they were walked through. Ambra had felt a stirring of dread, all those months ago, some sort of bleeding over from Misia before she even knew what it was.

Ambra opens her mouth to tell Gurlien, before a guitar strums through the speakers, echoing on the low ceiling and in among the cracks in the bones.

Sound slams into her, so loud it takes her breath away and she recoils back, and Gurlien hands her the bright orange earplugs from his pocket.

"Thought you might need these," he says, and she

hastily fits them on her ears, and they only cut through a bit of the sound.

It's a familiar thump of noise, one she vaguely remembers hearing through the floor of the lab here, as she bled and suffered.

Nalissa must've held her events even while cutting into her brain.

Gurlien surveys around, his eyes sharp even through the mask of eyeliner, before he nods towards the low roof.

There, amongst the femurs and phalanges, is the barest hint of a rune, painted, and there's no way Gurlien had spotted that on his own.

"Did you memorize the protection placing?" she whispers, and she can't even hear herself speak. He cranes down to her, before he nods. "Insane."

It's an easy rune to bypass, one that discourages fighting and destruction, pointing all the safety to those on the stage.

If Ambra wants, she could unravel it in a second, but it would almost certainly send alarms through the entire complex.

The complex they're now in.

Noise, rough noise and more noise, crams into the small space, denser than the human bodies surrounding them, and a cold sweat breaks out over Ambra's brow.

Even when they flew them, even when they marched her through the airport, it wasn't this crowded.

"Here," Gurlien shouts, barely audible through the din and the earplugs, and grips her by the elbow. "We're in, now let's go deep."

Deep.

The labs are deep underneath them, a few levels of music and noise and bone dust between her and the pristine white lights of Nalissa's experiment table.

And she has to get there.

She straightens, lifting her chin, and pulls Gurlien through the crowd.

Lights flash, striking out at them before skating through the crowd as someone screams something raw into a microphone, the racket chasing Ambra's thoughts down like a fox to a rabbit.

"The faster we're out of here, the better," she tells Gurlien, and has to repeat it twice before he can hear her.

He nods, his lips thinning, and they push their way through the crowd (and around a demon trap) to the next set of stairs.

There's a brief touch of cool air on the winding staircase between the two levels, and she gulps at it greedily. The noise, still ever present, dulls in the background.

Gurlien's hand on her elbow is tight, and his jaw twitches as well. "Three traps next level, two layers of guards, and a sensor scanner."

It's information she already knew, but it's more for him than for her.

There's sweat on the back of his neck, and another couple clatter into the staircase, breaking the small snap of peace.

They giggle, like they caught them doing something they shouldn't have, before the man slams the woman into the wall, kissing her with such a ferocity that Ambra flinches.

The woman kisses back, yanking on his hair, and it's wholly unpleasant. Bone dust settles down in their clothing at the impact.

Gurlien pulls her along, and his brows are raised, before the man stops, breaking the kiss like he's breaking through the surface of water.

"Wait, Gurlien?" the man asks, and his voice is raw, like he had screamed into the woman's mouth. His pupils are wide, blown out unevenly, and his sweat smells sour.

The woman giggles, befuddled, staring at Gurlien and Ambra. "Do you know them?"

The man's brow furrows, and the smallest of scans snakes out of him, not strong enough to come close to the scar inside of Gurlien's soul. It's a pitiful attempt.

"You must've got me mixed up," Gurlien says smoothly, his fingers tightening only briefly on Ambra's arm. "Sorry, mate."

"No..." the man trails off, but Gurlien tugs Ambra forward, into the next main space.

It's a long, low hall, a stage crammed far on one end, and the thrum of bodies dance as one mass, and Ambra has to swallow down her fear at it.

And Nalissa chooses to do this. Chooses to spend her time setting these up, listening to the noise, letting it invade her space.

And she's down here somewhere.

Ambra pushes past the sweaty malaise of humanity, Gurlien right behind her, skirting along the edge of the bone encrusted wall. "I didn't think you'd be the one people would recognize," she calls to him, and his mouth is in a grim line. "Should have done more eyeliner."

"Should've gone full face paint," he gripes, and the band hits a high note, a long wail through the dusty speakers, and Ambra flinches.

Before her feet cross an invisible line, and all the noise falls away, all her attention on the single narrowing focus of magic.

If she goes any further, she can't teleport out to run away, not without breaking the runes down and sending all the alarms ricocheting through the tunnels.

Which they knew would happen. They knew they would reach a point where they would have to unravel everything to get out.

She just didn't think it was this close.

She twists to look at Gurlien, and his face is lit by the neon lights strung by wire across the ceiling.

"Is this the teleport line?" he asks, because of course he memorized that.

She nods, mute, and he stares down at her, face serious.

If she crosses this line and things go south, she can't get them out easily.

Or, rather, if she crosses this line, getting out will be noisy, disruptive, and everyone will know she's here.

Gurlien shifts closer to her, shielding her from someone streaking by, so most of the light that hits her is shadowed by the bones.

She wants to warn him. Tell him to stay here. Tell him to get out, go save himself, in case this doesn't work. In case she can't pull this off. In case Nalissa is prepared for her, in case they're walking into a trap.

But the leash is still around his wrist, and the chance of her success without him is next to nothing.

"You ready?" he asks, barely audible over the thumping bass, the yells of people, the scream of the singers.

She's not, but she grabs him by the collar, pulling him down to her and pressing her lips against his.

And with the pound of the music, he cradles her chin, like this kiss is the most precious thing in the world, like he's holding onto the most delicate of treasure that will shatter if he makes one wrong move. Like in the proximity of her, all he can do is protect.

Which is manifestly hilarious, she's the overpowered one in this scenario.

She breaks the kiss, staring at him, then steps backwards over the teleportation line.

Immediately, the magic washes over her, sending goosebumps up her arms, and she shivers.

"You should do that if we're concerned someone spots us," Gurlien says, low, crossing to be side by side with her. "I think you distracted the guards with that, so I don't have to punch them."

"Why would you..." she shakes her head, clearing her thoughts.

He gives her a half sidelong smile and her heart jumps a bit. "It'll be more effective than punching them."

"Why are the two options kissing me or punching them?" Ambra asks, and despite the noise and the din and the strobing lights, there's a small moment of comfort with him. A small moment of security.

"Well," he drawls, "I figure if they're staring at your tits so much, one of those actions are appropriate and I like kissing you more than I like punching anything."

"It's because of your wrists," she says.

He laughs, as she takes a moment, adjusting herself to the magic of the room.

"You can't feel the line?" Ambra murmurs, and he shakes his head. "Be glad."

The line itself is a few stories underground, written in copper ink into the very grout of the tile, but it's strong enough to impact even up here.

Nalissa's always been the strong one. Not as combat forward as Korhonen, but strong.

Gurlien snags her hand as they walk, yanking her back

into a bruising kiss, searing into her, before he releases her, just as quickly, leaving her winded.

She gapes at him from behind the glasses, and he has the temerity to look smug.

"Distracted that guard," he says, pointing with his chin at a heavily muscled man turning away from them, an earpiece curving around his ear. "He noticed you."

"I don't think you can kiss me each time a guard looks at me funny," Ambra informs him, but despite it all, she finds herself smiling.

"It's worth a try," he says, self-satisfied, and some of it is bravado over a layer of trepidation. "I'll have to try it elsewhere."

It's a manifestly ridiculous conversation, but it carries her down another hall, through a cramped corridor where an impromptu bartender pours a toxic green drink for a mob of drunk women.

One of them's even wearing the same mesh shirt as Ambra.

There's a demon mark on the far end of the wall, traced over the ridges of skulls, to prevent her from getting into the room behind it.

Once, when getting the tour and Misia was still alive, they told her that there were protected books beyond that mark, and the curiosity had distracted Ambra a lot more than they thought it would.

But that's not their goal this night, even though the same burn of curiosity rushes through Ambra once more.

If they can do this subtly, if they can kill Nalissa and get out without anyone knowing, she'll send Gurlien into there. Grab whatever books catch his fancy and get out.

There's a bright ward at the top of the other staircase, an ugly shining gold thing, almost neon underneath the artificial lights, and a guard stands underneath it. A clear 'nobody allowed past here' sign.

The ward wouldn't stop her. It'd hurt, she'd have to shield Gurlien, but it wouldn't stop her.

The guard, with her large biceps and brownish hair scraped tightly back into a bun, scowls at a set of drunken idiots, who promptly turn away from trying to stumble down the stairs into privacy.

And there's something about her face that's familiar.

Ambra can't tell where, she wasn't one of the research assistants, she wasn't one of the guards assigned to the room when they cut into her, but she must've passed this guard somewhere. Seen her before, just enough to recognize but not enough to memorize.

Which means she must've seen Ambra, possibly before they even cut Misia out.

Deliberately turning her back on the guard, Ambra hooks her fingers in Gurlien's belt loops, pulling him closer. "Are you sure not a little bit of murder?"

His lips part and his eyes go down to her scar. "Please, only Nalissa," he manages after a long second, and his hand curves along the rise of her hip, the mesh shirt the only thing between his touch and her skin.

The touch feels right.

"Then this might go loud," Ambra murmurs, leaning in close to him like they're more drunken idiots.

For at the floor of the guard, magic swirls, subtle, a captivating curl that begs to pull Ambra's attention from everything in the room.

His lips part once more.

"I'll shield you," she says, and he huffs out a laugh. "There's a pain deterrent ward, you won't feel anything."

"That's less than reassuring, but sure." Despite the

sarcastic words, he cradles her face, his thumb swiping over the still sensitive edge of the necromancer wound. "Will you feel it?"

Unbidden, tears spring to her eyes at how gentle the touch, at the care he's giving her at this very moment. At how she's dragging him into danger and he's still taking his small motions to soothe her.

He might not even know he's soothing her, but he is.

She owes it to him to get them out of this alive. Alive and with one less handler, with one less obstacle in their lives.

"Okay," she murmurs, letting herself lean back against his hand for one briefest of seconds, before she steps back, facing the guard with the widest smile she has.

The guard startles.

"Hi!" Ambra says, as bright and as cheery as she can, and the guard squints warily. "Can we go by there?"

She keeps Gurlien's other hand in hers, and it's nice. She doesn't need both hands to defend him.

"No," the guard says, her brow furrowing, glancing between the two of them. "No entry."

Ambra doesn't want to break the moment to check Gurlien's expression, so she attempts a sunny smile up to the guard, who's about a foot taller than Ambra, and pulls Gurlien forward.

"I said no—"

Ambra strides across the ward, snapping the shield around Gurlien, and magic rips at her, stabbing into her chest and side and throat and—

Black sparking behind her eyes, she grabs the guard by the collar, slamming her into the door, opening it with a twist of magic and yanking the three of them into the staircase beyond it.

The moment her feet carry her outside of the shining

ward, the pain crackles away, leaving her breathless. Uninjured, but her chest heaving and her hands shaking.

The guard's lifting her hands, a strip of magic already in a needle, ready, and Ambra rips it right out of her hand, tossing the gold needle down the stairs.

"No," Ambra says, matter of factly, then flexes her magic, flooding the air pressure around the guard.

To her credit, the guard struggles against it, stronger than Ambra would've thought, before her eyes roll back and she slumps against the wall.

Ambra releases her collar, and she crumbles to the ground, limp.

Gurlien gasps, an aborted small sound, and when she turns to him, his eyes are wide.

"I didn't kill her," Ambra preempts. "She'll wake up with a bad headache in a few hours, and they'll know a demon did it."

He swallows, before nodding. "Thank you." He's unharmed, not even a streak of his eyeliner, and when she snaps a scan at him, the only thing hurting is the bones in one of his wrists.

Good. Her shields work.

With a nod at him, she starts down the stairs, and there's only the far-off thumping of the music now, some sort of sound softening spell, and she's definitely not going to break that one.

Pain still arches through her spine, almost as an afterthought, but she ignores it. She'll have time later, when Gurlien's not at risk and Nalissa's dead, to experience it and curl up on the bed, but not now.

Here, instead of the rough-hewn stone and bone, Nalissa fastened metal to the walls, as if this is a normal laboratory setting.

"It would've been easier if I killed her," Ambra mumbles. "All it will take is someone spotting the empty doorway and this entire place will lock down."

Gurlien inhales and, carefully, pulls the gun out of the hidden holster underneath his shirt.

"They'll have protections," Ambra warns.

"And all it'll take is you distracting one of them long enough to break those," he snips back, before the lights over them snap on.

Ambra recoils back, despite the tinted glasses, as the fluorescents hum, high pitched.

He catches her with a hand between her shoulder blades. "We got this," he murmurs, and there are whites visible around his eyes.

But now, Ambra can feel everything.

There's another demon trap, three hallways down and out of the way, and in the middle of it is a demon, half twisted half dead, the body they're forced into breathing through a machine. They respond to the touch of Ambra's mind, flexing outwards into a silent plea.

There's a complicated series of runes, the sort to keep out nosy Wights, and inside is a human, trapped inside a tube, unconscious.

Another demon, this one older and fiercer, snapping like an animal inside of a trap, snarling at the brush of her mind and promising death to her if she ventures close. They're in pain, so much pain it's twisted their mind.

Ambra recognizes that. Recognizes the panic of the pain and the desperation to do something, anything, to end it.

Also recognizes that the demon would almost certainly kill her if they think she could help the pain.

There's a human with them, half dead, unconscious.

"Bianci was right," Ambra murmurs, as she shakes

herself loose and resumes the cautious steps down the hallway. "Nalissa did try again."

Gurlien eyes her.

"How much of this place can I destroy?" she asks, and her throat is tight. Tight as if the sympathy tied the leash itself.

"Not much," he murmurs, pointing out a security camera, which Ambra breaks the glass with a flick of her fingers. "Not without destabilizing the city of Paris."

"I don't care about the city of Paris," she informs him, something akin to fury prickling hot underneath her skin.

He gapes at her.

"What, I don't," she says, surly.

"Well...I do?" he says, obviously fumbling for the answer. "Don't...please don't blow up Paris."

The other demon sends a trill of a scrape down her consciousness, a demand for attention, but she can't do anything about that. Can't do anything while they're inside the demon trap, can't do anything without alerting Nalissa.

But it means Nalissa is still trying, and that has to be stopped. Beyond just Ambra's revenge, beyond just ensuring her safety, it has to be for this person. For this demon held so insane with pain that they can't think, just act out.

Ambra understands that.

Gurlien's hand settles in her lower back, and she twitches in surprise.

"I'm okay," she preempts, the words falling from her lips automatically, and he gives her a fully unamused look. "This place is full of people like me."

He tilts his head, the question silent.

"Other demons being experimented on," she clarifies, as another claw reaches out to her. "I'm not sure if they're just not as far along...or if they didn't succeed."

"You are only the second success that is known," he says, and she wouldn't call herself a success on a good day, before he huffs out a breath.

In the fluorescent lights, the eyeliner is ridiculous, her shirt is ridiculous, the headache is ridiculous, but she still faces down the hallway.

This deep, it's familiar.

"Let's go," she murmurs, then takes off down the hallway.

It's only forty steps before the first turn, then another twenty before the first locked door, the ones that only some of the assistants had badges that could go through it.

And alarms aren't ringing. Yet. The lack of them itches under her skin, needling at her awareness. There should be alarms, someone has to have seen her by now, the cameras tracking their movements.

"This is too easy," he murmurs, echoing her thoughts.

"Far too easy," Ambra says, then lets her eyes flutter shut, snaking out a tendril of power towards the door.

It's double locked, with a chain on the inside and an electronic badge lock on this side. She easily severs the chain—that's almost comical—and after a few moments of finessing, cracks the badge reader off the wall, where it clatters to the tile.

Gurlien jumps at the noise, but the door hisses open.

"See, this would be a good place for Chloe," he says, waiting for her to scan the room before she ventures forward.

"Why?" Ambra asks, only half paying attention, nestling her magic into the nooks and crannies, testing for traps.

"Her specialty is actually traps and locks," Gurlien replies easily, like that's not insanely impressive by itself. "What, that's how we made it past the locking traps."

She pulls up short, crossing her arms at him. "What?"

"That's how we did that...what, did you think we had more help?"

Ambra hadn't actually thought much about how her rescue came to be, just that they were there and the alchemist had been damn impressive and exhausted.

"I am absolutely going to ask her questions later," Ambra informs him, before a tendril of her magic smarts, snapping back to herself.

There's a trap.

It's a small trap, designed to stop the unaware, one of Nalissa's favorites. One wrong step and it'd close around anyone, sticking their feet to the ground and stopping all sense of time passing.

It's also, of course, right in front of the door they have to get through, deeper into the laboratories.

The easy answer is to snap it, to unravel it, push onwards. It's not terribly far to where Nalissa stays, to her office where she sits for all of her events, they might be able to get through to there before they can muster up a response.

"Shit," Ambra mumbles, keeping an arm across Gurlien's chest, stopping him from moving forward.

She skirts her magic around it, testing the tiles, the grout, leaving little puffs of powder where the tiles give way, and Gurlien hisses in a breath.

"That you?" he murmurs, and she nods.

"Trap, trying to find a way around. If I wasn't..." if she wasn't stuck in a human body, it'd be simple, but that still gives no way for Gurlien to get over, and she's not leaving him. "I can destroy it, but there'll be alarms, so I'm trying to get around it, find a weakness."

"Which type of trap?" he asks, and she forgets that he's also intelligent, also just as learned as she is.

"Sticker type, just a nasty one, she would keep them in front of private things to keep people out..."

Almost at the edge of her hearing, there's a clatter of footsteps behind them, down the staircase with the unconscious guard.

They both straighten, staring at each other.

A startled yell, someone calling for help.

"Destroy it?" Gurlien asks.

"Yep," Ambra says, and before she can even do so, before she can even grip it in her hands, a low, lolling alarm tolls through the hallway, setting Ambra's teeth on edge.

"There it is," Gurlien mutters, and more footsteps echo their way.

So Ambra grips her power in both hands, digging it underneath the tile, and slamming the tile upwards until it crashes into the roof, sending dust flying through the room.

And thoroughly destroying the trap.

Gurlien jumps back, but Ambra grabs his wrist and hauls him forward, right as two more guards round the corner into the room.

Before she can think, she clenches her hand into a fist, dragging down the ceiling on top of the guards with a thundering crash.

Buying them a little more time. Not nearly enough.

She pulls him along, even as the dust tries to settle in their hair, and his eyes are wide, starkly wide beyond the eyeliner.

"Are you okay?" she asks, then coughs in the dust.

Destroying the walls in the Toronto base had significantly less dust.

He gapes at her. "I thought you said you weren't killing anyone?"

Still, they half walk-half run, now through the tolling alarm custom made to never disrupt any music above.

"We have to get to her office, we have to—"

Before she can finish the words, in between one breath and the next, with her lips forming the shapes of the letters and her hand still gripped in his, everything stops.

Everything stops, and the leash around her neck snaps tight.

Tight.

29

She gags, free hand coming up to claw at her throat, nails scratching at her skin—it's the same skin Gurlien had kissed—and she recoils back, thumping into him.

He says something, his voice meeting her ears but not registering in her mind, his tone distressed, his tone panicked, and—

White blanks out her eyes, crackling over her vision, and Gurlien's hand closes over her wrist, cool against the fever hot skin, as the leash twists its grip on her, pulling her...

With a snap so hard her ears pop, she teleports, feet sliding along new tile, Gurlien stumbling next to her. It's a short teleport, barely twenty paces away from where they were, but still, her mind stops, the heart stuttering in the chest until she gasps, all color blooming around her.

Nalissa always kept her office colorful.

The wall behind the desk—just a converted surgery table—is medicinal pink, glaring and bright under the white lights, up until it meets a line of skulls in the crease to the roof. There's a riot of a flower bouquet on the desk, held in an oversized glass beaker, and with every breath Ambra can smell them. Nalissa's flowers were always cloying.

The tile is a dizzying design in teal and orange, and Misia had stared at it for too long to attempt to figure it out, and Ambra never wants to see something like it ever again.

In between one gulp of air and the next, Nalissa crosses into her field of vision, her face open and soft.

Behind her, Gurlien makes a noise Ambra can't describe, before he throws his arms around her, keeping her back against him, rooting her in place.

Gurlien.

Ambra straightens, and Nalissa hasn't compelled her to act, other than the teleportation.

Nalissa's face creases into a smile, like she's glad to see Ambra. Like she's a friend, like she would soothe her with the conversation and discuss warmth and cozy things. Her hair is a little longer and a little grayer than the last time Ambra saw it, but it's been a few months since she's looked Nalissa face to face.

Usually, Nalissa faced her elsewhere. Usually, Nalissa faced her at a combat foe.

"Gurlien Banks, you're definitely not who I expected," Nalissa says, her voice extolling, like it's some praise.

Gurlien stiffens behind her, his arm tight around her, and it's a small protection.

Ambra cracks out a snap of power to Nalissa, but it crackles to the ground before it can reach her, bouncing off a shield.

No, not a shield, a trap.

Ambra forces herself to look down, and Nalissa had teleported them into a demon trap.

She couldn't move out of it, she couldn't use power out of it, just inside.

Nalissa smiles at her, gentle, like she's a child that did something right.

Ambra hates that smile.

"Don't worry, I didn't place you somewhere where you could do actual harm," Nalissa says casually, boosting herself up so she sits on the pink metal surgery table, next to the flowers and the ever-present picture of her collection of golden retriever dogs. "I wasn't going to give you the chance before we could talk."

Ambra stills herself, and Gurlien loosens his arms.

She misses the contact, immediately, throwing a look back up to him.

"I saw Johnsin's body, I don't blame you," Nalissa continues, voice still friendly. "He never did get the concept that you had a sense of self."

"What the hell does that mean?" Gurlien bursts out, obviously startling Nalissa, who blinks owlishly at him.

"He thought of her as a plaything," Nalissa says, after a moment of silence, obviously calculating, and Ambra doesn't like it one bit. Nalissa could twist her words, could get anyone to do her bidding, and the last thing she wants is for her to get her claws into Gurlien. "We all thought it was ghastly, but we couldn't stop him, we all had equal power over her."

Nalissa's eyes drop to Gurlien's wrist, where the leash is still tied and still obvious.

"And now you, too," Nalissa continues softly. "Somehow in this demon's mad quest to be free, she tied you into the mess."

Gurlien shifts behind her, and to someone unused to his motions, it must read as discomfort. As being insecure.

But he's reaching for the gun tucked into his waistband, using Ambra's body to block the view.

"You must know that she's not going to stop at us," Nalissa says, as matter as factly as if she's delivering a lesson to her apprentices. "Demons aren't logical creatures, they don't form attachments, she'll absolutely end you the moment she gets rid of me and Boltiex."

A laugh at the ridiculousness bubbles into Ambra's throat, but she squashes it down. Instead, she shakes out her arms, stepping forward, still blocking Gurlien from view, and opens her mouth to speak.

And without even a gesture, Nalissa cuts off her voice, closing her mouth again.

Oh, so she's not gonna let Ambra speak.

A fission of anger winds its way up her back, and she shivers.

"Did she have you work on your distance?" Nalissa asks of Gurlien, and her warm brown eyes are on him. Ambra remembers that gaze, how until she knew better, she felt special underneath it. Misia felt special. "See how far you can control her?"

"Twenty feet," Gurlien answers, and Ambra squashes another reaction at the lie.

He shifts, so the gun is tucked behind his back, easy to grab if he needs, but out of Nalissa's sight, then nods, ever so minutely, to Ambra.

So he has some sort of plan, some sort of idea.

Ambra attempts to speak again, but nothing comes out, not even a twitch of her face, and Gurlien's brow furrows at her.

"Makes sense, without any powers of your own, that controlling someone like her would be difficult," Nalissa sympathizes, but Gurlien just narrows his eyes at Ambra, like he could tell something is off with her, even something as mild as Nalissa controlling her words. "Probably why she picked you, no offense, I heard the rest of your 'crew,'" some real venom sneaks into Nalissa's voice at that, a hint of her real emotions instead of this manipulation, "were very powerful, leaving you as the odd man out."

Gurlien twitches his eyebrow at Ambra, then shrugs, facing Nalissa. "She said as much."

This time, Ambra's not nearly as worried that he's buying her words. Not like she was with Johnsin. Not after how easily he read Bianci.

The fact that the College disposed of him, even with all this knowledge and all this fluency and skills, is laughable.

Nalissa nods, full of sympathy, before she turns her gaze to Ambra. "And is he telling the truth?"

Whip fast, compulsion wraps its way around her throat, and Ambra physically recoils back for a split second before Nalissa controls that, too.

"I picked him because he had no power," Ambra blurts out, beyond her control, and the side of Gurlien's mouth tilts up.

But Nalissa just tightens the compulsion, choking her, leaving her sputtering. "Where have you been hiding?"

"The Paris house you found," Ambra says, digging in her feet and struggling against it. "Minnesota. Bellingham. Maine." Nalissa relaxes the compulsion long enough that Ambra can pull in a breath, ragged, before she tightens it again.

This time, the words aren't Ambra's own.

"Leave," she spits out at Gurlien, and Nalissa has just enough control of her to make the words sound real, make the sentiment echo.

To her equal parts horror and amusement, Gurlien just raises an eyebrow at her. "Uh huh," he says, visibly skeptical, then, to Nalissa, "do you think I can't tell when someone's controlling her?"

"How?" Nalissa breathes, and Ambra tries to recoil back, tries to move, but Nalissa holds her in place despite her distraction. "You shouldn't be able to, none of us can feel when another controls."

Ambra tries to twitch over to Gurlien, the hair on the back of her neck rising, because even if Nalissa doesn't have plans at the moment, this curiosity is absolutely how she would disarm him, absolutely how she would distract him.

Gurlien's gaze flickers to hers then, deliberately, takes a step towards the edge of the circle.

"You're massively overestimating my ability if you think I can sense something like that," Gurlien says, and Ambra wishes, ever so briefly, that she could read his mind. Could see what he's planning. "It's more subtle than that."

Nalissa's eyes skate over to Ambra, almost uneasy. "How well can he control you?"

Again, the compulsion.

"He can't," Ambra says, and it's technically true, but she blinks at herself anyways. "He can just disrupt, pull on the leash."

"Interesting ramifications," Nalissa murmurs, her fingers twitching, like she's reaching for a pen but her desk is too clean. "Pity we can't study that more."

Nalissa loosens her grip on the leash just enough that Ambra strikes out, her magic snapping useless to the ground at the edge of the shield. But all Nalissa does is smile softly at her, like she's merely a misbehaving child.

"Well, Gurlien, thank you for keeping her somewhat controlled, in a manner of speaking," Nalissa says, and Gurlien's face twists something awful for a split second before he gets it under control. "I'll write a report that you helped, get you reinstated in some research or another."

"No thanks," Gurlien replies, backing up another step, and as much as Ambra wishes she knew what that was about, wishes she knew how to interpret it, she misses the contact more.

"No, returning a valuable asset is enough, despite what happened in Toronto." Then, Nalissa smiles, and it reaches her eyes, warm and friendly. "Just untie it and I'll write a letter of recommendation."

"I can't," Gurlien says easily, though his jaw is tight and the line of his shoulders underneath the black shirt is tense. "I can't even see it."

"Is he telling the truth?" Nalissa murmurs, snaking out her compulsion again.

"Yes," Ambra spits out, struggling against it as if it's as physical of a gag.

With a nod, Nalissa paces Ambra over to Gurlien, an easy, casual motion, and Gurlien's eyes widen.

"Here," Nalissa says through Ambra's voice, even imitating the murmur, "give me your hand."

Gurlien recoils back even further, even as Ambra reaches for him, each little muscle controlled by Nalissa.

"You've done enough, you'll be free of this mess, go back to your friends," Ambra's voice continues, pouring out in such a good mimicry of her emotions, as Nalissa picks through her vocal cords and her small unconscious motions like an artist picking her paint. "We'll pay for your plane ticket."

It dawns on Gurlien's face, slowly, and his eyes snap up to Nalissa. "You need me to do this, don't you? Give this up willingly?"

Nalissa shrugs, easy and nonchalant. "It's a lot easier if you do, the death of the others has given...instabilities."

Ambra doesn't know how, but it gives her a little thrill, a little bit of fresh air, standing in front of him and glancing up at him. She can't look away, not with Nalissa controlling her like that, but...

They're unlikely to just kill him to take away the leash. Unlikely to just end him and snap her up.

Relief almost makes her knees weak.

"No," Gurlien says, then, and the relief is mirrored on his face. "I'm not gonna do that."

He had been scared, too.

"There are other things I can do to make you," Nalissa continues, as if he didn't say a thing. "Other things to convince." Her control winds its way back through Ambra's spine, straightening it with a pang of pain.

And Nalissa's awareness floods through Ambra, floods through her, picking apart every ache and pain, the flinch that runs through her with every thump of the music, the glare in her eyes, every small soreness in her back, where her feet are pinched in her boots, to the warmth of her shoulders at Gurlien's lingering touch, and...

"You slept with her?" Nalissa asks through Ambra's voice, and Gurlien blanches before getting himself under control. "That's...astoundingly stupid."

Nalissa steps Ambra forward again, and Gurlien takes another step back, towards the edge of the circle.

"This demon can't even form a bond, so any security you'd get from such a trade is gone," Nalissa says, leaving Ambra standing, mute, struggling for words and struggling to move. "She won't protect you if she succeeds in killing the rest of us."

Nalissa stares at her, though, her eyes pitying, and Ambra hates it.

"Oh Ambra," Nalissa says, soft as a lover, "you really should be dead. There was no reason for you to survive."

Gurlien opens his mouth, then closes it, taking another step back. He's planning something, he's planning something and she doesn't know what.

As if sensing his fear, Nalissa pours her control through Ambra, twisting the magic inside the circle around her, crackling through the air. It's a pretty trick, relatively harmless and useless, but visual chaos, making her seem far more powerful than she actually is inside the demon circle.

It succeeds, and Gurlien flinches back, his feet crossing the line of the demon trap, leaving her alone.

She can't reach him now. She can't lift her hand to touch him, not unless Nalissa compels her past the trap, and her ears pop with the fission of magic closing again around her.

"I could always have her torture you," Nalissa murmurs, but her eyes are deceptively sharp. "It'd probably distress her, too, she doesn't have the stomach for that sort of thing. We had her do that with Misia." Nalissa pauses, as if for dramatic effect. "Did she tell you about Misia?"

Rage, so strong it almost knocks her off her feet, floods through Ambra, and she twitches towards Nalissa, her hands coming up, before Nalissa smoothes the motion away.

Holding her still, holding her looking away from Gurlien.

Nalissa stares at her, hard, her warm brown eyes flinty in the overhead light, as the music up above thumps.

"Yeah, I heard about Misia," Gurlien says, and there's anger in his voice too, anger that she can barely pick up, even knowing him like she does, and Nalissa almost certainly misses it.

"Impressive," Nalissa says, still locked eyes with Ambra. "I thought she made herself forget that name."

Nalissa raises an eyebrow at Ambra, evaluating, and Ambra hates it. Doesn't want to give any sort of information to her, any sort of ammunition, nothing.

"Did you?" Nalissa murmurs.

"I tried," the words pour from her. "I tried."

There's a hot pit of anger inside her stomach, of shame and terror at the memories. Of when Nalissa made Ambra twist her own power against the body they were both in, of the agony they both felt.

And that Nalissa might make her do something like that again. To Gurlien, none the less. Gurlien who held her when they tried to take her back. Gurlien, who called his enemies who didn't like him for help, to help her.

Gurlien who kissed her, who held her against him in bed, who took her out to wine and food. And now Nalissa's facing Ambra in the other direction, she can't even look at him, can't even see his eyes or his hair or the flush of his skin.

"Twenty feet?" Nalissa muses. "Ambra, is that correct?"

Ambra digs her feet in, physically anchors herself away from answering, but the words are dragged out of her. "No."

And Nalissa smiles, showing all of her teeth. "Good girl."

Behind her, there's a whisper of fabric, a subtle motion, before the telltale click of a gun safety flipping off, a creak of metal, a hiss of breath.

The bang shatters all concentration, the bullet crashing into the wall behind Nalissa, sending plaster and bone dust into the air.

Nalissa flinches back, eyes wide, winding both hands around Ambra's leash, and between one breath and the next, with the same creak of metal and scrape of springs internally in the barrel—

Nalissa pulls, jerking Ambra to her up, past the demon circle, past the protections, close, too close, so close she can see the lines in her eyes and each gray hair in her curls and —

Another bang before Ambra can breathe, and pain sears through her, brighter than any lights.

She staggers, black blood spraying all over Nalissa, and there's red blood in a hole in Nalissa's shoulder, brilliant against the white lab coat.

Nalissa gasps, and Ambra can't tell if it's from pain or shock, but Ambra reaches up, twisting her magic up and around, and, despite the agony searing through her and the edges of her vision caving in, Ambra snaps Nalissa's neck.

There's a moment, there's a breath, where Nalissa's fingertips twitch, before she collapses against the medical table, lifeless.

Ambra staggers back, and Nalissa's body slumps down.

There's pain everywhere: in her chest, her lungs, her bones. Her knees feel weak, as if the very tendons keeping her upright are giving out.

Gurlien yells something, rushing across the demon circle to her, but there's a roaring in Ambra's ears, drowning out everything else, and she turns towards him.

Blood falls from a hole in her chest, just above her collarbone, viscous and terrible, and she stares down at it for a second.

Even as she does, she can feel the protections of the place unravel. The wards, the magic twisted into the walls and the bones, all unfurling with a snap outwards from Nalissa's death, rendering them useless.

"I can teleport out now," Ambra manages out, but fire

draws in with each breath and her own words are distant, off beyond the rushing roar, as Gurlien surges to her, bracing her.

She stumbles, her knees wobbling, her hands slipping as she tries to grasp Gurlien's arm, slipping on her blood.

Ambra's been shot before, even in this body, but it hadn't hurt like this. Hadn't echoed through the body, hadn't struggled the lungs, hadn't blacked out her vision.

Gurlien grips her, keeping her upright as her knees give out, pitching her into his chest.

It's bad. It's very bad, and she sends a tendril of power to the wound, but her grip on it is weak, ephemeral. Like it could escape her with just a thought.

Gurlien says something again, she can feel the rumble in his chest, but nothing reaches her ears, nothing beyond the vague panic of the body flooding itself with adrenaline, of the gaping lack of Nalissa dead in front of her, on the brilliant heat of Gurlien's hands on hers.

"I have to get you out," she mumbles, and the words are tinny to her hearing. Guards must be coming, guards will bang down the door and she can't defend him and—

She grips the collar of his black shirt, and does the simple most instinctive action a demon has.

She teleports.

Her knees crumple the moment she does, into snow and howling wind, and the last thing she sees is the burnt-out remnants of the motor home, before the black crowds her vision and takes her over.

30

There's cold against the cheek, something frozen and wet, and all she can muster is the twitch of an eyelid. Wind screams at her, stealing all warmth from her skin.

The world is bright, way brighter than the nighttime it should be, and pain echoes harshly in her chest, fighting against the lungs and the still-beating heart.

A voice reaches her ears, distant and panicked, but not talking to her.

Something hot, brilliantly so, brushes the hair away from the forehead, and she tries to unstick her eyes, but she can't.

Can barely move, none of the limbs follow her direction, and after a few moments of struggling, she slumps down into it again.

∼

Something moves the body, jolting, a rumble of machinery beneath her. There's a low murmur of voices, multiple voices, and she can't pick them apart.

There's a scrape against glass—windows?—and tree branches against metal, before the rumbling beneath her turns rougher, gravelly. She's still moving, even when held perfectly still, some sort of vehicle.

It had been so long since she'd been in a vehicle.

The magic is strange, here, the lines slipping in and out of contact, tasting of the wild.

The head is against something soft, and a hand shifts through the hair on the side of her head, gentle.

It's almost enough to distract from the pain.

A bright flash of necromancy, and Ambra surges upright, terror and hunger inside her, before her vision blacks out and hands push her back down.

Still, something ties itself around a wrist, and she knows she should be afraid.

The body lays in a bed, uncomfortable and hard, a sheet pulled up, itching against the scar beneath the breasts, and Ambra struggles to breathe.

There's something over the face, fitting cleanly over the mouth and nose, and air, sweet air, flows through it. A cold prickle of metal sings in the veins on an arm, and there's a bit of fear along with it.

But no pain.

After a few good long moments, Ambra cracks an eye open. The room is dim and pleasantly warm.

Wards swirl in the ceiling, fluently written, new ones on top of old, engraved into the very concrete and wood of the building itself. It's beautiful, if intense and overkill.

Ambra blinks up at it, and the figures blur in her vision, before she squints to focus them. They're odd, written in a hand she doesn't know, in a glittering gold and copper paint.

Someone must've craned their neck for forever to paint it, for it to exist like this, and a detached part of her marvels at it.

Right up until she tries to draw in another breath.

Pain wracks its way across her chest, and she jerks, gasping, but her arm's stuck in place, tied down, and—

Before she can think, before she can even comprehend what's happening, black crowds her out.

NEXT TIME SHE WAKES, the body feels more like her own, and while there's pain, it's more of a distant companion.

The paint is still on the ceiling, but she's more alert this time, alert enough to realize there's a demon trap around her, around the bed she's laying on.

And Gurlien's nowhere near by. She can't sense him, she can't feel his touch on the leash, nothing.

And no matter how much she tries to panic, no matter how much she tries to teleport out, she's stuck in place.

Neck stiff, she tilts her head over to stare at her wrist.

There, neatly tied and still shining gold, is a strip of necromancer power, gleaming. It's not hurting her, and it's pinning her wrist in place, next to an IV hooked up to the vein in her elbow, the plastic line trailing up to a bag on a stand.

And, right beyond the IV stand, sits a man.

Ambra blinks at him, but she can't make her eyes recognize him. His hair is wildly curly, pulled back into a bun, and he frowns at her through thin wire-rimmed glasses.

She stares blankly at him, and he frowns deeper at her, before she tries to open her mouth to speak, but...

There's still the mask over her face, muffling her, forcing air down her throat. She's stuck, she's tied down, she can't talk, she can't—

"Stop panicking," the man says, like this is a giant annoyance, and there's something wrong with him. There's something so completely wrong, he's not a human, not entirely, but he doesn't read as anything but human, but... "You'll tear open your stitches if you do that."

Ambra coughs, and everything hurts again, before trying to mouth, frantic.

"Where is he?" she manages out, and she can barely hear herself, so muffled, her voice a dry scrape against her throat. "Where is he?"

The man raises an eyebrow at her, but doesn't answer.

"Where—" She coughs again, before jerking as much power to herself as she can, stuck inside the demon trap, but the magic slips from her grip before she can do anything, the strip of necromancy shining bright.

She gapes at it, trying to jerk her hand out from it, but the pain sparks up against her eyes, slumping her back against the bed.

The man stands, scowling at her, before picking up a small piece of technology—a phone, no, a short-wave radio—and presses a button. "She's awake, can we get a familiar face in here?"

Ambra tries to pull in a breath, tries to force the lungs, but it's hard, forcing her to gasp.

"Please stop panicking, we're not going to hurt you," the man says, crossing his arms, still standing. "The necromancy is because you were fighting us while unconscious and you needed an IV."

And there are only two necromancers active right now, and both of them know Gurlien.

"Where..." she trails off, her mouth too dry, the air from the mask too forced.

"I am absolutely not telling you where we are," the man says, scowling. "You're not going to be hurt, we just needed to put in an IV." Then, his face softening just minutely. "You were unconscious for four days."

She blinks up at him, then towards the door. Four days is too long, Gurlien could be hurt, Boltiex could be trying to hurt him, trying to reclaim her.

"I'm the Mel that's been texting you," the man continues, more begrudging than not. "The necromancers aren't here. I'm not going to let you see either of them."

Ambra stills, his words filtering in her mind, before she swallows.

Even that is like glass.

"Right now, all you need to know is that you're safe, and if you keep on panicking, you're going to rip yourself open again."

The door clatters open, and Chloe rushes in, her eyes wide and hair mussed up, the Half Demon behind her.

"Oh my god, you're awake," Chloe blurts out, rushing over and grabbing Ambra's untied hand. "Are you okay, how do you feel, are—"

Ambra flinches away from her grip, and Chloe gapes at her.

The Half Demon runs a scan on her, some sort of flash

assessment, and Ambra bristles. He's not stepping inside the demon trap, very obviously so.

"You're doing better," he says, matter-of-factly, and Ambra vividly remembers their clash of powers in the bar, how he almost won that fight.

And now she's helpless. Every breath is difficult, her arm is pinned down so thoroughly she can't do a single thing, and all the magic slips from her.

The two men exchange a glance at her obvious attempt at grasping power.

"How are you feeling?" the Half Demon says finally, as Chloe stands, pale, to one side.

Ambra tries to speak, tries to say something, but coughs instead, her mouth too dry.

"Can we remove the mask?" Chloe asks, small. "She's trying to talk, but it's stopping her."

Which is entirely accurate, but being talked like she's not there just bristles something inside of her even more.

"I don't want to until Delina or Lyra give approval," the man—Mel—says. "Last thing I want to do is to upset Lyra with more pain."

Ambra blinks at him. If he's the one who's texting her, if he has some sort of demon past, now in this human body, he might understand her. Might understand the need clawing at her throat, the panic at not being able to know anything about Gurlien.

"Are you thirsty?" Chloe asks, and her voice is still small, such a big contrast with the last time they spoke. Unfitting for an alchemist of her power. "You're probably starving."

Her stomach is the least of Ambra's worries.

"Where is he?" She croaks out, muffled against the mask held so tightly to her face.

Chloe glances up at the Half Demon—Maison, his name

is Maison—and a pool of dread starts in Ambra's stomach.

"Is he okay?" she asks, and even she can't hear her voice properly. "Is he..."

"We're holding Gurlien downstairs," Maison says firmly, and Ambra gapes at him. "He's completely untouched."

Holding, like some sort of prisoner?

Ambra glares up at Chloe, like she could will her to understand her. Chloe's supposed to be on Gurlien's side in all of this, his one true friend, and she let this group put him in some sort of holding cell?

Chloe pales, but doesn't shrink back.

"He shot you," Mel, the other not-demon, drawls. "He shot you then brought a demon to a controlled facility with wanted necromancers. We're not going to let him run away."

It's entirely inaccurate, and Ambra wishes she could laugh, but with the mask and her throat, she doubts she could.

She shakes her head, and the three exchange a look above her.

"Ambra," Chloe starts, gentle, "you were shot by his gun, and it punctured your lung and broke your clavicle. A gun I told him would hurt you."

"You're not dead only because you heal," Mel says, clipped. "You almost died three times in the last few days."

But it was Nalissa who pulled her to block the bullet, and there would have been no way for Gurlien to predict that and they can't seriously be thinking it was intentional...

By the grim expression on their faces, they think it might be.

Ambra struggles to pull herself upright, and Chloe rushes to her, guiding her back against the cot.

"Here," Chloe says, pressing a button on the side of the mattress, and the head tilts upright until Ambra's in an almost sitting position, her wrist moving with her. "This'll be easier."

The position stretches at the pain in her chest. There's a white bandage over her breastbone, stark, and Ambra's just covered by a papery medical gown.

She wants to burn all medical gowns.

Instead, she lifts her free hand to the edge of the bandages, and the pain echoes at the touch.

"He..." she trails off, swallowing, before she scowls at Chloe, shaking her head and trying to peel the mask off her face.

It doesn't move, held down by straps on the back of her head, straps she can't reach, and even that effort winds her, leaving her panting into the mask.

"We should get Delina in here," the Half Demon murmurs. "See if she can speak without danger."

"We shouldn't do that while she's awake," Mel shoots back.

Chloe and Ambra make eye contact at that, at the frustration and incompleteness of the communication, and that seems to solidify something inside Chloe.

She stands up straighter, still close to Ambra, but even that motion is enough to draw their attention.

"Ambra, I'm going to ask you some questions, just shake your head yes or no," Chloe says, and a rush of gratitude floods through Ambra. "Are you going to hurt Gurlien?"

That's easy, and Ambra scrunches her face under the mask as she shakes her head no.

"No demon is going to answer that honestly," Mel mutters.

"Shut up," Chloe says with a scowl. "Did he mean to hurt you?"

Again, Ambra shakes her head no, and Chloe gestures at

her, as if that's the proof she needed in the argument.

"But it was his gun," Maison says, and Ambra nods yes. Because of course it is.

And that's not what matters, not really, and the idea of Gurlien just sitting there, probably worried, makes her jerk her arm again.

"You will say anything to get out of this right now, wouldn't you?" Mel says, voice low, and she scowls at him from beyond the mask. "Do you want us to drug you so one of the Necromancers can come in and scan you, or do you want us to wait until you're asleep?"

Ambra stills, a flutter of fear welling up inside of her again.

"Because I won't trust your word on this until I hear you say it, without knowing the story Gurlien told," Mel continues, and he's entirely correct. "And I'm not letting you out from the wrist tie, not this near to Necromancers, until I know for a fact that Gurlien isn't going to use you as a weapon against them."

"He wouldn't," Chloe mutters, dark, and Ambra likes her a bit more at that tone.

"You don't think he would," Mel shoots back, and Maison rubs his face, like he's had to hear this argument several times in the last few days and is tired of it.

Ambra sags back against the bed, which is at least more comfortable in the reclining position, and tilts her head to look at Chloe, before mouthing, 'Is he okay,' through the mask.

Chloe nods, slowly. "They're just keeping him in one place, they're not doing anything to him."

Ambra at least believes that Chloe would tell her the truth on that.

"We're not monsters," Mel drawls, and Ambra wishes

she had her phone with her so she could throw it at him.

Maison's jaw ticks, like he too is at the end of his patience, before he turns to Ambra instead. "Besides bringing Gurlien directly here, is there anything we can do to help your healing?"

"No," mutters Mel, and he's still not wrong, but Ambra dislikes that still. "She needs time, rest, and when she can breathe on her own without choking on her own blood, food of some sort."

All of those are exhausting, and Ambra closes her eyes, ever so briefly, as if that would stop the pain and the ever-present swirls of the wards above her.

It doesn't, so she sighs through the mask.

"Nalissa's death is definitely spreading around," Chloe says, and Ambra jerks with remembrance.

Right. She succeeded with that.

And she hadn't even thought of it since waking.

Ambra coughs through the lump in her throat, before grimacing at it.

With the worry about Gurlien, she hadn't even had a chance to feel the lack of the leash towards Nalissa. She hadn't even had chance to poke at it like she had with Korhonen and Johnsin.

And now there's just Boltiex left.

And Gurlien is out of range of the leash.

The three are staring at her, and Ambra must've let something sneak onto her face.

So instead of speaking, she runs a finger under the leash around her neck, tugging it, trying to indicate it.

"That's the other reason we kept you tied down," Maison says with a grimace. "They tried to take you, but the Necromancy prevented it."

Oh.

Ambra settles back down against the bed, and there's not even a bit of soreness around the leash that there should have been at an attempt.

"I don't like the idea of restraining you either," Maison says, and there's half an apology in his voice, an apology for her.

Ambra nods, at the sense it makes, even though the fear of it twists inside of her. Exhaustion creeps up her, despite everything, pulling at her bones and her eyelids.

Without another word, Chloe and Maison filter out, their faces grim, and Mel settles back in the chair.

They're not letting her be without someone keeping watch.

It should rankle her. It would've rankled her.

"I know what it's like," Mel murmurs into the oppressive silence, and she barely has the energy to tilt her head towards him. "Getting injured in a human body. It's limiting and haunting."

She can't speak back, just blinks at him.

"My first injury I thought I was going to die, and it was hilariously minor." His face is serious, and there's some trace of something Ambra can't quite interpret. "You get used to it."

"How long?" Ambra rasps out, and the mask muffles her tone.

"I've been in this body for almost two years," he says, just as solemn, and the possibility is dizzying, to be like this for that long. "Don't count your time in stasis, believe me."

She does.

"It gets far easier."

If she hadn't just had the last few weeks with Gurlien, she would never believe him.

"It'd be easier for you if you kidnapped someone actually decent," Mel continues, stretching out, and she summons the energy to scowl at him. "But that's more of your taste than mine, we just all think you're insane for it."

He leans forward, tenting his fingers together, like she's a bug under a microscope.

"They killed your bond?" he murmurs, and of course he could tell. "And are using it for control?"

She nods, the oft familiar pang of pain hitting somewhere beneath the bullet wound.

His face is serious, far more than it was before. "I'm sorry."

It's plain words, from someone who would know.

31

When Ambra awakes again, the mask is off, and the air around her chin is starkly fresh and the wards swirl above her again. A single bit of tubing trails across her face, laced into her nose, and breathing from that sends cold into her lungs.

Breathing hurts less.

A woman sits in the single chair next to the cot, reading a leather-bound book, and wild magic practically drips from her fingertips. Her dark hair is tied back in a braid, and her glasses are rimmed with gold, and there's a thoughtful expression on her face, one that Ambra has really only seen on Wights before.

"You're Alette from his stories," Ambra croaks out, and the woman jumps, clearly startled.

"I...yes," she says, blinking. "I suppose Gurlien would say something about that time. Here," she pulls a water bottle out, cracking the seal, and there's condensation around the plastic. "You're probably very thirsty."

Ambra is, and her hand shakes on the bottle. "I want to see him."

"Do you want me to call in Axel?" the woman, Alette, says, and she's perfectly earnest. "So you have someone familiar to talk to?"

Ambra manages a sip, and it burns down her throat. She sputters, coughing, but even that is easier than it was before.

The edges of her wound stretch less, though. The skin is knitting itself together, even without real direction from her.

"Nalissa teleported me to use me as a shield," Ambra says, as strong as she can. Which isn't much, at this point. "Right as he shot. He didn't mean to, I know that, let me see him."

She scowls at Alette, as if she could make her point through that.

"Oh you're just like Mel," Alette murmurs, which doesn't help, but she's pulled out a phone, tapping on it, and to see the wild magic interact with the technology is a little funny. "It's two in the morning, so I doubt anyone else is awake, but I've let them know you said that."

Ambra struggles to push herself off the bed, and Alette watches, as if waiting for her to fall, her expression never wavering, even after Ambra slumps back against the pillow.

"If you're as human as you seem, you should eat this," Alette says, pulling out one of those cursed protein bars, the type that Misia would buy. "Gurlien said you liked spicy food, so we can get you something after you eat this, but for now..."

Ambra has to set down the bottle of water for it, one hand still tied to the bed, and Alette tears it open for her.

"Stella is grateful," Alette murmurs, passing the bar to her, and Ambra automatically takes it, before freezing.

Stella. The little Wight she had been caged next to.

Of course this Alette would know her.

"Is she okay?" Ambra asks cautiously, unsure. The little

Wight was never taken out of the cage, never given the small reprieves that Ambra did, and Ambra heard her crying at night.

The sound had reminded her of Misia at first.

Alette folds her hands, and the intricate stitching of her coat catches Ambra's eyes. Even her coat has wards stitched into its hem.

"She's recovering," Alette says, picking her words very deliberately, and Ambra nods. "I think it will be an awfully long time before she is okay. She was there for six years."

Six years is a hell of a lot longer than Ambra had been.

"Still, she said you spoke to her through the walls," Alette continues, "nobody else there had tried to say anything, so we thank you."

"Who's 'we?'" Ambra asks, then tries to distract herself by taking a bite of the protein bar.

It's awful.

"Pretty much the entire Wight community of the Pacific Northwest," Alette replies, and there's a funny sort of smile on her face, like Ambra's doing something entirely predictable.

Her phone beeps, and she glances down at it.

Ambra sits with that, with the discomfort at the mention.

"She didn't..." Ambra starts, the coughs, twisting her face. "She didn't belong there."

She phrases it as a statement, but hears the question anyways.

"No," Alette says, shaking her head. "Not at all."

It's even worse. At least Ambra had all the instability and chaos and murdering to her name. An innocent twelve-year-old did not.

"I can talk to her when she's ready," Ambra murmurs,

thinking of the brief glimpse of them she got while hungover. "If it doesn't make things worse."

Alette watches her from behind the golden glasses, as if evaluating. "I'll tell her that, well, I'll tell her mother," she says. "Her mother isn't letting anyone near her without approval."

Understandable.

"She wouldn't even let Zoel talk to her without being there," Alette continues, and Ambra remembers with a jolt that she has to have a fucking talk with Zoel about Gurlien. "Don't be surprised if this takes a while."

"I can be patient," Ambra lies.

Another beep of the phone.

"Only people awake right now are Axel and T...Axel said that Gurlien is fast asleep."

Ambra tries to push herself off the bed again, but definitely fails at that.

"Do you want Axel to come up here?"

"That's a hard no," Ambra mutters, and Alette's lip twitches. "Do you trust that? He hates Gurlien."

"Hate is a strong word," Alette says, and Ambra just stares flatly at her. "They don't get along."

"He was an asshole," Ambra shoots back, then tries to take another bite of the flavorless bar.

"If he was just an asshole, he would just wake up Gurlien and make him miserable before bringing him up here," Alette says gently, and Ambra's suddenly reminded of all the times she went out of her way to not interact with Wights. "Axel doesn't actually wish harm against Gurlien, they occasionally would get together and commiserate."

"You mean yell at each other," Ambra interjects, then puts down the bar for another sip of the water. Every little action pulls at her chest, but even trying to grasp power to send it to healing slips from her. "They would get together and yell at each other."

"Alright, so Gurlien has been real honest with you," Alette comments, pulling open her leather messenger bag and rummaging through it. "I was worried he was just giving you a glorified version of himself."

"That suggests he likes himself enough to do that," Ambra replies darkly, and Alette's eyebrows flash up over the gold rimmed glasses. "He thought I would hate him after hearing the story. I thought he should give himself credit for going into something he thought would kill him."

Alette pauses, clearly unnerved, and Ambra presses that advantage.

"He thought he had to do this to save the world, and he thought he would die because of it, and everyone cast him off. I offered to be his weapon," Ambra switches gears. "I offered to do whatever he needs me to do, to defend him against whatever he wanted, to fight whatever battles, and do you know what he said?"

Alette remains silent.

"He said that people like him shouldn't have weapons." Ambra takes another heaving breath, and it hurts, so she slumps back against the chair. "I don't think he likes himself enough to even begin to try to make himself look better."

There's a stretch, a pause of awkwardness, before Alette hands her a small bag of candy, brightly colored and covered with a reddish powder. At Ambra's skeptical look, she says, "He told us you sometimes have issues with food. This'll at least taste better and we can move onto better things once you get something in your system."

That reeks of a deflection.

"We were worried that Gurlien might be trying to trick you," Alette continues.

Ambra snorts, which is painful and sets her off coughing.

"But I'm glad to see that he's been honest with you."

"He's been kind with me," Ambra pushes, taking another sip of water. It doesn't quite soothe the roughness of her throat or the ache in her chest, but it helps.

Another almost twitch of a smile, and Ambra's not trying to be charming. She doesn't want to be friends with this Alette, not if that's their opinion of Gurlien, not if they locked him up for four days.

"I can't believe Chloe let you lock him away," Ambra grumbles, then tries one of the candies.

Immediately, her eyes water, and a salty sweet spice hits her tongue instead of the cloying sugar of the other candies she's tried. It's a hard candy, so the spice sticks with her, utterly amazing.

"She protested, but Gurlien was willing to do so if we got you medical help," Alette says, not noticing or ignoring the miniature revelation Ambra's having with the candy.

"And that didn't give you the clue that maybe he really wanted to help me?" Ambra says finally, finishing that piece of candy and immediately digging out another one.

And here, Alette pauses. Actually pauses, like she's evaluating Ambra, piecing through her, and it's enough to make Ambra still, like she's a bug under a microscope.

"We have secrets here that I have no doubt the College would do much worse and much weirder to obtain," Alette says finally. "And I hope you finish with your quest so we can tell you. And here," this time there's a note of distaste in her words, as she places a small plastic bottle in Ambra's free hand, with the words 5-Hour Energy on the side. "These are beyond gross, but they will help."

Ambra eyes it, but it smells closer to the soda that Gurlien once gave her than anything bad.

"Drink it in one go, if you can, don't sip it," Alette instructs, her lips thin. "It'll give you a jolt of energy, your heart might beat fast, but it will help rebuild yourself according to Mel."

Ambra trusts that, at least, so she tilts her head back, shooting it.

It burns, and she coughs once, twisting her face.

Still, the door opens and in strides Axel, the same self-satisfied friendly smile on his face.

Ambra scowls at him.

"Less impressive when you're in a hospital gown and a bullet hole in your chest," he says easily, dragging another chair over to the other side of the bed.

"I want to see Gurlien when he wakes up," she forces out, and her voice quavers. Of course it does.

"Are you going to kill him?" Axel asks, and Ambra gapes at him. "It's a worthy question, he shot you, most demons aren't that forgiving."

"For fuck's sake," Ambra blurts out, and the force of it pulls at her wound, but both Axel and Alette grin at her words. "He didn't mean to, he's not a monster."

Alette and Axel exchange a glance over her, and Ambra hates it.

"He told her about what happened with the line," Alette says, and a sort of wordless understanding passes between them. "No glossing over what I can tell."

Axel's lips thin, but he nods, and they have a silent conversation, driving Ambra nuts.

"And that he wishes he could apologize but keeps messing it up," Ambra says, and as one, both roll their eyes at her. "He's a lot kinder than you were—"

"Once you finish your killing spree, I'll explain my questions and you'll probably understand," Axel replies, still casual, before he shrugs. "Though from what I've heard, they probably sucked."

It's almost an apology, and Ambra leans her head back against the makeshift pillow.

"He's okay?" she asks, after a few minutes of vastly uncomfortable silence.

"He's absolutely fine," Axel replies, amused. "Being an absolute prick about all of this, but he's fine."

And then, with them having a wordless conversation she has no hope of understanding, with a snap, the leash jerks around her neck.

She chokes, arching off the bed, her wrist tied in place.

"Shit!" Axel says, scrambling for her other side, as Alette grabs her by her shoulder, pressing her downwards.

Pain ricochets down her back, up her throat, reaching down to her fingertips, as the leash closes around her.

He can't. She's not recovered enough, she can't fight back, she can't—

An abrupt loosening, and she slumps back, keening, the edges of her vision black.

Each breath comes out in a rasping squeak, and the edges of her wound start to pull, blood welling up on the edges, even underneath the bandages.

"What was that?" Alette asks, almost imperial, like she's imitating someone with far more authority than she has, and all Ambra can do is gasp.

"Obviously, that was the leash, A," Axel replies, and she's not thankful for his translation, and both of their hands are tight on her shoulders. "Ambra, can you hear us?"

She manages a nod, and there are tears on her face, starkly cold. Her wrist aches, the line of necromancy twisting it down into position even when the rest of her body reacted, keeping it at an unnatural angle.

"I—" she starts, then takes another shuddering gasp, her lungs on fire. "Get..."

With another snap, the leash tightens, pulling her chin up and closing off her throat.

She struggles against it, trying to bring her other hand to claw at it, but Axel pins that shoulder down, pressing her into the cot.

A wire wrap of compulsion, yanking her away, teleporting, but the line of necromancy burns, viciously bright, and a scream builds up in Ambra's throat, caught behind the leash.

Before the leash abruptly goes slack, slumping her back against the cot, sweat coating her forehead.

"What do you need?" Alette says, her dark brown eyes completely serious. "Tell us what you need."

Ambra opens her mouth to speak, but the compulsion twists itself inside of her, cutting off her words.

It's not the leash, he's not pulling against her, just...controlling.

In the space of a few seconds, Boltiex's control floods through her, and he opens her eyes up to the room, immediately at the wards that circle the ceiling, then to the strip of Necromancy on her wrist.

Sharp, she can feel his curiosity.

He's seeing through her. He's observing, he's putting them in danger, he's...

"Interesting," he murmurs through her voice. "Untie that."

Alette freezes, staring at Axel again. "I can't."

"Hmm," her voice speaks, and he flicks her eyes up to Alette, observing her face, then to Axel, and his recognition thrums through her veins. "Alette Jyoshti? What are you doing in all of this?"

Alette jerks back, then her chin juts out to Axel. "Go get him."

"What?" Axel asks, but he's already scrambling back, releasing her shoulder.

He doesn't wait for an answer, fleeing the room and snapping the door shut.

"Is this your aunt's little compound?" Ambra's voice says, and horror spikes its way through her. He's going to find them, he's going to hurt them, he's going to—

"Of course not," Alette replies, and even though there's fear in her brow, her voice is even. "I would never bring a demon there."

Ambra doesn't know if that's true or not, and Boltiex pauses, giving her a chance to claw back her voice.

"Get me out of here," she chokes out, her breath rasping over her throat. "I need to go, I need—"

His compulsion rushes back to her.

"You're in the western Americas, somewhere north," Boltiex says through her voice, taunting Alette, who's mouth thins into a determined line. "Your aunt loved Vancouver. I can turn that city upside down to find my demon."

Ambra's gut twists at his possessive. They're not going to let her get away.

"Still, necromancy on a living demon, that's risky." He makes her observe the strip tying to the bed, and it pulses gold, fascinating him. "You don't know what you're getting into."

"I know an injured girl appeared, asking for my help," Alette responds. "Zoel takes care of the injured."

This catches Boltiex off guard. "She ran to the Wights?"

Alette nods. "She freed one so they would help her."

It's so laughably incomplete, and Boltiex rockets pain down her spine, jerking her, as if he could tell she's lying.

"Stop," Alette breathes. "You're hurting her."

He snaps the leash tight around Ambra's neck, cutting off her words, gagging her. He pulls her towards him, it's somewhere off to the west, but the necromancy twists her back into place.

Alette stares, her mouth grim, and there are footsteps outside of the door, running.

A cord strikes within Ambra the moment Gurlien comes in reach of the leash, and even Boltiex recoils from it.

"I need to leave," she blurts out to Alette, in the spare seconds between compulsion, "he'll come, he'll kill you all, he'll—"

The leash jerks again, closing off her throat, another vicious attempt at breaking out of the necromancy.

And simultaneously, she feels Gurlien twist his hand in it, relaxing the grip, and she gasps, air flooding in.

There's more than just Gurlien and Axel approaching, vivid down the hallway. Next to them, tall and willowy and brilliant against her awareness, is a Necromancer.

And Ambra knows which one, and Boltiex can't find out.

"Blindfold me," she pants out to Alette, who recoils. "He can't see her, he can't."

Alette's lips part, and wild magic swirls around her, sparking up in response to something Ambra's putting out, but she doesn't bother to question, tugging off her scarf and knotting it over Ambra's eyes.

She descends into soft darkness, almost a shocking lack of sense. It's not pressed against her eyes, pinning them into place, instead just blocking out all ability to see beyond it. Some light still filters through the navy-blue fabric, the dim shadows of someone blocking light and moving, but Ambra's not able to see it.

"Thank you," she mumbles, and there's still the chaotic swirl of the wild magic next to her. "I need to leave, he's going to track me down here, he's going to find you."

She pulls in another breath, and Boltiex worms his compulsion into her again, seeing through her eyes, expanding her senses, and she can feel his wonder at the brightness of the necromancer drawing ever closer.

Fast, he snatches her free hand to the blindfold, before Alette grabs her arm, pinning it to the bed.

He snarls through her voice, a wordless expression of anger, and that had always been his problem, the reason why the College made there be co-controllers. He couldn't help but react to things, couldn't help but respond to the immediate frustrations.

So, unable to teleport, unable to see through her eyes, he rockets pain down her spine.

Sharp, Ambra arcs her back, and he cuts off her air, too, gagging her again.

Gurlien twists his fingers in the leash, desperate even down the hall, and she pulls in one breath, before her throat closes once more.

Hot liquid seeps from the bandage on her chest, and Boltiex's curiosity snaps off the pain from her nerves, sudden.

"Who shot her?" he asks through her voice, as the door to the room slams open. "Who shot her and what gun?"

Even though she can't see, even though there's just the navy darkness over her eyes, the awareness of Gurlien rushing in steals all her attention, even after the Necromancer—Delina—skirts in after him.

"Get her out," Alette orders him, and Gurlien loops the leash around his arm, secure.

"That won't work," Boltiex says through her voice, almost sing-song, and Gurlien's sharp inhale is almost a music to her ears. "I'll still find you."

Before Gurlien twists his hand in hers, in the wrist pinned down, Ambra's breath is stolen away once more, by that simple action.

"Get me out—" she manages, before Boltiex yanks again, and blood prickles at her neck, at her wrist.

Sudden, there's a smudge on the demon circle surrounding the cot, some sort of exit route. Power floods back into her, in her grasp, the wild magic all around sparking up in her awareness, as natural with every breath, and she immediately claws it into herself, flash healing the cut on her wrist.

The grab of power creaks the entire building

"Ready?" the necromancer—Delina, her name is Delina, she needs to remember that—asks grimly, and Gurlien tightens his grip on the leash, weaving it through his fingers. Even with the direness, even with someone actively trying to take her back, she marvels at the difference. At how massively more gentle it is.

"Who is that?" Boltiex demands through her voice, and a trickle of fear from him sits in her throat.

He's afraid. He's caught off guard.

"There were only four more, who's that—"

Gurlien must've nodded, for in one brief second the Necromancer's hands are on her, before the binding on her wrist slithers off.

There's a moment, a breath, before Ambra snaps the magic around Gurlien and her, teleporting away.

32

Ambra staggers, her feet sliding against the floor of the large apartment, the air stale.

Gurlien catches her, half walking half carrying her to the too large bed, and the pain is like a dagger in her chest. He's controlling the leash, so tight that she can feel Boltiex tugging on the other edge of it, barely managing a twitch.

"I got you, you're okay," he mutters to her, and the blindfold still blocks out her sight, the world just a dark blue smudge. He presses her into the bed, into the cool sheets that still smell of him, and she's gasping, struggling for breath.

"Who's there?" Boltiex spits out with her voice. "Who's controlling her, everyone's dead."

Gurlien falls silent, keeping the contact with her shoulder, solid. He's in the bed with her, his body weight dipping against her, warm.

Ambra hadn't even been aware of how cold she had felt in the cot until that moment.

But he's here, he's next to her, out of whatever prison

they kept him in, and Boltiex gives one more brief, brutal yank of the leash, arching her up, until his touch vanishes.

Ambra sags against the sheets, gasping for air, before she reaches up and tears the scarf off her face.

"I got you," Gurlien murmurs again, and there are circles under his eyes, his hair completely a mess, sticking up in the back. "I got you, you're safe."

She's not, but she swallows. "He was gonna come after them," she croaks, and speaking pulls at the wound on her chest, at the barely healing crater against her lungs. "He was gonna find them, he was gonna—"

"We planned for that," Gurlien replies, his brown eyes flickering down to the wound, and for a split second he's dismayed, he's panicked, before he controls his face, smoothing it over.

She reaches up to cradle his chin, and there's a line of black blood on her wrist where the line of death cut into her, even after her healing.

He catches her hand, gentle, and there's a moment of silence. Of stunned peace, where Ambra's ears ring and her lungs rattle, but there's no other sound besides the soft whir of the air recycling around them and the wind creaking against the windows.

Before his lips part, like he can't believe the world in front of him.

"I'm sorry," he says, the words falling from him, almost too fast for Ambra to hear them. "You trusted me and I shot you."

It's so laughable, so far separate from the terror of Boltiex and the pain from the leash, but the edges of the wound pull at her, so she just blinks up at the familiar ceiling.

Boltiex will try again, and he's not going to give them

warning. Going to wait until they're asleep, wait until she can't fight back, then take her.

"I don't care," she informs him, after another stretch of silence, then coughs, her throat ragged. "You're okay?"

His face tight, he nods.

"They shouldn't have locked you away," Ambra mumbles. "You distracted her, I killed her, anything else is detail."

He blinks, rapidly behind his glasses, before he bends over, pressing his forehead against her hand, still held in his. "I'm so sorry. I'm so sorry."

"Stop," Ambra rasps out, but still she leans over as much as she can, wound be damned, until she can tilt her head against his, smushing his blond hair against her cheek.

He doesn't move, his breathing a bit ragged, and Ambra knows he just woke up. Probably disoriented and exhausted. He's been locked up, away from his friends, no way to defend himself.

"I didn't mean to," he repeats.

"Do you really think I'm mad about that?" she asks, and a whisper of Boltiex's awareness winds its way into her, and Gurlien tightens his hand on the leash in response until he vanishes.

"I shot you," he repeats.

She nudges his hand until he raises his head and looks at her, actually looks at her.

Deep purple circles rim his eyes, and the collar of his sleep shirt is a bit ragged.

She knows she doesn't look much better, with the bandage seeping with black blood and who knows the stage of her hair, but she locks eyes with him and keeps it.

It feels like some sort of challenge.

A million emotions flicker over his face, something she

can only pray to keep up with, but still, she holds herself as motionless as possible.

"I'm not angry," she states, then amends, "at you."

His jaw tightens, like he's actually about to fight her on that.

"You distracted her enough that I killed her," she points out, as she had to be reminded of it. "Then got me help. Who would be mad at that?"

"Many people," he repeats, and finally, there's something close to amusement filtering into his expression. "If they didn't press charges, most people would cut someone out for, you know, actively harming them."

"That's ridiculous," she informs him, and gets rewarded with a small smile, like he can't believe what she's saying. "If you had meant to hurt me, sure." She takes another breath, experimental, and it hurts.

He watches her breathe for a few moments, as if he's counting the seconds between the rise and fall of her chest. Idle, his fingers play with the leash on his wrist, a welcome sensation.

"They shouldn't have locked you up," she repeats, after the pain of her motion recedes like a wave. "You were trying to help and they treated you like shit."

His lips twist, something between amusement and loathing. "I showed up with a woman bleeding from a gunshot wound from my bespelled gun, that is suspicious as hell," he says, but he settles on the bed next to her. "They put me in an extra apartment. I had books and a stove and Chloe brought my cat, I was fine."

It's a little softer than what she had imagined.

"I'm glad Chloe was with you," Ambra says.

"Yeah, she..." Gurlien trails off, and for a split second she sees sadness on his face, some other form of loss.

"What?" Ambra demands, as imperiously as she can while being slumped against the bed.

With a wry smile, he shakes himself out of it. "She always talked about how she was going to go on and continue her research if she ever recovered her notes," he says. "We did that at the base. She's preparing to head out soon."

So the loss will be the ability to see his friend as easily.

"I'll teleport you to her if you need your friend," she says seriously, because of course she would. "That's hardly a problem."

A small smile. "I don't think she'll tell anyone where she's going."

"I can track her," Ambra says. "Probably." In odd with her words, she coughs, then grimaces.

"What do you need," he asks, like a vow, and he traces his fingertips on the leash, sending a shiver down her back. "He's not going to stop, what do you need to fight back?"

It's a hard question, one she doesn't fully know how to answer, beyond holding her down and stopping Boltiex from taking her.

"Food, probably," she replies miserably. "Rest. Energy."

"The other necromancer was going to compel you to not injure her and then let you take from her, apparently, but pretty much everyone shut that down," Gurlien says. "I met her, I do not understand her."

Ambra blinks at him. "That would be foolish," she says dryly.

Still, she closes her hand around his once more, and there's silence, just the two of them, and the closest she's felt to peace. He's here, he's safe, she'll heal, they'll fight off the College...

A twist of Boltiex and his awareness blooms in her eyes, her breath hitching.

Gurlien recoils, like he could feel it, too.

And all Ambra can do is blink at him, as Boltiex absorbs her vision, absorbs what she can see, absorbs the pain in her chest.

"Gurlien Banks?" he finally asks through her, flickering her eyes down to the leash in his grip. "There's no way you have the power to do that."

Gurlien's lips part, hesitating one moment, before twisting the leash in his hands, and Boltiex vanishes from her mind, leaving Ambra reeling.

"Okay," Gurlien says, "so he's going to just do this."

Wordless, Ambra nods.

In a sharp motion, Gurlien rolls out of the bed, pushing himself to standing, and Ambra immediately misses his contact.

"Stay," he orders, and there's no compulsion in it, but she still settles back as he strides over to the kitchen.

"He's gathering information," Ambra murmurs, and Gurlien nods. "You stopped him and he's gathering information."

"And I," Gurlien starts, and there's something dangerous in his voice, "have spent the last five days with some very knowledgeable people about demons, and we are going to get you back up and running."

She tilts her head to him, as he opens the cupboards he had stored food in, the non-perishable stuff.

"Mel was a dick," Ambra ventures, and there's a small smile on his face. "And I still don't like Axel. Alette was okay."

Alette followed her instructions in a crisis and held her

down, disparaging comments about Gurlien notwithstanding.

"I met Axel's girlfriend," Gurlien starts, making a funny face, "and so much more makes sense."

He pulls out a box from the cupboard, one she barely remembers him buying, and roots through it.

"You're going to have a lot to talk about with her when this is all done," he says casually, as if they're not in danger. As if Boltiex won't decide to pull her immediately, to control her and kill Gurlien, backlash be damned.

Giving up on the box, he grabs the backpack because they let him have the backpack before rescuing her, and she gets an irrational surge of gratefulness.

"Did you bring the gun?" she asks, struggling to push herself up to sitting, but he points at her until she settles back down.

"No, they took the gun," he says dryly, but he rummages through the backpack, pulling out a small yellow bag, too similar to the first aid kit that Misia kept at the motor home.

"I want one," she tells him.

"A gun that can kill you?" he asks, his brow furrowing as he unzips the bag, digging through it.

"Good self-defense," Ambra says.

"Jesus Christ, you're really not mad," he mutters, before laying the contents on the bed. "Good. They gave me a magician pack. You're gonna hate this."

He waves what looks like a foil tube at her, then tears it open and hands it to her.

"Glucose and caffeine gel," he informs her. "Used by marathon runners for energy."

She sniffs it, and it doesn't necessarily smell bad, if a bit chemical.

"Eat it," he orders, but again there's no compulsion and

she could shrug him off if she needs to. "Eat it and then focus whatever energy you can to healing."

She pushes a bit of energy towards her chest, and it resists, before the skin slowly crawls together.

"Yeah, that's still weird," he mutters, digging into the pack, laying out a variety of things. Another 5 Hour Energy Drink, something called "protein goo" and a bag of dried dates.

Moderately horrified at the display, Ambra attempts to eat the gel in front of her, and it's wholly unpleasant.

"Sure, you can shake the entire building, but can't eat something a little bit disgusting?" Gurlien asks, and she flatly raises an eyebrow at him.

"Did being around other people remind you to be caustic?" she asks, and he grimaces.

"Fair." Still, he watches her, his hands in fists on his side, an odd desperation in his stance, so she finishes it anyways.

Without even pausing, he hands her the protein goo, and it smells even worse.

"Why would you even have this?" Ambra asks, after ripping it open in a move that was rather unpleasant to her chest.

"Because suddenly running out of energy is a normal problem for magicians to have," he replies, his brown eyes a bit intense for her to eat under. "And Mel said it would be the same for you in that body, and absent a Necromancer for you to kill..." he gestures at the display of food, and there's a tremor in his hand, one she can't quite parse out. "I would keep chocolates and caffeine gel with me. Axel did the energy shots and cheese sticks. Alette apparently did tea."

She hates it.

"Chloe always ate candy," Gurlien continues, almost babbling, and she eyes him.

He's nervous, he's still worried.

"Delina didn't do enough for us to fully know, but when she raised Maison—" Ambra raises both eyebrows at that, "we gave her some chocolate chips and water, we weren't prepared for that."

"Was that before or after the bar?" Ambra mumbles, eating despite herself.

"It was when Karkohen tried to take down Delina himself, before he brought you out," Gurlien says, grasping on to the distraction with both hands. "He came alone once, with just an activated teleport spell and tried to kill Delina, Maison stepped in front of one of his bolts."

Ambra had the dim idea that the Necromancer had been way newer to her powers at the bar, but if she had already raised someone with a critical injury, Korhonen was more stupid than she thought at trying again with Ambra and expecting it to be so easy.

She pauses at the thought, but Gurlien just gestures her to continue.

It's another part of the body she'll have to get used to, so after taking a rather unpleasant gulp of the protein goo she twists the magic again, focusing on the edges of the wound.

"I've spent the last five days thinking you may die because of me," Gurlien says, voice low, his face pale, as she picks off the bandage to inspect the wound closer.

It's right underneath her clavicle on the right side, black blood crunching around the edges, and with the half-healed state she can see the flex of the body's lungs and the tremor of the blood vessels.

"Well, I unconsciously did a lot of this," Ambra

murmurs, poking at the edge of the skin and almost blacking out at the shock of pain. "Not bad."

This breaks him out of his direness, and he rolls his eyes.

"Can you get me a shirt?" Ambra asks, taking another deep breath and reinforcing the veins, smoothing them over. "I never want to wear a hospital gown again."

Without even bothering to go to the closet, he pulls out one of his extra shirts from the backpack, shaking it out.

It's the sky blue one she picked out on their very first attempt to shop, all that time ago. It's a bit wrinkled, but he places it around her shoulders like it's the finest of cloth, adjusting it so she can easily worm her arms through it.

It's been washed since he wore it, and it smells of his detergent, a scent she hadn't yet been aware of. That her entire existence, she hadn't contemplated that specific of scent.

She clutches it closed, then tilts her head up to him, sending another tendril of power to the wound. It resists her, the bespelled gun doing the damage it needs to.

But eventually, even the wound relents, knitting back together, the skin stretching fragile over the bullet hole.

The effort leaves her fingertips trembling, so she eats more of the protein goo under his watchful gaze.

It's dark outside the tall windows of the apartment, snow striking it softly, and he looks, exhausted.

"I think that shirt looks better on you than it does on me," he murmurs, like he's aiming for sarcastic and missing it completely, coming out on this side of earnest. His face twists, at the frustration of expressing himself, something Ambra understands completely.

"You're thinking something," she whispers into the stillness of the room. "You're thinking something and I can't interpret it."

Slowly, in a heartbreaking moment of peace, he sits next to her on the bed, folding his legs underneath himself, but still doesn't say anything.

The bed even creaks with his weight, louder than her beating heart.

"I—"

Loud, his phone rings, and they both flinch.

"Jesus Christ," he mutters, shoving his hair away from his face and digging it out of the pocket of his—actually fitting—pajama pants, before he freezes.

It's an unknown number.

"Nobody should know this number," he says, grim. "It's unlisted, it's protected, only people who I give it to should have it."

Ambra shakily grabs one of the dates. She's going to need more power, more stability in her limbs.

There's a detached fear sitting in her stomach, underneath the cursed food he's feeding her.

"I don't know when he's going to grab me," she says, trying and failing to keep the tremble out of her words. "But you should get dressed and have some food and be ready."

He leaves the phone, still ringing, on the bed next to her, and it rings twice more as he changes into a pair of his pressed slacks and the deep maroon button up, drawing the color to his complexion. It rings again as he grabs a protein bar and one of the five-hour energy shots, a grim determination fitting over his face like armor.

Gone is the rumpled, soft Gurlien, and now it is the Gurlien who is ready for battle.

"I still think you should have the gun," she says, as he flips the phone onto silent.

"Is your phone somewhere in Paris?" he asks, and she nods. "Good. I don't want him hacking that either."

"We'll go get it after," she says desperately, "and I'll take you to the library and anywhere you want to go."

It rings again, now a soft vibration against the bedsheets, the surface lighting up.

"Why call you instead of control me?"

"Two things," Gurlien says, holding up his fingers, "one, he thinks I can do more than I can, or two, he wants to intimidate me."

Ambra twists more power into her chest, to try to stop the quivering of her heart.

"Or, a third," Gurlien continues, "he wants to manipulate."

The phone screen lights up, a text, and they both pause to read it.

UNKNOWN NUMBER (4:02 AM): She will kill you after this, don't think you can escape.

Ambra scoffs, and for the first time, it doesn't hurt her chest. "I won't," she assures him.

His lips twitch. "I gathered that."

Another text.

UNKNOWN NUMBER (4:03 AM): I assume Nalissa tried to bargain with you?

UNKNOWN NUMBER (4:04 AM): I won't.

"He's going intimidation," Gurlien says, picking up the phone and gesturing with it for emphasis.

"You faced a ley line," Ambra says, and shakily buttons the shirt together before pulling on a pair of the pants they had left here. She palms the pants. The pocket knife's still stuck in the pocket, and she smiles at it, brief. "Why do they think words would scare you?"

He watches her, a funny sort of smile on his face, before he shakes his head. "I missed you."

It hits a chord inside of her, a chord of emotion she

didn't know she still had, and she swallows past the sudden lump in her throat.

It's brutal, the surge of sensation she's experiencing, and her fingertips shake from something completely new. Like her stomach had fallen out and her gut tightens and her heart aches all over again.

It's a little like losing Misia.

In the sudden dread, the sudden complete loss of control over the emotions, the rushed scrambling to make sense of the change. Of the stark terror that this could happen, that this is at all a possibility, of the certainty that everything is different.

And he's still standing in front of her, a fond half-smile on his face, next to an array of horrible foods and the backpack without a gun.

"Oh no," she whispers, and his brows flash up in alarm.

"What?" he asks, leaning towards her, grasping towards the bag. "Do we need to run, do we need to go, what—"

She shakes her head, the heart pounding, her mouth dry. "I'm..."

She doesn't have words for this sort of thing, not anymore, and it's wholly impossible for her to think them for Gurlien.

He leans back, gaze wary, and his hand goes to the leash, like he's testing for something.

"It's not him, it's not that, I just..." she trails off again, gaping at herself, then shuts her eyes, as if eliminating one sense could heal her. "Human bodies experience things different."

"I can't imagine a gun wound is very fun," Gurlien says, his voice still wary, like he's expecting this conversation to go wrong at any moment. "Not to mention any pain that comes with healing."

Healing. Right.

Ambra twists more power into herself, to brute-force the healing to be faster, to knit the skin together.

After a moment of watching her like a hawk, Gurlien slowly starts to repack the backpack, pulling a knife from the kitchen for self-defense, a few changes of clothing, and when he passes by her, the edge of his sleeve brushes Ambra's.

And that splits her willpower in two.

She grabs his hand, his skin brilliantly hot, catching him off guard, and pulls him close. He staggers, propping himself up on the bed, arms bracketed around her.

There's a moment, a quick inhale, before she curls her hand around the collar of his shirt and kisses him, straining her neck up.

He startles at her touch, and she knows it's stupid, knows it's beyond stupid in this time. She should be healing, she should be preparing, she should be doing anything else but—

With as much passion back, he opens his mouth to hers, his lips moving against hers, settling until he sits next to her on the bed, his clothes creasing in the bedsheets. A hand brushes the side of her scalp, where the hair there is now impossible to ignore, and his other hand circling on the small of her back.

He's careful, even so, not pressing against her wound and not bearing down against her, his restraint painted in every line of his body, every muscle in his legs and the taut line of his shoulders, but he kisses her greedily, like this too is something he missed.

Making a small noise in the back of his throat, he pulls away, and there's a flush on top of his cheekbones, but he smiles.

"Is that what humans experience different?" he asks, and his voice is a little lower, a little huskier.

She nods, unable to speak past the beating of her heart.

He must be able to read something in her expression, in the starry awe of her eyes, and he softens, settling back on the bed, until they're both sitting there, knees touching and heads bent close.

Gentle, he cradles her chin, like she's the fragile breakable human and he's the protector.

"I've spent the last five days talking about you to anyone who would listen," he informs her. "About how interesting and unpredictable you are, about how much you've shown of me and of demons and about everything else."

She hopes not everything, thinking of their night in Paris.

"Do you know what Chloe said to me?" he asks, still tilting her chin, his fingers warm. She doesn't, she doesn't think she could ever guess, but her heart flutters, completely separate from the injury. "She looked at me and said, 'I don't think you've ever talked about someone like this, what are you going to do to keep her after this is over?'"

After it is over.

Ambra can't find the words, instead leaning upwards and kissing him again, this time slow and languorous.

But he wants her to stay after as well. He wants to still know her, when the leash is untied and she is outside of the control. When everything standing in her way of her existence is gone, when she has to answer to no one.

His hand splays on her knee, a firming grip, before he breaks the kiss again. He smiles, actually smiles, genuine and disarming, and she wants to remember that forever. Remember everything about it, every little sensation, every crease of the bedsheets where they touch, every hair out of place on his head, every little freckle across his cheekbones. Every nerve tying her into place, every whisper of air across her skin, even the lights in the room and the dim rumble of the outside world as it wakes for the morning.

Leaning her forehead against his, she breathes in, ignoring the pull from the injury, the skin tightening on around the wound.

"I'll always be broken," she mumbles, in the mad rush to make sure he understands this, understands what she is no longer capable of. "I don't know how humans love, I only know how demons do, and I can't...there's no way. Not anymore."

He nods, still keeping the contact. "Melekai explained that to me."

"I'll always be weird, I might not adapt well, I'll be prickly and uncomfortable to be around."

"I know," he says, simple, and her heart stutters once more, at the easy acceptance and the knowledge behind it. That someone could look at all the facts of her and be okay with it.

"I—"

And in that moment, in the perfect whisper of air, in the skin touching and the prickle of awareness of her wound, the leash jerks tight, snapping her head back, away from the closeness and the comfort.

She scrabbles back, clawing at the leash, and Gurlien closes his hand over her arm and—

33

Ambra lands, butt against lush carpet, Gurlien fumbling into her, before her body snaps away across the room, breaking the contact between the two of them.

They're in a...room? In a house? It's unfamiliar to her, not somewhere she's gone before, but the carpet is beautiful and gray and the wallpaper is homey, floral. It's bright outside, almost as if the sun is setting directly out the window, golden light streaming in.

Gurlien recoils, reaching his hand for leash, and between one moment and the next, all sound falls away, all sensation of his fingers against the leash, everything, as the leash around her neck jerks her again.

She teleports, against her will, clawing at every moment, and the control spins her into....

Into a white cell.

Her feet slide beneath her against the tile and her ears pop, and she staggers. All connection to the outside world vanishes, all sensation of magic, of her powers, of anything that ties her into reality.

Instead, just a blank white room with bright overhead lights buzzing ever so slightly, and the air doesn't move.

She's been in this before.

She spins, and her own skin doesn't change, her own perception of pain and discomfort. The breath she pulls in doesn't impact her lungs, her blood stilling in her body, but her mind continuing to turn over, to think, to experience, and—

Stasis cells always have one wall that's open for observation, and so does this one.

Beyond the bright light of the cell, the world is dim, like someone forgot to turn a light on. Like a basement, the floor raw concrete and the walls untouched brick.

Panic starts to drip down her back.

"Gurlien?" she calls out, and her voice breaks, echoing around the room, deadening to anything outside. No words can reach outside, nothing.

She weaves her fingers against the leash, testing it, but there's no sensation.

It's the only stasis cell in the room, and she creeps closer to the open wall, to the pane of observation glass, and no other light spills out from anywhere else, even when she cranes her neck to either side.

She's alone, she's alone and Gurlien isn't here and—

Her breath, the completely useless breath that does nothing to help her body, hitches.

For a brief, heartbreaking moment, she lets herself crumble. She lets the worry and the pain and the terror wash over her, lets her legs dump her so she sits on the cold tile, hugging her knees to her chest.

If he's too far away, if she can't reach him, then this whole thing is for nothing, then...

She squeezes her eyes shut, taking another long useless breath, before opening them up again.

If Gurlien's too far away, then he's somewhere alone that she can't control, and he'll need her help.

He'll need her help, he'll need her to break out of this and get to him.

Still sitting down on the tile, she tilts her head against the observation glass, casting her eyes across the room. Water drips in the corner, further solidifying the basement sensation, and a dirty table with rusty tools sits off to one side.

So obviously Boltiex. He never cared for the condition of his tools and would buy new ones when his current set inevitably broke from overuse.

It does nothing to quell her fear, so she glances to the other side. A set of stairs, leading up to somewhere unlit. A single dark screen of some electronics, set on a set of wooden boxes.

The lack of rune boxes, the lack of basic sanitation, this is an unsanctioned stasis cell, one that Boltiex would be imprisoned if it ever came out.

She'll kill him before it does.

But it does tell her some interesting things. That he'd want to keep this quiet, keep her quiet. That he wouldn't want witnesses.

That he wouldn't have backup.

Careful, she presses her hand into the seam between the glass observation panel and the floor, and no air flows through. In one of the cells, the Korean one, air occasionally hissed through, and she would lay next to it just to feel some sensation.

The wound at her chest pulls, sending a pang through her awareness, but she pushes herself up to standing anyways. The glass is neutral warm against her palm, but that doesn't surprise her.

With her breath, the still jagged edges of her wound spark up at her, teasing at a madness of obsession.

That happened whenever she went into stasis. Any wound or injury, anything causing pain, tempts the mind into circling around it, swirling until it occupies every thought.

It did, for Ambra, the first few times.

Something in the basement beyond creaks. She freezes, squinting out past the brightness of the cell, but nothing's there.

Wait. Not nothing. Not nobody.

Deep in the shadows, so deep she can barely perceive, in a cage so small the figure has to crouch, is another demon.

Ambra tilts her head at them.

They're not in a dead body, instead far more incorporeal, but somehow still trapped. She can't see or sense the wards that must be everywhere around it, or else it would shatter the cage.

It's a cage meant for a dog.

"Can you hear me?" Ambra asks, even though most stasis cells also block noise from escaping.

No response, just a huddled figure, the shoulders hunched and unmoving.

She can't even tell if they're looking at her, not with these human eyes.

The stasis chamber was probably for them, and Boltiex evicted them fast to put in Ambra.

It's probably why she got that snippet of time with Gurlien, the time to press the heal into herself with the magician's energy 'food.' The time to breathe and get a little more of her power back. Boltiex had to prepare a space for her.

Makes sense. He wanted to get her into a place where she couldn't fight back as soon as possible.

It's one more thing making Ambra's blood run cold, and she shivers. Boltiex shouldn't have access to any demons, to anything, much less store them in a crate better suited for a large dog.

This is why they made five handlers. For all his brilliance and out of the box thinking, Boltiex is just another unstable scientist gone mad with the ideas of power he could control.

So gingerly, not pushing the wound, she prods at every seam in the room, her heart pounding uselessly. She has to get out, it's not a question, but every aspect of herself is cut off from the world.

The cell's not perfectly built, one edge of the floor sloping downwards, one of the walls a bit crooked, but all the connectors are flush, not giving her a single bit of leeway.

A light illuminates up the stairs, and she stills once more, letting her eyes flicker to it.

The easiest way out of here would be Boltiex coming down and doing something stupid.

But no footsteps echo downwards, and nobody appears before her.

Careful, Ambra lets her hand rest on her pants pocket, on the tiny multi tool pocket knife tucked inside.

Once, in the Toronto base, they had mistakenly left her with a metal clipboard that she broke into shards, and she carved up every surface of the cell with scratches. It did nothing to get her free, but they had to move her to a clean cell after that, the cell next to Stella.

She bets that this cell is a little less sturdy than that one.

Not telegraphing the motions, not trusting that she's not being watched in some way, she pulls out the multi-tool, flicking the screwdriver out, picking the one less likely to snap. Gripping it tighter in her hand, she scratches along the seam next to the sloped floor, and it digs into the tile.

So the very tile is softer.

Something between determination and hope, she sits next to it, gouging at the floor.

Until the single screen of electronics blooms to life in front of her, startling her into blinking out at it.

It's staticky, almost difficult to make out the picture, before it sharpens into a black and white surveillance image.

It's hard to make out, a figure sitting in a box of a room, before the figure shifts and she catches a glimpse of a familiar silhouette, a familiar set of the jaw.

Careful, she grips the pocket knife, continuing to work through the floor.

So he's showing her surveillance of Gurlien, and the horror settles deep into her stomach.

And, as Gurlien had said, manipulation.

She keeps her eyes locked on the screen, despite how much they ache with the bright lights. He's just sitting there, leaning against the wall, his legs awkwardly bent, his hands nervously fussing.

Whatever Boltiex has in store, he wants her to be off-kilter. He wants her to be reacting emotionally, easily prodded into whatever actions he wants.

She has to remember that. Not let herself get caught in the moment like with Bianci.

Another flicker of lights on the staircase, and she swings

her head up to watch a pair of shoes stomp on the highest step, kicking up dust.

So even if he held a demon here, he didn't come down to check on them very often.

Even more cruelty.

In the cage, the figure twitches.

"I'll get you out, too," she whispers, despite the danger. Despite the foolishness of getting anywhere close to another demon when she's like this.

Finally, the dim figure raises their head, and their eyes glitter in the darkness.

The shoes step lightly on the staircase, too light for Boltiex, so Ambra eyes the area. There's not enough brightness to see anything beyond shadows.

Until a hand on a light switch clicks it on, flooding the entire basement with harsh florescent.

The figure in the cage recoils back, but Ambra just blinks through the additional discomfort.

It doesn't go away, not in the stasis chamber, but...she adjusts.

On the bottom stair, not quite stepping onto the basement floor, a young woman hesitates.

No, not a young woman, barely a teen. More of a child. Same age as Stella, same gangly limbs of a recent growth spurt.

The hair on the back of Ambra's neck raises.

Her jaw is the same as Boltiex's, and her hair the same deep brown.

She tilts her head at Ambra, and that, too, is the same sort of motion of Boltiex.

"What the fuck," Ambra breathes, even though the child wouldn't be able to hear her.

The child shakes off whatever fear she had, then steps into the basement.

"My dad says your TV isn't working," she says, declarative in the way only fearful people are.

Nobody knew he had children. Nobody knew he had any attachments at all, it was part of what made him unpredictable.

Still, Ambra gestures to the TV, where the flickering screen still shows Gurlien.

The figure in the cage shifts, and the girl freezes, shying back again.

The pre-teen glimmers with some sort of potential, some sort of magic that Ambra's never seen before, and a quick glance to the demon in the cage catches them watching her sharply.

A fission of understanding passes between them, even with Ambra in the stasis chamber and him in the cage. Whatever this girl is, whatever the school of magic, it's weird and the other demon is not gonna let Ambra interfere with it.

Fine with her. She has more pressing things to deal with.

What sort of father would send his child into a basement with two living demons improperly restrained?

And if Boltiex is insane enough to do that, what would he do to Gurlien?

Ambra stands, walking over, then splays her hand against the glass of the observation wall. The girl stares at her, not getting closer, as if she's not sure how to approach Ambra, in the human body with hair that grows.

"It's okay," Ambra says, even though no sound could reach her. Then, "Free me?"

The girl shakes her head at that, which is fair. If she lives in such a state with her father, she would fear him far more than whatever monsters he has locked in his basement.

"I'll get you somewhere safe." It must be too many words for someone to lipread, for the child gives her a blank look.

It's words she said to Stella, in the last ditch attempts to get her to stop crying many times, and it never worked.

The demon in the cage twitches, and the hint of a hand curves around the bars of the cage.

Keeping a wary eye on the demon in the cage, the girl crosses to the television, bending behind it and messing with the cords that run to it. The picture flickers, but nothing else happens.

"It's supposed to play sound," Boltiex's daughter says, and in her tone is a hint of Boltiex's familiar frustration. "This won't work if it doesn't play sound."

The entire thing just got way more complicated. Now there's another demon and a child she has to get out, as well as Gurlien.

Slow, not spooking the child, Ambra retreats, letting her palm fall away from the glass, until she folds herself up next to the soft spot on the tile.

"Please don't do that," the girl murmurs, as if she could tell Ambra is trying to escape. "He'll be mad if you do."

Ambra bets he will.

On the screen, the familiar hunched shoulders of Boltiex cross the room, and Gurlien lifts his head. They're obviously speaking, and static crackles with one shift of the cords, but the sound doesn't connect.

The demon in the cage starts watching Ambra again, and she can't tell if there's malice or curiosity in that gaze. The moment she lets them go, there could be bloodshed or immediate retreat, and little in between.

Slow, the demon drops one hand to the floor and scratches the tile, sending a chilling creak through the whole room.

The child freezes, staring over at them with wide eyes.

The demon gestures, indistinct, and Ambra doesn't know how much the child can see of them. Either the child has more magical talent than most, or Boltiex has given the child the ability to see demons in their raw form.

Which is a cruel thing to do to a child on the best of days.

"I'm not supposed to go close," the girl says, Boltiex's familiar temper leaking through. "Stop it."

Another scratch on the floor, and the girl looks over her shoulder to Ambra, as if for back up.

Ambra just crosses her legs, her multi tool in her hand. Gurlien and Boltiex continue to converse in the silent video on the screen, and he's not approaching Gurlien, just pacing back and forth.

The screen flickers, static crackling. "I need you to—" it cuts off and the girl makes a huff of annoyance.

The demon in the cage locks eyes with Ambra, and makes another long scraping sound.

And it's been a while since she's had to communicate with someone outside of a body, but she can recognize a signal when she sees one.

So, even though the stasis chamber has ceased the nerves from flooding into her blood, she digs the tool into the floor again.

The sharp edge of the screwdriver skips along the tile, before hitting purchase, sliding underneath one of the tiles.

The motion tugs at her chest, at the half-healed wound, and she grimaces, pressing a hand against it over the shirt.

The sky-blue shirt.

The child glances at her, then at the other demon, then scowls at the other one.

"I told you, my dad will be mad," she scolds, even though there's fear in her voice, and the other demon grins at her.

But she doesn't recoil back.

So there's some familiarity, even with the fear.

"He's dealing with something," the girl says, with a nod at Ambra, like it's not evident. "You'll be back in there soon, this is just temporary."

Ambra can't imagine that the demon wants to be in the stasis chamber anymore than she does, but she moves slowly, digging her fingertips under the tile until it pops up.

Immediately, the child spins to her, her eyes wide.

Ambra holds up both hands to show her she means no harm, and even that action shifts the wound on her chest, sending sharp shivers of agony down her back.

And of course they don't cease, not at all. Once an injury happens inside of stasis, it stays there.

Boltiex's daughter looks at her, the other demon, the TV, then at her, like she's contemplating how she lost control of the situation, and Ambra doesn't want to scare a little girl, doesn't want her to suffer, but...

The demon taps on the bars of the cage again, then gestures the child close.

The hair on the back of Ambra's arms raises. That's too risky, she doesn't know this demon, she doesn't know their intention, but the girl crosses her arms and approaches.

"You're trying to scare me again," the girl says, her back fully to Ambra. "That won't work right now."

The demon gestures her closer, still indistinct, and Ambra hates it. Hates the situation, hates the danger, hates the fact that another child near her might be hurt, might suffer.

The TV sputters, and Boltiex paces close to Gurlien. On

the screen, he waves his hand and Gurlien recoils back, some sort of magic that the camera can't pick up.

Ambra stills. There's no blood, not visible.

She pulls the tile away, revealing soft packed dirt underneath, then jams the multi tool in it.

Gurlien huddles on the screen, clutching at his hand. The hand with the leash. From the set of his shoulders, Ambra can tell he's in pain, tell he's sheltering himself.

The demon says...something...outside of the range that Ambra's ears can pick up in stasis. If she was out, if she had access to her powers, she'd be able to understand easily, but here, with just her human senses, all she gets is a vague murmur.

"Shh," the child says, but there's a glimmer of something mischievous in her eyes, something so foreign on someone who looks so close to Boltiex. "That won't work, you know it."

A hint of a smile from the demon, and Ambra shivers again.

On the screen, Boltiex makes another strike, and Ambra digs into the packed dirt. If her heart was beating, it'd stop all over again from the fear.

She can't stall, she can't make this subtle, she has to hurry. And the demon outside can't distract her, and the child...

The child has to be protected but can't delay her.

Frustration builds in her chest, like emotion always builds in stasis, without any natural releases that come inherent in the human body. She's injured, she's at such a disadvantage, she can't quite stop the wave of despair that threatens to drown her.

And with another jam of the tool, she hits the limit of the stasis spells, tingling along her fingertips. Her ears pop, her heart jumps painfully, blood chugging to movement from her arm upwards.

She coughs, doubling over against her knees, and the girl spins to face her.

"What are you doing?" she asks, with the same fake imperiousness that everyone in the College always uses. "You shouldn't make noise!"

The demon in the cage settles back, their eyes shining in the dark.

The blood in her veins hits the wound, and despite all the healing she did at the apartment, it glistens in the light.

Ambra attempts to push herself up, but her arms shake all the same, as the blood slowly starting to pump hits her brain.

Prickles of sensation, warring with the pain and the dread, flood the body with adrenaline, and she hisses out a breath.

The little girl glances towards the stairs, like she's going to make a run for it.

"Wait," she croaks out, and Boltiex's daughter freezes. "Stay down here, you'll be safe."

It's a lie, she doesn't know what protections her father has built around the cage with the demon.

"I'll come back down and get you somewhere else," Ambra vows, and her voice quivers uselessly, like she's a newborn animal. "Anywhere you want, anywhere you need."

The girl glances obviously to the other demon, who watches them both. "Can you take me to my mom's house?"

Ambra nods, relief flooding through her with all the panic and the adrenaline and the pain. This child has another home, another place to go. "Of course," she says, and the girl scowls, like she's confused and doesn't want to show it.

The girl backs up, until her hand closes around the rusty bars of the cage, as if the monster in there will protect her from the monster breaking out of stasis.

With another dig of her nails into the packed dirt, Ambra folds more power into herself, creaking the ground underneath the stasis chamber, then teleports herself to right outside the glass observation wall.

Immediately, she knows she can't teleport outside the building, a normal two-story house with a basement. There're locks in the walls, traps to prevent her from going far. An entire building is a cage.

The child recoils away, towards the other demon in the cage, and Ambra puts her hands up, then points at the TV.

"How far away is that?" Ambra croaks out, and her skin shivers with the air brushing against it, derailing her thoughts.

The girl just cringes away, but...

The demon points up the stairs.

Good, they're in the same house.

Whenever she is brought out of stasis, the body dumps all sorts of chemicals into her veins. Panic, terror, fear, excitement, dread, all of the pent-up emotions from the chamber all at once. There's the leash, suddenly vivid against her awareness, slack. There's the itch of her scar underneath her breastbone, the gaping wound in her chest, her feet are cold against the concrete of the basement, and she's wearing Gurlien's shirt.

"I'll get her out," the demon whispers, and she can pick up their words now that she's out of stasis, pick up what they're saying. "I know where her mother lives."

Ambra inhales, but the girl nods.

And Boltiex strikes again, and this time there's some blood on the ground, fuzzy on the TV.

"There's a trap upstairs," they say, eyes glittering. "Unravel it and I'll get her to safety."

Ambra doesn't trust them at all, but she turns towards the stairs, her heart panging with stress as it attempts to cycle the blood sluggish in her veins.

Behind her, the demon laughs, low.

34

Without an accurate map of the building and with the traps built into the walls, Ambra can't pinpoint the exact location of Gurlien.

There's the awareness of him against the leash, faint, but neither of them are paying attention to it. It's hanging slack against her neck, and the lack of Nalissa on the other side of it hits her like a brick.

But she can't obsess over it.

Without the TV to give her information, without the visual of Gurlien and Boltiex, dread just pools in her stomach.

Gurlien is almost certainly hurt in some way, and her very bones vibrate with the need to get to him. To get to him, get him away, anything

Anything.

She creeps through a darkened room, the carpet crunchy against her bare feet, a sensation she didn't know was possible and never wants to experience ever again. The dim outline of a normal suburban living room, the sort found in the houses on the outskirts of the cities in most

Eastern European countries, surrounds her. The house is more narrow than the ones found in North America, but still functional, still has enough space to sit and turn around.

Pictures of a family without Boltiex lie in frames on the walls, each frame a different group of people, all too plasticky and perfect. It's the decorations of someone who wants to appear like it's a normal house, but can't quite comprehend the personal connection needed for such a touch.

Wards, in Boltiex's brutal script, line every windowsill and vent, forbidding entry and exit unless they come through with his permission. Anything that enters is trapped here, with no way out unless he allows.

Including, explicitly, written into the very protections of the house, his daughter, aged twelve. Couldn't even open a window, wave her hand outside, without her father there to allow her to pass.

It's another horror.

There's anti-demon, anti-Wight, anti-ghosts and spirits, anti-spells, everything. More protections than Ambra would ever think to tie into one location, and the upkeep must be an insane drain of power on him.

And somewhere, in this narrow house, is Gurlien.

Ambra exhales, pushing the air through her abused lungs, and it's not calming not quite yet. If the girl wasn't still in the house, she could expand through the entire space, fill it up, know anything and everything, but as it is, doing so would put them at intense danger. She'd be able to concentrate on one person, not so many.

And the other demon would almost certainly fight back.

Another room, this carpet lush against her toes, and it's the room he teleported them to before separating, the dusk light streaming in. Her throat catches at the site, at how different it is than the cold light of stasis and the dimness of the previous rooms.

It's like it's a different house entirely, momentarily disorienting her. More portraits, full of different families, line the walls.

She steps lightly onto some cold tile, in an unused kitchen. A thin layer of dust covers a kitchen mixer, and the stove has no stains of grease or food, the refrigerator unplugged and silent.

With each pace forward, her dread grows.

With each moment that he doesn't realize she's not in the stasis, with each option for him to discover that, the chance of getting caught increases.

But on the other side is another staircase, narrow and bare, with no pictures on the walls leading up.

Ambra palms her multi tool. It's not a perfect weapon, far from it, but it won't rely on her powers, which he could take away with a thought.

Not that he couldn't control her hand, either, but it's a little cool reassurance.

Her foot on the first step creaks, and she freezes, but there's no other sound. No sound of another person, no sound of a discussion or a battle.

In the opposite of Nalissa, he had hated extra noise.

He probably even warded it so that no noise would reach him unless he allowed. No distractions, nothing.

So following the blind faith that the demon hadn't lied, Ambra pushes herself up the stairs, clutching at the textured wallpaper to prevent herself from wobbling over. Her knees are still unsteady, protesting the motion, but still, she climbs.

The staircase narrows, the walls pressing closer to each other, until surely it must be difficult for someone with wider shoulders than her to comfortably pass. The skin on her elbows graze the textured paper, sending shivers across her body.

Still no other sound. Still no other evidence of Gurlien being here, other than the fact that it must be within 45 meters. Any of the doors on this floor could lead to him.

There's a single hallway, and all the doors are closed.

"Okay," she whispers, and her words deaden in front of her, completely falling away from her ears.

She didn't realize she had such strong opinions about child rearing, but something firm inside her rebels at the idea of making a house so you couldn't hear that your kid is in trouble.

Especially with some sort of demon in the basement.

Careful, she twists one last bit of power into herself to heal her chest a bit more, give her whatever advantage she can, then steps on the hall.

Immediately, wards swirl around her feet, mild ones, barely biting into her bare skin. They wouldn't hold back a demon, they wouldn't hold back a moderately competent spell weaver.

They might hold back a child who didn't understand it.

Lifting her head down the hall, she exhales, pushing her power out of herself, letting the tendrils creep along the floor, whisp along the wards, illuminating the path.

Footsteps glisten towards the last door of the hall, someone strongly powerful dragging another person, the afterimage of the magical trace vivid against her eyes for a split second before fading.

There.

Her heart jumps, her fingertips shaking, but before she can lose her will, she strides there, putting more confidence than she feels into her motions.

It doesn't matter that one of the faces of her nightmares is behind the door, so is Gurlien, and getting him to safety is more important.

Boltiex didn't even place any anti demon traps or wards around his door, he's that confident in his sloppily constructed stasis chamber. Just the anti-sound wards, a few trivial protections she could break, and the spells that prevent anyone from teleporting in or out.

Taking another deep breath that hurts, she grabs the magic trailing through the house and blasts the door open.

Her ears pop as it shreds through the anti-noise wards, crashing and clanging across the house. A glass breaks in the kitchen, a picture frame falls from the wall, a cheap stool splinters downstairs.

And in front of her...

Boltiex recoils back from the door, at the wood splinters flying in the room, and quick as she can, Ambra flashes a shield around Gurlien.

Gurlien, with blood viciously red dripping from his face and his arm, huddled against the ground. There's a tie around his ankle, a quick magic spell keeping in place, and Ambra snaps that, too.

He has a cut along the top of his eyebrow, a bruise forming around his left eye, and a clean and precise line of blood around the leash tied around his wrist. There's some sort of injury in his shoulder, he's holding his ribs like they hurt, and his eyes are wide, his pupils uneven.

And he's just as beautiful as he ever is.

His glasses lay broken next to him, the glass in them shattered, but Ambra can see the intellect racing across his face, the analysis, factoring her into his plans, his hand leaving the wound and going to the leash, and—

Boltiex recovers first, his hand flying to her leash, grabbing and pulling, cutting off all her powers and her abilities and everything.

There's a trace of blood on his knuckles, and it's not his. Rage, white hot, floods through Ambra.

"How the hell—" Boltiex breathes, and it's the first time hearing his voice in too long, grating along her ears.

Instead of answering, Ambra jerks at the leash, throwing him off balance, and Gurlien weaves his fingers through it.

His fingers are injured, shaky against the magic, but it's just enough to break a fragment of Boltiex's concentration, and Ambra uses it to shatter the wall next to Boltiex, shatter the sheetrock.

White dust blows outwards, choking them up, and Ambra ducks away, teleporting the small distance to Gurlien's side, dropping the multi tool and clutching at Gurlien.

His hand curls around hers, and even that grip is weak.

But there's a moment, a small breath, where his brown eyes meet hers and his lips part, as if to speak to her, before—

Boltiex grips her mind, grips her into his control, grabs Gurlien's arm and jerks the leash off his wrist. The knot unfurls with a snap, his hand going up to his wrist and his mouth forming a perfect 'o.'

And just like that, he's gone. All awareness of him is gone, all sensitivity and sensation from his side of the leash, gone. All of her sense of him is just her eyes, just visual, reflecting a completely normal person with a scar of magic burned out of him.

He recoils back, and she can't feel that. Can't feel any ghost of movement through the leash, any terror or control or motion.

Her heart drops, and Boltiex steps her back. He's

coughing still from her explosion of dust and wallpaper shreds, but his control is absolute.

"There," Boltiex rasps out, as Gurlien clutches at his wrist and Ambra's forced to stand stock still and stare at him. "Finally."

Gurlien pales, and this close she can make out the breaks of skin along his brow, the subtle crookedness of his nose. Boltiex had beat him, physically so, like nothing more than a schoolyard bully.

Ambra stiffens, just a little, and her brain tries to reach out and grasp at Gurlien, reach out to touch him, anything. Some sort of contact, some sort of recognition, something.

Her fingertips tremble, standing there, as Boltiex takes a few deep breaths, straightening himself.

"That was a lot easier than I thought, thank you, Ambra," Boltiex says, as if she had intentionally helped him, as if the sudden pain of the leash being gone from Gurlien's hand wasn't wracking through her spine, even with Gurlien standing right there. "Why didn't Nalissa just make you do that?"

He doesn't give her the opportunity to speak, doesn't release his control, just bends over double, still coughing from the dust.

Gurlien meets her eyes, and behind all the pain, behind all the confusion and weakness, he nods at her, something between a comfort and a command. He claws up to standing, still tied in place around his ankle, but something set in his jaw.

"How did you manage to control her?" Boltiex asks, honest curiosity in his voice. "You shouldn't be able to, not after..." he waves his hand at Gurlien, still out of breath from the dust slowly settling in the air. "It should've been beyond you."

Gurlien's jaw tightens, such a subtle motion of anger that Ambra almost misses it.

"She should've been able to escape your grasp in a second," he continues, and there's dust in Gurlien's hair, powdering it gray, and dust across the cuts on his eyebrow. "Ambra, kill him."

The words hang dark in the air, before the compulsion wraps itself wire tight around Ambra's throat, cutting into the skin on her neck, and she chokes on it, scrabbling her hand up to the leash and tearing at it.

And in that moment where she struggles, in that moment where she digs her feet in and fights, Gurlien stands there, his face open.

His brows raise, his lips part, and he looks at her as if he'd never dream of going anywhere else. In the face of almost certain death, in the face of her, he just gazes at her as if she's just as beautiful as she was on that night in Paris, as she was under the lights of the wine bar.

Ambra jerks back, the snap of anger tight against the leash, and Boltiex spins to her, watches her struggle with the order. Blood wells up in her throat as the leash constricts, as it pulls taut, choking her, coating her lungs.

Before Boltiex tilts his head, sliding his control into her stronger, smoothing down her actions, drifting her arms down to her side.

"Interesting," Boltiex murmurs, like it's something to be studied instead of horror and terror and Gurlien being right there, his heart beating. "So you have—"

In between one blink and the next, Gurlien surges forward and punches Boltiex straight in the jaw.

Ambra reels back, the control slipping from her mind in one blessed moment of peace, and she grabs at power, grabs at all the magic she can sense, twisting it up and around herself, something to insulate herself away from Gurlien, away from the danger, away from hurting him.

The house shudders on its foundation, cracking from the magic, and all the wards on the house snap apart. The weak stasis chamber three floors below, cracked. The cage around the other demon, shattered. The wards around silence, around stopping people from trespassing, from teleporting out, all gone in one crash.

Boltiex staggers back outside of Gurlien's range, his ears ringing so strong Ambra can taste it.

Ambra surges up with the magic, snapping it out at him. Boltiex manages to shield his neck, counteract her, but she twists her fist into another strip, slamming it into him, battering.

He grasps at her mind, his control filtering her enough that she falters, enough that she jerks backwards, the power flinging uselessly against the wall, showering her with more Sheetrock dust.

She snaps out more power, the house shuddering around her, before—

There's a gasp, a choked off sound of fear at the door, drawing her up short.

Right outside the door, her face pale, is the pre-teen. The child in the basement.

Her face is pale, and everyone stills, from Gurlien where he's scrabbling for the multi tool, popping out the knife as if it could do something, from Boltiex and his face streaked with blood, all turn to stare.

"Dad?" the child asks, her voice lilting up, and behind her, the demon in the cage rises.

Boltiex's eyes snap to the demon, to the nebulous state of a demon without a body to inhabit, and he jerks forward, clutching his daughter to him.

No, not clutching, hiding behind. Like the girl is another shield, just like the one he had to defend himself moments ago. Like the demon won't strike him if he uses his child as a buffer.

"Don't—" Boltiex starts, but the other demon surges up, surges past them, snapping Boltiex's neck where he stands.

It's loud, in the silence, before Boltiex slumps back, his arms falling away from his daughter as he clatters to the ground.

Ambra reels back, the sudden shock snapping through her mind. There's nobody, there's nobody on the other end of the leash, it's gone within one moment and the next. All bonds, all pressure, all control, gone.

Her neck, completely free. No tight constraint, no irritation, nothing.

The demon breathes out, and for a split second, Ambra can feel their eyes on her, feel their inspection and their appraisal, before they rest a clawed hand on the girl's shoulder, teleporting her away.

Ambra staggers, listing to the side, and Gurlien catches her by the shoulder.

Her ears ring, sharp, drowning out her gasping and the pounding of her heart, but she clings to him.

"Oh, hey, I got you," he's saying, and she can barely hear him behind the struggle for air. "You're okay, you're alive, you're okay."

As if in one final bit of resistance, her legs crumble underneath her, pulling them both to the ground in front of Boltiex's body, and she scrambles her hands to her neck.

There's no leash. There's no bond. There's nothing.

Just her own skin and her blood from the cuts.

She gasps, loud in the silence, before she twists her hand

on Gurlien's collar, holding him against her, holding him in place.

He flinches, before his arms go up around her, clutching her to his chest.

She still can't feel him, can't feel the awareness of him, nothing, but she buries her face into his chest so she can hear his heartbeat.

His arms tighten around her, like he's about to lose his grip. "Ambra," he whispers, her name a vow upon his lips. "Ambra, talk to me. Are you okay?"

She's not, there's something wild and terrible and terrifying without anything around her neck, but she presses her cheek against him.

Slow, his hand swipes the dust out of the shaved side of her head, gentle, and with a shock, she realizes there are tears on her face.

"I'm..." she chokes out, but her words escape her.

She's free. She's out of their control, she's out of everyone's control. She can run away, she can flee, she can do whatever she likes for the rest of her days for however long she exists. For however long it takes for the body to age around her.

Tender, oh so tender, Gurlien pulls away, cupping her chin his hands. His glasses still lay broke to the side, but his brown eyes flicker across her face like he could still read her like a book.

And they sit like that, limbs a crumpled heap on the floor, staring at each other, for a long moment.

"You're okay?" he says, the question an undercurrent in his tone. "Please, say something."

Swallowing, she nods, though it's fully incomplete, and tightens her hand on his collar. "You're hurt," she ventures, and her voice wobbles. "He hurt you."

"And something invisible killed him and then kidnapped his daughter, yes," Gurlien says, and just enough of his normal words filter in, settling something inside of her. "Do we need to go after them? Do we need to go save a child now?"

Ambra pulls in another breath, letting her mind wander out to that brief encounter, as far away as it seems. "They said," she starts, then has to gasp for more air, "that they would take her to her mother."

It all seems so remote, now that there's no leash around her neck, no control in her future, and she can do anything.

Her hand flutters to her neck again, and Gurlien sits back on his heels. He's still bleeding sluggishly from the cut on his brow, and they'll have to clean the dust out of it.

"Is the leash still there?" he asks, serious.

"No," she says, and the single word somehow makes it real. "No, I can...I can go anywhere. I can...I can do anything. There's no one on the leash, nothing..."

There's something on Gurlien's face, some sudden vulnerability that she can't quite parse.

"Anywhere," he echoes, and his voice is foreign a bit. "Anything you want."

Like he's worried she's going to leave him behind.

In a split second, she gapes at him, before she throws the pain, the grossness, the shock aside, throwing her arms around his neck and kissing him.

He shifts, pulling her onto his lap, his lips on her like she's the very air in the world.

"I can do anything," she says, between kisses, punctuating her words with touches to him. "I can go anywhere. Do anything."

Everything still hurts, but she twines her fingers into his hair, keeping him there with her.

And he kisses her back like she's the only water in the world and he's been left bereft. Like he's a starving man and she's the only thing he can consume.

"I can stay with you," she says, pulling away, and his lips are shining, relief in his eyes. "I can do anything."

EPILOGUE

After a few days of recovering, where she does little else but sleep and he does little else but fret, she dresses herself in one of the more comfortable sweaters, holding out his oversized wool jacket to him.

He takes it, his eyebrows raised.

"I don't want to sit here anymore," she says, declaratively. "I don't want to hide right now."

His lips twitch up into a smile.

"Where do you want to go?" she asks, and his eyes go thoughtful. "Back to that base? To Chloe?"

"Yes," he says, slow, plodding his words out, and by now, she knows enough to wait. "But first..."

His eyes steal to hers, stealing her breath.

"How about to that library?"

SNEAK PEEK OF THE GIRL WHO ONLY DIED ONCE

Chloe has a problem: she needs to die.

Sure, there are probably other ways to solve her demon problem, but when one has access to two Necromancers, this seems like the best way to go about it.

Others are less convinced.

"Absolutely not," Gurlien says, crossing his arms over his chest. His face is healing, a pinkish red scar above his eyebrow that pulls when he scowls. Chloe had teased him that it makes him look dashing, he had ignored her for an entire day after that.

He paces in the small library the five of them had commandeered in the compound. The other team of magicians had graciously let them stay there, but they all felt the same pressing need to have some space away.

It's awkward, to say the least.

The library's nice, of course, with red velvet couches and ornate rugs and too many breakable things that look old but are actually cheap reproductions.

Next to Gurlien, the person Chloe really wants the opinion of, Ambra, cocks her head at her, narrowing her red eyes. If the demon stuck in a human body thinks it is a good idea, then it has to be solid.

If Chloe gets Ambra on her side, she could deal with Gurlien.

"There are easier ways to see demons," Ambra says, brushing an idle hand against the shaved side of her head, and Gurlien scowls at her. "The other alchemist-" it still amuses Chloe how much Ambra dislikes Axel — "had some sort of fix onto glasses, into an earpiece."

"And glasses can be broken and lost, I want this fix to be permanent." Chloe shifts from foot to foot, as if movement could rid her of the restlessness.

Ambra nods thoughtfully, leading to a scoff from Gurlien, but she reaches out a hand to him and idly grabs at his palm anyways as he paces back towards her.

"The theory is there," Ambra says, which Chloe knows already. Chloe wouldn't ask something like this if she had doubts about the theory. "Alette says..."

"Alette had other advantages." Across the room, Maison chimes in. The half-demon is sitting on the fanciest of the red velvet couches, his leg propped up, still more injured than not. "She had a lifetime of being around an insane genius, no offense," Maison says, quick, to Delina, who's lounging next to him.

She shrugs her blond hair off her shoulders, unconcerned, but Chloe can see the little bit of interest in her eyes.

Chloe isn't worried about convincing Delina.

As a necromancer, Delina has had little ability to practice raising the dead, and Chloe knows the eagerness to stretch out muscles previously held back just fine.

Delina would absolutely raise her from the dead, no questions asked. Probably heal her sore shoulder, too.

"And there are spells," Gurlien interrupts. "There are spells and protections and runes and ointments that you could put on yourself until you find what you're looking for, and then you can take them off and not have to worry—"

"Some worry," Ambra murmurs, and he turns to her, almost aghast. "Spells aren't perfect, the good runes have awful side effects, and they're all hard to look at."

Chloe's not quite sure what that means, but she needs to actually be able to work with demons on this one.

Because whoever it is that has access to the spirit fox has access to a demon, and whenever she finds traces of her friend, she finds indisputable evidence of a captive demon as well.

And she can't fight, can't outsmart, something she can't see.

"As the only person in this room who's actually died," Maison drawls, "It's not exactly fun."

"You could already see demons, it's not fair," Chloe quickly shoots back. "This is about as low risk as it gets."

"Unless she can't finish bringing you back," Gurlien mutters, and she knows that's his fear. "Unless an actual demon - no offense - comes in and kills her before she finishes."

Despite holding his hand, Ambra bares her teeth at him for that comment, and Chloe definitely doesn't understand their relationship but is still massively amused by it.

"Well, there is another Necromancer," Delina starts, and Maison sighs and shuts his eyes. "And she practices within circles, and we have Ambra, and we have Maison."

"I will definitely be anywhere else but here," Ambra shoots back at her. "I am not signing up to be around Necromancer stuff."

"I was gonna ask you for the easiest injury to heal,"

Chloe says, almost wheedling, and Gurlien scowls at her once more, despite the interested look his girlfriend is giving her. "I figured you would know better than all of us."

"Absolutely not," Gurlien interjects, and Ambra shrugs in return. From what Chloe's been able to gather, Gurlien can no longer control her in any way, but Ambra tends to take his word at a much higher consideration than literally anything else.

Considering how Ambra makes Gurlien smile, actually smile, Chloe thinks it's charming.

"I'm sure Alette or Lyra would know the best way," Chloe says, forging onwards with an encouraging smile to Ambra.

"Why is this so important to you?" Ambra asks idly, and both Gurlien and Chloe immediately fall silent. "That's what nobody has explained to me."

On the couch, Delina and Maison exchange glances. The two of them don't know either, but they at least have more social grace than to just ask aloud.

"It's her research," Gurlien answers for her, saving Chloe the internal agony of trying to put it into words. "She can't figure out a way around this block without it."

"If you're going after demons you should take his gun," Ambra says offhand, as if the same gun hadn't caused her horrific injury. "A deterrent, at the very least."

"Oh my god," Gurlien mutters, then rubs his eyes, and for a split second she glimpses exhaustion in her best friend.

And for a split second, Chloe feels bad.

READ MORE HERE!

ALSO BY ALESSA WINTERS

The Magic of the Living and the Dead

1. The Girl Who Brings the Dead
2. The Girl Who Has Already Died
3. The Girl Who Cannot Die
4. The Girl Who Inherits the Dead
5. The Girl Who Should be Dead
6. The Girl Who Only Died Once

The Ghost of Riverside County

1. A Ghost of Her Own
2. A Ghost to Haunt Her
3. A Ghost to Free Her
4. A Ghost All Alone

The Paranormal Organization Series

1. Marked By The Demigod
2. The Succubi's Choice
3. Katya and the Young God

Summer Reads

1. The Man of the Lake: A Merman Romance
2. The Man of the Isle: An Alaskan Merman Romance

Follow her on twitter at @writerLyn

Want a Free book? Sign up for her Newsletter here and receive a previously unreleased Novel!

Printed in Dunstable, United Kingdom